A Whisper of Freedom

A Whisper of Freedom

A NOVEL

TRICIA GOYER

MOODY PUBLISHERS
CHICAGO

All Scripture quotations are taken from the King James Version.

Published in association with the Books & Such Literary Agency, 52 Mission Circle, Suite 122, PMB 170, Santa Rosa, CA 95409-5370, www.booksandsuch.biz.

Cover Design: David Carlson, Gearbox (www.studiogearbox.com)
Cover Images: Bettman/Corbis, Image 100, PhotoAlto
Interior Design: Ragont Design
Editor: LB Norton

Library of Congress Cataloging-in-Publication Data

Goyer, Tricia.
A whisper of freedom / By Tricia Goyer.
p. cm. — (Chronicles of the Spanish Civil War ; bk. 3)
ISBN 978-0-8024-6769-0
1. Spain—History—Civil War, 1936-1939—Fiction. 2. Americans—Spain—Fiction. I. Title.

PS3607.O94W47 2008
813'.6—dc22

2007041725

ISBN: 0-8024-6769-5
ISBN-13: 978-0-8024-6769-0

We hope you enjoy this book from Moody Publishers. Our goal is to provide high-quality, thought-provoking books and products that connect truth to your real needs and challenges. For more information on other books and products written and produced from a biblical perspective, go to www.moodypublishers.com or write to:

Moody Publishers
820 N. LaSalle Boulevard
Chicago, IL 60610

1 3 5 7 9 10 8 6 4 2

Printed in the United States of America

To Moody Publishers
You believed in me. I am forever thankful for that.
Thank you for allowing me to share these stories of my heart.

Dear Reader,

A few years ago when I was researching for my fourth World War II novel, I came across a unique autobiography. One B-17 crew member I read about claimed to have made it out of German-occupied Belgium after a plane crash due, in part, to the skills he picked up as a veteran of the Spanish Civil War. Reading that bit of information, I had to scratch my head. First of all, I had never heard of the war. And second, what was an American doing fighting in Spain in the late 1930s? Before I knew it, I uncovered a fascinating time in history—one that I soon discovered many people know little about. This is what I learned:

Nazi tanks rolled across the hillsides and German bombers roared overhead, dropping bombs on helpless citizens. Italian troops fought alongside the Germans, and their opponents attempted to stand strong—Americans, British, Irishmen, and others—in unison with other volunteers from many countries. And their battleground? The beautiful Spanish countryside.

From July 17, 1936 to April 1, 1939, well before America was involved in World War II, another battle was fought on the hillsides of Spain. On one side were Spanish Republicans, joined by the Soviet Union and the *International Brigade*—men and women from all over the world who volunteered to fight Fascism. Opposing them were Franco and his Fascist military leaders, supported with troops, machinery, and weapons from Hitler and Mussolini. The Spanish Civil War, considered the "training ground" for the war to come, boasted of thousands of American volunteers who joined to fight on the Republican side, half of whom never returned home.

Unlike World War II, there was no clear line between right and wrong, good and evil. Both sides committed atrocities. Both sides had deep convictions they felt were worth fighting and dying for.

So on one side we have: the new democratic Spanish government, Communists, Socialists, the "Popular Front," anarchists; freethinkers, artists, musicians; peasants, workers, unions; the Republicans, the International Brigade, Thaelmann Battalion (German Communists), *La Marsellaise* (French-British battalion), "the people," the Basques of northern Spain, Basque president Aguirre, "the Reds," Fernando Valera, Steve Nelson. The Soviet Union backed the Republicans. A number of volunteers made their way to Spain to fight under the Republican banner, including the English-speaking Abraham Lincoln Brigade from the United States.

On the other: General Franco, General Mola, the Nationalist Rebels, Fascists, Hitler's Nazi forces, Mussolini's Italian troops, the Spanish military, Moroccan cavalry, the established Catholic Church, the monarchy, "right-wingers," wealthy landowners and businessmen. Fascist Germany and Italy supported Franco.

During the Spanish Civil War, terror tactics against civilians were common. And while history books discuss the estimated one million people who lost their lives during the conflict, we must not forget that each of those who fought, who died, had their own tales. From visitors to Spain who found themselves caught in the conflict to the Communist supporters. Basque priests and Nazi airmen . . . each saw this war in a different light. These are their stories.

Tricia Goyer

Summaries

Summary for Book #1: A Valley of Betrayal

A Valley of Betrayal tells the story of Sophie, a young woman who is filled with romantic notions and dreams of walking down the aisle in a blue wedding dress and living happily ever after with her fiancé, Michael. In July 1936, Sophie reaches the border of Spain as civil war erupts.

With the border closed, Sophie must rely on the generosity of a mysterious stranger, Walt Block, to get her into Spain. Her reunion with Michael is bittersweet and he urges her to leave the country for her safety. While Sophie wonders if Michael's passion for her has cooled, she finds herself in love with the Spanish people. Yet even though she understands more about Spain, she questions all she once knew about Michael—especially concerning his relationship with the beautiful Maria Donita.

Spain is divided between two major political regimes. The Nazis are exerting their influence, supporting strong-arming Fascism led by General Franco. At the same time, Russia is enticing the ordinary, Spanish people with the idealistic vision of Communism. What was once a thriving paradise has become a battleground for fascist soldiers fighting against Communist-supported Spanish patriots.

The brutal realities of war provide a rude awakening, and Sophie uses her art as therapy for the children of the city, teaching them to express their visions and fears of the war through painting. Sophie also begins to paint pictures of war-torn Spain in order to alert the world to what is happening.

Michael is shot and killed by a sniper's bullet, and after she discovers Maria Donita is pregnant with Michael's child, Sophie agrees to be escorted out of the country by Michael's friend José. A wrong turn and a sniper's bullet nearly kill José, too. This causes Sophie to seek the help of a stranger—an International Volunteer and fellow-American named Philip. Now on the front lines of the battle, Sophie finds purpose in nursing the wounded and in painting the war's events and people in order to support the patriots' cause.

Philip Stanford had also journeyed to Spain for reasons having nothing to do with the war. Philip is an athletic trainer for his friend Attis Brody, who plans on running in the Workers' Games. Refusing to run in the Olympics in Berlin for political reasons, they are disappointed that the Workers' Games are called off because of the conflict. Instead of returning home, Philip and Attis put aside their track shoes and pick up rifles for the Spanish Communist cause. Philip and Attis start out in Barcelona, but end up in the trenches of the Spanish countryside fighting as members of the Internationals—volunteer soldiers from many different countries. Attis is killed in battle, but Philip chooses to continue his fight.

One day, in a forest marked by enemy artillery, a woman appears like a vision. Philip rescues Sophie and becomes her guardian. They build a friendship. Just when their care for each other seems to be blossoming into something more, they are pulled apart when Philip is accused of providing aid to an enemy flyer. Philip survives imprisonment and later finds Sophie in the bombed town of Guernica where she has gone to find out the truth about Michael's death.

In Germany, pilot Ritter Agler—a family friend of General

Goering—joins the secret German Luftwaffe. A Nazi pilot, Ritter fights for glory and the favor of his girlfriend in Berlin, shooting Russians out of the sky and bombing the cities and villages of Spain.

Shot down on a mission, Ritter finds himself in Communist-controlled Spain. In an effort to save his life, Ritter poses as a German volunteer who has been injured fighting for the Communist cause. In the hospital, he is befriended by a beautiful American nurse and painter. Though Ritter tries not to care, his heart is stirred by Sophie. When Ritter is finally mobile again, he steals a plane and escapes back to his airbase. Once there he takes part in the bombing of Guernica.

After being raised under segregation, a young black man named Deion Clay decides he cannot sit back and do nothing about the civil war in Spain. Deion hops a train to New York and joins the Communist party. With Communist support, he sails to Europe and hikes over the Pyrenees into Spain, entering the fight against the Fascist oppression. He finally feels part of something greater until an injury takes him away from the front lines. Deion ends up as a driver for the American painter, Sophie, and their last destination is the worst experience of the war. They arrive near the outskirts of Guernica in time to see the horrific bombing of the village by German aircraft.

Father Manuel Garcia ministers to a congregation in the Basque countryside, yet he is troubled by the complacency of the people—both toward the war and their Lord. When war comes to Guernica, Father Manuel feels hopeless. So many are lost . . . and without his people to serve, Father Manuel wonders what plan God has for him next.

The book ends with the bombing of Guernica. Although Sophie, Philip, Father Manuel, and Deion have survived much, they question their next moves. Is it possible that ordinary men and women can make a difference in a war that seems impossible to win?

Summary for Book #2: *A Shadow of Treason*

After witnessing the bombing of Guernica, Deion helps to rescue survivors from under the rubble of the buildings. Seeing the destruction confirms that his duty is to fight for Spain's freedom before many more innocent people are lost.

Sophie discovers that nothing is as she first imagined. When Walt, the reporter who helped her over the border, shows up again after Guernica is bombed, Sophie is given an impossible mission. Walt tells Sophie a tale of priceless Aztec and Inca gold stolen from bank vaults in Madrid. If found, this gold could pay for weapons to help the Republicans' fight against the Fascist Nationalists. The only person who knows where the gold is hidden is Sophie's ex-fiancé, Michael, who she discovers had not been killed after all.

Walt confesses that his job for the past two years has been to track Michael and his associates, knowing they have their own plan for the gold that has nothing to do with saving Spain.

Petra is a young girl raised in a wealthy family. After the bombing of Guernica, Petra has no one left. She dresses as a poor girl and hides away in a truck leaving Guernica. Her plan is to travel to Bilbao in order to find her friend Edelberto—the one person she has left. Yet when she arrives at his parents' estate, she discovers he has escaped to France with his family. With nowhere to go, ranch hands Pepito and Juan—and Juan's son José—take pity on her and care for her. They all build unlikely friendships.

To save Spain, Sophie must reinstate herself in Michael's life and find out his secrets. To do this she must leave behind Philip, the man she's fallen in love with, and return to the man who betrayed her. Sophie knows that she must hide her heartache over Michael's betrayal in order to get information about the gold. Whatever happens, she cannot let Michael realize she knows the truth about Maria Donita's child or about Michael's part in stealing the gold.

Walt also works behind the scenes to bring Father Manuel to Paris so the world can hear the truth about the German bombing of Guernica. Once in Paris, Father Manuel is befriended by a young Spanish man named Berto who helps Father Manuel find a place to stay and introduces the priest to Picasso. Picasso is eager to hear about the bombing of Guernica since he is painting this event for inclusion in the World's Fair being held in Paris.

Sophie connects again with Michael and attempts to find the information Walt needs. With each new day, Sophie discovers more layers to this international espionage scheme. She is determined to find the information that could turn the tide of the war and help protect the soldiers in the International Brigade, including Philip and Deion.

When Sophie discovers photographs that she believes are clues to the gold's hiding place, she must get this critical piece of information to Walt in time. As she ventures out to meet up with her contact, Sophie is caught. Thankfully, she is saved by the guardian sent to watch over her.

With the help of an old friend, José, Sophie is able to send Walt the information he needs. Then, with the front lines moving closer, Sophie escapes to Madrid with Michael. She only hopes that Walt can get to the gold before Michael does.

Asked to return to Germany, Nazi pilot Ritter Agler is given a new assignment—to travel to the United States and steal the plans for a very important bombsite that could help the Germans. Since Ritter hid himself so well among the Americans the first time, Goering believes he is the perfect spy for the job. Ritter travels to the United States and completes his mission.

Philip returns to the front lines with the International Brigades. Throughout the many battles, he prays to make it out safe so he can be reunited with Sophie again. After one battle, Philip is given leave and he travels to Madrid. He is shocked when he sees Sophie at the train station on the arm of Michael, her fiancé, who he thought to be dead.

Walt has kept his eye on the numerous players in this international espionage game for many months. Thanks to Sophie, he now knows where the gold is hidden. The question is if he can reach the treasure before Michael. Walt travels to southern Spain where the fascists are hard at work trying to build a tunnel to connect Gibraltar with Africa. Walt knows that the gold is hidden in the tunnel and he uses his acting skills to get him inside.

Once inside, Walt discovers the gold, Michael, and Sophie. An explosion leaves Michael injured, and when Walt prepares to rescue Sophie and the gold, Michael begs to come. At the airfield, it looks as if Michael once again overcomes the odds and flies away with the stolen gold. But after the cargo plane flies away, Sophie discovers that the soldiers at the airfield are on Walt's payroll. Not only is the gold saved, Sophie is reunited with Philip, whom Michael had taken as prisoner.

Now Walt, Sophie, and Philip are together. They have the gold. The question is . . . can they get out of Spain in order to help those who need it most?

Characters

Sophie Grace, twenty-five, American, aspiring artist, in Spain to join her fiancé

Walt Block, American newspaper correspondent who has been behind much of Sophie's adventure from the onset; a.k.a. **James Kimmel**, a pro-Franco reporter
Marge and William, Walt's adoptive parents
Philip Stanford, American, soldier in volunteer Abraham Lincoln Brigade, Sophie's new love
José Guezureya, childhood friend of Michael (son of horse trainers who worked for Michael's family)
Ramona, José's wife
Juan, José's father
Pepito, fellow "ranch hand"
Michael, Sophie's ex-fiancé and reason she originally came to Spain
Walter, his father
Cesar, his bodyguard
Adolfo Vidal, Michael's uncle
Edelberto, Berto, Adolfo's son (Michael's cousin)
Father Manuel Garcia, a priest who fled Guernica, now staying in Paris with Edelberto's family
Petra Larios, orphaned daughter of wealthy family of La Mancha, has joined up with José's family
Deion Clay, African-American, also in Abraham Lincoln Brigade
Gwen, a nurse with whom he falls in love

Maria Donita, young Spanish woman whom Sophie once felt was a threat to her relationship with Michael, now married and with a child

Carlito, her son

Ritter Agler, pilot in German air force, a.ka.

Hermann von Bachman

Isanna, the woman he wanted to marry

Xavier, the man Isanna married

Sebastian, son of Isanna and Xavier

Hermann Göring, German general

Monica Schull, American, Ritter's lover

Guerilla fighters for Republican side; enlist aid of Walt, Philip, and Sophie

Emanuel

Domingo

Salvador

Tomas, spy on the "inside" who pretends to be Sophie's uncle

Diego

BRIEFLY MENTIONED

Attis Brody, Philip's best friend, deceased

Benita Sanchez, friend of Michael and Sophie

Luis, Benita's husband (deceased)

Eleanor Winslow, (deceased) American author of letters given to Sophie

Mateo, Eleanor's husband

Gregory Wiersbe, English soldier with Republican volunteers

Hans, German soldier fighting with the Thaelmann Battalion

Oliver Law, African-American officer fighting for Spain

Steve Nelson, Croatian-born leader of Communist party in U.S.

"There is no getting away from a treasure
that once fastens upon your mind."
~Joseph Conrad

"For where your treasure is,
there will your heart be also."
~Matthew 6:21 KJV

Chapter One

The ominous, glowing eyes of a human face stared up at Sophie from the embossed coin. Ancient treasure lit by harsh lamps and protected by thick glass was a common sight at the museum of art back in Boston—but this was the first piece of priceless history she'd ever held in her hand.

The coin was heavier than she'd imagined and more intricately designed. It warmed her hand with its radiance. The pure, soft, and deep yellow metal had been sought for centuries for its symbolic and real value.

Only the movement of the truck broke her trance. She took one last look at the coin, shuddered slightly, and gave it back to Philip. He glanced at her, his blue eyes resting only a moment on hers before he looked away and slid the coin into his pocket.

Sophie knew there was no turning back. Since she'd arrived in Spain a year ago, there were a dozen times when she could have escaped. But she was in too deep now. She had helped to steal Spain's greatest treasure. She'd turned her back on Michael. She'd put her complete trust in Walt . . . and she'd dragged Philip into the mess. This final adventure would either bring all things right, or ruin everything.

Warm air with a hint of moisture blew through the open window. The sun overhead filtered through the trees, creating patterns of light and shadows on the narrow roadway before them. She rolled up the sleeves of her shirt as far as she could, but sweat still glistened on her skin. She brushed back damp hair from her cheek and scanned the roadside for any sign of life. It seemed important to get her mind off the urgent. To let her worries dissipate the way the dust behind the truck tires settled after they passed.

It was no use. The roar of questions that filled her mind seemed even louder than the noise of the truck engine. And the silence of the man on either side of her told Sophie her concerns were not unique.

She glanced at Philip. His wrinkled brow and tired eyes proved his weariness. Though only inches separated them on the seat of the large cargo truck, the wall of tension seemed too much to penetrate. She whispered a silent prayer that they'd find a safe place to hide their truck for the night—and that she'd have a chance to talk with Philip, to explain her seeming betrayal.

On her other side, Walt, too, was silent as he drove, and Sophie wondered if he was thinking through their options of escape and forming a plan. She hoped so. If anyone could take them to safety and get the gold into the hands of those who would make sure the people of Spain benefited, it would be Walt.

If they succeeded in transporting the gold safely across the borders, to the hands of eager collectors, it meant more funds to buy arms. It meant hope for the battle-weary Republic. But if they were caught with it in Nationalist-held territory, the gold would profit Franco and the Fascists. The treasure had already cost so many so much.

Sophie still worried about Michael. The wound from the blast wasn't something to be taken lightly, and she hoped he'd found a doctor.

But as she thought about Michael, anger overwhelmed her worry. Her mind flashed back to the last time she'd seen him injured—dead, she had thought . . . but in reality faking.

Who would do such a thing? Who would put another person through such pain to save his own skin—or more accurately, his own hunt for treasure?

There was a time she'd believed Michael loved her, but obviously that wasn't the case. If he had, he wouldn't have left her alone in Madrid when she first arrived. He wouldn't have left her fate to the mercy of Nationalist soldiers just hours ago.

The truck's movement over the uneven road jostled Sophie's body between Philip and Walt. The truck bed, laden with the heavy gold, creaked with each jolt.

Sophie took another quick breath of the dusty air as it blew in the window. "I have the strangest, creepy sensation, don't you?" She searched Philip's stoic face. "Maybe it's just that I'm being driven through enemy territory, feeling the creaking of this truck as it carries priceless gold"—she switched her gaze to Walt—"with no idea of how or when we'll make it out of Spain."

Walt cleared his throat and glanced at her for the briefest moment. "Yes, there is danger. But perhaps the sensation is due to something more."

Sophie glanced at Walt's fingers as they tightened around the steering wheel. "What do you mean? All that I'm worried about isn't enough? Is there more danger I should know about?"

Sophie felt Philip tense next to her. He'd been silent most of the trip, but from the way he crossed his arms over his chest and set his chin, she knew he wasn't happy. The worst part was knowing she'd caused his pain.

"People have always felt small in comparison to the great universe," Walt continued, ignoring Sophie's question. "They made up legends and myths to make sense of the world—the Greeks with their myths, the Jews with their stories about God. The Aztec nations paid a lot of attention to omens. If the moon was red before a battle, they believed the blood of their enemies would flow. They looked for signs of danger ahead and worried their actions would be displeasing to the gods. I imagine when they saw this gold they felt the same as we do." Walt sighed. "I can imagine them shuddering with each step, wondering if they were making the right moves."

"And if they'd be struck down with lightning if they weren't?" Philip scoffed.

"Or captured before nightfall?" Sophie studied the road ahead intently. A chill moved up her arms, and she wished she hadn't held the coin or looked into its eyes. "Of course, I don't believe in omens," she quickly added. "But if I did, then surely the fact that we outsmarted our enemy is a good sign."

Philip mumbled something under his breath, then said aloud, "If we are caught, the only reason will be our foolish haste. I can't believe you didn't think ahead, Walt—didn't have a plan for where we'd go with the gold once we got it back."

As if not hearing him, Walt continued to manhandle the overburdened truck along the narrow mountain road that Sophie was sure wasn't designed for a load of this size and weight.

Finally he glanced over, looking past Sophie to Philip. "I thought you'd at least thank me for saving your life. You'd be dead, you know, if it weren't for me."

Sophie could see both their points. She also knew the determination of both men and decided it best not to take sides.

The road climbed a small hill. "Besides . . ." Walt angrily shifted the truck into a lower gear as the engine lagged. "I wasn't even sure the plan would work." His voice was firm. "I'm only one man, and my connections only go so far. Be thankful I was able to figure out which airfield the shipment would leave from. The fact that everything fell into place surprised even me."

Getting the truck miles from the airfield as soon as possible had been their first priority. With that accomplished, Sophie hoped Walt had plans to stop, rest, get cleaned up, and maybe find something to eat.

His voice interrupted her thoughts. "I see a creek ahead. You ready for a rest stop?"

"Yes, fine. Then we need to talk about a plan." Philip's fingers tapped against the door handle.

"I would love to stretch my legs." Sophie pushed all thoughts of Michael from her mind. That was the last thing she needed to worry about. Michael had left her as he escaped to France, because she'd made a different choice . . . to stay with Philip, the man she truly loved. And the most important thing was to set things straight with him.

Walt pulled to the side of the road and parked. The truck still took up most of the dusty dirt road, but it didn't seem to matter. They hadn't seen any traffic for the past hour, and Sophie hoped they wouldn't. Though if they were stopped, Walt could likely talk their way out of danger. His quick thinking and persuasive speech never ceased to amaze her.

The men opened their doors and jumped to the ground, stalking away in separate directions. Sophie sighed, looking out at the countryside. In other circumstances she would appreciate the fact that this was one of the most beautiful places she'd seen in all of Spain. The narrow road had been cut through a valley where rolling hills met. Trees covered the hills, and sharp mountain peaks rose on either side.

As she climbed out of the truck she noticed white and purple wildflowers dotting the grassy fields next to a burbling creek. Beautiful—a perfect place to set up her easel and pull out her brushes. But she had neither—only the few items left in her satchel. Besides, those things almost seemed to belong to some other girl in another life. She had more challenging things to worry about.

The way Walt and Philip swung their arms and stomped away reminded Sophie of two boys who'd just been pulled apart from a playground fistfight. They noticed neither the mountain vista nor the wildflowers they tromped beneath their feet.

Philip walked briskly into a field and then stopped, as if realizing he wasn't in a hurry after all. Sophie quietly followed him. She had to defend her actions, had to make him understand why it had been so important to return to Michael, why she'd turned and walked away from Philip at the train station in Madrid three days ago.

She ran a hand through her hair. Had it only been three days? A lifetime of travel and betrayal had taken place since then.

The ground in the meadow was softer than the hard dirt on the road's surface, slowing Philip's agitated pace a bit. His head ached, mostly due to a lack of food and sleep over the last three days when he'd been held by Michael's men. Sleeping while tied to a hard wooden chair wasn't the easiest thing to accomplish. And he'd hardly eaten any of the food brought to him. Not that he wasn't hungry. The idea of being dependent on his captors—of needing them for food, water . . . life . . . disgusted him. He hated being helpless, and they reveled in that very thing.

He glanced back over his shoulder and noticed Sophie jumping down from the truck and heading his direction. He should have figured she would follow him. Anger stirred in his chest. Not just at her, but at Michael. Before last week, Michael had been only a name, a foreboding presence. From the moment Philip first saw Sophie, he had seen the pain in her eyes. Then the man who'd hurt her turned up in the flesh.

Philip replayed the moment at the train station once again. Michael at Sophie's side. Tall, handsome, walking with a commanding presence. He had placed a protective hand on Sophie's back as they moved through the jostling crowd. Philip instantly hated him—and immediately understood him. Maybe it was because if the roles had been reversed, Philip knew he might have done the same thing. He would have hurt Sophie's heart in an effort to save her life. And he would have tried to prove himself again to win her back.

It was hard enough seeing Michael with Sophie. It was even worse when the man walked into the small room where Cesar, Michael's bodyguard, held Philip. Michael tossed an orange back and forth between his hands. He didn't look cruel. In fact, he'd approached with gentle steps. "Untie him. We need to talk."

At first Cesar had refused, but Michael didn't give him a choice.

"I want to know the whole story. I want to know when you met Sophie. Tell me how close you are."

And for some reason, Philip complied. He told Michael about the accident on the battlefield and how he'd been assigned as Sophie's protector as she painted at the field hospital.

Michael listened intently, then nodded. "It seems we love the same woman. And that is no fault of ours. The problem is that I hurt her. And I'm afraid she'll never be able to forgive me." He pulled up a chair and settled across from Philip. "I'm sure that if you've been with her, you know what I did."

Philip jutted out his chin, knowing that if he angered Michael it could mean his death. He didn't care. "You betrayed her. You staged your own death. You abandoned her. And you hoped she'd leave Spain."

"Yes, I did. And now I regret it. I would kill you, but I've hurt her enough." Michael rose and strode away.

Philip hated himself because he understood. He tried to sleep that night, sitting tied to the chair, and the next. Instead, he couldn't stop thinking of what he would have done if he'd been in Michael's position.

Michael was a thief and a liar, yet it also was possible he loved Sophie—or at least thought he did. Philip tried to imagine if the roles were reversed, and he believed that the only way to save Sophie was to fake his death. She was determined and often let her heart lead over her common sense. She'd do anything to protect a friend. Anything to protect those she loved. In fact, she put herself into dangerous situations time and time again in hopes of furthering a cause.

Maybe Michael knew what Philip now realized—it took a lot to get Sophie to back down. Michael had deceived many for his own gain, but the more he thought about it, the more Philip understood his actions.

In the end Philip concluded that he'd do the same. And he hated himself because of that. He also realized that though he grumbled at Walt because of their predicament, the thing he was maddest at was his own heart.

Because deep down Philip worried whether Sophie might still love Michael as much as Michael obviously cared for her. And Philip wondered where he fit in. The answer to that question mattered far more to him than the fate of the gold.

❖ ❖ ❖

Sophie fixed her eyes on the grassy meadow, breathing in the scents of warm grass and sunshine. A small blue butterfly danced from flower to flower ahead of her, as if leading the way.

She watched as Philip scanned the poppy-dotted hillside, but she could tell from his set jaw and sad eyes that he really didn't see it. He glanced at her and sighed, fixing his light blue eyes on hers.

His look ripped at her heart, and more than anything she wanted him to open his arms to her and tell her everything would be okay. Instead they hung limply at his sides.

She had a lot of explaining to do. It wasn't just that they'd been apart for a month, but that she'd spent that month with the first man she'd ever loved. A man she still worried about despite all he'd done to hurt her.

"Philip, I'd like to try to make you understand."

"Yes, please do."

She took a step closer. "I'm so sorry you got involved in all this. I don't even want to think about the things that must be going through your mind. . . ."

He offered her a half smile, but it didn't hide the confusion in his gaze. "Well, I was praying that I'd get to see you again. I guess my dad was right—you'd better watch what you pray for." He subconsciously rubbed his wrists, chafed raw from the ropes that had held him prisoner.

She wanted to touch him, to sooth his wounds. Instead she plucked a tall piece of grass and twirled it in her fingers, finding it easier to focus on her own hands than to risk his gaze. "I suppose God is in control. It's just that at times like this it's hard to see how."

"Or why," Philip added. "Why did I get pulled into this mess?"

Sophie frowned, hoping by *mess* he didn't mean her.

"I can't go back now, Sophie—fighting with the brigade. They already accused me of being a traitor once. It was because of one man's kindness that I was given a chance to try again. If I told them I was captured, kidnapped, and taken to Fascist territory by men who wanted to steal some gold coins, no one would believe me. It sounds ridiculous to my own ears.

"It's not as if I ever planned on being here. Or planned on not being able to leave. I thought I'd done the right thing by volunteering to fight with the International Brigades, but every time I try I fail. I didn't sign up for this, and now . . . now I'd just rather be on the first ship out of here."

"You're right. You came to Spain for one thing and got another." She glanced back over her shoulder toward the truck. "More than you imagined, I'm sure. Yet I think there's a reason you're here, Philip. Why our paths crossed near Madrid. I need you." She hurriedly continued. "Walt needs you too, even though he might not act like it."

Sophie's mind turned to something that had comforted her when she was still with Michael and didn't know what to do or where to turn. Something that was more reassuring to ponder than omens and being captured.

"Maybe God knew our hearts, and how tender they would be for the people here." She spoke quickly, firmly, but deep down it was as if she were trying to convince herself. "It's an honor, if you think of it, to be trusted with so much. It kind of reminds me of how Jesus' mother must have felt—overwhelmed with the responsibility of such treasure given to her, yet in a way thankful that God would put her in His plan. Not that this gold can in any way be compared with God's Son . . . or our cause as worthy as His, but you know what I mean. I don't think it's any accident that we ended up in Spain, or that we are now in control of this treasure."

"I see. I should accept *everything* that's happened . . . and be grateful?" His eyes narrowed. "Just accept it as God's will? I'm still getting used to the idea, but you've had a lot more time to think about it." He turned his head. "Time to think about the gold, I mean."

"Yeah, well, those last days with Mi—" Sophie caught herself. "I went back because Walt asked me to. He told me that finding the gold could help the people of Spain. I didn't realize how long it would take. More than that, I never expected to see you at the train station. Never expected you to see Michael and me together. I never wanted to hurt you like that."

Philip's eyes darted to hers. They narrowed, and his look jabbed at her heart.

She wished he would say something. That he'd yell at her or confess his hurt. Anything would be better than this mute anger. Suddenly a new fear crept out from her darkened mood. What if they couldn't get past this? What if he couldn't forgive her? She searched his eyes for a hint of the affection he'd once shown. The comfort he'd given her when she had no one else to turn to.

"I have thought a lot about it. The gold, that is," she said. "And I think that it's worth it. If my actions can make a difference for the people of Spain, it will be worth all the hardship I have to face. But I never intended to hurt you."

Sophie turned and walked back toward the truck, hoping Philip hadn't seen the tears pooling in her eyes. She saw Walt coming around the side of the truck and moved in his direction, certain that she'd abandoned whatever budding relationship she'd had with Philip the moment she'd allowed Michael's arms to embrace her at the train in Guernica.

"Time to head out," Walt called. "We don't know how long it will take Michael and his friends to figure out they've been duped. The farther we can get from the airfield, the better."

"Do you know yet where we're going?" Philip asked him.

From the look in his eyes, Sophie could see Walt didn't.

"Not exactly, but I believe we're heading in the right direction. This back road is working for now. It has little traffic and plenty of tree cover to hide us from the sky."

"Do you think they'll send out a plane to find us?" Sophie scanned the sky.

Philip answered for Walt. "I'm sure they'll use whatever resources they have. It's not like they'll just shrug their shoulders and let us get away with this."

Walt shook his head. "I'm not sure how quickly they can pull together people to search for us. Our advantage is that Michael trusts very few people."

He opened the passenger door for Sophie and helped her inside.

"Everyone who did Michael's bidding did so by his trickery. Even the men who drove the trucks carrying the stolen gold knew nothing of the cargo. They were paid off and are living handsomely somewhere far away from the front lines."

"But this road will take us to safety, right?" Sophie found her spot in the seat and was soon sandwiched between the men.

Two doors slammed shut, and Walt started the engine.

"Well, it's not the most direct route, but it's taking us away from the seat of Nationalist control . . . and toward our best option. I think our best chance is to try to make it to Barcelona. I have good contacts there. I know we can get the gold out through their ports, but in any town closer . . . I'm uncertain what type of help we can get."

Chapter Two

The truck continued on with only its clunking, groaning noises to interrupt the silence between the occupants. Long shadows from tree branches spread over the road, telling Philip they were driving east and north. Beside him Sophie slept. Her head, cocked at an awkward angle, rested against the seat behind her and tilted to the left and the right with the movement of the truck over the road. Philip knew she'd be more comfortable if she rested her head on his shoulder. She didn't ask, and he didn't offer.

For weeks he had prayed to be reunited with her again, but now it seemed like someone was playing a joke on him. More than anything, he wished for space. For time to think and pray. Of course, that wouldn't happen unless he ditched her and Walt to head out across enemy territory on his own. No, he was forced to stay. Forced to follow this thing through, wherever that led.

When he and Sophie parted at Guernica, there was an apology in her gaze. Now he knew why. It hurt and humiliated him at the same time. What a fool he'd been to think she truly loved him. He should have learned from his first girlfriend in Seattle. He'd loved her too, yet she'd married someone else. Such beautiful, talented women would never love someone ordinary like him.

Sophie. He couldn't help that his heart warmed as he glanced at her. Yes, she no doubt appreciated his saving her on the battlefield. She seemed to have grown fond of him over those months he'd protected her. They'd grown close as she amazingly transformed oil on canvas to tell the story of the field hospital's carnage and of the faces of the desperate and dying volunteers who were so dedicated. Yet even though they experienced so much together, Philip realized he could never replace Michael. Even though the man had betrayed them all, Philip still saw the concern in Sophie's eyes as she spoke of him.

It was another cruel joke that their destination now was Barcelona. The city's name was enough to cause Philip's stomach to constrict. He thought back to his first days in Spain—training for the Workers Games, striding down the boulevard in his workout clothes with Attis by his side—as hungry for his friend's victory as he'd been for the authentic food that had saturated the air with its aroma. Stupid smiles had filled their faces, ignorant as they were of the developing political situation. Instead hopes of athletic victory pounded in their hearts with each beat. Had it only been a year ago that he'd dreamed of leaving Spain with a gold medal around Attis's neck?

Philip patted the gold coin in his pocket. Carrying a piece of history was an amazing thing, but he planned to return it at their next stop. Although he didn't buy into Walt's talk of omens and curses, he felt strange holding it. Perhaps that was because hundreds, even thousands, of people had lost their lives trying to possess it. From the people who first crafted it to the Spaniards who stole it, how many men had died fighting over these riches? He'd feel better knowing the coin was back in the box where it belonged. And after that, knowing collectors would take care of it, instead of allowing more little men to fight for the power and wealth the gold objects brought.

Walt cleared his throat, and Philip glanced over at him. Their irritation at each other had subsided as they'd both had time to calm their minds with the fresh air.

Walt nodded toward Sophie, who was snoring softly. "She's sleeping hard."

Philip couldn't help but think it was the most beautiful snore he'd ever heard. "She's been through a lot."

"That she has. And what about you? Are you okay? I swear the color drained from your face when I mentioned Barcelona."

"Next time I'm rescued, I hope it's not by a spy. It seems like I can't keep anything to myself—even my private thoughts."

"Fine. Next time you're rescued, you can make sure of that. But what about now? You still haven't answered my question."

"I'm fine." Philip let out a long sigh. Yet even as he spoke those words his knees trembled slightly. "I just had no idea I'd ever have to go back to Barcelona. It's ironic, don't you think? I went there once in search of gold of a different kind, and now I'm returning in an effort to protect that very thing."

"Don't let your feathers get ruffled just yet. We can't just jump on a turnpike and arrive in a day or two. First we must make it to Granada. There's a castle, a fortress, overlooking the city, with tunnels that lead to different parts of the city. Maybe we can find a place to hide the truck and the gold. At least it's a stopping place."

"Granada? Isn't that in Franco's hands?" Philip's fist balled in his lap as he said that name.

"Yes, the Nationalists have captured the city, but the Republicans still hold the rest of the province."

"How far away is it?"

"We've been traveling northeast, and we're nearly to Málaga. That means we're halfway."

"Really? That close?" Philip straightened in his seat. "Still, will we have time to travel all the way without being found? If . . . those guys who are after the gold are smart, they'll figure out where we're headed."

Philip could not bring himself to speak casually about Michael, even if the others did. He didn't understand how both Sophie and Walt could talk about him as if he were just a lost soul in need of discovering the truth.

"I don't think so. If the plane has landed, they may just now be discovering they were fooled. But also, it helps to remember how things work in Spain." Walt smirked. "*Mañana*. Whenever possible the business of today is put off until tomorrow. The way

I figure it, we have another day to get to Granada and hide the gold."

"Let's hope you're right."

Philip glanced at sleeping Sophie one more time. She looked like an angel, the way her hair fell across her cheek.

"You'd better be right," he added with more conviction.

José knew the mountains well, and though the journey on horseback up the steep hills had sapped the energy from his father and Pepito, and had taken a toll on the horses, they'd all made it. They now rested in a high pasture, off the beaten path, where he hoped they'd be safe for a time.

Petra did a fine job making sure the men were comfortable and fed. She was young, José knew, but she carried a strength that couldn't be denied. He chuckled to himself at the way his father diligently obeyed when told to wash up for dinner or to peel a few potatoes from the sack of supplies they'd brought with them. Juan Guezureya had never been one to follow another, or hold his tongue, yet he didn't seem to mind following Petra's orders. For that matter, Pepito didn't either. Each had his own reasons, José was sure, but they seemed to appreciate the young woman's care.

José set up a small camp and then he set out on foot, returning the way he'd come. Curiosity drew him to Bilbao. But more than that, fear forced him from his precipice of safety. What if something had happened to Ramona? What if she had been injured or . . . ? He didn't want to think of what else happened to women by invading armies. He knew he would never forgive himself if his wife experienced such a thing.

The trees thinned as the forest around him ended at a large cliff overlooking the coastal valley below. Two deep river valleys led to Bilbao. One valley came from the direction of Eibar and Durango, the other from Orduña, some miles to the north of the main Burgos-Vitoria road. High mountains, reaching to 4,500 feet, rose in every direction.

From these peaks José had witnessed the horror unleashed upon the coastal cities. With little opposition, the Fascists had penetrated the valleys winding through the mountain regions. First the air force and the artillery had bombarded the slopes nearest to Bilbao; then the enemy troops advanced. The opposition had staged a spirited fight, but there were not enough weapons or good men to hold their cities. José knew without a doubt that if the people had had more weapons, more manpower, the Nationalist High Command wouldn't have had a chance. Instead he'd seen them easily moving forward, steadily gaining ground. Nationalist troops had white patches sewn on their shoulders so they could identify each other. They also carried flags for the aircraft to recognize the units from above.

José had wanted to join the fight against their approach, but what could one man do? Instead he had grieved as he watched the gold and scarlet Nationalist banner carried to a high point where it fluttered from the top peak of the Urquiola range—the one ridge Franco's men dared to climb.

The Basques had done what they could, digging miles of trenches and spreading out barbed-wire belts, but somehow the enemy invaders had known the easiest penetration points. Once through, nothing—no one—stood in their way. Most of the defenders were forced to retreat. And soon, the town fell.

Days ago, as he watched the Nationalist flag unfurl above Bilbao, José's gut ached as if someone had slugged him. Even now tears ran down his face as he leaned against a tall tree for support. "Ramona, Ramona . . . How could I have abandoned my wife?" he muttered as a thousand possibilities raced through his mind.

He didn't know how much time passed as he wept. It seemed all the tension that had mounted since leaving Guernica refused to be dammed any longer. Perhaps there were other, older heartaches he'd been holding inside, too. The pain of discovering the truth about Michael, his friend since childhood. The pain of traveling to Madrid and leaving those he loved behind. The heartache of helping Michael fake his death in order to rescue Sophie from his grasp, but failing at that as well.

In fact, it seemed in every way he tried to help he simply

brought more pain, more heartache, to those he loved. He was ready now for things to be different. For once, he hoped, he would protect his wife as a husband should. And keep safe those in his care, despite the dangers around them.

Minutes passed on the quiet hillside, maybe an hour, as he looked upon the captured city below. All José knew was that when he rose and turned back up the mountain, he had made a promise to get his father and the others settled as best he could, and then return to find Ramona. He refused to allow the enemy to harm that which was most precious.

Chapter Three

Ramona's endless steps brought her to the top of a small rise, her feet aching in the broken-down shoes she'd worn for the past six months. The hot, dry road stretched before her as it had from so many other small rises she'd ascended. When would it end? Not just this stretch of the journey, but the war. Her back ached from leaning over countless war-ravaged casualties—individual human beings who'd looked to her for healing, for hope. Her heart hurt too, but that was nothing new. Nothing she wasn't used to.

Her feet continued moving one in front of the other, linked to her conscious mind only by the pain of each step. Small dust clouds formed with each footfall, rising to join the choking large cloud caused by the thousands of other feet trudging along the side of the paved road. The sun bore down on her without the slightest stirring of air to carry away its heat. She wiped her sweaty brow with the handkerchief, now as rough as sandpaper, and tried to find her way to the edge of the walking mass. Maybe there was a breeze to be found there.

A caravan of trucks had carried the other nurses, but Ramona gave up her place so one of the injured could find a way out. She was young and could walk for a while, she told herself, hoping for another truck to come along. But none came, so she continued on. Just one in a sea of many.

She replayed in her mind the weeks before the fall of Bilbao. She'd carried a tray of food to one of the ill nuns just as the first wave of bombers appeared over the mountains. German planes. Like those that had attacked Guernica. Soon the church bells pealed, but the terrified cries of the people were louder than the bells.

In Guernica, before the bombers came, Ramona thought the war would simply pass, just like the numerous little battles she'd experienced while growing up, and then they'd all get on with normal life. She believed if she worked hard and helped those she could, then she would make a difference. And since those around her worked as hard as she, together they would find victory. The war was hard on all of them, but the fight was worthy. She'd lost many close to her, but the war had also brought José back to her from Madrid.

Instead, food shortages had caused many to grow sick and weak. And though she helped all she could, trucks transported the dead from the front lines, depositing their ghastly cargo in record numbers. It seemed they lost more soldiers than they had time to bury.

Ramona trudged past a small oxcart and nodded to the older man and woman who sat under it, seeking shade and rest before they continued. From somewhere ahead she heard the cry of an infant and wondered if the mother had enough water for herself and the baby—not that she could do anything if they didn't. Ramona had drained her own waterskin over an hour ago.

She thought back to the first time she'd heard that José had returned to Guernica. His injury had reunited them, and in a way she felt it was God's hand—to bring them back together when so much threatened to keep them apart. They could stand anything for a short time, including their most recent separation. They would get past this too, and be reunited. All of Spain would get past this and find the peace they all longed for. Or at least that's what she had hoped.

But the bombers told her differently. First in Guernica, then in Bilbao. It was the bombers that proved to her that the mountains could no longer protect her people. It was the bombers that forced José to return and care for others he felt a responsibility for, both two-legged and four-legged.

She felt guilty for feeling thankful that his injury was bad enough for him to be brought to her care. At least it hadn't damaged him permanently.

And because she firmly believed God had brought José to her, when the bombs fell she had decided to stay at the hospital to help care for the injured who were brought in, instead of leaving with him. Surely if God had saved José once, He'd do so again.

She had heard that tragedy brought people together. Instead it had pulled them apart. José still embraced her, but she could see a distance in his gaze, as if there were a part of him that had died that day . . . something she didn't understand, but that had affected him all the same.

The Germans knew what they were doing. They knew war that killed and injured women and children touched men in a way that battlefield casualties couldn't. And their hellish strategy had worked, changing José because he couldn't protect what he felt responsible for.

While she traveled to Bilbao with the injured, he'd gone another way—back to the place where his father was . . . and the horses. To be with them, to protect them. He'd run to the one place he hoped he could make a difference.

Even though she told him to go, her heart wanted him to stay. And even when she claimed she'd be okay, she wanted more than anything for him to realize how much she needed him. Why couldn't he see that? Why couldn't he fight for *her*? Protect *her*?

She'd wanted him to stay because it was in his heart—not because she had asked. But instead he left. He embraced her, turned, and left.

Yes, her body was fine, but Ramona's heart hurt. It felt as if a bomb had exploded across it, shattering it into a million little pieces and then burning what remained.

"But what difference does that make now?" she muttered as she continued on, moving one foot and then the other. "He is gone and I am alone."

She looked down at her nurse's uniform, now stained and soiled, and then repeated herself, though there was no one close enough to hear. "I am alone. I'm surrounded by strangers, but alone all the same."

The man walked by with a baguette on his shoulder. The whiff of it, the wonderful scent, brought tears to Father Manuel's eyes as he considered the poor and the hungry of Spain. Why should he be healthy and well fed when those God gave him to shepherd lived in hunger, poverty—and now bondage?

The newspaper was spread open before him on the small café table, and he read the headlines as if reading a letter from home, so urgent to his heart was the news. Bilbao had been taken. The city was now in Nationalist control. Most had escaped and moved to the next town, and the next, hoping to stay one step ahead of the troops. But could they? Could they outrun the inevitable?

Feeling the weight of his people on his shoulders, Father Manuel rose from the cast-iron chair by the small café table and strolled down the boulevard. Paris was a beautiful city filled with sharply dressed people attending the World's Fair. Yet he knew if it hadn't been for the kindness of a stranger, that reporter Walt Block, he wouldn't be here at all. He'd be with the others, running, hiding, hoping for escape. Why had he been plucked from the fire? It was a question he couldn't shake.

And what about Berto? The young man had shown up at the train station the first day Father Manuel had arrived. Many were there that day, all waiting for word from Spain, and when Berto discovered Father Manuel was also from the Basque region, he'd offered help, for which Father Manuel was thankful.

Through their time together, it was clear that Berto's heart was for the people of Spain. Father Manuel knew that the young man was another evidence of God's provision. It was clear God wanted him here, even though he did not know why.

He considered retreating to his small room, but knew his

Lord would take no pleasure from his hiding away there, worrying about events that he could no longer influence. Besides, during the day his room offered him no comfort. In one of the other rooms a guitarist played Spanish music, fast and painful, playing what Father Manuel dared not voice. More than that, if a musical instrument could scold, this one did.

Remember Spain. Do not forget. Fight. Remember. Fight.

He continued walking until he reached the beautiful church he'd noticed from a distance. Cathédrale Notre Dame de Paris. Our Lady of Paris.

A hedge circled the small grounds. It was trimmed so perfectly flat it could have served as a table. Most visitors lingered outside, taking in the well-known and admired architecture. People came from all over the world, he'd been told, to view the church. Yet this made little sense to him. How could one care for the elaborate towers and spire but ignore the purpose of its construction? A great cathedral pointed to a great God, did it not?

The church bell tolled three solid rings, and Father Manuel grunted as he walked up the brick steps, as if answering the echoing gong. *I'm coming, I'm coming.*

He was far from home, but not far from God. And perhaps instead of trying to make sense in his mind as to why he was in France, it was time to ask God's opinion on the matter.

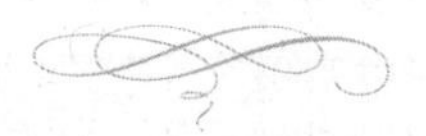

Night had come, and they'd found a place to rest. A meadow that allowed him full view of the truck and a long stretch of the road each direction. Still, Walt's focus wasn't on the road.

He looked to Sophie, curled on her side in a tight little ball. She looked so small, so fragile, lying under the tree. On the other side of her, Philip lay close to the base of the tree, his back to her.

Walt had known many beautiful women in his life, but that was all they were. Just a shell. But Sophie was so much more. Her spirit. Her strength. Her trust. Her trust in him was overwhelming.

Yet she no longer looked brave. Instead she appeared like an injured lamb. Her heart had been broken by Michael's betrayal. And by Philip's anger. And Walt had no answers, no plan to keep her safe. He knew when he got into this treasure hunt that there was a chance he could lose the gold. But now so much more could be lost.

He let out a sigh and plucked a blade of grass. It had been easy to pull Sophie into the conflict when he didn't know her. Or rather, when he thought she was part of Michael's team. Later, when he knew she was an innocent victim, Walt—for the first time—felt his foundation crumble.

As someone who prided himself on being in control and unemotional, he questioned if his motives were right—and if his plan would succeed. Until today he'd always acted with determination, but it was clear that Sophie and Philip had witnessed the crumbling of his façade. He had the gold, but it was almost worse than not having it. Keeping it, transporting it, was the problem now. And Sophie was again pulled into the middle of the danger.

Oppression bore down on Walt, and he suddenly wondered why he was doing this. His life was entrapped in the middle of a tangled web.

His mind replayed every contact, every idea.

In the past he'd consider all his options, and one would rise to the top. Like a miner in days of old, he would swish the ideas around in his mind, washing away the silt until only a nugget of gold remained.

But not this time. This time his muddled mind wouldn't process. There was no easy answer. More than that, there were two more people who depended on him. He wasn't used to this sort of prolonged contact. His modus operandi was in and out of people's lives. No entanglements, no ties. But, Sophie . . . and now Philip. It was all different.

Weariness overcame him, and suddenly he didn't want to be in charge anymore. Maybe he'd talk to Philip in the morning and get some ideas. Or maybe he should just walk away. Or take the truck. Risk getting caught by himself. Philip and Sophie would think he'd abandoned them to keep the gold, but it might save their necks. Philip had crossed Spain before; no doubt he could do it again. Sophie would be better in Philip's hands than Walt's at this moment.

Because the truth was, there was more to the story than they knew. Yes, he had followed Michael, but not for the gold. For something far more precious.

❖ ❖ ❖

Sophie had no blanket. No pillow. But she did her best to find a comfortable place under the trees. For a pillow she used an old shirt that had seen better days. Thankfully the air was warm and smelled of pine, and the grass that grew thick formed her mattress under the tree. She closed her eyes, but sleep eluded her.

Not more than ten feet away Philip curled to his side, his back to her. He wore a blue and white jacket and had tucked an identical one under his head. He had other things in his pack that had been useful. A tin they used to heat water over the fire. A waterskin they'd refilled in the creek. He even had some dry crackers to share. That, with the few fish that he'd caught in the small creek, had taken away the hunger pains.

But even as he did his best to make sure Sophie was safe, comfortable, and fed, he'd said little to her. Every time she looked at him guilt stabbed her heart, and she wondered if they'd ever reclaim what they once had. She missed the way they used to talk so easily. The way they laughed and joked. She missed his hand taking hers and the feel of his breath against her neck as they embraced.

During the time she'd known Philip, they'd been apart nearly as much as they'd been together. And now the ten feet separating them seemed like an abyss.

Sophie sighed, rolled to her stomach, and imagined snuggling next to his back. She wanted to know he still cared for her. She wanted his assurance and his warmth.

She heard him stir and hoped he would scoot a few feet closer. Maybe then they could talk in the darkness of the night. Maybe that would be easier, so they wouldn't have to look at the pained expression on each other's face.

Instead, in the light of the moon, Sophie watched as Philip stood and turned in Walt's direction.

"I'm going to sleep in the cab of the truck," he said. "You don't mind, do you?"

"Not at all. If you think it will be more comfortable."

He walked in the direction of the road, and Sophie heard the cab door creak open.

Minutes passed, and the sounds of crickets rose from the nearby creek.

"Do you think he's asleep?" Sophie whispered to Walt.

"I doubt it. I'm sure he's trying to come to grips with all that's happened." Walt had settled on the other side of the clearing, close enough for Sophie to know that he was there if she needed his protection.

She lay for a few more minutes, trying to find shapes and constellations in the stars. "Maybe I'll go talk to him. We need to clear the air."

"I don't think that's a good idea, Sophie." Walt's voice sounded weary. "Leave him alone. Give him some time to sort things out."

"Yeah, well, I hate this tension between us." She ran her fingers through her hair, feeling a small twig caught in it. "Neither of us will be able to sleep unless we talk."

"He doesn't think the same as you. You want to talk so there won't be conflict between you. Philip *doesn't* want to talk because he already knows there is conflict. He's not ready to hear what you have to say."

She patted the ground and readjusted the shirt she'd tucked under her cheek. Then she yawned. "Maybe you're right. Forcing him to talk when we're both tired and worried wouldn't be the best idea."

"If you care what I think, hiding in Nationalist territory with a stolen, hunted treasure probably isn't the best time for two people to talk about their relationship—" Walt's voice stopped abruptly at a rustling in the bushes near the creek.

Before she knew what was happening, he was on his feet. It was dark, but not too dark to notice the moonlight glinting off the handgun he held pointed toward the noises in the night.

Chapter Four

Michael cursed as he paced in front of the cargo plane, waiting for his parents. He had sent a telegram ahead telling them to meet him at the airfield. And what did he have to show for it? Rocks. The white ammunition boxes held nothing but rocks.

In the distance, the lights of Paris caused the night sky to glow above the city. He used to love this place, but not anymore. He'd do anything to be back in Spain, and not have to face the fact that he'd been made a fool.

Across the landing strip, he saw his father walking toward him. That tall frame, those stiff shoulders. And just a hint of gray hair peeking out from under the fedora he always wore.

"Your mother couldn't make it. You know how stress weakens her heart."

"It's better that way." Michael lifted the lid showing the rocks where there should have been gold. He didn't need to explain. The disappointment in his father's gaze was clear.

"They tricked you, didn't they?" The older man shook a fist in the air. "I told you to stay away from that woman. From the first I thought she was a distraction. But I had no idea it would come to this."

"I'm going back. We'll find them. Get the gold." Michael remembered Sophie's look the last time he'd seen her. She'd been hurt. And she was determined to stay with the volunteer, Philip. Obviously she believed she cared for the man. But her eyes had shown no trickery.

"I imagine she thinks she will be rich. She'll use the gold for her own gain!" his father spouted.

Michael didn't argue. But he knew, deep inside, that Sophie believed he had flown away with the gold in the cargo hold. She was just a pawn in the hands of that man, Walt Block. He'd targeted Sophie even before she'd crossed into Spain. It was because of Walt that the gold would again be at the bidding of the Republicans—to be sold to Communist Russia and melted down into gold bars, despite its value.

Foolish woman . . . open your eyes to what's happening!

"I'll make sure we get the gold back. Nothing will happen to it," Michael repeated. His voice was firm, but he knew better than to raise it in the presence of his father.

"Who will ensure this? You and your bodyguard? Do you have the ability to cover the entire country in your search? I thought I could trust you, Son. Your mother . . . what is she going to say? Can you imagine how she'll feel to know that the priceless artifacts are once again lost?"

Michael didn't want to think about that. His mother could be the kindest person on earth if she got what she wanted. And when she didn't . . .

A new emotion came over him—pity for his father. Pity for any man forced to face his mother's wrath.

Weariness also washed over Michael. Pain from the wound to his leg and weakness from losing so much blood. His father hadn't even asked about his bandaged leg. Didn't he care about his son's injury?

No matter how hard Michael tried, nothing changed. His parents were concerned about what mattered to *them*. They cared for their son . . . if he shared *their* concerns. Never a day passed that he didn't strive for their approval, long for their praise. But whatever he accomplished never seemed to be good enough.

"How could this happen?" His father paced, throwing his

hands in the air. "When did they make the switch?"

"At the airfield. That reporter, or spy—whatever he is—must have more connections than I realized. I thought the guards loaded the gold, but they were on his payroll instead."

"Which makes reclaiming our booty even more difficult. Who knows who else is under his control! The gold is most likely at the port right now, being shipped to line their pockets. Shipped to the melting pots." His father's face fell. "What will I tell the collectors?"

"Tell them nothing." Michael limped closer to his father. "Not yet. Simply say that the war in Spain is making transport more difficult than we thought."

Michael could not tell his father that half the gold had already been claimed by Franco, even before they had a chance to rescue it from its "safe" place in the tunnel. To his father, Franco was Spain's savior. Telling him the truth would only shame the older man and feed his anger. Michael's only hope was that the collectors would be so enthralled by the beauty and worth of the ancient treasure remaining that they'd forget that what he offered was far less than first promised. Or perhaps that was just wishful thinking. Perhaps he'd been doomed from the start.

Pain shot up Michael's leg. He caught himself on the door of his father's automobile, using all his strength not to crumple to the ground. Then he straightened, forcing himself to be strong in his father's eyes.

His father looked toward the bloody shirt wrapped around Michael's leg but still did not ask about the wound. "You have two months to find the gold. Two months to get it to France. And to get rid of that woman, Sophie." He spat her name. "And finish off her friends. Nothing less will do." He wiped a drop of sweat from his lip. "What will I tell your mother?"

"Tell her that . . ." Michael's voice caught in his throat. His words escaped with a heavy breath. "I am sorry, and I will not fail again."

"Fine, but if I were you I wouldn't show my face until that promise comes to pass." His father looked away. "Her words can slice deeper than any knife."

Walter opened the door, climbed into the automobile, and

started the engine. Michael hobbled two steps back, then watched him drive away without another glance.

Cesar approached, and Michael saw the pity in his gaze. It was the last thing he wanted.

"We need to return to Spain as soon as possible."

"And find help from where?" Cesar questioned. "It's obvious we can't trust the police or Franco's men. Besides . . ." He stepped forward and wrapped an arm around Michael's waist. "We're going nowhere until you get that leg looked at and find your strength. Many have already died in search of the gold. Let's not add your name to that list."

Ritter settled on the stool in front of the bar and rested his weight on his arms. He was happy to be back in Germany. Happy that the plans for the Norden bombsight had been delivered and that Göring had been generous in his reward.

The strong smell of beer caused a weary smile to curl on Ritter's face, and he knew that its numbing warmth would soon spread its wings over his anxious mind.

The bartender acknowledged his presence with the faintest of nods. He offered Ritter a tall glass, filled to the top with frothy cold beer, and then turned back to a man who claimed he'd just arrived from Thuringia.

"You should see what the fuehrer has planned for the enemies of the Reich." The man's words slurred, and his eyes were bloodshot. Ritter wondered how much longer the man would be able to sit at the stool at this rate.

"I was asked to come and tour the place myself—a new concentration camp that will be opening in a month," the man continued. "They have plans for a thousand inmates, maybe more. Some prisoners are already there, building the very walls that will confine them! It is not a good time to be an enemy of the Reich." Laughter spilled from the man's lips.

Ritter opened his mouth to ask more questions, but another

man spoke before he had the chance. This man spoke German, but with an American accent.

"Perhaps if such a cleansing of one's enemies had been done in Spain, their civil battle would not have escalated as it has." He spoke with the slow, even tone of a politician.

"I've been in Spain," Ritter said, hoping to impress. "The people are mad—both sides. And the ideas they die for pale in comparison to those of our new Germany."

The American raised one eyebrow. "The Spanish war is only an outward indication of the disease that is inflicting mankind—it is not the disease itself. The fault lies in the Treaty of Versailles. Upon signing it, those conquered in the last war were labeled second-rate. It robbed them of any hope for a better future."

"Germany was one of those nations, but not any longer," Ritter replied. "And though it seemed as if we were robbed, that is no longer the case. We have grand hopes, grand dreams." He leaned toward the man. "Dreams many are willing to fight for, die for."

"*Ja*, because you have a great leader. Hitler has emerged at the right time, with a message that twenty years of despair has primed the people for."

Ritter studied the man's face, surprised that the American's views matched his own.

"Men and women living as second-class citizens, due to the mistakes of an earlier generation, will embrace the first opportunity to free themselves." The American turned to the man who had spoken of the building of the camp. "And in this case, their freedom hinges on locking up those they feel threaten that freedom. It's a step." He took a long drink from his tall stein of beer. "Only a first step."

Ritter nodded his agreement. "Better to lock them up than blow them up. I've seen the destruction bombs and artillery can do to a country."

The men drank in silence.

"So where does that leave us?" Ritter finally asked.

"I, for one, am returning to my country to relay my thoughts to any who will listen. I'll urge my country to stick to the treaties, but also understand those who do not. In my opinion, the conflict in Europe—that which is already happening and that which is to come—will right the wrongs the other nations have imposed. Yes, there will most likely be more battles, more deaths, and more camps . . . but when the dust settles we'll discover a greater peace than we've ever known."

"I hope you are right." Ritter ran his finger along the droplets of water pooling outside his glass. "I can think of nothing greater than to settle down with a good mate and live a good life." He took another drink as his brooding thoughts turned back to Isanna, who was doing just that—with someone other than himself.

The first man rose and staggered across the room to tell another table of his news, and the American ordered another drink with a flick of his finger.

Ritter did the same, and as the bartender approached, he peered over Ritter's shoulder toward the door.

Ritter turned and nearly fell off his stool as he saw Monica Schull approaching.

"Ritter, darling." Her voice rose excitedly. "Your uncle said I might find you here. He's disappointed, actually, that you didn't choose to spend the evening with him. But he was pleased and excited to know that I'd come—that I just couldn't bear to stay away."

"Monica." Ritter opened his arms for a quick hug. "You've followed me home, like a puppy looking for its master."

"I'm not sure about that, but I am here. New York was boring without you, darling." She gazed up at him with large blue eyes and adjusted the red hat that perched on her blonde curls. "I hope you don't mind."

"Mind?" Ritter patted the barstool next to him, motioning for her to sit. "You are far more entertaining than the politics these men prattle on about. And far more appealing to the eye as well." Ritter let out a long sigh. "Why ever would I mind?"

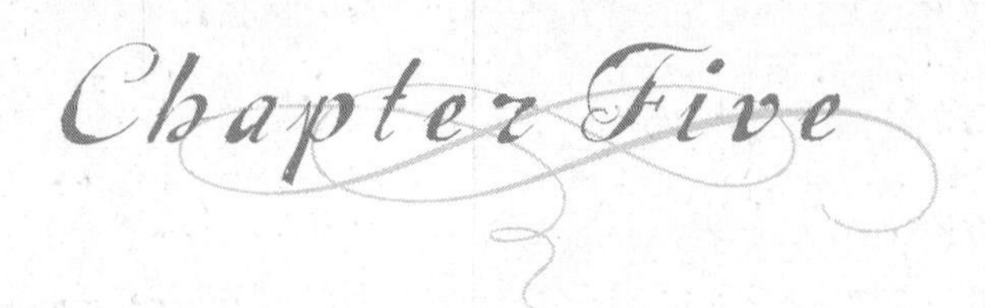

Chapter Five

Sophie watched with wide eyes as a lone man exited the woods, his footsteps steady despite the darkness. His hands stretched into the air when he noticed Walt's gun fixed on him.

"Do not shoot. I come as a friend, señor! I come in peace."

"Come closer. Let me see your face." Walt motioned with his free hand.

There was nothing distinguishing about the Spaniard. The deeply creased wrinkles on his face told Sophie he was most likely as old as her father, but he moved with the energy of a much younger man.

"You drive a truck from Franco's men, but I know you are not one of them. We've been watching you. We'd like to offer help."

Walt cocked his head to the side, but held the gun steady. "How do you know we aren't with Franco?"

"Because only those who hide from Franco use this road. There are more direct routes to take if you are working for the general. Also, we noticed the man's jacket. The one who now sleeps in the truck. It was for the Workers Games, was it not? And the men who were in those, they believe in the cause of the people, yes?"

"You are brave, coming to us like this. It could have cost you your life." Walt lowered his gun.

The man shrugged. "That could be said of many things. No place is safe anymore. My hope is that you have supplies for fighting against Franco. Am I right?"

"Sí, you are correct. I—"

"Sophie? Walt? Are you okay?" Philip's voice interrupted Walt's words.

"Yes, come here. We have a visitor."

Philip came closer, and his eyes widened as he spotted the Spaniard. "I thought I heard a strange voice."

"Strange, sí, my wife says the same thing. I am Emanuel." He moved forward eagerly to shake Philip's hand. "I've come to provide help, señor. Perhaps you need a place to rest for a few days? Maybe someplace to hide your truck?"

Philip looked toward Walt. Even in the dim moonlight Sophie could tell he questioned whether the man should be trusted.

As if understanding the look, the man continued. "I used to work in a coal mine deep in these mountains. It has been shut down for a while. Now many of us live off what the land and forest provide. We have opposed Franco from the beginning, but no one bothers us up here. We are like fleas to them. No more than a small annoyance."

"You say you have a place where we can hide our truck, our . . . supplies?" The breeze blew slightly, and Sophie tucked a piece of hair behind her ear. A warm peace settled over her, and for some reason she knew this man—his offer—was an answer to her prayers.

"Sí, I can give you directions." Emanuel turned to Walt, as if knowing he was in charge. "It's only a couple hours' drive by truck. We can get there faster on foot, if we are not limited to the roads. It is my job, you see, to know who travels through our hills and why."

"I have paper in the truck. I'd better write these directions down." Walt turned to Philip. "You don't mind, do you, if I take over the cab for a while?"

"Not at all. I . . . I need to talk to Sophie anyway."

The man followed Walt. With excited words he described

many of the ways they'd ambushed Franco's troops and stolen weapons from his armories in the nearby towns. When their voices were out of earshot, Sophie turned to Philip.

They were alone, and his look held compassion. Sophie tried to think of something to say, another way to apologize, but Philip didn't give her the chance.

He took her hand. "I know I haven't been the easiest person to get along with, Sophie. But I have to tell you that I fell asleep as soon as I lay down on the truck seat, which is a miracle in itself."

He paused, as if replaying a memory, then spoke again. "I thought I was praying, but it must have been a dream. Anyway, dream or not, I was praying for God to make a way for us, when I could almost hear Him speak. 'You're asking Me to help you, but you haven't forgiven Sophie yet. Hurry now. Go right now and forgive her.'"

Sophie felt her heartbeat quicken. "You heard that? In a dream?"

"Strange, isn't it? And then when I came to find you, to talk to you, I heard another person's voice. All I could think of was that something was going to happen to you, and you'd never know I cared. Never know I've forgiven you. I have, you know. And now I ask, can you forgive me?"

Sophie squeezed his hands. "You? But you've done nothing. I was the one who lied to you. I should have told you where I was going and why."

"And I should have trusted your heart. I know that you're not perfect, Sophie, but you try to do what's right."

Sophie didn't know what to say. Instead she offered Philip a quick embrace and stepped back. "Yes, I forgive you . . . I'm glad things are okay between us. They are okay, aren't they?"

Philip was silent for a moment; then he shrugged. "It's still painful for me, knowing you were with Michael all that time." He swallowed hard as he said that name. "But over time you can tell me more. I'm sure it wasn't easy for you either, especially after all you've faced. Soon, Sophie, I want to hear what you went through while we were apart. But not tonight. We better get some rest. Tomorrow, it seems, will be another challenging day."

With the directions tucked in his pocket, Walt approached Philip, who had resumed his first position at the base of the tree.

Philip was awake, and Walt wasn't surprised. He knew he also wouldn't be able to sleep, knowing they'd been discovered. It made no difference that they'd been discovered by a friend rather than a foe. Thankfully, Sophie trusted their decisions, and her gentle snore was carried along with the sound of crickets.

Walt pointed in the direction opposite her, and Philip rose and followed him.

When they'd moved far enough away that their voices wouldn't be heard, Walt placed a hand on Philip's shoulder. "What do you think?"

"What do you mean, what do I think? I was going to ask you."

"I'm not sure. Emanuel seems sincere enough. But it could be a trap."

"Then again . . ." Philip ran a hand down his face, rubbing the shadow of a beard. "He could be an answer to our prayers."

"Do you believe that?" Walt studied Philip's face. He wished he had the same faith. But to have faith in God now, he had to accept the fact that God had been there all along. A silent figure who did nothing to step in and change the one thing Walt had wanted most—which wasn't the gold.

He felt a glimmer of peace inside him. It was like nothing he'd ever felt before. It wasn't there, and then suddenly it was. Something inside that was telling him everything was going to be all right. He moved toward the nearest log and sat down.

"I don't know. He seemed genuine," Walt repeated.

"I sure hope so. I'll take the first watch, just in case." Philip straightened his back and crossed his arms over his chest. "This isn't only the gold we're talking about." His eyes were fixed on Sophie.

Two hours after he and Philip had talked, Walt knew he should have been sleeping. They had an answer to their problem.

As strange as it was, it had come to them, walked to them, in the night. He'd never believed in God. Never given it much thought. But could this be just a coincidence?

It hadn't started this way. He never thought so much would be at stake—especially the lives of people he considered friends. He'd just wanted to find the truth about the treasure Michael sought, and a way to redeem himself.

It's been about me all along, Walt realized. *I told myself the gold should be saved. I told myself the money would help the people. But the fact of the matter is, I wanted this for myself. I wanted the glory.*

The large canopy of black velvet stretched before him. The closest stars were thousands—or was it millions?—of miles away. The large expanse put him in his place. The inner condemnation did too.

Who are you to think that the lives of others should be sacrificed to fill your needs? Yet even as he asked himself that, the inner peace remained. And in a strange way he somehow knew that things had turned out just as they were supposed to. It wasn't an accident.

It was too much for Walt to comprehend. He closed his eyes, hoping again for sleep. Sleep to take him away. To calm his worries and fears. And to make him forget the peace that he feared even more than the questions. Because with it he ached to understand why he had it and where it came from.

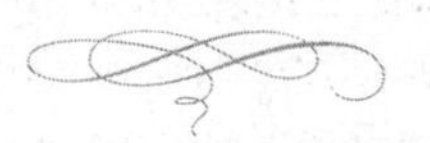

José arrived back at their campsite tired, but happy to discover all was well. The sun had already lightened the sky, and the first direct rays stretched their fingers over the high peaks.

Yesterday, before returning, he'd journeyed farther up the mountain, finally coming across the caves he'd found long ago by accident. Ones that would provide shelter for his father, Pepito, and Petra, and also for the horses. The more challenging aspect would be to find enough food and fresh water, but at least they'd have shelter. In the middle of summer, sleeping outdoors wasn't a problem, but he had to think long-term. Who knew how long it would take before . . . ?

Before what? José asked himself. Before the Republicans won back their land? No, that would not be easy. Before winter came, and traveling in the mountains would be impossible and surviving nearly so?

The more he thought about it, the more he realized there was only one thing to do. He had to get Ramona and then find a passage out of the country for those he cared for. But where could they go? Where would they find the help and safety they needed? Those were just a few of the questions that plagued him.

Then, just as the dew on blades of grass evaporated under the sun's rays, his worried mind calmed under Petra's gaze.

It was just a simple gesture, Petra smiling up at José as he handed her a piece of stale bread. And her words were simple too.

"Where are we headed today?" she asked.

They were words of dependence—on him. And the look was one of pure trust and gratitude. It was only bread. And her willingness to follow, not knowing what waited ahead, caused José's chest to swell with warmth.

"There are some caves I remembered exploring as a boy with . . . a friend." He didn't mention Michael's name, although Petra would make no connection even if he did. For the briefest second a thought flickered through his mind. Perhaps Michael, too, would remember the caves and guess that's where José had gone. Yet Michael had made it clear that he cared little about the horses. In fact, José knew if things had gone as planned, Michael was now far from Spain. The Michael of today cared little about anything except for the size of his bulging bank account.

The sound of footsteps neared, and José turned to see his father approaching. Juan Guezureya's color appeared normal again, not as flushed from the heat of the sun. Still, his legs wobbled from the long days in the saddle. José could tell his father was trying to walk straight, and he realized how difficult it must be for one who trained horses and commanded stallions to have to submit to an aging body.

He searched his mind for anything witty to take his father's mind off his obvious embarrassment, when Petra jumped from where she sat on the cool grass and approached him.

"Do you have a minute, señor, to help me with a problem?" She slid her hand in the crook of Juan's arm and led him to a fallen log, brushing off debris. "Erro, you see—I still don't think he trusts me completely. Maybe it's his hesitation when I pull on his lead that gives me that idea. Or the evil eye he gives me when I saddle him. I have the feeling he still thinks he's in charge, and that's he's just being nice to allow me to ride him."

José watched his father's countenance lift. His feeble body was forgotten, and a new energy lit his face.

"Sí, I do." Juan patted Petra's hand. "Listen closely, and I'm sure within a few days' time, the horse will understand just who is boss."

Perhaps because she knew that safety was only a few hours away, Sophie was even more nervous about being spotted. She tried to forget the danger as they drove along the dirt road, and thought only of the fact that Philip did care for her. A smile graced her lips as she scanned the views of the Spanish countryside.

Their truck rumbled past a large tree, not far off the road. It looked to Sophie to be an oak, but strangely, from the ground to the branches most of the bark had been stripped away.

Walt must have noticed her curious gaze. "Cork trees. Their bark is stripped every summer and used for wine bottles and other things, like soles for shoes."

The tree's branches spread upward at odd angles. It was hauntingly beautiful in its nakedness. Again Sophie's artist's heart wished she had time to paint these new sights, even though that was the last thing she should be thinking about. "I never thought about where cork comes from."

"Yes. And while that is interesting, there are a few things we need to discuss," Walt stated. "If we are stopped and questioned, the story we will all stick to is that we are Americans volunteering for Franco."

"Are there such people?" As soon as the words spilled from her mouth, Sophie thought of Michael.

"Do you think it is only the Republican side that has gained the sympathies of Americans? Many have come to fight for Franco—mostly Roman Catholics outraged that the Spanish Republic has disestablished the church. They believe in Franco's cry for the defense of 'Christian civilization.'"

"I wonder what Father Manuel thinks of that?" Sophie commented.

"Father Manuel?" Philip asked.

"A priest I met in Guernica right after the bombing. You should have seen the horror on his face as he looked at the destruction of his town. I bet he'd have something to say about Franco fighting for a Christian nation."

"Yes, well," Walt commented, "most volunteers for Franco do not know that side of the story—of all the destruction Franco has done in the name of Christ. All they've heard about are the church burnings and lynching of priests by the antifascists during the first months of the war."

"Something I witnessed with my own eyes in Barcelona," Philip said. "I saw a church burn. I didn't ask what happened to the priests."

A deep sadness caused his face to fall. Sophie could see in his eyes that his memory took him back to that place.

"Like the volunteers on the other side," Walt said, "most of the Fascist volunteers know no Spanish, and virtually nothing of Spain itself."

"Yet, once they get here . . . can't they see they are fighting against the Spanish people?" Sophie asked.

"Are they? Imagine it from their point of view. Who are they fighting?" Walt glanced at Philip, and Sophie tried to put herself in the mind of a Fascist volunteer.

She thought of those she'd helped in the field hospitals. She thought of her former driver and friend Deion, a member of the Communist party.

"I am sure they believe they are fighting against Russia.

Against the Soviet Union invading. Against foreigners trying to take over their country."

"You are very observant, señorita."

"I've thought of this before, but . . . well, it makes me wonder what would have happened if my journey into Spain had led me to Nationalist-held territory. Would I now be fighting equally as hard for their side?"

"Maybe, maybe not. Of course, I didn't give you that opportunity, did I?"

Sophie laughed, yet even her laughter seemed stilted due to the pain she still noted in Philip's gaze. "No, I don't suppose you did. Like a fish biting on to bait, I was pulled from a safe pond into a huge ocean of conflict. Then again"—she patted Philip's hand—"I wouldn't have it any other way. As odd as it sounds, this is exactly where I want to be—no matter the number of times I've questioned this very thing."

Walt cocked an eyebrow. "So this is your idea of a vacation, huh? You like knowing that people are hunting us down as we speak?"

"I meant to imply that I am thankful I am in Spain. . . . I could do without being in the territory of the enemy. But more than that, I'm with exactly who I want to be with."

Walt cleared his throat. "Well, just as long as you're not afraid to change who you are."

Sophie looked toward Walt and cocked her head, puzzled. "What do you mean?"

"Remember our first plan? When we were in Madrid, and we figured out that the gold was hidden in the tunnel near Gibraltar? I told you to make an excuse not to go with Michael, and then I'd come for you and you'd travel to southern Spain with me instead?"

"Yes, you said you would get fake identity papers for me."

Walt continued to steer with one hand as he slid the other into his shirt pocket. He pulled out an identity card and handed it to Sophie.

She opened it. It was her face, but bore the name of another.

Philip leaned closer. "Eleanor Howard, huh? It says here you are a museum owner and artist, and you've come to volunteer for Franco."

Walt shrugged. "I wanted to make sure it was a role she'd fit into nicely."

"So . . . if we are caught? What am I supposed to say?"

"If I cannot convince them that Philip and I are volunteers for Franco, then you will say that you had just arrived in Gibraltar when we kidnapped you."

"Are you joking? There is no way I could abandon the two of you."

"I'm not saying it's going to happen—but if it does, that's the story you're going to stick to. Understood?"

She turned to Philip, hoping he'd agree with her. "Philip, tell him—"

"I agree." Philip's voice was firm. "You don't need to worry about it. But if that happens . . . if it's the last resort, then you must do as Walt says."

Sophie refolded the identity card and tucked it into her satchel, though she felt like throwing it out the window. She knew better than to argue—she'd never win with these two.

"Fine," she said. "But only as a last resort."

And though her words seemed to appease the men, Sophie had no intention of doing as she was told. She wouldn't abandon them. She couldn't.

"One more thing, Sophie. I need your old identity papers. If they're found on you, they'll ruin everything." Walt's voice was firm.

Sophie dug them out of her satchel and then handed them over. Her fingers clutched the paper for the briefest second, even as Walt tried to take it; then she released her grasp. "You're taking my life, you know. By giving you this, Sophie Grace no longer lives in Spain."

"Is it such a bad thing," Walt asked, "to start over completely? Your life is yours to design from this moment on. You can choose what you want to bring with you. And whom to leave behind."

Sophie knew he was referring to Michael. She also knew what her response should be. Yet without Michael in her history, she would be a different person. And for a time, for the briefest moment, it seemed that clinging to the pain was better than stepping out without a past.

Even though she'd faced many hard things because of her relationship with Michael, she also knew for certain that for a time she had been adored. And in a strange way, knowing that was enough to convince her that when the time came, she would drag the pain with her into her new life as Eleanor Howard.

Chapter Six

Deion didn't budge until he heard the movement of the others around him as they stirred. They had slept in the upper story of a whitewashed house made of stone and bricks. The bottom story was something of a barn with a small door in the wall leading into darkness. He had peered inside by the light of an oil lamp the previous night, checking for enemy soldiers. Finding the barn empty hadn't stopped the dreams from invading his sleep. Dreams of the Fascist troops finding them here.

Even now Deion resisted the urge to climb from his mat and peer out the window, which consisted of four small frames of dirty glass. He told himself no one waited outside, eager to arrest him—or worse, kill him and the other members of the Abraham Lincoln Brigade.

Then, as he lay there, another face filled his memory. It wasn't one from his dream, but rather the face of the nurse who had cared for him. The strength and meekness that shone through her eyes, her shy smile—all made his heart beat faster.

He rose and slowly ambled to the window. He bent low to look out; from his vantage he could barely make out the roof of the field hospital in the distance. He dressed quickly, then grabbed his rifle and moved to the dirt-packed street, leaving the other soldiers behind to fully rouse at the sound of the breakfast call.

A donkey cart was the sole occupant of the road, carrying a small load of oranges.

The farmer offered Deion a one-armed fisted salute, then tossed him an orange. "*Salud.*"

"*Salud,*" Deion responded. He caught the orange with a smile, anticipating its juicy sweetness. He ate it quickly, wiping his sticky hands on his pants, and hurried on.

It was hard to believe that just days ago he'd been so near a mortar shell's blast that it had completely knocked him out. He'd been carried back to a waiting ambulance by fellow volunteers—or so he'd been told. Then, in his unconscious state, he'd been moved up through the mountainous interior.

Only upon awakening did Deion realize he'd discovered yet another part of Spain. Its beauty overwhelmed him. He'd been taken farther east up the coast, deeper into the mountains, where the doctors and nurses running the field hospital hoped to find protection from Franco's ever-advancing troops. Tall cliffs and bare rock formed the tumbled landscape, much as he imagined the Rocky Mountains would look.

With quick strides, Deion hurried to the field hospital. Upon opening the door, he was struck by a feeling of celebration.

"Double rations of Lucky Strikes and Hershey bars. Ah, the simple pleasures in life."

It was a female voice that spoke to him, one he recognized right away. He turned and met Gwen's gaze. If he weren't mistaken, he saw color rising to her cheeks as their eyes met.

"Double rations?"

"It's the Fourth of July. Did you forget?"

Deion scratched his forehead. "S'pose I did . . . but I'm all for celebratin'," he quickly added. "Got plans for tonight?"

"Nothing different from usual. When I get off work, I usually listen to the radio for a while and then write a letter home." She moved to a cabinet and rearranged the bandages. One came undone, and she worked to wind it back up, making sure the clean cloth didn't touch the dirt floor.

Deion plunged his hands deep into his front pockets. "So, there's someone special at home?"

"Oh, yes, he's wonderfully special. He says I'm his pride and joy. He's a real catch. . . ."

Deion hoped his face didn't betray his disappointment. "You don't say. Sounds like a great guy."

"My mom thinks so. She's been married to him for the last thirty years."

Gwen laughed, and Deion couldn't help but smile at the twinkle in her eyes. He almost forgot that just days ago he'd been injured in the fight to protect Bilbao's Iron Ring. That they'd retreated, and that the area they'd held had been lost.

It's a strange thing, he thought, as he watched the beautiful nurse move toward an injured man, *how easy we forget.* One day he was fighting for his life, and the next trying to catch the interest of a pretty girl.

Well, almost forget, he corrected himself. Because deep down in the pit of his stomach there was a nagging feeling. He'd learned one thing in Spain, and that was how quickly things changed. How happy thoughts could be gone in an instant. One enemy aircraft overhead. One planned attack, and cries of terror would replace the laughter.

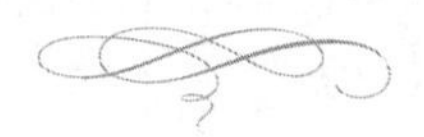

Walt slammed on the brakes and the truck skidded, barely stopping just before sliding into the washout in their path.

Sophie sat stunned as both Philip and Walt jumped from the truck. With reluctant steps, she followed.

A nearly ten-foot stretch of the road had been washed away. A stream of water from the mountainside formed a small, wide river. Dead branches and chunks of earth mixed with small boulders, telling Sophie that some type of mud slide from above had caused the destruction. There was no way to pass.

Surely that man last night, Emanuel, must have known that. Her eyes scoured the hillside, almost expecting a band of men to attack at any moment. After all, Walt had told the man that the truck carried weapons. And weapons were nearly as valuable as gold in Spain these days.

"Do you think it's a trap?" She turned first to Walt, then to Philip. "You said this morning our fuel supply was dwindling. And it is a long way back. We'll surely run out of fuel before we make it out of these mountains. Not to mention those guys tailing us. They'd love to find us where we started."

Neither man spoke, but Sophie could tell by the intense looks on their faces and the way they scanned the hills they were considering her words.

Walt's gaze returned to the washed-out section of road. "Well, we could try to fix it. But I imagine that would take a couple of days."

"If it were a trap, they'd be here by now, taking what they wanted. I think Emanuel didn't know about the washout. It looks to me as if it just happened." Philip took Sophie's hand.

"We could go for help. Maybe the others can help us build something—a bridge of sorts that would make this passable." Walt sighed. "Then again, if word gets out about our whereabouts, we'll be found easier. It's better not to draw attention to our plight."

Sophie looked back at the truck. "The size of the truck is a huge hindrance, plus the weight of the gold. How could we ever engineer something that could hold up under that? And it's not like we can explain why our truck is so heavy. *Anyone* can turn on us, and . . . well, I just hope Philip is right, and the man from the forest had good intentions."

She pressed her lips together, refusing to voice her fear of being betrayed again. She knew too well the pain of discovering that a friend—no, more than that—the man she loved was actually her enemy. The thought of a friend turning out to be an enemy cut her to the core even more than the thought of being caught by enemy soldiers. At least with the Nationalists she knew where she stood. She couldn't stop the shiver that traveled up her spine.

She moved to a fallen log, brushed aside some of the dust, and sat down.

Philip ran his fingers through his blond hair and focused his eyes on the scattering of clouds in the sky as if hoping to find his answer there. "Walt, you know the area—and you have connections. Maybe you can hike out for help."

"Connections I can no longer guarantee." Walt pushed his fedora back from his head. "Michael is a smart man. He no doubt will figure out, if he hasn't already, that I've been playing both sides. Journalists are rarer than the soldiers who have flooded into the country. I'm sure with a few phone calls he could easily discover that Walt Block and James Kimmel are one and the same. No, I don't think that is an option."

Walt moved closer to the hillside. He shielded the sunlight filtering through the trees with his hand and studied the terrain, as a draftsman would view a proposed building site.

"James Kimmel?" Sophie's eyes widened as she remembered the name she'd read in the paper. "You're the one who wrote that piece about the destruction of Guernica being caused by *Russians* on the ground?" Heat coursed through her, and she thought again of the photos she'd taken of the German bombers and other planes over the small Basque town. "Is that why you wanted me to give you the photos? You had no plans of seeing them published, did you? You just wanted to make sure they didn't make it to the press and contradict what *you* were writing about the explosives on the ground."

A trapped feeling gripped her chest. She'd trusted Walt time and time again, but should she? She turned to Philip, to see his reaction. More than anything she wanted to see support in his gaze, and maybe shock that Walt, or James—or whoever he was—was the one who spread those reports. Instead Philip looked away, as if his mind were focused on something else.

Walt sighed. "The photos were published. . . . I can show you the papers if we ever make it back to the safe zone. And as for James Kimmel, I thought I told you about that."

Sophie pressed her fists into her hips. "No . . . um . . . that would have been an oversight on your part."

"Well, all that drama to say that although I still have connections, I doubt I can count on my cover. Also, I don't like the idea of leaving the two of you here, even if I could count on finding help." He tapped his finger to his chin and hurriedly continued, not giving Sophie time to continue her tirade.

"Our biggest asset is that I truly believe the man was on the Republican side. I've heard about groups of men in the mountains who've escaped from the towns Franco's troops invaded. Also, the stories Emanuel told me last night are consistent with the guerilla warfare I've heard of in this part of the country—"

"We have another asset." Philip's words interrupted Walt, his voice rising with conviction. He pulled a small stack of letters from the inside pocket of his jacket, tossing them onto one of the smooth rocks on the edge of the road. "We have God on our side. We have prayer. God knows who we are and what we are. He knows our desire to use this gold to help the war-battered people of Spain. He has not forgotten their plight, and He has not forgotten ours."

"You're right, of course." Sophie knew his words were true, but it really annoyed her at this moment. She crossed her arms. "But doesn't it seem like a huge obstacle, getting this gold out? It's impossible. We have to figure something out, or this river will be the end of us." She stood and kicked a dirt clod into the rushing water. "Every moment we sit here gives Michael's guys more time to find us."

Philip took her hand and tugged her back to the log. "You've allowed the Fascists to get too big in your eyes."

"What do you mean, too big? They are big. They control the territory we are in. The ports and airfields and the roads—or at least the passable ones. That seems pretty big to me."

"In Madrid, right before I saw you, Sophie, I'd received a batch of letters from my father. I only had time to read a few. These were still in my jacket pocket—and somehow that henchman, Cesar, missed them when he went through my things."

Sophie didn't need to ask what had happened to the rest of the letters. Michael had taken them, no doubt. Her stomach ached just thinking of Philip's loss. News from family back home was something every soldier treasured—just another thing she could add to the list of hurts Michael had caused.

He picked up the letters. "My father told me to remember David fighting Goliath."

Sophie snorted. "I know who Goliath is. But we're no Davids."

"Well, we're not the great warrior King David, but don't

you see? David was just a young man when he killed the giant. It wasn't *his* strength." He sat down on the log and looked up at her. "David was the one person who saw differently."

Sophie's throat tightened. For some reason she almost felt as if she were going to cry.

"It was—"

She interrupted Philip. "I know. I know. It was God's strength. This just seems so impossible. Sometimes I trust that God will help us, and sometimes . . . well, I don't." She sighed and wiped away a tear.

Philip put an arm around her shoulder.

She leaned in. "I guess I'm focusing on the impossibility—making this situation look large in my eyes. When really, a great God is over it all."

"God may choose to rescue us, as He rescued David. Or He may not. But I think He'd be pleased to know that we see Him as greater than our enemies. Greater than the borders and boundaries."

"And greater than this hole in the road, too," Sophie added. She let her gaze fall to her hands clenched in her lap.

"If He so chooses, we will discover a way of escape. But if there is none, then we have to trust that He has another assignment for us." Philip offered a soft smile. "One that involves being stuck behind enemy lines."

Sophie tried to think of what such a thing could be, but her mind couldn't comprehend it. Her chest tightened again as she considered hiding and running. What could God possibly do with that?

Still, Philip's words stirred something within her. She couldn't help but think about Benita, her faith and prayers. Staying with the older woman and Luis—dear Luis now gone—had been an exercise in faith. No, more than that. It had been the planting of the first seeds of faith that had grown in her as the months passed and the war progressed. The only problem was that too often she forgot to turn to the source, like a gentle, sweet spring of hope, when the salty waves of war pummeled her.

"I think Philip's right." She turned to Walt, ignoring his patronizing expression. "I know you're not a praying man, but would you let us . . . turn to God? Seek some direction from Him?"

Walt didn't seem overly excited about the idea, but he didn't mock them either. He simply shrugged. "What could it hurt?" He hunched down near Sophie and Philip.

Sophie let her eyes flutter closed; then she opened them for just a second and grasped the hands of the two men sitting on either side of her. Then, in the sweet stillness of the forest, accompanied by the muddy, small stream of water gurgling over the rocks, Philip began to pray.

"Lord, You know where we are and You know our problem, too. Neither surprises You. What surprises me, God, is how often I forget to turn to You when I need help. . . ." He squeezed Sophie's hand. "When *we* need help. You know the situation we're facing. After all, Lord, You made Spain and created each of its citizens. You also know the history of this gold, and You alone know its worth and whether it will be used to help the people's plight. You also know the way out of the wilderness. And the right path we need to take.

"God, I remember the story of Your leading the Israelites while they were in the desert—a cloud by day and a plume of fire by night. We don't need a plume of fire exactly, but we do need deliverance. Please either show us how to fill this hole or show us another route. Anytime You see fit would be great. And if it's Your will that we stay stuck, help us to trust You anyway. In Jesus' name. Amen."

Sophie smiled, gave Philip's hand a squeeze, and then released it. "Thank you," she whispered.

Walt also quickly released her hand, but he just sat there, unblinking, as if trying to figure out what the big deal was.

They waited a few minutes more, each lost in thought, until Walt finally spoke. "Well, I don't see the clouds parting or hear a voice. But I see only one option, so let's give it a try."

Sophie stood, but Philip didn't move. Didn't crack a smile. Instead, calmly, assuredly, he picked up the letters and returned them to his interior pocket. Then, with a gentle pat to ensure they were safe, he let the corners of his lips curl into the smallest grin. "Yes, well, maybe that option—whatever it is—*is* the answer to our prayer. Ever think of that?"

Chapter Seven

Walt's idea seemed simple enough. All they had to do was turn the truck around and follow one of the side roads they'd seen not too far back. They spent thirty minutes inching the truck forward and backward, turning the tires, until they eventually got it turned around on the mountain road. Sophie would've given anything for a dimly lit café, a glass of cold water, and a plateful of the chicken and rice Spaniards cooked so well. Her stomach growled at the thought of it.

Walt motioned for the others to get into the truck. The cab reeked of body odor from their hard work in the sun. Sophie knew she smelled just as much as the guys, and if she weren't so desperate to find shelter and food, she would insist they use some water from the stream to clean up before continuing.

Instead Walt turned the key and they were off again. The engine hummed, and his gentle whistling bolstered Sophie's confidence that this adventure would work out.

"Remember how I told you we were nearly to Granada?" Walt said, wiping the sweat from his brow. "The city itself is in Nationalist hands, but the Republicans hold the surrounding area—so the farther we journeyed down the road, the closer we came to friendly territory."

"Well, that's good news." Sophie wiped her own brow.

In a few minutes, Walt found an intersecting side road. It was merely two tire tracks and some gravel, but at least there were no washed-out areas in the way.

"Okay, this road is taking us . . . somewhere, but we still don't know what we'll find. What if we aren't as close to the Republican territory as we thought? Should we start getting our story straight about who we are, and why we're in the middle of nowhere?" Philip rested his arm on the seat back behind Sophie. His fingertips barely brushed her shoulder.

"Well, being this far out has its advantages. Many don't hear news reports or read the papers. In Granada and other Nationalist-held towns, our way will be more difficult." Walt glanced from Philip to Sophie. "In my opinion, our greatest benefit is that no one knows your faces. Sophie, some key people may know your name and the connection with your paintings. We'll worry about that when we get to the city. For the most part you can pass as Eleanor without question. And even for those who have met you before, what type of spy would I be if I couldn't create a simple disguise?"

A burst of laughter flowed from Sophie's lips before she could stop it. "Hmm, for some reason that statement scares me."

"And Philip." Walt cocked one eyebrow and glanced at his face. "Even fewer know you. If we can just find a good cover . . . another name."

"Attis," Philip said promptly. "As a first or last name I don't care, but use the name Attis."

Sophie's heart sank at the pain she saw in Philip's eyes. Pain upon pain, actually, because the glimpses of heartache he'd carried with him since first seeing her with Michael hadn't faded. Yes, she was forgiven. And Philip was trying to make the best of the situation, but much still plagued his soul. If only she knew what to do about it.

Deion wasn't sure if Gwen was aware of the way she tapped her fingers on the pistol's handgrip as she talked, venting her frustration. Her happy-go-lucky attitude from the morning had faded to a memory. Soon after they'd settled under a tree to enjoy their rationed Hershey bars, two ambulances had arrived with more injured. Not just soldiers, but women and children who were hurt as the Fascists took over their small town.

He felt helpless as he watched Gwen race from one person to another, trying to decide who was urgent, who could wait, and who wouldn't survive despite the efforts of the doctors and nurses. Hoping he could help, Deion followed, fetching things she needed and helping her move patients, lining them up in the right order for surgery.

"We don't have the instruments and supplies we need. There isn't enough gauze or bandages to dress the wounds. And not a drop of novocaine, although some may arrive in the next shipment." She moved to the window and folded her arms across her chest. "I never realized that X-ray film was such a luxury. We have to work by touch to determine fractures. Do you know how hard that is?"

Deion didn't answer, and Gwen scowled at him.

"Hard, I s'pose," he finally croaked. Emotions flooded, and he grew angry with himself for being so captivated by this woman. She cared for many men, and in a few days' time he'd come to care for no one but her.

"They say I'm the only colored nurse in all of Spain," Gwen said, as if reading his thoughts. "And you're one of the few colored soldiers I've seen. I suppose it's only natural to feel attraction."

Deion bit his lower lip. He wanted to ask if it went both ways, but he didn't have the nerve. Besides, he could see it in her eyes. Beyond the frustration and the weariness, Gwen enjoyed having him there. Still, he couldn't believe she could move from the subjects of bandages to their feelings in the span of two sentences.

She walked to the sink and pumped the large handle. Splashes of foggy water trickled out, and she washed her hands. "I'm itching to get on the road. Do you think you could drive me to the first-aid station closer to the front? I hear they've hit some of the villages."

Deion watched as the woman's eyelids lowered to half-mast, as if struggling against a memory.

Finally she sighed. "You know, last time I went near the front, a young woman approached me. She asked where I'd been. Her new husband and baby had both been injured and died the day before. I always think of that. The difference one day could make."

"Don't take that on. It's not your place." Deion meant the words to provide comfort, but Gwen stiffened.

"What do you mean? I came here to save lives." Her chin jutted out.

"You can help, but you can't save people. Only God determines if they gonna live or die."

Anger flashed across her face. "Oh, is that what you think? Then I might as well go home."

"Didn't mean that. But you can't feel every death is one you coulda prevented. People have lived and died for thousands of years, Gwen. If you're gonna carry that weight on your shoulders, why stop with Spain?" He placed a hand on her arm. "'Stead, think of those you do help."

"Never mind. I'll find someone else to take me to the front." Gwen turned and stalked away. Her fingers drummed the handle of the pistol on her side.

The small road wound through another mountain valley, and as she gazed at the chains of mountains, or sierras, Sophie truly understood what the word *breathtaking* meant. Not a shrub or tree dared thrive on the summits that pierced the sky. Sharp rock peaks sliced into the clouds like the spires of a great church.

"You'd be surprised how the people in those mountains live. Towns and villages exist in the most unlikely places—like eagles' nests in the cliffs. And in some places there are remnants of the watchtowers built by the Moors when they controlled this part of Spain hundreds of years ago," Walt commented. "I was a young twenty on my first trip to Spain. Hopped on a bus and told myself I'd ride it until the end of the trail—which turned out to be a valley not too different from this one. The people were simple but friendly. They thought it was a wonderful thing to have someone from the outside world visit them. Now I know why. Few journey this far out without knowing their destination first."

The truck made its way through the green mountain valley, and they came upon a herd of bulls. Sophie recalled the day in the arena when the bullfighters had surprised her with the beauty of a sport that was also an art.

"They are destined for the arena," Walt said before he was asked.

"Do you think they know they are raised to die?" Sophie asked.

A few bulls lifted their heads and turned in their direction, but none of them moved more than a few steps.

"All they know their whole life is a hostile environment—the high mountains, hot summers, hard winters. They rarely interact with people, except for the herdsmen who watch from a distance."

"I'd rather watch lambs." Philip chuckled.

"Everyone has a duty. What appears dangerous or odd to some seems commonplace to others. I suppose if your father and grandfather had such a job, you'd think nothing of it."

They continued on, and Sophie didn't know if it was the warmth penetrating the windshield, the gentle rocking of the truck, or the soothing sound of the men's voices, but she drifted off to sleep.

Soon she awoke to the sound of the engine shutting off and a door opening.

"Let's stop here and stretch," Walt said, jumping from the truck.

Sophie opened her eyes to find they'd stopped in a pleasant green meadow surrounded by hills blanketed by trees. Walt ambled toward an elm tree, and Sophie followed. Soon she could make out the sound of a bubbling creek. On the other side, in a grove of trees, small caves had been dug into the hillside.

Like small, furless bears emerging from hibernation, people

began wandering out of the caves. Soon a dozen curious folks approached with wide yawns and tired expressions. Sophie realized they'd disturbed their afternoon siesta.

Walt went back to the cab and pulled out a box of cigars to distribute to the men. The people didn't seem to care which side they fought for. They didn't even ask. Or maybe they could tell already. Surely that was the case, because soon one man started speaking about the coming triumph of the Republican army, as if assuming they were on his side. Walt talked about war news, and Sophie noticed he didn't show his leanings for one side or the other.

"Come, *por favor*, to my home. My daughter is preparing dinner." One old man took Sophie's arm with eagerness. "You visitors must come."

She glanced toward Walt.

"Sí, señor, thank you. We would be delighted," Walt answered.

The man tugged harder, and Sophie had no choice but to follow.

The cave smelled of earth and was dim and damp. Sophie tried to suck in a breath, but the stuffiness almost overwhelmed her. The furnishings were as simple as the earthen dwelling. An old chair, a bed. A long bench served as a table, and the woman's thinness told Sophie their one cupboard was mostly bare.

"I keep telling myself we will not be here much longer," the woman said cheerfully. "Once we have beaten *the Fascists*"—she whispered the last words—"the better off we will all be. Someday we'll move into a good house, with a tree outside to give us shade."

Sophie's mind traveled back to the tree-lined streets of Boston. She had never been rich growing up, but what she'd had seemed like a palace compared to this woman's meager home.

Sophie studied the old man as he talked with Walt. She was sure he'd witnessed many changes in the government, and this was yet another. He ate his simple meal with a decorum that showed he had not always lived in caves or hills. He spoke simply, but Sophie found his speech picturesque. It reminded her of José, who said he was a poet but never shared one poem with her. That was most likely because their friendship had centered on survival and not pleasure. This man's phrases, too, rang with poetic rhythm in a way she couldn't explain.

Sophie took a bite of the warm bread and then slurped the thin soup with a wooden spoon. She ate slowly, savoring each bite, knowing there would be no seconds—what the people shared would have lasted the two of them a couple of days if it weren't for the surprise guests.

Walt sat near her, talking with the man, but Philip sat just outside the door, watching over the truck.

"If you need a place to hide your truck," the old man said, "I know a good spot."

Walt nodded his interest, and Sophie wondered again if they could trust these people. It seemed too easy. Unless . . . maybe it was an answer to prayer.

"There was a woman who used to live up the road. Her husband was a foreman at the mine. They had a house—a real house—not like our dugout. She passed away last week, leaving it abandoned. I have thought of going up there myself, but it is too far. My daughter enjoys her friendships here, and we have planted our garden. But up the road there is a large barn also—a rarity in these parts. It is big enough, I believe, to hide your truck."

"It is something to consider." Walt locked eyes with Philip, and Sophie wished she could read their thoughts.

The young woman placed her spoon on the table and reached for Sophie's hand. "If you are worried about the others, we will make sure no one knows you are there. They will think you passed through. We are God-fearing people," she added. "We only speak the truth."

"In that case, I do not think we can refuse," Walt commented. "We will finish our lunch and then move out." He turned back to the old man. "Would you be willing to meet us down the road and point us in the right direction?"

"Sí, señor." A smile filled the old man's face. "I will serve you as if I serve my Lord. He has sent you to us, indeed He has. Just this morning I was praying how I, an old man, could contribute. I have no doubt you are my answer." And with that the man clapped his hands in excitement and motioned to their plates on the table. "It is settled. Eat, eat. Let us celebrate how God provides."

Chapter Eight

They found the house and the large barn down the road a few miles and up another winding road, just as the man described. The house was small—no bigger than one of the suites at the hotel Sophie's father managed back in Boston—but it looked well tended. The rough-hewn planks had received a fresh coat of whitewash. A small chicken coop stood to the right of the house. A dozen thin chickens squawked as the truck rumbled up and parked in front of the barn.

"Sophie, you stay here. Philip and I will check the premises before we settle in."

The men got out of the truck and moved together, like two soldiers scouting the area for the enemy—looking first in the house and then the barn, and finally the area surrounding the buildings. After twenty minutes they returned.

"It looks good. Almost too much so." Walt climbed into the cab and started the engine. "There is a garden in back, a well for water, and a creek less than a half mile away. It's a perfect setup really, with everything we need."

A way to heat bathwater? Someplace to sleep other than the ground? To Sophie, this was the center of comfort, and it was safe

. . . an answer to prayer. Though she was thankful, she wished that somehow she'd also find clothes not faded and mended. And boots that hadn't traipsed from one end of Spain to the other. But she knew better than even to wish for such things.

"A creek, that will be nice. And to sleep in a bed will be wonderful. There is a bed, isn't there?"

Walt turned the truck around so it backed up to the barn. "Yes, one bed. Philip and I have already decided we'll sleep outside to guard the gold."

For the briefest second Sophie felt a tinge of guilt that she'd have a bed and pillow, and they wouldn't. She thought about suggesting they take turns, but she knew these men. They wouldn't hear of it. Besides, it was the only thing to do. She couldn't sleep one night in the bed and the next with one of the guys.

Philip jumped from the truck and opened the two large barn doors. Slowly Walt backed the truck in, the large tires crunching the hay. When he'd made it all the way back, Philip shut the door most of the way, so just a crack of light illuminated the truck.

Sophie let out a long sigh. "Amazing. How come I feel as if a weight has been lifted off my chest?"

"Well, it's a good start—that's for sure." Walt opened the door and jumped down. His eyes didn't meet hers, and she sensed that something bothered him. Something he wasn't telling.

"We can't stay here long," he commented, his voice more cheerful than she'd ever heard it. "But it will give us time to make a plan, find more supplies, and rest. Then we can get the gold out of this country and sell it to the right people." He pulled off his hat and rubbed his forehead. Dark circles under his eyes and worry lines creasing his forehead made his face appear older.

Sophie climbed from the truck, sneezing at the cloud of dust that stirred on the floor of the barn. "When you say rest . . . do we also have time to look at what we have back there?" She pointed to the back of the truck.

The initial feeling she had of not wanting to see or touch the gold had subsided the farther they'd driven from the airfield. It was as if the thin blanket of security she felt piqued her curiosity.

Philip had approached and heard her question. "I imagine there are people who would give anything to view our load. Most of the Aztec and Inca goldwork found its way into the Spanish melting pot hundreds of years ago."

"The gold sent on to Russia has most likely met the same fate," Walt added. "This is all that's left." He opened the back and jumped onto the truck bed, lifting the lid off of one of the boxes. "Philip, can you get that lantern?"

Philip took the lantern from the wall, pulled out a lighter from his pocket and lit it, handing it to Walt. Walt set the lantern on the lid of another box, illuminating the cargo. Rays of light glittered off the gold, as if the pieces glowed with light.

Sophie and Philip joined him, running their hands through the coins, jewelry, and other gold treasures.

"So, how many antique artifacts remain? Not counting these, of course," Sophie asked.

"Well, let me put it this way. Just five years ago a treasure hunter, Dr. Alfonso Caso, discovered the undisturbed tomb of a high Mixtec official. What he found doubled the ornaments held by collectors—which tells you that there aren't many pieces."

"What about the pieces held by Spain? Did they include those in the count?"

"No, they didn't." Walt held up a coin, studied it closely, then returned it to the box. "Not many people even knew it was there. The Spanish government hasn't been stable in years. Bank officers come and go. Perhaps if someone had a good friend, they might have been able to get a look at the treasure hidden in the bank vaults. The greatest fear of those who understood was that others who had no idea of its worth would sell it or melt it down."

Philip held up an object that appeared to be a cob of corn . . . a pure gold cob of corn. "Which is exactly what happened. And why these pieces are so valuable."

Walt held some pieces of jewelry in the light. The necklace and ring were bulkier than Sophie had expected, and much more interesting, too. The double chain of the necklace held a three-tiered pendant that reminded her of an inverted layered wedding cake. Within each tier was a precise pattern of small circles. She couldn't even imagine how long it must have taken a craftsman to create a piece like that.

Walt gave a low whistle. "I know one thing. Cortés understated the talent of the Mexican goldsmiths. This work is finer than I expected."

"Can I see?" Philip opened his hand, and Walt placed a ring in his palm. "I studied South American culture in college, and I can see some of the same design elements. In fact, if I had to guess, I'd say these pieces were Inca. But you probably know more than I do."

"I can see why you would think that. Some of their techniques came from Ecuador or Peru and migrated up the Pacific Coast—but this workmanship tops the best of the older goldwork."

Sophie ran her fingers over a necklace. She tried to picture it around the neck of an Aztec or Inca queen. What type of life did that woman live? Was this a gift from her husband? Father? What would she think of the fact that the society she ruled over had been completely wiped out—partly due to the greed of foreigners who longed for the very necklace she wore around her neck? What would she think of the idea that her jewelry would survive long after she did and would be sought by so many?

The necklace had been stolen during the conquest—and how many times since then had it changed hands? And now it was in Sophie's. Its fate depended on them. Would it be okay to pray for gold pieces that had been crafted in the worship of false gods?

"I can't help thinking about the beliefs of the people who crafted this," Sophie said. "The items were made and given in worship in great temples, and now they're hidden in the back of a truck and cared for by us. Maybe their bad omens did come true—I mean, look how things ended for them."

"That reminds me of a story by Diaz that I used to tell my students." Philip sat back on his haunches. "Diaz claimed that on the night when Cortés retreated from Mexico in the mid-sixteenth century, he took his share of the treasure and then turned the surplus over to his troops.

"Of course, the natives didn't stand for their temples being robbed. They chased the Spaniards out of their towns—towns that were very confusing to maneuver through, since they were lined with numerous canals. Most of the men tried swimming the canals in order to escape." He paused and looked at Sophie.

"But the men's pockets were filled with gold . . . they would've drowned!"

"That is exactly right. You, my dear, get an A for today's assignment!"

"What about this Diaz? How did he survive to write about it?" she asked.

"Well, Diaz was smart. He knew the Aztecs believed jade was more valuable than gold. So when he left, he took four pieces of jade instead of the gold treasure. He later traded the jade for food and care. He didn't return to Spain with great wealth, but his awareness of the people and what they valued most saved his life."

Again, a strange feeling flooded Sophie, and she returned the gold necklace to the box. "That's fascinating. I'm sure your students loved it."

"Well, they certainly seemed to learn more when I taught history through stories than when I forced them to memorize names and dates."

"And someday, when you return, you can tell them stories about your own adventures in Spain!"

Philip laughed. "I'm sure they'd think I made it all up. Their history teacher fought in trenches, rescued a beautiful woman on the front lines, aided a Nazi spy unawares, was kidnapped by a thief, and helped to protect ancient treasure."

Sophie's laughter joined his, and even Walt smiled and shook his head.

"They'd believe you had too much Spanish wine, my friend," he said.

"Still, it is nice to think that we'll go back someday, isn't it?" Sophie studied Philip's face. "I'd love to go see the school where you taught. See the track where you used to race. Meet your parents, too."

Philip nodded. "I think that can be arranged."

Walt cleared his throat. "Well, it's nice to know that you two lovebirds have your future all set, but I think we need to find out what's in the house, see what we can use, and start thinking about our plan of attack for *now*. The way I see it, we won't be safe here for long. News about a truck passing this way won't stay quiet when so many people know of it. We need to consider our assets and our liabilities."

"Reminds me of the Boy Scouts," Philip commented. "The first step in making a feasible plan is to figure out what can help you and what hinders you."

Walt nodded and placed the lid back on the gold. "Yes. And what could help Spain the most is now our biggest hindrance."

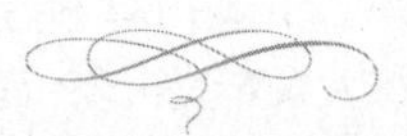

Deion felt like he was coming home as he slid into the seat of the old Russian truck. The back was filled with supplies for the soldiers. The seat next to him was empty. He'd offered Gwen a ride, but she refused, stating that she wouldn't travel to the front lines after all, since she was needed in the operating room. Deion knew she didn't like what he had told her. And because of that, she now didn't like him.

But he knew what he'd said was true. For a while carrying the weight of the world could be a good feeling. Personally, with more responsibility, he'd taken more pride in his worth. Yet he had learned the hard way that anyone under that pressure would grow discouraged. He only wished he had walked away seeing the twinkle return to Gwen's eyes.

Just before the truck pulled out, the commander motioned for Deion to wait. A moment later, a young German soldier climbed into the truck. The man appeared friendly, but Deion's skin crawled. He remembered another German he'd cared for—only to discover he was an enemy pilot. Ritter had fooled them all, and Deion wondered if this man was the same—a liar, a spy trying to gather information for his own cause.

It wasn't until Deion read his assignment papers that he discovered he'd been assigned not with his own Abraham Lincoln Brigade, but as a driver for the German International Brigade—the Thaelmann Battalion.

The truck creaked and groaned as Deion drove through the night. The man beside him slept, and as the hours passed he realized the weariness of the soldier was not unlike his own. Deion struggled to keep his eyes open. He would do the best job he could, even if he didn't enjoy it.

When the German awoke, he worked hard to communicate. Hans had light brown hair and a handsome face. He didn't understand Deion's silence, and treated their lack of communication as a puzzle to figure out. First he'd try a word in Spanish, to see if Deion understood. Then he'd try to remember the English word. He'd hop all around the word he meant until Deion would finally blurt it out, much to the young man's delight.

Somehow, through bits of English mixed with Spanish, Deion learned that the man's family were Socialists and locked up in Hitler's concentration camps. Only then did his heart begin to soften.

"They hang dark men from trees in America?" Hans asked, his most clear sentence yet.

"Yes. People just *think* it's a free country."

Deion thought of his own family back home in Mississippi. They were fenced by the same type of hostile feelings this man's family faced, though they didn't live behind barbed wire. Instead they were held in by signs that said WHITES ONLY. And their deaths often came by the rope.

Deion didn't share his insights with Hans. Instead he told him about his work in Chicago washing dishes, and his train ride to New York with the other hobos on the rail. He told him about the group of friends he discovered in the Big Apple—a few of whom traveled to Spain. He didn't know how much the German understood, but the man nodded and listened.

Finally, they arrived at the Thaelman outpost and unloaded their supplies. The German volunteers shared some stew and bread with Deion, and gave him many pats on the back for successfully bringing their supplies.

Before leaving, Deion sought Hans out. Giving him a firm handshake, he cleared his throat. "Great meetin' you. I'll pray fer you."

Hans nodded and smiled, and Deion laughed out loud, realizing the communication barrier again won. It didn't matter, though. He knew the man understood enough.

As Deion climbed back into the truck to make the return ride alone, he missed Hans's chatter. He also realized what a strange day it had been. A pretty nurse, a friend, had become an enemy. And a perceived enemy had become a friend. No one ever said things were easy to figure out in Spain.

Chapter Nine

Father Manuel stood at the doorstep of the palatial apartment building, certain he had copied the address wrong. The weight of his meager possessions taunted him in the presence of such luxury. He moved his bag to the opposite hand and let out a worried sigh.

A few days prior, he had entered a great cathedral with hopes of hearing from God. At the time, he had no idea his prayers would lead him here—to the home of Berto's family.

The cathedral's massive scale and solemn beauty had intimidated him; it wasn't the same as seeking God on the hillsides surrounding Guernica. For the grandest of man-made objects, even the sacred paintings and stained glass windows, paled in comparison to the smallest pinecone, perfectly designed, or the awe-inspiring delicacy of a bird's wayward feather as it fluttered from a nest high in the trees.

But even though the cathedral wasn't the setting in which he felt most comfortable, Father Manuel had known his prayers were heard, and he trusted God's purpose for his time in France. He'd left the cathedral with no answers, but instead a sweet peace had settled in his soul. And somehow, when he returned to his rented room and spotted Berto—the young man who'd first greeted him on his arrival in Paris—sitting in the hall by his door, he realized that they could help each other. Father Manuel was a stranger in a strange land, and Berto provided friendship. On the other hand, though Berto's physical needs were being met in Paris, perhaps Father Manuel could offer direction for the young man's soul.

So when Berto offered Father Manuel a place to stay with his family in the fine neighborhood of Le Marias, Father Manuel agreed. Now he breathed in the scent of flowers as he walked through the courtyard, awed to be transported into a private haven in the midst of a large city.

Three dozen large windows faced the courtyard, and just when Father Manuel had decided to turn around and go back to his small rented room, he saw movement in the window closest to him. Before he could take another step, the door swung open, and he found himself in Berto's warm embrace.

"Father Manuel! You found us. I apologize for not meeting you and carrying the bags myself. My mother discovered my tutor was not as diligent in his hours as she had hoped, and I am the lucky recipient of his eagerness to please her. It seems I have studied all day." Berto laughed heartily as he took the weathered satchel from Father Manuel's hand and motioned him inside.

Father Manuel's plain black shoes squeaked as he strode across the floors that shone like glass, and he followed Berto down the hall to the right of the entrance. His robe swished as the black fabric trailed over the geometric pattern of the floor. A maid hurried by, pausing briefly to bob a curtsy.

"It is a fine place, I suppose. It is only a short walk to the Place des Vosges, or to the best boutiques in Paris, if you care about those things." He glanced back at Father Manuel. "Which I suppose you do not, with those vows of poverty and the like." He laughed again. "If you would believe it, my favorite place to live was our summer cottage in Santander by the sea. It was small but nice, and just a stone's throw from the water. I miss it. We were just packing to go there last summer when the war erupted." Berto paused before a closed door and pulled out a key.

Father Manuel glanced back over his shoulder and counted

—it was the fifth door down the long hall. The last thing he wanted to do was end up where he wasn't welcome. He felt uncomfortable enough as it was.

"No, I have not done much shopping in Paris," he commented, clearing his throat, "though they do have fine things."

Berto unlocked the door, then handed the key to Father Manuel. "My father, he is very different from me, and he appreciates his privacy. He anticipates his guests feel the same. I hope you do not mind."

Berto entered the room and set Father Manuel's satchel on a small bench by the doorway. "But if you happen to lose it, there is a master key." A grin curled on Berto's face. "I have used it before. But that is a story for a different day."

He flounced upon the bed, unconcerned with disheveling the fine layers of bedding. "I like to explore the city—not the shops, but visit with the people. That is how I met Señor Picasso, you know. A friend of a friend. And though I try to keep track, sometimes I lose more than a key, much to the dismay of my mother. *Por favor*, do not ask about the numerous textbooks she has replaced."

"No, of course not." Father Manuel pretended to lock his lips with the key, bringing another burst of laughter from his young friend.

"Well, then." Berto rose. "Dinner is in an hour. I will give you time to rest. I always like to check out the menu ahead of time." He winked as he hurried to the door. "Or rather the young maids who help serve." Berto's hand flew up to cover his mouth, as if just realizing to whom he spoke.

"Of course, I understand. A young man, old enough to be married, must appreciate beautiful young women. Then again . . ." Father Manuel reached out and patted the boy's shoulder. "That is not something I really do much, either."

Berto's laughter filled the hall as he hurried away with a wave. Manuel closed the door, hoping that someone would come get him when it was time to eat. He could always follow his nose to discover the dining room, but that might lead him to off-limit places, something that his host wouldn't appreciate.

Father Manuel recalled the day he'd met Berto. The young man had led him away from the reporters at the train station and found a small room for Father Manuel to rent. At first the priest had questioned Berto's motivation. Later he discovered the young man's political leanings drove his compassion.

It was Berto who'd taken him to the Workers Parade on May Day to see the thousands crying for support for the Spanish people. It was Berto who'd ushered Father Manuel into the private studio to meet Picasso. The great master had asked him to give a painful, eyewitness account of the bombing by German planes. And now . . . it was Berto who once again sought to help a simple, Spanish priest who questioned why he'd been saved when so many others had perished.

Father Manuel noticed a basin of water on a small table in the corner and washed up, drying his face with a towel that smelled of lemons and lilacs. Then, as gingerly as possible, he folded down the layers of blankets and bedding until only one sheet remained.

He kicked off his shoes and stretched out in the center of the bed. His glance darted from here to there, taking in the crown molding on the ceiling, the rose-patterned wallpaper, the fine burgundy drapes. His being here still didn't seem real. A poor country priest far from his people and home. Or whatever remained of both.

His mind wandered to the canvas of Guernica he'd seen earlier that week. He was amazed that the horror of the event could be captured by such abstract forms and shapes, representing the people and animals of the town. He also thought of the photos and paintings of the young American woman; had she escaped? He would look for her art, in hopes his worries were for naught.

Still, the ache in the center of his stomach that came each time he thought of the beautiful young American finding herself in war-torn Spain would not leave him. His teacher had once told him that sometimes the Spirit of God moves in such a way—as a reminder to pray. He closed his eyes and brought her needs before the Savior Jesus, whatever those needs were.

He also asked for forgiveness for not kneeling to pray at the side of the bed. For some reason, his body felt weary. Perhaps from the miles he walked in the city each day, but more likely from the overwhelming feeling that God had indeed brought him to Paris, but Father Manuel had somehow missed Him and headed the opposite direction from where he should be.

"Oh, Father," he prayed, "how has it come that I have found my way here? And am I right to believe that a young boy's heart is the assignment you have for me now?"

Father Manuel's words were cut short by a knock at the door. He rose, straightened his clothes, and opened the door, expecting to see Berto. Instead a taller man with dark hair and green eyes stood there. A camera bag hung from his shoulder as naturally as if it were a part of him.

"Excuse me, Father, for interrupting. I am Edelberto's cousin, and I've just arrived from Spain. I am not a patient man, and I am eager to meet the priest that my cousin says witnessed the bombing of Guernica."

The man spoke with an American accent, and didn't look Spanish. He shifted his weight, and Father Manuel could tell he favored his right leg. On closer inspection, Father Manuel noted bulkiness near the man's thigh, as if his leg was bandaged underneath his clothes.

Father Manuel stretched out his hand. "Edelberto? . . . Yes, I see . . . he calls himself by a nickname."

The man's hand was warm and his handshake firm. Father Manuel liked him.

"I am Father Manuel, and I am happy to meet you. I am sorry, but I did not catch your name."

"Michael," the man said with a smile. "My name is Michael. Come, and I will lead you to dinner."

Michael moved with slow, sure steps through the house, and Father Manuel found himself trying to keep track of the direction they walked and also follow the conversation. Not an easy task.

"So, Padre, I hope you do not mind me being so bold, but I have a friend who was also in Guernica at the time of the bombing —an American artist named Sophie. You would not have happened to have seen such a person there, now would you?"

Excitement stirred in Father Manuel's chest. "Why, yes, I did, just minutes after the bombing ended. She approached me with tears in her eyes and said she was looking for a friend. José something."

"Immediately after the bombing?" Michael cocked an eyebrow. "Are you sure it was not the next day?"

"No, I am very certain. Even in the shock of what happened, I could not forget the sight of an American woman and a Negro driver."

Michael chuckled softly, yet his eyes told Father Manuel that something was amiss. "No, I am certain one would not."

They resumed walking, and Father Manuel's stomach growled as the scent of chicken and other heavenly aromas filled the air.

"So my friend was with her driver. That makes sense. Did you happen to see her with any others? I am trying to find her, you see, and any help you give would be very much appreciated."

Father Manuel's footsteps slowed as he tried to think back. Then a tension caused his limbs to tighten as he remembered the woman had been with the man in the black hat—the very one who asked him to come to France, the one who also urged Father Manuel not to tell anyone of their meeting. Still, a priest could not lie. Besides, maybe this was an answer to the prayer he'd prayed not an hour before, prayer that the American woman would be okay. Yes, he was sure of it now. This man would help her.

"Yes, I saw her with two others. An American volunteer and a man with a black hat. I saw them talking often in the garden, though I could not hear them." Father Manuel shrugged. "I wish I could tell you where she is now. I only hope she is okay."

"I am sure she is fine. It seems those very men care for her now. And it is also helpful to know that she was looking for help from her friend José. Thank you for your assistance." He paused for a moment. "And now I can be assured that these three men have accompanied her all along. It helps me to piece some things together, and maybe—it is my hope—to find her."

"Sí, I am happy to offer such help," Father Manuel said as they entered the large dining room. "And when you do find her, can you tell her that I am praying for her? Can you do that?"

Michael nodded and pursed his lips. "That I will, Padre. That I will."

Chapter Ten

Sophie used clean water and a little soap she found to scrub the kitchen of the small house. It wasn't really a kitchen, just one corner of the main living space. But it contained a sink and a hand pump for fresh water. A cookstove, a few cupboards, a table with two chairs, and a large window looking out the front of the house completed the area. On the other side of the room sat a rocking chair and a store-bought sofa. Sophie imagined it was quite the purchase, considering that the rest of the items, and the house itself, appeared to be made from scraps of material most likely gathered at the job site. She turned to attack the film of dirt on the windows when she heard footsteps.

"Stop!"

Sophie's heart leapt. She turned to see Philip standing in the doorway, extending a hand toward her.

"What's wrong? Are you trying to scare me to death?" She set down the rag on the small wooden table and placed a hand over her racing heart.

"It's just that we don't want it too obvious that anyone is here, that's all. Clean windows and a swept front porch will give it away. Walt's working outside to hide the fact that we're here."

Sophie took a step closer to the window. Sure enough, Walt was sweeping a leafy tree branch across the tire tracks in the driveway.

She placed a hand on her hip. "I suppose these precautions make sense. But did you forget a small community already knows we're here?"

"Actually, they don't. They saw us earlier, but they don't know we stopped here. The man and his daughter promised not to tell, remember?"

"All right." She nodded her chin toward the other room, set off by a door. "Can you help carry the feather mattress outside to air it? I found clean linens in the bedroom."

Philip didn't wait for Sophie to grab the other end. Instead he flung the mattress over his shoulder and carried it outside, laying it over the wooden fence behind the house. Then he sank to the ground, patting the green grass beside him for Sophie to sit.

Sophie sat next to Philip, shoulder pressed against shoulder. She tried to imagine what it would have been like to live here. The old man said the woman's husband had worked at the mines. She imagined a simple existence caring for this property, feeding the chickens, growing a garden, and awaiting the arrival of the man she loved at the end of the day.

Perhaps the woman walked down the road to meet with friends. Or maybe, like Eleanor—whose Bible Sophie carried—her closest friend was the Lord.

Sophie plucked the small wildflowers that grew within arm's reach and created a bouquet. The sweet scent of the flowers perfectly matched her mood. She turned to Philip.

"Can I ask you something?"

"Hmm?"

"The name you picked today . . . well, you told me before about your friend, how he died here in Spain. But you've never really told me about your past. Did you meet through your track-and-field training?"

"No. Attis and I were childhood friends. We lived right down the street from each other. Every memory I have of my growing-up years seems to involve him."

Philip grew silent, and Sophie could almost imagine the pictures floating through his thoughts—two little boys . . . their laughter, their play, their mischief.

"Sometimes it's hard to remember he's dead, and this war cost him his life. One bullet to the forehead, and he never took another breath. I guess I haven't had much time to stop and think about it, with the war, the fighting, the running. But the last few days, well, I've had time to think."

"I can't imagine losing someone so close . . . I don't want to." As she said those words, the unwelcome memory of Michael's funeral filled her thoughts. She quickly pushed the pain-tinged memories out of her mind. "I've seen a lot of battlefield injuries. I've heard the pleadings of men who begged me to kill them."

A shudder traveled up her spine, and she refused to let the images of crying men and broken bodies reclaim her thoughts. "At least your friend's death was something quick. He didn't suffer, right?" Sophie was grasping for the right words, but she didn't know what else to say.

"Actually, I'm not sure if it was better. If an illness had claimed him, I would have had time to adjust. I could have said everything I never had a chance to say. I could have told him how much he meant to me. I could have asked his advice about women." Philip chuckled, though the sadness remained in his gaze. "Attis was married, you know. And I still can't make myself write Louise. It's cowardly."

Sophie didn't rush in with words. She waited for him while he dug the toe of his boot into the dirt, letting him figure out how to say what he'd held inside so long.

Finally Philip cleared his throat. "He was there. We were laughing and joking, and then he was dead. Just like that. I wasn't gone more than thirty minutes. It seems like a bad joke. And you know what? I can't cry about it. I feel bad, so why can't I cry?"

"I don't know. I wish I had an answer. Sometimes I wonder the same. Knowing Luis is dead—because of me. Wondering about José. Thinking about . . . well, how I was deceived."

Philip didn't reply, and Sophie didn't need him to. It was enough they were together and sharing their pain. Sophie knew things weren't back to where they had been when they both left

Guernica. Their excitement of mutual attraction had died down, but perhaps it was better this way. Now they chose to care, each knowing the other was far from perfect. A lot had happened that they still needed to talk about. But this was a start.

After a few minutes, Philip tapped his fingers on his knee, no doubt to some melody that played in his head. Sophie glanced at his wrists—still raw from the rope. She wished she could take his large hand between her two smaller ones. Wished she could tell him that they'd get out of this, the gold would be saved and the profit would help the people who had little hope. That in the end they'd be together. And then, when the conflict in Spain faded into a memory, they could start anew and explore the budding feelings of love they'd previously confessed.

But she could make no promises. To do so would be foolish. God had a plan; that was one thing she knew for sure, but to assume the plan meant she and Philip would end up together . . . She couldn't presume on God like that. She'd tried it once before . . . and, well, she decided that instead of running toward a relationship, she'd give her love and then leave the results up to God. Love worked no other way.

Walt rounded the corner and paused when he spotted them. His jaw dropped slightly. "Glad you two feel the day's work is done," he called. "Sorry to ruin your siesta, but we need to round up some food for dinner, and then we need to talk." He ambled toward them. "I'm hiking out tomorrow—leaving for the closest town. We need to plan and"—he pulled out a revolver and handed it to Philip—"talk about what might need to take place to ensure the gold is protected."

Philip took the revolver and nodded.

Then Walt lifted his head and scanned the sky. "I know this place is deceptively peaceful, but we can't forget the real dangers out there."

"You're right." Philip rose and brushed his pants off; then he turned and offered a hand to Sophie. "No more fun. No more heart-to-heart talks until we're safe."

Her eyes widened, and then Philip laughed.

"Fine, then." She placed her hands on her hips. "I'll keep all my deep thoughts to myself until we're safe." With a toss of her hair, she moved toward the henhouse. "Anyone know what to do with these hens? I'm tasting eggs Benedict. Some ham—lemony hollandaise. Yeah, and maybe just a fried egg will be fine."

Laughter carried her steps forward, and Sophie walked with a lighter step. Walt's comment was a good reminder, but it did not put a damper on the warm feeling that now spread through her chest. Philip trusted her—he'd shared his heart.

❖ ❖ ❖

The sky was steely gray, and the first rays of dawn stretched their fingers over the crest of the mountain peaks. Sophie stepped out the front door, noticing a refreshing chill in the air. She was thankful the day wouldn't be as hot as yesterday. Walt wanted to leave today, and she hated the thought of his hiking through the heat.

She moved to the henhouse and peeked in. Most of the hens slept, their heads tucked under their wings. She hated disrupting them, but her stomach rumbled, and she didn't want to wait for the sun to rise before starting breakfast. With so much happening, last night's dinner had left them wanting. She'd only managed a thin soup made from a few potatoes she'd found in the garden. It hardly satisfied, but they'd been too tired to care.

They'd fallen asleep before the sun had even set, Sophie in the bedroom, Walt in the barn with the truck, and Philip on the sofa in the living room. Sophie didn't know if it had been for her protection or because the sofa was soft that he had chosen to sleep there instead of the barn, but knowing he was there helped her to sleep better. Through the thin walls the sounds of his occasional snoring had comforted her, especially when she awoke and remembered again where she was.

The hens welcomed her with low cackles, and Sophie smiled, wondering what her mother would think of the city girl learning country ways. She slid her hand under the nearest hen, who clucked peevishly.

"Don't sass me." Sophie shook her head. "You can share your eggs, can't you? It's better than being someone's chicken dinner."

She checked under each hen and gathered six eggs, imagining how proud Philip and Walt would be when they saw her bounty. Casting one last glance at the nestled hens, she moved out of the henhouse and quietly latched the door.

Before she took one step, a force knocked her to the ground. A low growl filled her ears, and Sophie felt a scream rising in her throat.

She called Philip's name and covered her face with her arms for protection. Yet instead of attacking her, the hungry beast lapped up the now-broken eggs with wolfish greed. Even in the dim moonlight she recognized it as the thin mutt that had been wandering around yesterday.

"Stupid beast. Now look what you've done!" As if in protest, her stomach growled. She raised her hands and pushed the dog out of her way. His skin clung to his bones, and immediately her anger turned to pity. Poor thing.

She wondered if this had been his home—wondered if he'd been abandoned when his master died.

"Sophie?" Philip's voice called to her. "Are you all right?"

As he rushed toward her, she heard a *click*—the cocking of the pistol Walt had given him.

"I'm fine. It's just a dog. Don't hurt him. He meant no harm."

Philip approached with slow steps and gazed down at her. His eyebrows lifted at the sight of the dog still licking at the dirt and the bits of eggshells. "I suppose that was our breakfast."

"Unfortunately." Sophie lifted her hand, and Philip took it and pulled her up.

"And I was hoping to get something decent in Walt's stomach before he headed out." She sighed.

"Too late. He left an hour ago. He tapped on the front door and told me."

She wiped her hands on her skirt, noticing how they stung, and then brushed off her backside. "Really? That's what must have woken me, without my realizing it."

Philip squatted and scratched behind the dog's ear. "Poor thing."

"You shouldn't do that." Sophie took a step back. "You don't know what kind of bugs that thing carries."

"As if we don't?"

Sophie crossed her arms over her chest. "Good point." She stepped on the eggshells on the ground, crushing them into fine pieces. "Still, if you're too nice he'll want to stay."

"Yeah, you're right. What should we name him?"

"Are you serious?"

"How about Badger? Or maybe Sonny?"

"I think I like Badger better . . . little weasel, taking our eggs. Or maybe Weasel?" Her tone was playful; she couldn't help warming to the dog. He was no taller than her knee and had black fur, and brown and black whiskers that gave him the appearance of an old man.

"He *is* an ugly thing," she mumbled, but her heart warmed to see Philip acting so tenderly to a dirty, mangy beast.

"Yeah, but he's so ugly, he's cute. Isn't that right?"

The dog's tail wagged in agreement.

"Still, we have no breakfast."

"Well, maybe I can dig around the garden. I think I saw a few more potatoes. We can fry them up." He stood and brushed his pant leg. "It can tide us over anyway, until Walt returns."

"Boy, are you a dreamer," she said with a sigh. "I saw some flour and oil in the pantry, too. I can try for pancakes. Still, I would give anything for some fresh yeast rolls and Boston cream pie."

"How about smoked salmon from the Pacific?" Philip added as they strolled back to the house. "And just think, I used to complain to my dad when we'd have fish *again*."

They slowly made their way to the small cottage. Philip opened the door for her and she paused, staring up into his face.

"So do you think we'll ever get back? To the United States. I mean, even if it weren't for the gold, there is the war, and . . . well, the border seems farther than when we started, not closer."

He reached up and brushed her hair back from her temples. "Yes. I have faith that we will get home someday." He leaned close as if to kiss her forehead.

The dog scratched sharply on Sophie's leg, interrupting the tender moment. She jumped back. "Ouch, that hurts." She pushed the dog away, but he didn't stop. Finally, when he saw he had her attention, he raced through the backyard, under the fence, and toward a small hill behind the house.

"I think he wants us to follow." Philip jogged after him.

"Wait . . . I'm hungry!" she called. "And I was liking the feel of your hand on my face," she mumbled more softly.

Then Sophie crossed her arms, realizing it was the second time the dog had ruined a good thing. She was just about to enter the house and start the pancakes anyway when Philip's voice broke the silence of the morning.

"Sophie! Come quick!"

Chapter Eleven

The blue and white flyer in Father Manuel's hand read *Paris on Display*. Most likely Berto had slid it under his door. Truth be told, he had no interest in venturing out again. His heart weighed too heavy. He missed serving God and the people.

He felt emptied. More than anything, he needed living water. Christ offered to penetrate his weary soul, and he now realized how dry it had become.

And so, with sure steps, he found his way to the courtyard and took a seat on the polished wooden bench, placing the paper on the bench and folding his hands. The morning sun settled on his shoulders like a warm blanket. The grass had been neatly trimmed, and every bush shaped in precise arches along the border near the gate. The flowers danced in the breeze, and the song of birds in a nearby tree reminded Father Manuel of the first garden tended by Adam. Father Manuel had always pictured a lush, untamed wilderness—like the one he walked through back home. But what if Adam had also liked to manicure his surroundings? Maybe he, too, appreciated control and design in his private garden—a small reflection of the creative nature of his God.

Prayers spilled from Father Manuel's lips, and soon he

slipped from the seat to kneel in the soft grass, lifting his arms in prayer. He wasn't sure how much time passed as his lips mouthed prayers to the Lord, but eventually the morning sun hovered high overhead—beaming warm rays upon his head.

He rose, struggling to his feet like an old man. He chuckled with the memory of the first time his legs had fallen asleep during prayer. It didn't seem right. He wished that when it came to kneeling priests, God would void the laws of nature, the laws of blood circulation—a small reward for those who served with dutiful diligence.

As he stood, Father Manuel noticed movement in a second-story window, and he nodded to the man he saw observing him. He was older than Berto's cousin Michael, but their features were similar. Father Manuel decided it was Berto's father, who'd unfortunately missed last night's dinner.

Father Manuel lifted his hand to wave, and the man took a step backward as if startled that he'd been seen. He offered a quick wave in return, then moved to close the heavy drapes. Father Manuel wasn't certain what that was about, but he did hope to meet the man soon. He had much to thank him for. In fact, the overwhelming feeling of undeserved mercy rested upon him.

Though yesterday Father Manuel questioned if he should accept the offer of a free room, today he was glad he had. His soul already felt refreshed, his mind clearer. Worries about receiving this gift disappeared from his soul as he realized one thing—God had brought him here, to this fine house and these fine people, for a purpose. In fact, the more he'd thought about it, the more it felt like a mission. The discovery that Berto's cousin knew the very woman he'd urgently prayed for confirmed that. He was here to provide something even more valuable than what he received—but to whom he'd bestowed his favor he did not know. Berto? Michael? Berto's father?

Father Manuel knew one thing. Though these people had their every physical need taken care of—and much more—they needed the new hope found in Christ. A gift greater than any treasure. He would find the recipient.

Father Manuel trusted God with the rest.

As he rose, the front gate opened, and a man hurried in. He seemed surprised to see the priest, but continued along his path to the front door.

He was a young man, wearing some type of uniform with a sharp-looking blue cap. He knocked firmly, and when the door opened he asked for Señor Vidal. Father Manuel noticed the telegram in the man's hand.

The housekeeper answered and must have offered to deliver it, because the man spoke firmly. "What I have in my hand is for Señor Vidal, and him only."

The servant ushered the young man in, and Father Manuel offered one last prayer—that the news the man bore would benefit his host, and bring hope and not harm to the generous Spaniard who'd opened his doors to a simple priest.

Though a spacious office spread around him, ornately decorated with the souvenirs from his numerous travels—a handmade drum from Africa, a beautiful wall hanging from South America, a wooden ship from Boston—Adolfo Vidal felt as if the walls pressed in. Perhaps the image of the priest on his knees in the courtyard added to his already unbearable burden. The image of the man, so humble and unassuming, had both drawn his interest and burdened his soul. How a man could abase himself so openly was something he would never understand. Yet the faith . . .

He envied the clear trust on the man's face. So much so, he had to block the view from his vision, lest the priest cause him to question all he'd dedicated his life to for the past three years.

The heavy drapes blocked most of the sunlight, but even in the dim room the volumes of books on the shelf drew his attention. History books, tales of adventure, diaries of Spanish conquistadors who had parted from family and homeland in hope of discovering treasure in a distant land. He'd read them, absorbed them, since childhood. Even as a young man, he'd often taken one of his family's white stallions and searched the hills in hopes of finding buried treasure there.

He'd found nothing in those hills, no matter how many caves

he ventured into or holes he dug. Yet the older he grew, the more a subtle knowledge grew—deep in his gut—that someday he would. Just as Columbus believed he'd discover a new land, Adolfo trusted he'd be the adventurer who'd unearth the discovery of all discoveries. He opened his desk, removed the large map, and spread it across the oak surface. The map was nearly as ancient as Cortés himself, and Adolfo knew it contained mysteries. Yet, if all continued to go well, the light would invade the dark obscurities, revealing long-awaited answers.

The stolen gold in Spain was key to it all. The bankers of Spain found value in the weight of the gold alone. Michael and his parents, collectors and businesspeople, saw the value in the worth of the artifacts—knowing collectors would pay well for them.

But only he saw their value not in their intrinsic worth, but in their ancient symbols, which could lead him to the unfound treasure still hidden in South America. While others looked at the surface, he, an adventurer and history lover at heart, searched deeper still.

When he'd first learned of the maps and the symbols—which were all that remained of the travels of ancient adventurers—he dedicated himself to uncovering their truth even if it took thirty years. With the right people, he would eventually discover the secrets of the coins. But in the end, he found he needed only one man—the man he trusted with everything. The man he hoped hadn't turned on him.

Three sharp knocks sounded at the office door, and Adolfo Vidal's heartbeat quickened. He strode to the door and took the telegram with a nod. He paid the delivery boy and added a generous tip.

"Wait here. I might have a return reply."

For days he'd been unable to eat and had hardly slept. He only hoped the news was what he hoped for.

GOLD SAFE STOP HIDDEN FOR NOW STOP TWO OBJECTS FOUND WILL SEARCH FOR OTHERS STOP GRANADA NEXT STOP SEND WORD OF NEPHEWS SEARCH IMMEDIATELY STOP HOLD HIM OFF AT ALL COSTS STOP WALT

Feeling his legs grow weak, Adolfo sank into the chair. For a time he'd worried the gold was lost. Then, when Michael had arrived yesterday with an injured leg, he questioned what had taken place. He had prided himself on being the one person Michael could turn to . . . and he questioned why Michael held back this time. Had he successfully retrieved the gold? Had he brought it to French soil? Or had Walt somehow intercepted it as planned? From the anxious look on Michael's face Adolfo believed the latter had happened. He hoped that with time Michael would turn to him for advice as he'd always done in the past. But until that time he'd be forced to wait and wonder.

Of course, if that was the case, what had become of the shipment? He'd replayed the questions through the night, coming up with a hundred different scenarios. And when morning dawned, he still had no answers.

Walt Block was a resourceful fellow; he'd accomplished more than Adolfo thought one man could, but still . . . Adolfo questioned himself again for placing so much responsibility, so much knowledge, in one person's hands. After all, Walt could have taken everything for his own gain. He knew which objects—which coins to find amongst the boxes. He knew their use. The only thing he didn't have were the maps that led to the ultimate treasure, but Adolfo knew a man like Walt could find a way to get those, too.

Adolfo had risked much. He'd left his home and his prized horses. He'd used up most of his family's wealth with hopes of finding more. And while the treasure had tempted, the puzzle—the adventure—drew him unceasingly. From the first moment Michael came to him for advice, Adolfo knew there was more to his sister's request. She asked much of her son, to steal what was safely locked away. No doubt she hoped the discovery of the gold would line their pockets, not to mention boost her social status.

Only when Adolfo himself started digging deeper did he discover that though the treasure itself contained value, seven unique pieces had far greater worth than all the gold in Spain. They were the coins that would usher him into greatness. They would ensure he left his mark not only in the elite circles, but in the history books. When men spoke of great Spaniards, Picasso's name would be listed beneath his own.

Adolfo rose and scribbled the message for the return telegram on a piece of paper.

KEEP ME AWARE OF MOVEMENT STOP NEPHEW IN PARIS WILL KEEP HIM FROM SOUTHERN SPAIN STOP WILL SEND RESOURCES TO GRANADA STOP SACRIFICE ALL TO RESCUE OBJECTS OF GREATEST VALUE STOP A. VIDAL

Adolfo rose, opened the door, and handed the paper to the telegram delivery boy.

"Send this as a reply quickly. No delay."

As the young man rushed away, Adolfo gathered his coat and hat, moving down the polished hallways with quickened steps. He had a visit to pay. A doting uncle should apologize for missing his nephew at dinner. He should also be there to care, to offer advice, and to listen to the poor soul who worked so hard for his parents' approval, yet rarely found it.

He would help his nephew see that he'd done all he could, and perhaps it was time to count one's losses and walk away from the gold lest he lose more than he already had—his time, his resources, his fiancée, and his health. Surely a doting uncle would offer no less.

Chapter Twelve

Though it wasn't even lunchtime yet, Michael poured himself a glass of wine and settled into the plush armchair. The house was simple, but when he'd seen it, he'd known at once it was perfect. Not only was it situated next to a large park, it also had an enclosed back porch—a rare thing in France, but perfect for Sophie's art studio.

He took a sip from his glass and rubbed his aching leg. The doctor hadn't asked Michael how he'd received the wound; he simply removed the large chunk of metal and stitched the gash. And Michael didn't offer an explanation.

Even more than his leg, his heart ached to think it was Sophie who'd betrayed him. Who'd stolen the photos. Who'd chosen to stay with those she hardly knew instead of leaving Spain with him.

His eyes darted to the painting on the wall—the self-portrait she had done for him as a wedding gift. Hoping to surprise her, he'd retrieved it from the hotel near the border where Sophie had stored her things before she'd crossed into Spain.

In the painting, Sophie's dark hair cascaded over her shoulders, and she wore a light blue dress. The softest smile curled on her lips. She'd painted the eyes so intricately, it almost seemed as if she stared down at him.

He'd made many mistakes. He knew that now. He should have spent more time with her when she'd first arrived in Madrid. He'd chased information. He'd made friendships with key people and used others to do his bidding, in hopes of obtaining what his parents had wanted most—not that it mattered now.

The gold was lost. Sophie knew him as a liar and a thief, and he sat in Paris alone.

Michael rose and moved to the kitchen, slicing himself a piece of fresh bread he'd picked up from the market and thinking again about the priest. At the market, he'd skimmed through a half-dozen newspapers, reading the stories of the towns that people had abandoned in the Basque country, leaving them free for the taking. He wondered if the priest knew what had happened to his home. More than that, Michael wondered if the priest still prayed, even though his God refused to answer.

Michael didn't understand the Basque people. Maybe if they took the war seriously, they would not have lost everything. He'd read that Basque officials had let some of the Nationalist prisoners go before the officials fled town. In other places they'd protected the Fascist prisoners still locked up until the invading troops arrived. It made little sense. Did they not understand that when it came to a war they shouldn't protect those who in the end could hurt them? They shouldn't place food in hands that could chop off their heads?

Yet the Basques were mainly concerned for themselves. Whether one side or the other held power seemed to matter little to them, as long as they were not affected. Let them keep their language and their president, and all would be well. The problem was that things would not work that way. The Nationalists wanted total control. *Total.* And this meant, Basque or not, Franco's troops would take what they wanted.

Michael limped across the back patio, ignoring the pain from his injured leg. Also ignoring the easel and paints he'd purchased. The ones that waited. The ones that would always wait. He moved to the backyard. The sky held not a cloud, and the day appeared peaceful, unlike his soul. Unlike the soul of Spain.

In his opinion, the war had been lost long ago. The swing in the Nationalist favor had started with Italy and Germany sending support to Franco. Then, when the Army of Africa arrived on the mainland, it became just a matter of time.

Truth be told, the winner of the fight mattered little to him either. His one concern remained the gold artifacts. He knew either side would sell the gold if that meant more money for their cause. Anger boiled within him at the thought that Franco had done just that—taking what Michael had promised to share with him for a little help in hiding it, protecting it, and getting it out of the country.

Fools. They had no idea the treasure they possessed. That's why his plan had been to take as much of it as he could as quickly as possible. And at first he had succeeded.

In the Republicans' haste to get more supplies from Russia, they had become sloppy with their plan to export the gold. They had two men per vehicle; that was all. Why, it hardly dented Michael's bank account to pay off the drivers to unload a few boxes from their loads. After all, they believed they were transporting weapons. Better to line their pocketbooks. What were one or two boxes? No one would even notice.

But someone had noticed. His closest friend served the enemy.

He had trusted José. And instead José, his childhood friend, chose to support Walt—a foreigner who appeared out of nowhere. What Michael still didn't understand was who funded Walt's venture. Who else knew about the gold? Michael had been assured that only a few—those he trusted with his life—knew his deeds. He had been sloppy to let José get too close, and Sophie too. But that still didn't answer who knew about the gold from the very beginning. His father and mother had presented the idea to Michael. And other than his parents, only a few art dealers knew of the treasure hidden within the Bank of Madrid.

Not only did he not know the traitor, Michael questioned how he'd ever find the gold again. He considered his options. He could travel to southern Spain and find nothing. Searching for them over the miles of roads and in the numerous villages would be, to use the common phrase, like hunting a needle in a haystack.

Or he could travel to Bilbao, in the north, and find José.

The last Michael heard, José had left—taking the horses to the mountains. He likely thought he did a good thing by protecting the beasts, but Michael wondered if José was also trying to save his own skin.

Michael strolled down the rock path to the flower garden. He plucked a rose from a bush. He'd thought Sophie would enjoy painting a flower garden . . . instead she'd become a thorn in his side.

When he first saw her in Boston, he thought she'd be a pleasant temporary distraction. Instead she'd found her way into his heart—which made him even more angry at her betrayal. He'd loved her . . . how could she support everything he opposed? Perhaps he should show her just what she had chosen—prove to her that she'd made the biggest mistake of her life by choosing Walt over him. She'd pay—that he knew. She'd pay.

"Women," Michael muttered to himself. "How they complicate our lives. At least I didn't marry her." He looked at the flower again. "José, on the other hand . . ."

Yes, José had left, but as far as Michael knew, José's wife, Ramona, remained at the hospital. He knew if he could find her, he'd get to José.

Michael dropped the rose to the ground and crushed it under his heel. It made sense. José had taken all that was most precious to him. Michael's pride. His plan. His worth. And he'd helped to further alienate Sophie. Now it was Michael's turn.

He knew he could hire people to help him find the truck, but that would make too many people curious. He'd send his key people to watch the ports and airfields, but he'd put his efforts into undermining the core of the betrayal. He would journey to northern Spain, perhaps to write a few articles about the field hospitals there and take photos of the dedicated nurses.

Michael limped to his house, moving as fast as his leg would take him. His mind was racing with thoughts of how to return to Bilbao when a knock sounded at the door. He paused, and then moved to the window in order to get a closer look at who waited on the front step.

He released the breath he held when he saw his uncle. His

uncle, Michael knew, would always be there for him, always help—no matter if he achieved great successes or equally great mistakes. Unlike his mother.

Everyone said Michael and Uncle Adolfo were similar in looks and temperament. That is what perhaps first built their bond.

Michael opened the door. "Uncle, please come in. To what do I owe the pleasure of your company?"

His uncle laughed. "I just came to apologize. I wasn't feeling well last evening, and I wanted to give my regrets in person." He entered and settled comfortably in the armchair. "Besides, Berto said you had your own house. I wanted to see for myself. It is beautiful, wonderful. Something I'd choose for myself if it weren't for your aunt's extravagant tastes. But I have to say I'd hoped you'd stay with us. The summers just don't seem like holiday without my favorite nephew brightening my day."

Michael laughed. "Sí, although I'm not missed by everyone. I see Berto has already filled my bed. At least this time the guest room has a worthy occupant." Michael sat in the chair, facing his uncle, feeling a peace settle over him, knowing again that the older man provided unconditional care.

"The priest? Well, maybe his presence will bring a special blessing upon our home." Adolfo winked.

Michael nodded. "It can't hurt. Besides, I won't be there long. . . . I'm heading back to Spain."

His uncle sat straighter in his seat. "Are you sure? You are not well. You should wait until your leg heals."

"I thought I'd return to the north and check on the horses. And see how my friend is doing, of course."

"José? I remember him. Juan's son—the horse trainer. Northern Spain, you say?" The features on his uncle's face softened. "You never were one to stay away from danger. Are you sure you don't want to go to southern Spain? I hear there are not as many battles there. Most of the area is in the hands of the general."

From the look in his uncle's face, Michael knew his uncle remembered José better than he let on. And there was something else in the older man's gaze . . . a piqued interest that Michael didn't understand. Why would it matter to his uncle where he traveled?

"No, I really need to check on things in the north. I'm thankful my press clearance allows for that."

The pinched expression on his uncle's face seemed to relax. Adolfo leaned forward and placed his elbows on his knees. "Make sure you give yourself a few days to rest. And you might need help—a driver and bodyguard—don't you think? I know a few people who might be willing."

"Really, uncle, I don't think that would be—"

His uncle raised his hands, halting Michael's words. "No. I won't hear otherwise. I insist." Adolfo rose and strode over to where the painting of Sophie hung, studying it closely. "Besides, it is the least a devoted uncle can do for his favorite nephew. The least."

Ramona had first left Guernica behind, then Bilbao. But not the bombers. They came five at a time. Then four. Then three at a time. Even as she and the other doctors and nurses worked in the makeshift hospital to care for the wounded, their roar never ceased to make her heart pound.

For safety, most of the women and children were taken to the railway tunnel—although dodging the infrequent trains provided its own risks. The planes bombed frequently, but never the center of town. In Bilbao she'd found it strange at first that the bombers never hit the Altos Hornos steelworks or the shipbuilding yards across from the train tunnel. Later, after more than one hasty retreat, she understood. The Nationalists thought ahead and refused to destroy the factories and rails they planned on using soon.

The last of the patients had been taken care of, and Ramona returned to the large building that just this morning had been filled with the voices of dozens of children. She blew out a long breath, noting the blankets, shoes, and clothes left behind. She strolled to one row of cots and picked up a doll that lay half hidden under the bed. Her mind turned to the child who must miss this precious object. But at least that child, and the other orphans, would be safe.

Earlier that day, she'd walked the short distance to the harbor, herding the little ones onto a large ship. One had caught her eye, little Cristiano. His mama had died in a bombing only a week ago. He must've been barely three, and her heart had been stolen by his mischievous smile and few words. She'd never forget how he hugged her when he said good-bye. "Mama," he'd said. And her heart broke. She wanted to keep him. She said a prayer for him.

As she walked away, she heard two men talking. These were the last children they could take. The resources for saving the little ones had been exhausted.

In all, over thirteen thousand children had been sent away—to France, Belgium, Switzerland, England, and Russia. Their safety mattered, but so did the fact that there would be more food for those who remained. Thinking of the young soldier she'd patched up last night, she was glad for the rye bread, chickpeas, and fish they ate for every meal, even though she was sick of eating the same things.

Last night over dinner another nurse said she'd heard the chickpeas had come from Mexico. God bless the Mexicans.

Even though this new town varied from the one she'd left, her routine had not. She'd lived with the other nurses in a house in the city center, and every time the bombers flew over they hurried down to the first floor where mattresses had been piled against the windows. It wasn't sufficient shelter, but it was all they had. And just as bad as the bombings was the moment when they stopped. That meant the Nationalists were in their midst.

The Basque Ring of Iron had been pierced a few weeks prior. The Nationalists had gotten through by attacking at Larrabetzu, where their fortification efforts had not been finished. The Nationalists knew where to strike, she'd heard, because the key engineer for their defenses had defected to the enemy. Who better to disclose the weaknesses of their ring than the man who'd designed it?

But when it came down to it, the concrete pillboxes and the wide and straight trenches had not been designed well in the first place. The Fascists would have figured it out sooner or later. Besides, what good was a single line of defense anyway? Once pierced, there was nowhere to fall back to.

Thankfully the planes had not hit Bilbao with the same force used in Guernica. The hills of pine trees burned, but not in the area where she knew José had retreated with the horses.

Ramona finished cleaning up the large room, even though it would never be used by the hospital. It went against her nature to leave a mess. She smiled, remembering how José had teased her during their last day in Guernica.

"Wonderful. You did a fine job cleaning up for the invaders. I'm sure they will be thankful," he had teased.

How she wished she could hear his voice now—see his face, touch his hand.

She placed the doll on one of the straightened beds, then changed her mind. All she had was lost. Even the smile on her husband's face was now only a memory. She picked up the doll again and pulled it close. She needed the reminder that the peace she once knew in childhood could be hers again. That it was okay to hope for such a thing for her future, for her own children yet to come.

By tomorrow, or maybe the day after, they'd be on the move again. She prayed José had found a safe hiding place in the mountains.

Though she didn't want to leave her duties, Ramona knew the time would come when she had no choice. Tomorrow everyone would retreat to Santander, their next haven of protection. This time Ramona knew better than to give up her place on the truck.

While the International Brigade had returned to the area surrounding Madrid, she hoped that someone, somewhere, would send the help they needed. Ramona hated to believe things could end this way—running and running until there was nowhere left to run.

"Where are you, José?" she said into the empty room, clutching the doll to her chest. *Are you keeping track of me? Do you know where we're headed? Will you come for me again?*

Then she turned to the door, exited, and made her way through the streets, knowing it was time to pack again.

Chapter Thirteen

Good job, Badger!" Sophie scratched the mutt's ears, to his yipping approval.

Sophie knew they'd never have found the root cellar if it hadn't been for the dog. Camouflaged behind a hedge of flowering bushes, it had been carved into the rolling hillside behind the house and secured with a solid wood door.

This confirmed that the dog had belonged to the previous homeowner. He'd led Philip straight to the spot.

Sophie noticed a hole dug in front of the door. "Why were you digging, huh?"

Philip patted Badger's head. "There's not food in there, is there?"

Dried meats and strings of garlic hung from the ceiling. They discovered a bin of potatoes, in addition to bags of flour and salt. They even found coffee—as close to the real stuff as they'd drunk in months. Numerous cans of food also lined the shelves.

Sophie felt overwhelmed, as if God had provided a bounty of goodness for their journey. Philip must have thought the same.

"Like manna in the desert," he mumbled. "We can use what

we need, then make a special delivery down the hill before we head out."

Forgiving Badger for breaking the eggs, Sophie fried up some bacon and made American-style pancakes with the supplies. While she cooked, Philip gave Badger a bath in the river. They both came home soaked from head to toe.

"Dumb dog. He's stronger then he looks. I had to tackle him before he allowed me to scrub him down."

"Looks like you washed yourself and your laundry in the creek as well." Sophie winked. "I think you wanted to kill two birds with one stone."

As Philip changed into dry clothes in the bedroom, Sophie leaned down and set a plate of food before Badger. She smiled as he wolfed it down, his scruffy tail wagging excitedly.

When Philip sat at the table, his damp hair was the only hint of his morning "soak." His eyes widened as she placed a plate of food before him, and his enjoyment was nearly as obvious as Badger's when, after a quick prayer, he began to eat.

Sophie took a sip of her coffee. She'd even used a little sugar to sweeten it and enjoyed the warmth contrasted with the crisp morning.

Philip's smile broadened with each bite. Once finished, he leaned back in the chair with a satisfied look on his face. Then the smile turned into a serious gaze.

Sophie felt the same angst. As her grumbling stomach now felt satisfied, their predicament roared back to the forefront of her thoughts.

"Ever since we had that conversation about the gold, I've had a strange feeling about what Walt said," Philip began. "He kept talking about gold found in Mexico—Aztec gold. But personally, I think most of it comes from South America. I also think we have only a glimpse of the truth."

"Do you think he lied to us?"

"No. But maybe he didn't tell us the whole story. He says he wants to get the gold to collectors, then use the money to help the people's fight. His story is no different from Michael's, really. The only difference is that Michael wanted to line his own pockets, whereas Walt is concerned about helping the people . . .

which is actually the thing that bothers me most."

"What do you mean?"

"Did you ever hear of El Dorado?"

Sophie thought. "Isn't that a place where a warehouse of treasure is supposed to exist?"

"Yes, but before that, there was a person named El Dorado. Not long after Columbus, a rumor circulated about a Muisca Indian king in what is now Colombia. He would cover himself in sap or oil and then roll in gold dust. That's where his name came from —El Dorado means 'the gilded one.'"

Badger spun three times, then plopped at Philip's feet. Sophie could see that despite the struggle in the creek, Philip had found a new best friend.

"The Gilded One was an image of god on earth. During ceremonies he would throw gold items into the lake as a sign of sacrifice. Sometimes he'd jump in himself."

Philip's eyes brightened as he talked, and Sophie thought she was seeing a glimpse of what he must be like as a teacher. He shared his knowledge with such passion, she wanted to know more.

"Wouldn't the gold wash off?"

"Yes, but the next day he'd just apply more gold."

"Seems like an expensive costume to me!"

Philip smiled. "I agree, if it is true . . . and many people believe it is. Around 1520 the Spanish tried to drain Lake Guatavita in Columbia to recover the gold. They didn't succeed, but I've heard that gold artifacts have been found in various lakes."

He reached down and scratched Badger's ear as he talked.

How nice this is, Sophie thought, taking another sip of her coffee. *To be here together, well fed, with our devoted dog, talking about things we've read and heard about, wondering if more secrets are yet to be revealed.*

And she knew it wasn't going to last.

"Since then people haven't stopped hunting for the treasure," Philip continued. "In fact, that's why so many Spanish explorers traveled to South America. They could care less about the continent. They wanted the gold. They found some, mostly religious or architectural objects."

"And let me guess . . . they melted it down into ingots and brought them back?"

"Yes, that was the fate of most of it," Philip answered. "But some survived . . . some of which we have today."

"Surely people still can't believe in such a place as El Dorado—a treasure house?"

"Maybe, maybe not. But even if there is no treasure house, there has to be a mine. They got that gold from somewhere. And many believe the mine still exists."

Philip paused and rose to take his dishes to the sink. He pumped water and put them in the basin to soak, then turned to Sophie and took her dishes too. "I keep asking myself why Walt would get so involved in all this. Sure, an employer may pay him, but what happens when the gold is delivered? Will he just fade into normal life, happy with the money paid? Even if they sell the gold and help the people, it seems he and his employer would want some benefit. Since Walt seems sincere in wanting to help, my only guess is that he could use the gold for something else before selling it. I think they must believe the gold itself holds clues to . . . something. Maybe a mine, or maybe the treasure house? If that were the case, Walt could get the information he needed, save antiques—making collectors happy—and help the people, too. It's a way that everyone wins, except the Fascists."

"Do *you* think the gold has clues?"

"It doesn't matter what I think, Sophie. The people we're involved with—on both sides—mean business. How long did you say Walt has been keeping track of all the players? Three years?"

Sophie nodded.

"If they are willing to finance Walt's work, what else do they have invested? The truth is, it doesn't matter what they believe. What matters most is they'll do anything to follow it."

"So now what? Should we continue on as if we don't have questions? Or when Walt gets back do we tell him we want to know the truth?"

"Oh, we'll find out the truth, all right." Philip finished washing the dishes; then he took the basin and tossed the dirty dishwater out the open window. "But we won't ask about it—we'll watch for it. The truth is the truth, no matter what someone shares. Also, Walt's actions will follow his beliefs. If he believes the gold treasure leads to something greater, we should be able to see it—by the way he talks, acts, and reacts."

Sophie stood and placed her hands on her hips. "You *have* thought a lot about this, haven't you?"

Philip stepped closer, reached for Sophie's waist, and pulled her toward him. "I used to try to figure you out. But that was too much work. I've moved on to deciphering Walt's mind and the mystery of the gold. It's much, much easier."

Sophie frowned and playfully punched his arm as laughter spilled from Philip's lips. She reached her arms around his waist for a hug, and her hand felt the pistol he'd stashed there. She jerked her hand back, and the playful moment dissipated as the seriousness of their situation struck her. This was not pretend. They could not afford to let down their guard. Sophie knew that getting the gold out of the country would bring more danger than she'd faced so far.

From the moment Ritter received the invitation to Göring's dinner, he knew he shouldn't attend. Seeing the little men in their ornament-covered uniforms made his stomach turn. The only thing that forced him to accept was Göring's handwritten note on the back of the invitation.

Meet me in my office after dinner. New venture to discuss.

Ritter wasn't sure if he wanted a new venture. His reward for stealing the plans for the Norden bombsight would tide him over for a while. Still, the intrigue of the general's request clung to him, and so he found himself seated at one end of a long table. Göring sat on the other end, but it made no difference. The conversation never changed. Men and women who'd never traveled to Spain, nor knew anything other than what they read in the paper, rehashed the same stories with the confidence and bravado of Franco himself.

Ritter took a bite of his herb-crusted duck, enjoying the

flavor that filled his mouth, and tried not to let the dinner conversation spoil the enjoyment of the fine food before him. He grew tired of the fact that whenever people talked about Spain, they spoke of Guernica. Of course, those at his table did not know of his personal involvement in the bombing raid. Even Monica, seated on his left and as beautiful as ever in a red satin dress, remained unaware.

An older woman in a silver evening gown, with shiny gray hair that matched, lifted one thinly drawn eyebrow and raised her voice. "I just returned from Paris myself, and I could not leave without a look at Picasso's newest work. It disturbed me deeply, I tell you. As do the news reports. They say children were among the casualties. Can you imagine?" She lowered her voice, and leaned in so close that her necklace grazed her duck. "And some say we were involved?"

Ritter placed his fork and knife on his plate and wiped his mouth. "It's a painting . . . done by someone who wasn't there. But didn't you ever consider that war brings death—even of the innocent?"

Her eyes narrowed and her mouth opened into a wide circle as if she couldn't believe he would speak to her in such a way. Instead of hindering him, her look of anger mixed with incredulity urged Ritter to continue.

"So what if hundreds were killed? So what if Guernica was bombed as they say? Does anyone ever talk about the Reds' bombardment of the public gardens of Valladolid, which killed many children? Or about the Republicans bombing Saragossa, killing over a hundred women and children? War means war. You cannot control rebellion unless you show your fighting power."

"Well said," the man next to Ritter chimed in.

Ritter picked up his fork and knife again, but suddenly the finely displayed food on his plate no longer appealed. He knew the arguments. And he spoke with conviction, but it didn't help him sleep at night.

Monica touched Ritter's hand, as if feeling his anxiety. "I too wouldn't put any weight on one painting done by a Spaniard who doesn't live in Spain. Personally, I don't think a bombing happened at all. How convenient that the newspaper people were brought in at night after the city was already in rubble," she continued. "Or rather, burning. They were simply told what had taken place. Of course it was also convenient that witnesses were brought forward to confirm these stories. Like that priest, supposedly from Guernica, who was all over the newspapers? I saw his photograph. He didn't look like a priest to me. Too young. Too handsome. Besides, why should anyone believe he'd even been there? He was interviewed in France. Then there was the young boy who said he was sure he saw the pilots leaning out of planes tossing hand grenades. . . ."

Ritter chuckled at this. "Truly. Ask any airman, and you will know this is nonsense."

Another gentleman spoke up, his voice building with excitement. "I have a correspondent friend, and he entered the town himself—as he'd done with other bombed Spanish towns, like Burgos and Valladolid. He said when those towns were bombed, the roadway was scarred and pitted, and the houses had collapsed. At Guernica there were houses burnt out, but they were not pitted by bomb fragments. And the roadway was just fine. My friend saw it himself. And he had photos. I wish I had copies."

Ritter was about to comment again—he was actually enjoying the foolish banter—when Göring rose.

"If you will excuse me. I will meet everyone on the patio for drinks in no more than thirty minutes. But first, I have a pressing meeting that I must step out for." Göring's eyes met Ritter's. "Herr Agler. Would you join me in my study?"

Ritter nodded and rose, feeling all eyes on him. He couldn't help but feel his shoulders straighten and his steps lengthen with a sense of importance as he left a crowd of murmuring guests in his wake—great men who realized just then that they'd been in the presence of someone important, unaware.

Chapter Fourteen

The sound of the front door opening with a loud squeak drew Sophie from her sleep. She sat up with a start, straining to see in the dark. In the night she'd dreamt of Michael. In her dreams she had been there when the plane touched down. There when he'd discovered the gold was missing . . . replaced by heavy, worthless Spanish rocks. Hatred had filled his gaze. Murderous eyes peered from the face she once loved.

She placed a hand over her pounding heart, wondering if the dream was sent as a warning. Then she rose and dressed in the dark of the windowless room.

Opening the bedroom door, she saw that the light of dawn flooded the front room of the cottage, and there seated at the table was Walt.

He refused to look at her, diverting his gaze. His foot tapped an irregular beat, and he quickly tucked something into his pocket. "You're awake."

"I thought I heard something."

Something looked different about him. He'd set his hat on the seat of the chair. His hair hung over his forehead, making him look younger than before. His uncertain glance gave her a sinking feeling.

She wondered if Philip was still sleeping in the barn. She thought about waking him, but Walt spoke before she had a chance to ask if she should.

"Sophie, you'd better come sit. I need to talk to you." He rubbed his brow. "The Nationalists hold Bilbao now, all of it. Thousands have tried to flee to the coast of France, but failed. Overcrowded boats have sunk in the Bay of Biscay."

Walt was rarely one to show his emotion, but she saw tears pooled on the bottom edge of his eyes. Yet somehow she wasn't able to connect his words with his emotions. Surely there was more than he was telling. She could see it in his eyes.

"And José?" Sophie searched his face. "Was he one of those?"

"No. From what I can gather, he has gone into the hills with the horses. The mountains are dangerous, but so is the enemy. The city fell so quickly because of the fifth column—Franco's supporters on the inside who took over the key buildings. They were just silently waiting for the right time to strike."

Sophie didn't need Walt to explain that Hector and the other men she'd lived with during the past month had been part of this inside contingent.

But why tell her this now? How did the events happening in Bilbao affect them here?

"The traitors within, that's what brought it down," he repeated again. "It's the silence you have to watch for. You think you know a person. . . ."

He didn't continue, and Sophie waited. She crossed the room and moved the hat, then sat down.

She knew if she asked, Walt would tell her what was really going on. But for some reason her mouth wouldn't move. The words wouldn't form.

"Sophie . . . I . . ." He paused. Then he blew out a breath. "Yes, well, I am back. And I've had a little time to think."

"About how we're getting out of here?"

"Yes, and other things."

Sophie stood and unwrapped a loaf of bread. "I baked this

yesterday. It's actually flat, flavorless, and heavy, but I'm guessing you're hungry."

He took a piece from her hand, not really seeing it. "Those that succeed in their plots are the ones willing to move slowly and bide their time, waiting for the right opportunity. To make sudden moves or hasty plans will only end in disaster. We won't travel out with the gold—not yet anyway. Michael will be expecting that very thing. The people he works for will use their resources to watch every harbor. Every airport. We will follow the example of the fifth column in other ways also."

"Such as?"

"They had something more important than treasure, and that was information. They sent it out piece by piece in some of the most unlikely ways." Walt stood and gazed out the window toward the barn, and she could tell he spoke more to himself than to her. "They will expect a large shipment to leave the port, but they will be unconcerned about small packages. How do you eat an elephant? One bite at a time? And how do you ship a large cargo hold of gold?"

"Little by little." Sophie clenched her hands on her lap, remembering her conversation with Philip.

Listen, watch, Philip had urged her. *What Walt believes about the gold—his ultimate goal—will come out in his words and plans.*

She rose and looked again to see if there was any movement from the barn. *Where is Philip now? Why didn't he wake up and come in? For that matter, where's Badger? He's always the first awake, running around.*

She turned her back on Walt, pumping water into the tin coffeepot, hoping he didn't notice her trembling hands. "Yes . . . but how long can we stay here safely? Surely word will leak out. Where can we hide? It's a big truck."

Walt nodded and rubbed his chin. "Yes, I understand these things. But plans, too, must be worked out piece by piece."

Sophie added a scoop of coffee to the pot, noticing Walt didn't ask where she'd found it. She thought again about waking Philip.

Sophie returned to her chair and sighed. "Every time I think about it, I can't believe how I was deceived by Michael. And . . .

to be honest, how easily I trusted you when I first crossed the border. I was so naïve. . . . I suppose I didn't understand that Spain would split in two before my very eyes."

She searched Walt's face as she said the words, trying to see his reaction. Trying to assure herself that she was not being deceived again. "I've failed more times than I can count. You'd think as an artist, I'd see the world a little better."

Walt rubbed his knees with two hands as if he were an old man whose joints ached. "You didn't fail, Sophie. You see the world through eyes of truth. You believe what you see, and that is why you can reflect it back onto the canvas. You believe the destruction, and you paint it. You believe the pain, and we feel it in your work. Of course, you believed in love, only to find it limited and weak. You believed I was a fellow passenger who was kind in offering you a way across the border. That was the layer of truth I showed you, and you had no need to look any deeper."

"And you, Walt? How do you see the world? Through deception? Do you second-guess everything?"

"That's my nature, I'm afraid. I'm not sure I can change. It reminds me of my grandfather. He was a soldier as a teen and faced many battles. Any loud noise would bring him to his knees, covering his head with his arms. As small kids we thought it quite funny. Now, of course, I regret all those times we dropped horseshoes on the cobblestone streets just to see him react. He knew what we were doing, and he was ashamed of his reaction, but still he saw the world through the eyes of that frightened soldier. It colored his existence. As for me, I also—"

A dog's bark pierced the air. Sophie looked out the window to see Badger bounding between the barn and the house. Behind him Philip closed the large barn door.

Walt stood and moved to the door, reaching for his gun. "What in the world is that beast doing?"

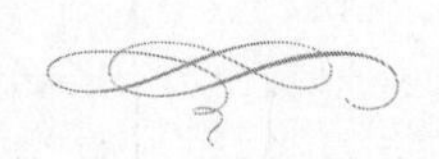

A knock sounded at the door only moments after Father Manuel had risen and dressed.

Berto entered and closed the door behind him, almost shy. "Father . . . if it is a good time, I would like to talk to you about something. About *God*," he whispered.

Father Manuel nodded and motioned to the chair across the room. Instead of sitting in it where it was, Berto moved it to sit across from Father Manuel. So close their knees nearly touched.

"I wanted to thank you for the way you changed the subject last night when my mother asked about our friendship—and about how we met. I should have told you sooner that my parents aren't aware of some of my leanings . . . like that day in Picasso's studio when you shared your story. My father wouldn't approve if he knew I'd been with *those people*."

Berto was a handsome boy. Anyone could see that his outgoing personality would be a draw to the young women—both the Spanish girls and the French lasses he interacted with. And while he seemed to be playful and flippant, Father Manuel guessed that beneath the surface was a mind that didn't stop thinking and weighing the concerns of the world around him. And a heart that cared much more than he let on.

"He doesn't know those friends, does he? Are you saying your father is for the Nationalist cause?"

"My father thinks that God works best in a well-ordered society—such as the Spanish nation he grew up in. To him the order of the property-owning class and religion are one."

"And you don't believe this?"

"Please tell me if I'm mistaken, Padre, but from what I saw growing up, there are times the church seems more concerned about the outward show. I was brought up not knowing the love of God. Instead I focused on the worries about purgatory. I've tried to discover God for myself."

Father Manuel leaned back in his chair, realizing that for years he'd longed for someone to share these same thoughts. He could hardly believe that in this house, this country, where he felt so out of place, God had answered his prayer. "And have you, my son, discovered God?"

"I think so, Padre, at least from what I've been reading. You see, I found in our study a copy of the Bible, and I've been reading it for myself." By the look on the young man's face one would think he offered a confession. "Even though I am young, I have known the romantic love of many young girls—not physically, but emotionally. In thinking about these relationships, I've begun to see that the Word of God is a bit like a romance—God loves, and then loses His love to another, only to find a way to win His bride back."

Father Manuel straightened his back and sat up, surprised, mainly because this was the most candid conversation about God he'd had in years. Also because, though the boy sought his guidance, he felt as if he were receiving much in return.

"I think you are right. I have thought of the love of God often myself. It is not enough to love; love's nature is that you take that thing for yourself. Loving from a distance doesn't seem to be true love at all."

"I knew it. I knew you felt the same. Then you too have known the love of God deeply?" Berto's eyes filled with wonder, and a smile curled on his face.

"Sometimes I've wondered if I were the only one. It was a lonely road at times," Father Manuel said. "I met God in the mountains as a boy. It was there that His reality seemed so clear to me. I devoted myself as a priest, because that is how I believed I could prove my affection. Yet sometimes it seemed I served for no purpose. It was like trying to share a great treasure with those content to live in poverty."

"That is why I have asked you here. That is why you cannot return." Berto must have realized his voice rose in volume because he lowered it again, leaning forward with elbows on knees. "Spain is not a place for you anymore. The Basque region is being taken over piece by piece. Soon there will be no place safe. I've heard recently that the insurgents have shot fourteen Basque priests in Guipúzcoa. And they say they're 'for God and for Spain.'"

Father Manuel felt his stomach grow sick at the news. He had no doubt that if he had stayed he'd have been one of those whose blood spilled onto the Spanish soil. He had thought his mission had been to spread the news of Spain, but perhaps it had been to save his life.

But save it for what?

"I'm sorry. I did not mean to upset you with the news." Berto rose and paced toward the window. "I just . . . needed someone to talk to. Sometimes I feel as if I don't fit into this family at all. Other times I question if I'd set up this image of God in my mind, but it doesn't really exist."

"I know what you mean, all the questions and doubts. And I thank you for trusting me with them. I will share mine with you. . . ." Father Manuel heard heavy footsteps outside the doorway, and he paused. "But not today. Today I think we must both seek God and pray. I have no doubt that God has brought us together for a purpose—what an unlikely pair we are. And I'm sure He will reveal why in His due time."

"Thank you, Padre." Berto walked to the door with a smile spreading across his face. "It is a good thing to know that in this world—in this very home—another man will be lifting up prayers to God. It is a very good thing."

Chapter Fifteen

Ritter arrived in Vitoria. He landed the Junkers Ju.52 trimotor and stepped out on Spanish soil for the first time in months. He'd felt an affection for this country that he couldn't explain as he'd flown over the blue gray mass of hills, the somber clouds, the ancient vineyards. Even the scarred landscape, where little men dug trenches for protection, seemed more familiar to him than the hustle and bustle of the Berlin streets.

He looked around the airfield and realized nothing much had changed—the same aircraft, mechanics, and pilots strode across the dirt runways after finely executed missions—yet in a strange way everything was different. A new solemnity permeated the airfield, despite the victories on the Northern front. It was here on the third of June, just a month prior, that General Mola, the most brilliant military advisor, had met his death.

The general had left the Vitoria aerodrome in his own communication plane with two members of his staff and his personal pilot. Ritter believed the man had gotten the pilot's job because of his friendship with the general, rather than because he had superb flying skills. And perhaps that was the problem.

Ritter strode across the field, tucking his flying helmet into his pocket. He removed his heavy jacket, lest he melt under the Spanish sun. On the day of the accident, the weather had been extremely bad and visibility poor. Which was hard to believe since this day was so beautiful.

The accident had occurred only a few minutes from Burgos when the pilot descended, looking for the signals from the airfield. Being lower than the pilot thought, the small aircraft flew into the side of a hill. It was a tragedy for Spain and for the German pilots. General Mola had often smoothed things between the Spanish high command and the foreign generals, including those from the Condor Legion. More conflict existed now between the groups. Ritter was thankful he was not here to join in the battle. He answered only to Göring himself.

Yet last night in Göring's office, Hitler's general had another request. A simple one, it seemed. He asked Ritter to be a ferry pilot between Germany and various parts of Fascist Spain. He was to deliver specific items and pick up others for the return trip. No questions. No need to know the identity of the items he delivered or their purpose. Only obedience. And a healthy paycheck.

Though Ritter had skirted most of the northern coast on his flight from Germany to Spain, the clear Spanish sky made it possible not only to watch the bombs descending on the Basque towns in the distance, but also the artillery shells. Heavy shells from the howitzers streaked through the sky, appearing almost pretty if one did not realize what they were. Even the three-inch trench mortars arced at a high angle, upward, like silvery birds.

He had no doubt the war would end soon. It was only a matter of time, and he wondered how much the "materials" he transported would help make that so.

Ritter checked in at the main office, then—as Göring requested—watched as unmarked crates were hauled from the aircraft to a secure area. He didn't ask about the contents. He didn't care.

In fact, Ritter cared about little these days. Once the last box was delivered, he ran his fingers through his hair and considered heading toward the nearest tavern to unwind before finding a spare bunk to sleep in. As he walked toward the auto pool, hoping to beg a ride to town, a man's voice interrupted his thoughts. He spoke in crisp German, with an air of appreciation for Ritter's position, which caused Ritter to smile.

"Sir, can you come to the office, please? My commander wishes a word with you before you depart."

"Of course; lead the way."

Ritter sighed as he entered, realizing he now had the upper hand. He had free entry into Göring's office, and no doubt more Spaniards would ask favors of him. The thing was, Ritter determinedly heeded Göring—and Göring only. Anything less would waste his time. Göring considered him more than a pilot. He was an asset to the German cause . . . and with authority came responsibility. Something he did not take lightly. He would do the bidding of Hitler's general.

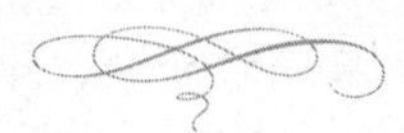

Deion had only spent a few days driving the truck for the Thaelmanns when he was told that someone had messed up, and he should, in fact, return to the front lines with the Abraham Lincoln Brigade. While they waited for their next orders, he thought about visiting the hospital again to talk to Gwen, but his feet refused to carry him that direction.

The battlefield was no place to spark a romance, he told himself—even if Gwen had gotten over her anger. It was easier if things ended now, before they really got started. He knew if he let himself fall for her, he couldn't live with himself if anything happened to her.

A strange uneasiness hung in the air. Perhaps because the commanders checked and rechecked their troops and inspected their weapons—just in case. Or maybe because the troops had received double the amount of food for dinner. A last meal before the big battle to come?

They finished their dinner, and he washed his face and brushed off his dusty uniform the best he could. Then the word came. They were leaving tonight. He'd have no time to say goodbye to friends in the hospital or, for other soldiers, señoritas they'd been seeing in town. They had to pack up and head out. Not a minute could be wasted.

Major George Nathan called the men to order, then stepped out from the cluster of brigade staff, clearing his voice to speak. "Battalions stand ready to move out!" He relayed no grand plans other than that they would head to the front lines. Still, another word traveled through the groups and brought excitement to their limbs. *Offensive*. After a year of defensive warfare, it was their turn to make the move, to lead the fight.

They headed out on foot because they heard there were tens of thousands of Republican soldiers and International volunteers merging on the Nationalists. As Deion set out, keeping time in stiff, creaky boots, he had never felt so conflicted. Fighting had been his main goal, to make a difference. Yet he couldn't deny that if he had a few more days, he most likely would have paid another visit to the pretty nurse. There was something about her he couldn't shake. And now he left, without the chance to say good-bye. It seemed foolish, but in a very real sense his heart was another victim in this foreign war.

The man to his left sipped from a canteen, and Deion could tell by his trembling hands he'd already seen the front lines. Those who had witnessed the death of friends, and suffered injuries of their own, gathered the nerve to march forward. As Deion had seen through his seven months in Spain, they faced their own fears on the battlefield as clearly as they faced the enemy. Others—those new to the brigades—walked taller, with straight backs and sure smiles.

"Where you from?" Deion matched his pace to the man beside him.

The soldier was stocky, with a freckled face and reddish brown hair that stuck out from beneath his cap.

"Stockholm. I never thought I'd miss it." He turned to Deion as he spoke, wiping his red eyes.

The man's breath smelled like alcohol, and Deion knew it was cognac, not water, in his canteen.

"Can ya believe it?" Deion tried to act as if he didn't notice the way fear caused the man's eyes to dart wildly. "We gonna be the one surprisin' the enemy this time."

The man was silent for a while as they walked along, and Deion wondered what he was thinking. When the sun set over the ridge of the distant mountains, his companion finally spoke.

"The last time I was on the front lines, we was sitting there when this young man came up—a Spanish lad. We chatted for a while, and he offered us cigarettes. Then he headed back out across no-man's-land."

"A scout?" Deion asked, replacing the face of the boy in the story with a dozen others he had met and seen.

"So we believed. Not two minutes later, a guy from the staff came by. Said the boy was sneakin' round for the other side. They headed out after him, but secretly I hoped he made it back. I heard that happened in the Great War, too. Men saw the enemy face-to-face, only to discover you can't hate the guys on the other side once you joked with them. I think about that kid every time I fire my gun, and hope my bullet's not heading his direction."

Deion's footsteps slowed slightly, and he questioned why he'd even started this conversation. His mood was bad enough as he replayed his own misgivings. Not talking to Gwen one last time, knowing his last injury—a concussion—was just inches from being more serious. Not to mention the bullet to his leg that caused stiffness and aching even now.

Third strike you're out! He tried to push the thought away.

Another guy approached Deion, passing out Hershey bars. He moved on, making sure each man had one.

"Is this what they call a good-bye gift?" the man from Stockholm mumbled. "Something to enjoy because tomorrow we die?"

"Don't talk like that," Deion spat out. His words came out harsher than he'd intended. "I been injured twice. You think I wanna go out there again?"

A foul attitude settled over him, and he didn't know where it came from. Just hours before he'd been eager to fight, and now . . . the more he marched, the more faces of the dead flashed through his mind. Guys he'd known for such a short time.

As they marched on, morning came, and then the hot sun was high in the sky. The path they followed sloped, like a gully now; so many boots had marched through it.

No clouds shadowed the sky, and Deion wasn't sure when he'd ever felt so hot. They passed a row of poplars, and for a brief time found relief. The trees curved over the road as if offering a moment of shade and protection. But soon they too disappeared, and nothing remained except a solemn house and Spanish fields that also seemed to wilt under the sun.

A layer of sweat covered his body and soaked his uniform. And when they approached a square of a small town, they found no relief.

"Wait here, men; we have a special surprise. *La Pasionaria*, Dolores Ibárruri, will visit us soon! In fact, she plans to travel down the entire front of soldiers as they prepare to advance."

Deion settled to the ground, but didn't remove his boots for fear that he'd never get them back on his swelling feet.

"I've heard of her, but no disrespect . . . it's hot out here," he mumbled.

A bespectacled man with a long, thin nose looked at Deion as if he'd just cursed the Virgin Mother. "Dolores Ibárruri is a great woman—a leader to the people. She is the daughter of an Asturian miner. She even led the coal miners' strike of 1934."

"Yeah, I know," Deion stated, curling onto the patch of dirt and dried grass. "But do she come with shade and water? My canteen ran dry hours ago." Deion lay there in distress, realizing he had become just as miserable to the others as the Stockholm man had been for him.

The stirring of the men around him woke Deion from his fitful sleep. And as he rose and stood with the rest, blearily blinking at the woman standing in front of the men, he realized why the commanders felt an audience with *La Pasionaria* was worth the wait.

She spoke of the hardship to come and the solidarity of the people of Spain. More than that, they now knew why their offensive was so vital. It seemed Franco's armies continued to press into the Basque region, conquering one town after the other. In addition, Nationalist artillery did not let up on Madrid. The Republicans believed that attacking Franco's army just west of Madrid would relieve both sections. Perhaps they could end the siege against the capital!

Hope blossomed in Deion's chest.

"We will go forward under the banner of the United Front," she proclaimed. "We will smash the Fascist generals."

She said more, but Deion could hardly hear her over the roar of approval from the men around him. Her words encouraged them, strengthened them for the fight.

She ended her speech by extending a fisted hand, and the men responded in kind. *"Viva la Republica!"* they shouted, and Deion joined them. "*No pasaran!* They shall not pass!"

Chapter Sixteen

Gusts of hot wind blew over the tall, pointed sierras, flowing down the hillside to meet Sophie as she climbed by Philip's side. Badger ran ahead, darting around the trees and then circling back again. Sophie wished she had the mutt's energy. Her legs burned, and she wondered what had possessed her to tackle the hillside behind their cottage. She paused and moaned, grabbing on to a small tree lest she tumble back down the hill. "Why are we doing this again?"

Philip turned and reached back, extending his hand toward hers. "Walt says on the top of the hill on a clear day we can see a Moorish outpost. It's been here since the time the Moors ruled this part of the country four hundred years ago."

Sophie took his hand. His palm felt soft and sweaty. He tugged, and she felt herself being dragged up the hill. The landscape around them stretched brownish green in every direction, with dark green brush appearing like freckles on the face of the mountain.

Badger approached with a stick in his mouth. Philip took it and flung it as far down the hill as possible. "There, that should keep him busy for a while."

From somewhere a bird sang, yet Sophie couldn't place the location, nor the melody. It was unlike any she'd ever heard. Small pebbles rolled under her feet, causing her to catch herself more than once. Yet in front of her, Philip strolled with poise and ease as if he walked down a cobblestone path. Even pulling her along with him didn't hinder his pace. Her feet moved quicker to keep up.

"Okay, this works. Why didn't we try this sooner?" she laughed. "From now on, this is the only way to hike."

The hill leveled off some, but Philip didn't release her hand as they walked side by side.

"You know, what I'd really like to see is the coal mine," she said. "How far do you think it is?"

"I'd guess about five miles. Down that first road we were on, remember?"

Sophie nodded. "Do you know why I picked the name Eleanor for my new identity papers?"

"Actually, I do. It's because of the nun who gave you the Bible. Or her grandmother's Bible. Eleanor's."

Sophie's feet stopped, and she tugged against his hand. "How did you know?" For so long Eleanor had been her private friend—and the Bible her secret treasure. "Did you look through my things?"

"That day in Guernica. The nun told me you needed to rest. She set up your room, and then she showed me the Bible."

"Hmmph. And to think all this time I thought you were the one who put my concerns first."

He glanced at her and grinned, the blue of his eyes matching the brilliant sky above. "Well, a guy needs help sometimes—to know what to do."

She held his gaze and smiled.

He let out a deep sigh, and then turned and continued up the hill. Sophie frowned, wondering why he was so quick to break any moment of tenderness between them.

After a few minutes of silence, Philip spoke. "So, have you thought about what we talked about? I spoke with Walt. I don't know what he said to you, but he told me he'd like to send the gold out a little at a time."

"He said the same to me. It made me consider what you said about the gold itself—certain pieces at least—being key to a great treasure. That's all very interesting, but it seems so unlikely. I mean, why would Walt risk losing the treasure he has for the hope of something that could be made up?" Sophie paused, and her eyes widened. "Unless what he found was enough to convince him that it was the real thing."

"You may be right. What if you were in Walt's shoes? What would cause you to sacrifice the treasure we have in our grasp by just sending out—saving—a little at a time?"

"A hope that key pieces could be clues to a greater treasure, of course. It only makes sense." With that realization, troubling thoughts filled her mind. "But it's like that old saying, 'a bird in the hand is worth two in the bush.' If this is truly Walt's motive, he may be seeking something that may not even exist, or at least may never be found."

Philip released her hand and stretched his arms wide, as if the vista surrounding them helped prove his point. "But don't you see? It all comes down to faith. Think of all the smirks—the looks—all the comments he's given us when we talk about God. He chided you for putting your faith in what you can't see . . . when, in truth, he's doing the very same."

The path leveled off to a wide plateau, and Sophie turned in a half circle. Her eyes took in the vastness of the view around her, and she suddenly felt very small. Then in the distance, a white, man-made platform caught her eyes. Like a rock terrace to a great castle, it had been built in the side of the mountain opposite them, no doubt for the purpose of a lookout against invaders.

She sucked in a deep breath. "Yes, I'm starting to see it more clearly. I'm getting a better view of how Walt sees things. As you said the other day, what we believe colors our world and the view of it. If this truly is what Walt believes—"

Philip picked up where she left off. "Then the last thing Walt is concerned about is making sure we get out of this, or in that case, making sure all the gold *does* . . . no matter how much it is worth." He squeezed her hand tighter. "I have a feeling, Sophie, that we're on our own. We can't count on Walt to get us out, no matter what he says."

Sophie nodded; then she sat on a large rock and wiped her brow. She studied the outlook built by the Moors hundreds of years before. They'd reigned for a time, but their kingdom ended. And generations of people had lived since then . . . each person with his or her own goals and dreams. All of them living out their beliefs, seeking their own treasure—whether it was someone to love or something to achieve.

Sophie thought about all she'd faced trying to find worth in someone else's arms. There was so much that she held deep inside still—so much she couldn't tell Philip. Because of her own secrets, Sophie had compassion for Walt. She knew how easy it was to hide things from others—especially if one believed that it was for the good of the other person.

She sighed. "I wouldn't give up on Walt just yet. He's always been there when I needed him. He has never left me stranded. He even showed up with more fuel for the truck and maps of the mountain roads. I don't think he's going to let us down. We could be imagining more than what is there. But, still, it makes me think about where I put my hope."

Philip drank deeply from his waterskin, filled with fresh springwater. Then he handed it to her. She took it and smiled, hoping he couldn't see the concern in her gaze. It wasn't only concern for Walt, but also worry that Philip would turn his questions away from their mysterious companion and to her.

Exhausted from the hike, and with her mind more settled with the knowledge that God had a plan for Walt, Philip, and even herself, Sophie had gone to bed early. Through the thin walls of the cottage, she heard Walt and Philip outside tossing sticks for Badger. And as she collapsed onto the bed, the darkness caressed her as if it were night, even though they had just finished dinner.

She drifted easily off to sleep. But she didn't know if five minutes or five hours had passed when she suddenly awoke with the knowledge that she'd been calling out in her sleep. The door to her bedroom creaked open, and she saw a man's form moving toward her.

"Michael?" she whispered, both surprise and fear pounding through her mind.

The man paused, then knelt by the bed. By the light of the moon, she saw it was Philip's face, filled with compassion and confusion.

"Did you dream about him again?"

Sophie hadn't told Philip of the other dreams. The ones where Michael chased her down a dark alley. Or the others—more frightening yet—the ones where he loved her, and she gladly returned to him.

She hadn't mentioned these dreams to Philip, and she wondered how he knew. Had he seen the confused look in her eyes in the morning? Had she called out Michael's name on other nights?

"I'm sorry. I don't know why. I don't *want to* dream about him, believe me." Sophie studied his face and hoped he believed her, because it was the truth.

"What do you want, Sophie?"

She saw that Badger had followed Philip into the room, and she motioned for the dog to jump onto the bed.

"I don't understand. I want to stop these dreams, of course. I want to stop these feelings for him."

"Are you sure?"

She sat up straighter, and the dog curled next to her. She could feel his warmth through the blanket.

"Why wouldn't I? Why would I want to keep dealing with this over and over again?"

"That's what I want to know. I want to know if you really do, or if you're just trying to make me believe it. Maybe you're even fooling yourself. It seems as if you get something from the pain. Maybe justification for the way things are turning out?"

She reached for Philip's hand, but instead of clenching hers as his fingers had earlier that day, it felt lifeless. Badger licked both of their hands. His tongue scratched the surface of her skin.

"If I could erase every memory of Michael, I would do it. If I could tear out every bit of feeling toward him I would.The anger. The fear."

Philip refused to meet her gaze.

She released his hand and took her sheet in her fingers and twisted it, tighter and tighter as if it were possible to rip away the thoughts of him from her heart.

"I know, Sophie. I trust that you love me."

"I do, you know," she whispered.

"Didn't I just say that?" He sighed. "I also know you didn't plan for any of this. You didn't know what you were getting yourself into. But think of it this way. If it hadn't been for him, you'd never be in Spain. And we wouldn't have met. We wouldn't be together now."

Sophie noticed Philip didn't speak Michael's name. It was as if he kept the idea that Sophie had loved another at arm's distance. Or rather as if it were some entity that plagued her instead of a living, breathing man. A man that, no doubt, hunted them even now, eager to reclaim what he desired most—which, Sophie knew, was not her.

"But why can't I just forget? Every time I think of him I push him out of my mind. Every thought, every memory. But I can't control my dreams. Why does he still plague me?"

Philip sat down on the dirt floor. He folded his legs in front of him, and his tight fists rested on his knees. Seeing those clenched fists made her realize that he was bothered by that fact too. The look in his eyes spoke something else. That he wanted to come to her and hold her, but this was not the time and the place. Sophie was thankful he honored her.

Philip blew out a breath. "I've thought about it. And I tried to imagine what it would be like if, for the past three years, all my dreams, thoughts, and hopes had been centered on one person. I imagine if that were the case, I'd be having the same struggles. It's not just that the emotions were one-sided, Sophie. He drew you in. He promised you his love. You'd planned to marry."

Philip was silent for a moment, and he turned from her to the open door. It was only then she saw the tears on his cheeks.

"I'm praying, with you, that the emotions will go away. But you've watered them, tended them for a long while. I'm sure they can't be uprooted easily, no matter how much I wish they could. But I'm praying God will do a work in your heart as only He can.

And that someday—hopefully not too long in the future—you can look me in the eyes and tell me that your heart is undivided. That your love for me has overgrown all those old places. I'm praying that same day those longings will be just a memory."

He didn't wait for her to respond, but rose and left the room, shutting the door behind him. Badger followed, casting one last look at Sophie with a wag of his tail before the door closed.

At that moment Sophie's heart swelled with love for that man. How did she deserve someone so wonderful and understanding? Someone so wise. She didn't know, but she knew he was right. It wasn't as though she *wanted* to admit she still had feelings for Michael. But the truth was she'd loved him for a very long time. And even after all the pain he'd caused her, glimmers of it still rested deep in her soul. Glimmers that had reemerged during their days before she and Michael had been found by Walt at the cave. Moments together that caused her throat to tighten with emotion whenever she thought of them.

Sophie thought back to Eleanor. She thought of the letters Eleanor had written to her past love, Jeremiah. They weren't letters of passion or longing. Instead they told Sophie that it was okay to accept the past for what it was. It was okay to face the realization that two hearts had connected.

But Michael was still living and breathing out there somewhere. Sophie knew that in her case, it was time to turn those same feelings over to God one by one. She'd think of Him as a master gardener, digging out the deep roots that no longer belonged. She closed her eyes and pictured it . . . God with His small shovel digging in her heart.

Then with an ache to her gut the image changed. And in her mind's eye she pictured a mechanical tractor instead—the sharp blades digging deeper, working faster than a hand shovel alone. It hurt. It dug deep, but God would take care of it, in His time.

"Take it, Lord," she whispered into the dark night. "Take what doesn't belong. I know the memories will always be there, but if there are any emotions . . . or even ties that don't belong, dig those out, as only You can."

From somewhere outside the cottage Badger barked, reminding her of his protection—and the care of Walt and Philip, too.

She knew that somewhere beyond the mountains, tall peaks formed a wall of safety around her. Men, volunteers, sat in trenches, defending their lines and fighting for their convictions. But closer, deeper, inside her, Sophie knew that her fight was no longer her own. God was taking care of her. Digging in.

Yet even though she prayed, and she knew God took care of the inner stuff, outwardly she had to keep fighting. Michael was out there—no doubt looking for her. Or rather, seeking out what she had, what he treasured most. The gold.

Chapter Seventeen

Before the sun had completely risen over the mountains, Sophie left the cottage and wandered down to the creek. The air was cool and fresh, and as she walked she almost expected to come upon Philip and Badger. Neither was in the house or surrounding area when she'd left, and she wondered if Philip too had trouble sleeping after last night.

She settled onto the damp grass, tucking her skirt around her knees. Above her, two birds fluttered from limb to limb in the branches of a tree. She watched them squawk and flutter away. Then she heard the thump of Badger's feet and Philip's footsteps clomping down the trail.

He approached, hands in pockets, and sat on the grass beside her, his leg gently brushing against hers. Badger wasn't as gentle. He danced by her side, then jumped on her knees, finally plopping down half on her lap and half on the grass. Sophie smiled and scratched behind his furry black ear, waiting for Philip to speak.

"Sophie, we have to talk."

She looked at him and waited. She knew he wasn't waiting for her to respond, but instead seemed to be trying to figure out what to say.

"Is it about last night? Our conversation?"

The dark circles under Philip's eyes told her he hadn't slept. And she knew that although he'd said all the right things to her in the dark hours, he wasn't at peace.

He plucked a blade of grass and tore it into small pieces, letting the pieces flutter to the ground. "I want you to know how much I care. I meant what I said, but—"

"But you have questions. Things you were hoping you didn't have to ask. Concerns you wished would diminish in time?" She thought about taking his hand, then changed her mind. "You can ask me, Philip—even though I was hoping you wouldn't. But we need to get it all out. You have a right to know."

"Know what, Sophie? What happened during those three days after I saw you that you were with Michael? I saw the difference in your eyes. You seemed more attached to him than before."

She had expected Philip's questions, but his bluntness surprised her. She opened her mouth and then closed it again. Apprehension rippled through her chest. More than anything, she wished she had a different story to tell Philip. Anything but the truth.

She turned to him and noticed the color fading from his face.

"Your silence scares me," he whispered.

"I thought I could just forget it. Once I left him, I thought I could leave all that behind."

"Something happened, didn't it? I was with Cesar. Walt found his own way down to Gibraltar. And you—"

"I almost got married." There. She'd told him. And she would understand if he decided once and for all that she wasn't worth the heartache.

Philip's brows furrowed, and a deep sadness filled his eyes. "What are you talking about?"

Sophie's hands trembled, and she tucked them under her quivering leg.

"I told Michael that we knew where the gold was—that Walt and I figured out it was near Gibraltar. I told him that I loved you," she hurriedly added, "and I wanted to be with you. He said he didn't believe me. He told me to look in his eyes and say it was over."

Sophie dug her toes into the cool dirt. She looked away, wishing the birds would return. Anything to distract them from what she couldn't avoid. Philip remained silent. The only sound was the beating of her heart and the rustle of leaves as a soft wind blew.

"I couldn't do it. The first day. Then the second. Every time I opened my mouth, I couldn't do it." Sophie's throat felt hot and dry. She couldn't look at Philip, couldn't bear to see his face.

"After days of being unable to sleep, I fell asleep in the car. I thought we had to be near Gibraltar. I didn't even wake up when the car stopped. Or at least not right away. All I remember is being alone, waking up all sweaty from the heat coming through the windows. I opened my eyes, and the automobile was parked in front of a church. I . . . I didn't see anyone around, and I knew the only place Michael could be was inside."

She turned to Philip, and his eyes searched hers. She lowered her gaze again, tracing her finger on the flowered pattern of her skirt.

"I thought about running away, but I had nothing. He'd taken my satchel, and I had no money—not even my identity papers."

"Which was likely a good thing in southern Spain."

"Yes, well, I didn't know what to do. I walked to the church and opened the door, and there he was. He was speaking to the priest. He turned and looked at me. And he actually smiled. I swear. It was the dream I had since I was a child. The priest was there, and Michael was standing at the end of the aisle. He turned and looked at me and stretched out his hand." She swallowed hard. "I walked up the aisle. I don't know why. It's almost as if I did it without thinking. I had come to Spain for that moment. It was all I ever dreamed." She turned away. She knew she couldn't face him.

"What did he say?"

"He said, 'Let's do it.'" Tears ran down her face. "'This is what you came for. Sophie, will you marry me?'"

Footsteps sounded behind them, and Sophie knew it was Walt. She quickly wiped the wetness from her cheeks.

"And then what happened?" Philip touched her arm as if urging her to continue.

"I told him I couldn't. I told him I loved you, Philip—for your goodness, your heart. Michael didn't say anything, but his face—" A cry caught in her throat. "He didn't say a word, and then we got back in the automobile and drove to the tunnel. Only hours later, when we prepared to leave, Walt showed up. Michael was injured. We drove to the airport. And the rest is history."

Sophie glanced over her shoulder and noticed Walt standing in the distance . . . giving them space and time to finish their conversation.

Philip coughed faintly. She dared to glance at him and found his eyes fixed on hers. "Thank you . . . for telling me." He wrapped an arm around her shoulders. "Thank you for choosing me." He held her gaze, and then turned to Walt.

Responding to Philip's nod, Walt approached. "Sorry to interrupt, but I'm heading out again." He tucked his hands in his pockets and shifted his weight. "I . . . I'm going to try to find a ride to Granada—to check out what's ahead. I'm going to see if there is someplace we can drive the truck."

Philip pursed his lips. He nodded once and rose. Then reached his hand behind his back and pulled out a pistol from the waistband of his pants.

"Really, Walt?" Philip's voice was tense. "I don't think so. Not until we talk."

Walt's eyes widened in surprise, and he lifted his hands in the air. "Philip, you—"

"What are you doing?" Sophie interrupted, jumping to her feet. "Put that gun down!"

"Walt, quiet. No, Sophie. I'm tired of this game we all seem to be playing. Tired of hearing the truth in pieces. I want to know it all. Now. No one is leaving until I do."

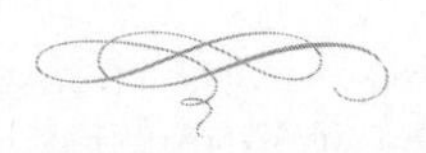

The crackle and boom in the distance caused Deion's shoulders to tense. Still, his footsteps didn't waver, and his aching feet plodded forward as he left the last sign of civilization behind. At least the tension of his neck took his mind off the hollow ache in his stomach from the lack of rations. Or perhaps from fear.

Deion readjusted his hands on the thick rope laid over his shoulder and pulled harder, dragging what seemed like dead weight.

They'd been given steel helmets—thick and heavy, yet not as heavy as the burden Deion pulled through the soil behind. It was said the Italians, fighting for the Fascists, had tractors that pulled their antitank cannons to the front lines. Deion only dreamt of such a thing. Instead, their cannons were pulled by the strength of Deion's back. His and a handful of other men. Nine on each cannon—but not nearly enough for the weight.

One of the men, Jerry from Cincinnati, told Deion the name of the village they'd just passed through, but five minutes later Deion had forgotten it already. He could barely remember his own name, so numbing, so oppressive, was the summer heat. Thinking back, fighting in the treed hills around Bilbao seemed preferable compared to the plains that stretched before him now. Not a tree in sight; only blinding rays that cooked his skin until he was certain he couldn't get any darker.

He supposed he should be thankful for the 45-mm gun. It wasn't pretty, wasn't easy to work, but he'd heard it was effective. And that was the most important thing.

The explosions grew louder as they pressed on. The familiar odor of gunpowder stung his nose. Overhead, a thin layer of gray haze, lower than cloud cover, told him they neared their objective.

And *his* goal? To make it out alive, one more time.

Next to Deion, Jerry blew out a long breath. "Dang, it seems like this gun grows heavier with each step."

Deion nodded and licked his dry lips. "I was just thinking that."

"Anyone got anything to eat?" another commented.

"I heard them say that over the next hill they're gonna set up a command post. And a mess tent."

"That's worth continuing." Another man beside Deion wiped his brow.

Hours later, Deion shook his head at the phrase *the next hill.*

It was farther than they'd thought, and reaching it had taxed the measly strength that remained.

He placed his hands on the small of his back and let out a low moan as he straightened.

He glanced around him. He couldn't see the far target, but in the distance, the cool mountains. He knew the ocean waves crashed far beyond this place in the other direction. The ocean. An ocean breeze. He took a breath and sighed.

"*Vamanos!* Set up the cannon!"

As a team, the exhausted and sore soldiers set up the gun, and then Deion scurried into a nearby foxhole. A different hill, other guys, but he knew soon the same type of battle would replay.

The large *ba-boom* of the gun caused earthquake-like vibrations to move through the ground, as if the very rocks under his feet had taken on a life of their own. As soon as the gun fired, Deion and the others stretched their necks to see if they'd hit their mark. Cheers erupted as an enemy machine-gun nest exploded in a cloud of smoke and debris.

Behind the big guns, the infantry waited for their cue to move forward. With the voices of the infantry, the rumble of a few tanks added to the music of war.

The first set of machine-gun nests was blown. They moved forward again. More enemy troops spotted. Additional fire from their big guns. More cheers.

Pride grew within Deion's chest each time their offensive gained ground. For too long they'd held the defense lines—restraining the enemy. This time he was a part of those leading the fight.

He hunkered down again—pulling the metal helmet tight to his head—as the big guns did their work, and he remembered the days back in Chicago. The first news report of the Spanish War came back to him, as if he'd read them yesterday. He could think of nothing else as he'd cleared the dining tables, picking up after rich folks who didn't notice the colored man's serious expression.

Deion smiled. This time they would carry news of this offensive. In Chicago and New York. Even as far as California. Surely the papers would have bold headlines telling the world that the tides had turned. The Spanish people had hope once again!

But then he thought of the reality. How many times had he seen those men in business suits reading the international news section? No, they skimmed to the business section first. Fancy Chicago women flipped through the lifestyle and gossip columns. How many really cared about Spain? Or about international affairs?

Then again, maybe if these troops succeeded . . . even gaining one small victory . . . people would take notice. If Deion and the others were able to show what dedicated volunteers could do, then surely the people would send support.

These hopes replayed through Deion's thoughts, giving him strength. When the dust had settled they received word to head out again, and he picked up the rope, taking the lead—thoughts of victory lightening his load.

"Just think. Maybe tomorrow or the next day they'll print what's happenin' here. Whole world'll see we're not beat yet," he said to Jerry.

"It's nice to think about, but will it really happen? And even if it does . . . no one will know it was us." Jerry wiped at his red eyes, brushing away the dust that blew in his face as the wind picked up.

"But we'll know." Deion tugged harder on the rope. "And at least they'll know we haven't given up."

Though the others didn't comment, he could feel their pace quicken, and it brought the slightest smile to his face.

"Do you think they'll say the Abraham Lincoln Brigade is involved?" asked a man named Howard. "My mother would like that. She never put up with bullies. She'll know I'm here fighting."

Houses and buildings soon cropped up on the plains. Every so often, as they dragged their guns forward, they spotted burnt-out tanks—more cause for celebration. Deion tried to ignore the fact that men's bodies most likely lay burnt within the metal frames. War was war, and for once his part mattered.

They moved down a small village's main dirt road, and Deion noted foxholes and concrete defenses littering the area. Most enemy soldiers had already abandoned their positions. Only the scattered lifeless bodies testified that just hours before, this ground had been controlled by the enemy.

It stirred eagerness inside Deion, seeing they were making progress. But it also made him realize how crazy their advance was—they'd crossed a dozen fields. They'd made it a few more miles down the road. All that work for so little. Then again, didn't every inch count? Sure, it only made sense. They would win inch by inch. They couldn't give in. Not a little.

The sky, which had gleamed blue all day, turned a gray white as Deion helped to set up the large gun in an abandoned cornfield. He heard a noise from inside one of the white brick houses. A vulture had landed on the roof, knocking over a loose brick. He saw what the vulture waited for. An enemy soldier sprawled in the dirt below it. The man's legs were bloodied, and even though he tried to appear dead, Deion saw his eye blink open. The vulture waited for him to die.

But before Deion could decide what to do about that, machine-gun fire erupted from somewhere inside a row of stone houses.

Looking up to see what they were firing at, movement caught his attention, and Deion looked to the trees across the field from where the enemy had retreated. *Stupid. I've been thinking too much, not watching enough. I should have known. . . .*

The spaces between the tree trunks became a solid mass formed by the blue color of enemy uniforms. There were two times—three times—more enemy soldiers than Deion's group.

"Everyone down!" The words were out before he realized it. "Moors!"

The glint of the sun on their rifles told Deion the Moors were lifting, aiming modern guns. Accurate guns. Unlike their own.

The *rat-a-tat* of bullets split the air, and Deion covered his ears.

As he dropped, the golden stubble of grass blocked his view of the trees. His fingers dug into the reddish clay as he scrambled to turn and retreat.

His head turned. His body was slow to follow. *I've gotta get out of here.*

Around him men's bodies dropped in succession like bowling pins, struck down, tumbling. *How did the fire miss me?*

Deion tried to move through the others in his group toward the row of houses. A man dropped before him. A pained expression deformed his face.

One man still stood. Jerry. He peered down in amazement, or perhaps disbelief, as blood spurted from the bullet wounds in his gut. *Stupid. Get down. What are you doing?*

Deion scrambled over the injured man to get to him. As he heard the cries of his friends, Deion wondered if the hospital had come closer. If anyone could help. *Gwen. Are you near? Will you help?*

Deion reached for Jerry. "Get down! You'll get us killed. You're a perfect target."

He watched, as if in slow motion, his own hand reaching. He snagged Jerry's bloodied, torn shirt. Anger filled him, and he cried out again, "What do you think you're doing!"

Anger at Jerry for being so stupid and not getting down soon enough. Anger that another friend was hit.

Jerry submitted to Deion's tug and crumbled at an awkward angle.

"Don't make me responsible for this. Don't make me responsible to save you!" Deion shouted in his ear.

Jerry's face was within inches of Deion's own. His eyes blinked and his mouth opened, but no sound emerged.

"Don't look at me like that. Don't look at me like you're dying!" Deion's trembling hand covered his face, unsure of what to do, where to go.

We should have known. Why were we so bold?

"They always leave the Moors—leave them to clean up the mess," Deion mumbled as he ripped his shirt off and quickly wound it around Jerry's stomach. He cinched it tight, hoping to stop the bleeding.

"Everybody back to the trees. To the buildings!" Deion didn't know what possessed him, but he knew he had to get the others—mostly new recruits—out of the danger zone. Before he could second-guess his plan of action, he jumped to his feet and lifted Jerry into his arms. Then he ran as fast as he could toward cover.

"To the buildings. Now!" he shouted again, unable to turn to see if the others followed.

In his arms, Jerry moaned. Deion felt the warm, sticky blood seeping through the shirt and onto his skin. More gunfire erupted, and Deion held his breath, expecting to feel the sting of the bullet at any moment.

Without stopping, he ran through an open door into a small house.

"Medic! Medic!" he called. Yet he knew even as he said the words, there was no help. The emergency workers were still back with the infantry. Deion's group had been eager—too eager to move ahead, to claim new ground.

What was I thinking? It's my fault. I shoulda said something. I shoulda stopped the advance.

Deion laid Jerry on an old dining room table, praying it would hold under the man's weight. It creaked, but it held.

He saw that Jerry was shot in the side, rather than the stomach as he first thought. His mind raced, trying to remember the medical training he had received when he first arrived in Spain.

Stop the bleeding. Protect the wound. Treat for shock.

Chapter Eighteen

Deion had worked for over an hour to stabilize his friend. After the blood flow eased, he made a nest of old bedding and clothing on the floor for his friend. Dusk had come upon them when Jerry finally drifted off to sleep, and Deion did too.

The droning of planes overhead woke Deion from his slumber. Morning light flooded through the windows, but the sound of gunfire outside told Deion that someone still battled.

Though Jerry's face was pale, his breathing remained steady. Deion released the breath he'd held. He sat up, then crawled toward the window, hoping more than anything that he'd see Republican planes in the sky. Instead, the aircraft were unlike any he'd ever seen.

"Italian," Jerry muttered. "I can tell by the sound of the engines." With slow movement, he tossed Deion a wayward shoe. "Here."

Deion glanced at it, unsure.

"Get down and stick that in your mouth," Jerry mumbled. "Now!"

Deion didn't question him, but it almost seemed surreal that the near-dead man was giving him an order.

With an earthshaking explosion, the first bomb hit twenty feet outside the small house, and one wall seemed to fold in, in slow motion. Deion felt as if his whole body was encompassed in the blast. Immediately, intense pressure hit his ears. He bit down on the dirty boot, and the pressure relaxed.

Brushing debris off, he sat up and noticed Jerry didn't move. Deion thought what the bullet hadn't achieved, the blast had. He didn't have time to check on his friend, because for the next ten minutes one explosion after another shook the house.

Eventually the explosions ceased and the droning disappeared. Deion was thankful the house still stood. He pushed the debris off himself, then brushed bits of plaster off Jerry.

As if just waking up from a peaceful sleep, the man's eyes fluttered open. "How are yer ears?" Jerry mumbled.

"Aching but good."

"If yer mouth had been closed, you'da lost them for good. Now we're even. I saved your hearing. You saved my life."

Deion nodded; then his face fell to the man's side where fresh, bright blood seeped through the bandages. He looked to Jerry's face and noticed the color draining.

Realizing what was happening, Jerry's eyes narrowed and his forehead tightened.

"Not yet, buddy. My job's not through, but I'm gonna save ya." Deion immediately applied pressure to the wound. "I'm gonna save ya."

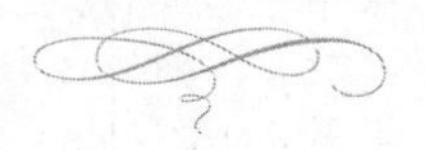

Sophie reached a hand to Philip. "You need to put down that gun." They were back at the small house, and Walt sat at the table. Philip still held the gun steady, pointing it at Walt's chest.

Philip ignored Sophie. Instead he neared Walt, stretched his arm, and narrowed the space between the gun barrel and Walt's body.

"I want you to know I consider you a friend," he said without emotion. "But I've already lost one friend in Spain, so that wouldn't be anything new."

Sophie took a step back, her hands trembling. She looked around for something, anything to protect herself and Walt. "What do you think you're doing?" She reached behind her back for the tin pan used to hold wash water.

Philip spoke to her, though his eyes were on Walt. "Sophie, I'm not going to tell you again. . . . I need to know the truth. If I have to lock you in the other room I will."

"I've told you the truth." Walt's voice was calm.

"You've told me part of the truth. I want to know all of it. If we are going to risk our lives for this gold, then we deserve to know why."

"The truth." Walt stared at the gun barrel directly. He sighed deeply. "Though I truly doubt, Philip, that you would use that gun on me, I do owe you the whole story. You and Sophie both. Can you put it down?"

Philip lowered the gun slowly; then he moved to sit across from Walt. Sophie returned the dishpan to the counter.

"So." Walt crossed his arms over his chest. "Do you want to know about the gold first . . . or why I got involved with it?"

"Why you got involved," Sophie blurted.

"The gold." Philip leaned one arm against the table.

Walt shrugged, and then glanced at Sophie. "I'm sorry, señorita. The man with the gun wins." He took a deep breath. "Since the conquistadors, treasure hunters have journeyed into the mountains of South America searching for a great treasure, never to return again. My employer is such a treasure hunter. He had also given up trying to find the treasure when he heard about the special pieces."

Sophie pressed her fingers to her temples. Philip had been right. There was more to the gold than Walt had first told them.

"My employer told me about a region where they think a great treasure, greater than anyone can imagine, is hidden. The craggy Llanganati Mountains are rugged beyond belief and cloaked in fog. In addition, they seem to be alive with electricity and earthquakes. Perhaps that is why there are so many legends surrounding them."

"What type of treasure?" Sophie dared to ask.

"To understand the treasure, you need to know about their ruler—the Lord Inca, who they believed descended from the sun. Everything belonged to the Sun King—the gold and silver, the land, the people themselves. Gold was considered 'sweat from the sun.' It was not treated as money, but as religious symbols. They fashioned it into ornaments, plates, utensils—all in honor of their Sun King.

"Amazingly, the Inca land was ruined by its own civil war of sorts," Walt continued. "Two brothers wanted to be king. They had a five-year war, and just when the winner, Atahualpa, defeated his brother and was about to become king, the Spanish conquistadors arrived in Peru. The goal of the conquistadors was to seize the gold and silver, claim the land for the king of Spain, and convert the Indians to Christianity."

Goose bumps rose on Sophie's arms. "Am I the only one who thinks this story sounds like something from yesterday's newspaper instead of something that happened four hundred years ago? The same war is happening around us."

"And the same fight for the gold and silver," Philip added with a sigh.

"What happened after that?" Sophie sat on the dirt floor, her focus intent on Walt.

"Well, there were so few soldiers that the Incas considered them more a curiosity than a threat. Pizarro invited the Inca King to meet with him in the village square. The king met him, considered it a peace meeting."

"How many Spaniards were there?"

"Sixty-two horsemen and 106 foot soldiers. The Inca king showed up with six thousand armed guards. Before the end of the skirmish, thousands of Indians had been killed and the Inca ruler captured. From his prison cell, King Atahualpa bargained for his life. He told the Spaniards he would fill two large rooms—one with gold and the other with silver—if they would let him go free. They agreed."

Walt paused and he leaned back in the chair, seemingly pleased by their curiosity. He turned to Philip. "You're the history teacher. I'm sure you know what happened next."

"Remind me." Philip leaned forward in his seat.

"The king called to all his land, asking for a ransom. The people obeyed and brought ceremonial gold and silver from the temples of the sun and moon. For the next few months, treasure poured into Cajamarca. The Spaniards melted down most of the objects into ingots to be transported back to Spain by ship."

"What a waste! Did they let him go?" Sophie scooted closer, anxious to hear what happened next, eager to know the connection with the gold they carried.

"Even after the people fulfilled the request, Atahualpa was not freed as promised. Instead the Spaniards decided to murder the Inca king."

Sophie felt anger stirring within her. "But why?"

"First, they feared General Ruminahui would attack from the north. Second, they wanted to ransack all of the temples—the gold the people brought wasn't enough for them."

Philip shook his head and snorted.

"They fastened the Inca lord to a pole and strangled him. And before the Inca king's troops could attack, they set out to raid the empire. But what the Spaniards didn't realize was that at the very hour of the murder, a caravan of sixty thousand men was on its way to Cajamarca. They transported all the gold from every temple and place in Quito. It was their last-ditch effort to free their king. Leading the caravan was the general himself."

"Oh, my." Sophie placed a hand over her heart—not only at the unimaginable worth of the gold, but at the dedication of the people to their king.

"Our dedication seems to pale in comparison, doesn't it?" Philip mumbled.

"So I assume the gold wasn't delivered?" Sophie asked.

"No, it was hidden in the mountains by the general. He'd grown up in a mountain hamlet and knew the area better than anyone. The general was later captured and tortured, but he never revealed the location.

"Yet . . . there is a story about one Spaniard, years later, who discovered the location after he befriended some of the people. Once he had the information, he realized three things. First, if he turned over the information, others would become rich—not him.

Second, once he disclosed the location, he too would most likely be killed. He also knew he would not be able to retrieve the great amount of gold alone. His plan was to travel to Spain and assemble his own group of men to return and retrieve the treasure."

"So did he?" Philip moved the gun to the other hand, and Sophie now knew he had no intention of using it.

"This man was very wise. He took some of the ingots and had them fashioned into special coins. There were seven of them, and each one held one clue that would disclose the hiding place. He hid them amongst the Inca treasure being shipped back to Spain. In this shipment they transported Inca artifacts, too—not just ingots—so no one realized their worth. His plan was to retrieve the coins upon arriving."

"Let me guess." Sophie sighed. "He never made it."

"That's correct. Unfortunately, he died on the journey. My employer believes the coins made it into the treasury, where they have languished for hundreds of years."

"And was he . . . or she . . . right?" Sophie asked.

From his pocket, Walt pulled out his fist and opened it to display five coins. "I don't have them all, but this is more than I expected. I'm not sure when the others were lost, but these . . ." He blew out a breath. "These are the key to a greater treasure than anyone thought possible."

"I don't believe you." Philip's words were sharp, and Sophie turned to him. Her jaw dropped at his response.

"What about Valverde's Guide? It seems you forgot that part."

Walt's eyes widened in surprise; then he broke into a smile. "You seem to remember more of the story than you let on."

"Valverde's Guide?" Sophie looked to Philip. "You've completely lost me."

"Yes, well, a few years *before* this incident, a poor soldier—another Spaniard—married an Indian woman. She was from the same town as the general. Her father was an Indian priest—"

"A *cacique*," Philip interjected.

"Sí, a *cacique*." Walt nodded. "It is said that the priest led him to the treasure and he became a rich man. Later he returned to Spain. On his deathbed he wrote *El Derrotero de Valverde.*

Valverde's Guide. It describes in detail how to reach the treasure. There are many copies of it in print."

"So if there is this guide, why are the coins needed?" Sophie's head throbbed as she tried to soak up the information.

"For four hundred years men have tried to use the guide, but they all have failed. They all reach a point where they get lost in the dense jungle and the strange mists. They come to a point on the journey where the guide no longer makes sense."

"As I was saying before Philip interrupted, the man that I spoke of—the one who discovered the gold and fashioned his own coins—did so in such a way that the coins only work with Valverde's Guide. You see, even though the guide is very clear at the beginning, it gets more confusing toward the end. The coins are symbols that begin at the confusing part. These—" He shuffled them in his hand, causing the coins to clink together. "These are . . . well, priceless. I cannot even begin to describe their worth."

"Wait a minute." Sophie stood. "Okay, first of all, you pulled me into this mess because you thought I was working with Michael. Then . . . you used me—you asked me to return to him —because of the gold. You said that he was involved in a plot to steal it. You said the gold could be sold to collectors and used to fund supplies for the people. . . . And now . . ." Sophie placed her hands on her hips. "And now, it's not just the value of the gold, or the value of the artifacts, but it is the value of *those five coins* that matters most. *Those five coins* are what this whole thing is about? Those are why I was pulled into this?"

Walt nodded.

Sophie closed her eyes and tried to will away her frustration. Then she opened them, took a step closer, and gazed down at the coins. "May I touch them?"

Walt nodded. "Yes, of course. I wouldn't have them without you."

Sophie ran her finger over the face of one. On it was imprinted the image of a waterfall splashing into a narrow valley.

Philip's gaze was still fixed on Walt. "Do you believe it? Do you think the story is true?" he asked.

"Well, before I found the coins I wasn't so sure. Now . . . well, they seem like evidence that the story is true."

"Yes, but how did you keep going when you didn't know for sure?" Sophie looked at another coin that showed a mountain. The peaks were an odd shape and almost looked like a woman lying on her side.

"Like anything one chooses to believe in," Walt continued. "I came to a point when I had to make a decision. I've seen people . . . friends . . . killed because I put them in harm's way. And soon I knew the only way I could continue was to have faith." Walt removed his fedora and rubbed his forehead.

"Faith?" Philip eyed the man, then glanced at Sophie.

Walt shook his head with a laugh. "No, no. Not that kind of faith. At least now I can see the gold and touch it. Your faith is based on anything but reality. A man dies, and thousands of years later He's supposed to help me. It's foolish."

Sophie glanced down at the third coin, which showed a log bridge crossing a stream. She felt warmth spreading through her chest, urging her to speak.

"Jesus is the greatest treasure, Walt, but He's not just something you obtain—He is *the way* to the greatest treasure of all—our salvation."

Philip glanced up at her with a smile, but he didn't speak.

Sophie handed back the coin. "Jesus is like this symbol. He's a bridge . . . crossing to the other side, from death into life. Jesus is that bridge for us, Walt. Remember that transporter bridge? The one in Bilbao?"

"Yes. There are very few like it in the world."

"Exactly. There are other bridges you drive across. Or you walk over. You use the vehicle's power, or your own, to carry you. But that one—it is different. You trust in its power to take you. You climb on, and that is enough. The bridge, under its own power, carries you to the other side."

She took Walt's hand, wishing her faith could flow into him with one touch. If only it were that easy.

"That is what faith in Jesus is," she finished. "It's knowing that your efforts, your strength alone, cannot take you to the other side. But believing in Him and climbing on that promise can. In fact, it's the *only* thing that can."

Though Walt said nothing, she could see in his gaze that he

was considering her words. As he always did, Walt was taking in the information, filing it, and tucking it away for a time when it would be useful. Sophie only hoped that time was sooner rather than later.

He slid the coins into his pocket and turned to Philip. "So now that you know, I suppose you can guess what I've been asked to do."

Philip nodded. "Leave the rest of the gold behind—and us with it. Which, of course, I'm not going to let you do."

Walt seemed almost relieved. "Yes, I figured you would say that." He stood and moved to the window, cocking his head as if scanning the yard for Badger. "I suppose we need to figure out another plan then."

"We'll get to that." Philip returned the pistol to the waistband of his pants. "But there's another part of the story, one you haven't told us." He approached and placed a hand on Walt's shoulder. "Who is your employer, Walt, and how did you get involved?"

Walt turned, and there was pain in his expression—pain that cut Sophie to the core. "Okay, I'll tell you. But Sophie, you better sit down for this."

Chapter Nineteen

Walt insisted they eat breakfast before he told them the rest of his story.

Sophie ate her bread and omelet. Walt picked at the food on his plate. His eyes appeared clouded over as he moved his eggs from one side of the tin plate to another. After Philip cleared the dishes, Walt leaned back and entwined his fingers behind his neck, staring at the ceiling.

"I've never told anyone this story. And I'm not even sure I should now." He looked at Sophie. "But I guess you could say this whole thing started before I was born."

He let out a low breath. "Before Michael's father traveled to Madrid, he was engaged to another young woman, also from Boston. She found herself pregnant and didn't want anyone to find out. She turned to a former teacher for help and traveled to Chicago, where the teacher lived. That's where I was born."

Sophie felt her stomach drop as she tried to piece together what Walt was saying.

"Wait a minute." Philip leaned forward. "Are you saying Michael—"

"Is your brother?" Sophie finished.

Instead of answering, Walt continued. "For years I didn't know I was adopted. The teacher, Marge, and her husband, William, raised me. Their friend Camille would visit every summer. One summer, when I was twelve, I heard Camille and my mother fighting. Camille wanted to tell me the truth, but Marge wouldn't have it. I followed Camille to the train station and told her what I'd overheard. I didn't want to hurt my parents, so I didn't tell them I knew."

Sophie's hand covered her mouth. She studied Walt's face, trying to convince herself that what he spoke wasn't true; but the more she looked at his features, the more she saw the resemblance. Michael was darker, due to his Spanish mother, but their build, the set of their eyes—even their noses looked similar. And the more she looked at him, the more Sophie was convinced. He resembled Michael's father—far more than Michael did, actually.

"I wanted to know more," Walt continued. "William was an investigator for the Chicago police. He always came home with stories of gangsters—cops-and-robbers tales. I wanted to learn all I could from him, for one purpose—to find my father. After graduating from high school, I moved to Boston to go to college. It was the hardest thing I ever did. I saw the pain in my mother's—Marge's—eyes as she realized I knew the truth."

"And did you find her? Find Camille?" Sophie's fingers clasped together on her lap.

Walt lowered his gaze. "No. Camille died of tuberculosis a few years before I moved to Boston. She'd never married. Never had any more children. She'd lost her heart completely to a Spanish dancer, and lived her whole life under a cloak of self-pity.

"But in my search, I found a neighbor who'd kept some of her things. It wasn't much, but it was enough to lead me to my father. I remember the first time I saw his house. There he was with his beautiful wife and son. Michael was not much younger than I. They lived less than a mile from Camille in Boston, and I wondered how often she had witnessed their life and wished it were hers."

"That's horrible." Philip scratched Badger's ear. The dog flopped to his side and fell asleep at Philip's feet.

"Watching them, following them, became my obsession.

Then one day everything changed. Michael's uncle approached me. He had been in town visiting his sister. He demanded to know who I was and why I stalked his sister's family. I suppose I hadn't been as careful as I thought. At first he was angry, rude; but then he took a closer look at me and figured it out. He said I looked just like my father."

"Then . . . did you meet them? Does Michael know?" Sophie thought back, trying to remember if Michael had ever spoken of a brother.

"Not as far as I know. Adolfo set up a meeting with my father. He thought it best he wasn't around—that it was something we needed to do without his presence. My father was kind enough, but his wife was a difficult woman. I was tossed out of their home before I had a chance to speak. Adolfo was distraught when he found out. He searched for three days until he found me. At the time he had no children, but desperately wanted them. He didn't understand how someone could allow his own flesh and blood to be turned away. And he never liked his sister's choice for a husband, so I think his care for me was half to fill his need and half to defy my father. Then Adolfo brought me to Spain. Though I never met his family, he paid for my schooling. I fell in love with the country. I studied languages and built friendships."

"So when did you get involved with the gold?" Philip leaned forward and rested his elbows on his knees.

"It was on a different trip to Boston that Adolfo first heard about it. Michael asked him for advice. Adolfo looked into it himself; then he asked me to help him. Together, we learned the truth about the coins."

Walt stood and strode to the window. He tucked his hand into his pocket and pulled out the coins, squeezing them in his fist. "Adolfo asked me to return to Boston. I learned about the meetings with investors and their plans for getting the gold. They wanted to sell the antiques to collectors, but they had no idea about the seven coins."

"You were there? At the museum?"

Walt turned and met Sophie's gaze. "Yes, Sophie. That day you met Michael. I saw you together . . . and I thought you were part of the plan, too."

Sophie was glad she was sitting, for suddenly she felt her body grow weak. Her romance, or what she'd believed was true love, had been watched and scrutinized from the beginning. Nothing had been hers alone. Nothing.

"Of course, at first I didn't care about the gold. I just needed an excuse to stay close to my family. By this time both Marge and William had passed away. Adolfo was all I had left. He wasn't family, but he was the closest thing I had. It was only later I came to believe the story was real."

Walt folded his arms across his chest and leaned against the wall. "I plotted with Adolfo until the gold became an obsession. Soon, I wanted the treasure house more than anything. It was my way to prove myself . . . to my father. I wanted to give him what Michael failed to find."

"So you did all this out of revenge?" Philip stood and paced. "We're here because you wanted to be the better son?"

Walt straightened his shoulders. His voice deepened in anger. "Partly, but also for the honor of Adolfo, who took me in. He cared." Walt's features softened. He looked again to Sophie. "I thought you were in on it. I was sure Michael used you. It seemed too convenient that you worked at the museum. Then, when you came to Spain, I knew my theory was true."

"Well, maybe I am in on it." Sophie bit her lip. "Maybe I've fooled you all." She threw up her hands.

Walt chuckled, and his eyes brightened. "I wish. Maybe then I wouldn't feel so guilty for all the pain I've caused you. Especially since you were simply a woman in love."

Philip stopped his pacing as Walt said those words, and Sophie saw the pained expression on his face. She lowered her head to her hands, wondering if they could ever get past this. Wondering if Michael would invade every conversation.

Walt hurriedly continued. "That's when I knew I had to get you out of the country, Sophie. I talked to José, and he agreed to help. He convinced Michael to fake his death. We knew you wouldn't leave otherwise."

"You helped?" Sophie lifted her face to his. "It was all *your* idea?"

From the guilty look on Walt's face, Sophie knew it was true.

"Wait a minute. There's something more important here," Philip said. "So now what's your motivation, Walt? If that's even your name. Is it wealth? Revenge? Approval?"

Walt turned his hat over in his hands. "I don't know if you'll believe this, but like Sophie, I too have fallen in love with Spain. I honestly hoped to get the gold out of the country, sell it to collectors, and use the money to help the Republican efforts. Adolfo agreed we could use the money this way if I helped him find the coins he wanted. And, yes, my name is Walter. I'm named after my father. Michael's father."

Philip approached him, peering down. "If that's so, and you just want to help the Republicans, why were you going to leave with the coins? Why leave us behind?"

"Who said I was? Those were my orders . . . but I couldn't pull it off. For the first time, I questioned myself."

"You grew a conscience?" Philip raised an eyebrow.

Walt shrugged. "Yes, I suppose I did."

"Where does that leave us now?" Sophie looked from one man to another. "This is an amazing story, but we're still stuck with millions of dollars' worth of gold."

"I'm racking my brain to figure out an answer to that."

Walt's face looked pale, and his voice was shaky. "I've always thought ten moves ahead. This whole thing has been like a chess game, as I moved the players around." He pressed his fingers to his forehead. "Not this time. I can only think of one more step. The next step . . . and I just hope it's the right one."

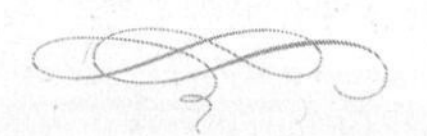

Something seemed to die within Deion as he tossed the last shovelful of dirt over Jerry. He left a wooden cross he'd formed with sticks as a marker and retreated to where the infantry was reforming after the bombing.

"Men, this offensive could make or break us," the commander said to the group circled around him.

He was shouting, but Deion could barely make out his words

over the wobbling *thrum* of shells exploding in the distance. The flickering night clouds—the flashes of explosions—caught his attention.

The commander talked on, and by the end Deion knew their tactic had not changed. They would march into the Guadarrama Valley. They'd seize Mosquito Ridge, which dominated the area as the high spot.

After he'd dismissed the others, the commander approached Deion. "I heard about you. You're the one who carried your friend off the battlefield."

Deion nodded. He didn't tell the commander his efforts had been in vain.

"I need someone like you." The commander pointed to the first ridge. "I need you to deliver a message for me."

Deion listened intently, but his mind and emotions were numb as they set out again, and he determined not to talk to anyone. The last thing he wanted to do was get to know any of the other men. The ache in his gut from Jerry's death grew stronger as he neared the battlefield.

He felt like he was wrapped in a nightmare as he once again found himself on the front lines. He hurried to the ridge, determined not to stop until he reached it.

The air was thick with the smell of gunpowder and the dust from the explosions. A violent fit of coughing overtook him, and another bomb fell—a terrific blast as hot as a furnace. The sky around Deion flashed white, and then everything went dark.

The earth rumbled again, and Deion felt his body flying through the air. He imagined the force of hitting the ground, but instead his body landed and was surrounded by a sweet coolness. His lips parted, and muddy water seeped into his mouth, and he realized he'd landed in the shallow river. He struggled to stand, but his legs wouldn't cooperate. He moved his arms to swim toward shore, but it was as if he were swimming in wet cement.

As he struggled to hold his head above water, Deion thought of the piles of bodies. He remembered Gwen studying their faces. And he imagined her pain if she found his face among the others.

He wouldn't let that happen. Maybe, when all this was done,

he'd find her again. Renewed energy surged through him, and he struggled to the bank. He pulled himself to his feet, feeling suddenly tired. More than anything he wanted to lie back down and sleep. His eyelids grew heavy. The clay felt like a soft mattress under his body.

The double *thwack* of the antiartillery pulled him from his slumber. Whether he'd been out for five seconds or five minutes he wasn't sure, but he awoke with the iron-tinged taste of blood in his mouth. His sore tongue told him he must have bit it hard.

He touched his face, certain the blast had melted it off. Instead, he discovered his eyebrows were missing. Heat warmed his cheeks as it had when he was a child and spent too many hours in the sun.

It was then Deion remembered, as bright and urgent as the flash of explosion, the message he was supposed to tell the others.

"I gotta get to the machine-gun team on the hill," he whispered.

He moved up the slope. Around him Spanish troops straggled back from the ridge.

"Hold your position!" Deion gasped, unsure if they could understand his English words. He motioned to the others. A few paused and looked at him with a dazed expression. "The commander sent a message. Hold your position!" He pointed to the small ridge. "You can't retreat. Do not retreat!"

Understanding flashed in one man's eyes, and he quickly spoke to the others. Without hesitation, they hurried back to the ridge.

Deion hurried up the slope. A chaser whistled overhead and to the right, toward the town of Brunete. He struggled to give the message to the other Spanish troops. "Hold your position."

Shrapnel bursts hit all around like fireworks at a Fourth of July celebration back home. Deion felt clumps of debris hitting his steel helmet and bits falling on his shoulders, but it wasn't enough to slow him down. He worked with the others to dig into the ridge of rock. Below them more explosives hit the oaks, causing dark shadows to bend and flex. Bullets caused the moonlit trees and vines to tremble, but he was safe. He was alive. And they held.

Chapter Twenty

Badger's barking interrupted Walt, Philip, and Sophie as they discussed their next steps. Walt peered out the window to see the man and his daughter from the small community down the hill approaching.

"Señors, señorita," the man said when Philip opened the door. "My daughter and I wondered if you were still here. If you need help or information." He approached the front door with a smile. "Of course, we did not ask the others if they knew. They have no idea you ever stopped here. Your secret is still safe with us."

They stayed the morning, and Sophie enjoyed the female companionship, especially the small talk as they discussed simple things such as gardens and the Moorish outposts in the surrounding hillsides. It was nice not to focus her attention on stolen treasure and their duty to Spain.

They sat in the shade by the creek, enjoying the food Sophie prepared. As Sophie talked and laughed with the young woman, she wished she could tell her about the food cellar, but now wasn't the time. From the way Walt stood and paced, he was counting down the minutes until the visitors left.

Finally, when the sun was high overhead, the two yawned

and headed home for their siesta. Only then did Sophie follow Philip and Walt back to the house, where they resumed planning around the table.

Philip spoke first, but from the look on Walt's face he spoke for both men. "If what Walt says is true—and I trust it is—maybe we should escape with the gold coins only."

Sophie opened her mouth to speak, and Philip took her hand. With his free hand he pointed his thumb in the direction of the truck.

"Getting the truck to Barcelona is a long shot. And maybe that's not even the reason we were caught up in this in the first place. I have to agree with Walt—the fact that he found the coins leads me to believe the story is true. I can't even imagine the impact a discovery like that would make."

"I don't know." Sophie rubbed her tired eyes with her free hand. "I think you're missing the point. We're not doing this because we want fame or to make the discovery of the century. We're doing it for the Spanish people, right?"

She turned to Walt and focused her eyes on his. "That's what you told me when you asked me to return to Michael—you said that national security depended on it." She returned her gaze to Philip. "Weren't you the one who only a week ago talked about David seeing God as bigger than the problem?"

She tried to stand, but Philip refused to let go of her hand. "Yes, I know what I said, but I'm worried—mostly about you, Sophie." He hesitated, weighing his words. "I don't think I could live with myself if somehow we made it out with the gold . . . and not each other."

"I agree," Walt chimed in. "That's why I came back. Even if I pleased Adolfo, impressed my father, and discovered the gold of a lifetime, I'd never be able to live knowing I'd abandoned my friends."

"If you're not going to listen to me, then never mind." Sophie stood and kicked her foot against the dirt floor. Her gut ached and, as if a veil were descending over her eyes, she suddenly didn't want to think anymore—she was tired of carrying the weight of Spain on her shoulders. "Forget it. If this is the fastest way to get out of the country, let's do it."

She crossed her arms over her chest and closed her eyes. She thought of her last night in France before entering Spain. The soft bed and fresh, clean sheets. The tub filled with warm, perfumed water. Her hair, clean and styled. Clothes that made her look like a woman.

She thought of waking without worrying that an enemy hid around every corner. Or behind every set of eyes. She considered setting up her easel in a park and painting for the mere joy of it. Oh, to hold a paintbrush in her hands.

She also imagined phoning her parents and hearing their voices for the first time in over a year. Taking a stroll, her hand in Philip's, without a care in the world, except for the desire to know each other better.

Sophie opened her eyes and nodded her head. "Yes, I'm in. Let's figure out how to get those coins out of the country. Then maybe, from the outside, we can find a way to help Spain."

"By getting the coins out, won't we accomplish both?" Philip released her hand and rested his elbows on his knees as he always did when he was deep in thought. "If these few items can lead us to an even greater treasure . . . then we do both. We accomplish much with so little."

"Somehow that sounds too good to be true." Sophie sighed. "Even if Adolfo does take the coins to South America, how will he know what the clues mean? We have to trust him to find the treasure—if it's still there. Plus, will he really give the gold to Spain? And let's not forget that this man betrayed his own family—he took the information Michael gave him in confidence and found a way to steal the gold from his own nephew. He used Walt . . . and risked so many lives for his dream."

As she spoke, the taste she had for all the good things she longed for suddenly soured in her mouth. "There are no easy answers, are there? Either way we are at risk. Who really knows what will benefit the people most? Who really knows if any of it will succeed? Or if we have the right motives? Or . . . if I'm just rambling because I'm tired? I don't know about you, but today I'm taking a siesta."

"And maybe, like Jacob, God will speak to you in a dream?" Philip rubbed his brow.

“Who knows? He can do anything He wants. Maybe we’re thinking too far ahead. Maybe we just need to do the one thing He’s asked at the present.”

Philip looked at her curiously. “And what’s that?”

“Trust that no matter how this thing turns out, God still has a plan. His love for the people of Spain, and for us, will never stop. And . . . though it’s hard for me to believe sometimes, God can use even my failures for a greater good. So, no matter what tomorrow brings, I can trust—we can trust—we don’t have to face it alone.”

And with that Sophie made her way to the old bed and fell asleep with the image of God’s smiling face filling her mind. His smile was not due to anything she had done or would accomplish, but merely the fact that she was His. For the moment that was enough.

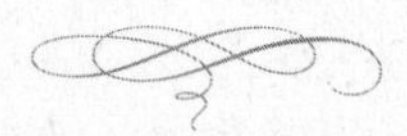

The horse’s breath smelled of chewed grass. His coat glistened like newly fallen snow, and Petra wondered how she could fall in love with an animal. But she had, and she was glad. She wiped the dew from Erro’s saddle and attempted to hoist it up.

The sound of hoofbeats punctuated the air, and Petra turned with a start. She breathed a sigh of relief to see it was José on Calisto, and not an enemy soldier.

He rode up the narrow path where she stood, then swung down from the saddle in one smooth motion, dropping Calisto’s reins. There was no need to tie the stallion up; he had been trained to stay where he was unless José ordered otherwise.

“Here, let me get that for you.” José’s dark eyes gazed heavily at Petra as he took the saddle from her hands, his fingers brushing against hers.

She put a hand on his arm. “Thank you, but I need to learn to do this, especially with you gone. I was just going to ride around the hill to get my bearings. I’d like to know what’s around me—more than just the inside walls of the cave and the path to the creek.”

"I'll be back." José's voice was defensive.

"Oh, I have no doubt." She smiled and tilted her head. "It was just . . . never mind. Thank you for helping me." Petra kept her voice light and teasing, but José's frown only deepened, and she wondered what she had done wrong. For as long as she'd known him, José had been kind and sincere. It was hard to see this other side of him—a serious and worried man who seemed to frown at everything she said.

He's just worried about us, Petra told herself. *He has a lot on his mind.*

Her father had been the same way. It could be the weather or the comment of a local merchant that caused his face to redden and his eyes to narrow. Her mother told her that it was difficult enough to be the head of the family, but her father was also the protector of an entire estate. The people relied on him for harvests, wages, and wisdom. Petra only wished they had understood that. Instead they focused on his heavy hand and his requirements. They didn't realize that what they considered unfair was most of the time for their own good.

She gazed at José, for a second seeing him as he truly was. Not as a hero, but as a man who made mistakes. Her stomach ached as she thought of it. She also thought of what his own pride had cost him—leaving his wife in the valley. Thankfully, his plan was to right the wrong. The idea of José returning with Ramona pleased her, but caused an ache in her heart at the same time. She refused to meet his gaze; instead she stroked Erro's nose.

"Your wife—does she know you're coming?"

"No, she does not."

Petra watched as José cinched Erro's saddle. He glanced at her, and she clearly saw his affection for her—mixed with a tinge of guilt. She could not deny that she wondered how things would be if José were not married. He cared for her, she knew, but he was also a faithful and dedicated man. She appreciated that about him. After all, anyone of lesser character could easily have walked away—especially when Ramona refused to come to the mountains.

"It will be a nice surprise when you show up." Petra took the reins and climbed onto Erro's saddle.

"I hope so." José looked away before Petra could read his

reaction. "I just don't know what I'll find when I get there."

"You'll find your heart," Petra commented with a smile. And without waiting for a response, she nudged Erro with her knees, and the horse trotted away. Though the sun beat down on her shoulders, a dark cloud descended over her heart. Petra didn't want to think of what would happen if José didn't return. She also didn't want to think about what he'd do or say when he discovered she'd followed him into the valley.

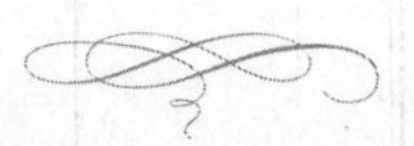

Deion never appreciated rest as much as he did the day after battle. Many had fallen due to heatstroke. Others reorganized and prepared for their next attack. They also buried thirty dead from among them. And from the crest of Mosquito Ridge, the Nationalists bombed their positions, reminding them they still held the coveted position.

Somewhere in the midst of those days, Deion heard news he never expected.

"They've gone and killed Oliver Law," reported a soldier. His face bore the pinched look of a man suffering from a stomachache.

Deion had hoped that one day he would have the chance to meet the Negro officer who had become the battalion commander after the battles at Jarama, but now he never would. Battle commander Steve Nelson took his place.

While the others cleaned their weapons and packed their supplies to return to battle, Deion gritted his teeth and pretended he didn't want to cry like a woman. And though he kept his lower jaw firmly set, his shoulders quivered like a leaf in the wind. How many days had he been in Spain? How many men had died? The days, the fighting . . . it forced Deion to lose all track of time.

Still time, after all, didn't matter. Survival did. And with every announcement of another soldier's death, Deion knew the odds of his survival narrowed.

He wiped his face and returned to pack his things. The next orders awaited him.

Chapter Twenty-One

The answer came while she slept. Sophie awoke to a knock at the bedroom door and men's voices. She rose from her siesta, opened the door, and rubbed her eyes against the light. A gasp escaped her when she discovered Emanuel waiting there. He had feared for them when he saw the washed-out road, and was looking for them when he happened on the old man and his daughter walking away from the house.

The man's timing came from the hand of God. He not only reassured Walt that he wanted to help, but he'd already prepared a hiding place for the truck and had "obtained" fuel for their journey.

Now the truck rumbled down the road, with four passengers crammed in the front seat. They neared the hills surrounding Granada, and Sophie saw a castle on a tall hill. Emanuel directed them through the mountains, but Sophie questioned every turn. The roads were no more than wide paths, winding through the hills. Eventually, just as Emanuel had promised, the narrow road opened up to a series of caves.

"It was the long way, but it got us here." Emanuel jumped down from the truck.

Sophie followed, with Philip's help. He took her hand as she jumped to the ground. Sadness filled his eyes.

"Are you worried about Badger? He'll be taken care of." She gave his hand a squeeze.

Philip pushed his hands into his pockets. "I know, I know. And that's why I agreed he should stay at the village. He'll be fine there. . . ."

Walt parked the truck in a large cave.

Emanuel approached Walt as he climbed down from the truck. "Although you cannot see them, there are friendly guards posted all along the road. Most of Franco's soldiers don't come in this area because it's too easy to get lost. Others don't come for the reason that those who *do* enter these hills often don't return."

He smiled as he spoke, and Sophie's eyes widened as she wondered how someone so friendly could also be so fierce.

Emanuel swept his arm in the direction of a smaller cave. "Follow me. I would like to introduce you to the others." He took two steps and paused. "They are willing to help, even though they do not know the nature of your shipment."

"I appreciate this." Walt placed a hand on Emanuel's shoulder. "Just trust that your group will be richly rewarded for their help."

Philip stayed back. "I can wait here." He glanced toward the truck.

"Nonsense. We're safe. The truck is safe." Walt motioned him forward.

Sophie entered the cave, and the first thing she noticed was a handsome man stirring a fire. The glow lit his face. He had a thin moustache, and a black and red bandanna graced his neck. A huge pistol hung from a belt over his shoulder. His face was kind, though she could imagine from his muscular frame and square jaw that he could be fierce if necessary.

Sophie sidled up to Walt. "I don't understand what this place is."

Emanuel answered. "It is the center of our partisan activity. We are teaching people to sabotage behind enemy lines."

"Those on the front can only do so much, and much of their effort is thwarted because the soldiers see them coming," Walt added. "These men work behind the lines—and they have great success because the element of surprise is on their side."

"Come, I will show you." Emanuel motioned to the back of the cave. "I will teach you first to make switches. Then detonate fuses. Finally, to set them."

Sophie turned to Philip.

He held back a laugh. "You prayed for this, didn't you? Prayed that we'd be able to transport all the gold and use it to help the people?"

Sophie crossed her arms and then rubbed them, as if trying to brush away the damp, eerie feeling of the cave. "Well, if I did, I surely didn't expect this answer."

Philip placed a hand on the small of her back and led her forward. "Don't worry. I'm sure you'll do fine. Your fingers are used to the delicate touch of a paintbrush. How different do you think working with thin wires can be?"

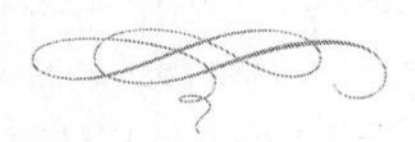

José eased back on the reins, motioning for Calisto to stop. In the distance, dense columns of smoke rose from the town of Camargo. He'd witnessed the bombers descending mere hours ago and hoped the damage would be minimal . . . but the destruction surpassed his worst fears. His heart pounded as he wondered if he'd arrived too late.

Townspeople were leaving with suitcases and bundles on their backs as they toiled in the mud from last night's rain. The feet of one man, burdened under his load, slid backward on the uphill path, and José's heart hurt for him—for all of them.

He motioned Calisto forward, approaching a different man. "Excuse me. Is the hospital still in town?"

"Hospital? No. There is nothing. Just an occasional patrol."

It wasn't until Calisto trotted away that José realized he hadn't thanked the man. He hurried toward the town, staying close to hedgerows, taking advantage of every bit of cover he could find. He saw a large oak and guessed he'd get a better look into town from its branches. He dismounted, then climbed up the tree. But another sight caught his attention—Petra coming up the road on Erro.

José cursed under his breath and then scampered down. As he ran to her he chided himself for trusting the girl. She was too strong-willed for her own good. Just like Ramona.

"What are you doing? Do you want Erro to get taken? If the enemy sees him . . ."

"Wait, José. Just listen. I wanted to help. I've discovered something. There is some type of truck up ahead, with nurses in it. I saw it from where I was. It is stuck in a muddy pit leading out of town."

"Nurses?"

"They were wearing uniforms and caring for injured men. I thought perhaps . . ."

"Sí. You leave this to me." He nodded, hoping she understood he was thankful. He turned his horse. "Head back into the hills with Erro. I'll meet you there."

"Can't I go with you?"

He slowed and turned. "No. Petra, please, won't you listen?"

"Sí, José. I'm sorry." She turned and rode the horse back up the hill.

José watched till she disappeared from view within the covering of trees. He shook his head. He didn't know why he so easily grew angry with the girl.

He rode in a field along the road, past a small farmhouse on the edge of town. Pink roses rambled across the dark fence. Behind him, from near the church, he could hear the crack of bullets fired. José hoped it wasn't at him, and he signaled with the sides of his calves for Calisto to pick up his pace.

Up ahead, he noticed the truck Petra spoke of, but now there was only a driver keeping guard.

"The nurses, where have they gone?" José asked hurriedly.

The driver eyed him cautiously. Eyed Calisto, too.

"Señor, one of them is my wife. Ramona . . ."

"Ramona, yes." The driver nodded down the road. "They moved the patients there."

José spotted a small house half hidden behind an overgrown and untended hedge.

"Thank you." José motioned Calisto forward.

Reaching it, he tied up the horse and walked around the corner of the house, looking cautiously through a window. More rifle fire sounded from where he'd just come. He thought about moving Calisto, finding a safer place, but he knew he couldn't waste time. Through the window he indeed spotted nurses, but Ramona was not one of them.

José hurried to the door and entered without knocking. Before he could speak, a man—the doctor most likely—lifted a gun toward José's chest. José stopped in his tracks.

"José!" came a voice from somewhere in the back of the room.

A woman hurried toward him, but it was not Ramona. His heart sank. It was Ramona's friend—a bridesmaid at their wedding, if he remembered right.

"José, what are you doing here? Why aren't you with Ramona?"

"What do you mean? I came to find her. To take her with me."

The woman's face scrunched into a frown. "But I don't understand. Your friend, he came to get her not more than an hour ago."

"My friend?"

"Yes, the American. He said you were taking care of the horses, and he had come for her. He was taking her to you."

"Michael. Are you talking about Michael?"

The nurse nodded. "Yes, that was his name. He said you'd been friends since you were children. He had a camera. He said he was a correspondent or something."

The energy drained from José's limbs.

"José? Are you okay?"

"Tell me; did he say where they were going?"

The woman turned to another nurse. "You heard the conversation. Did the American say?"

"No, I'm sorry," the woman answered. "All he said was he was taking her to you."

José hurried out of the house, trying to think of all the possibilities. He rounded the corner, then stopped in his tracks. Calisto was gone.

Chapter Twenty-Two

Emanuel had offered only the briefest explanation of handmade explosives before he and some of the others left on a night mission.

Though she knew she should sleep, Sophie found it hard to rest amongst a half-dozen men of various ages; plus it was difficult getting used to the strange place and hard-packed ground. She was thankful to have Walt and Philip by her side. One of them—if not both—never strayed more than a few feet away.

Sometime in the night Sophie heard noises from outside, and the men around her stirred. The man closest to the door lit a lamp.

Salvador, who stood far taller than the others, hunched over in order to enter the cave without hitting his head. A smile brightened his wrinkled face as he entered. *"Formidable!"*

The one word told Sophie his mission must have been a success.

The men following Salvador hauled in sacks filled with food. One man also carried an armful of rifles.

Though it was the middle of the night, the excited voices of the men filled the air as supplies were handed out.

Sophie scooted back and leaned against the wall, taking it all in.

Emanuel caught her gaze. He came over and sat beside her and handed her a tin of sardines. "We are our own army of sorts, but our work is important." He pulled a bottle of whiskey from the inside pocket of his coat, took a swig, then offered it to her.

"No, thanks." Sophie glanced around at the others. She chuckled as one man lifted another and twirled with joy over the supplies. "I'm waiting for them to sing."

Emanuel nodded. "We get some food from the army, but little else. We must purchase our own supplies and more food. Or steal it when that is our only choice. It has been many weeks since we've been so successful. Franco's armies won't know what hit them."

One man stood off from the rest, holding what looked like maps. With eagerness, he lit another lamp and unrolled one. Others watched him respectfully but did not interrupt.

"That is Domingo," Emanuel commented. "He studies the positions held by both sides. Watch. His most prized possessions are his colored pencils. He marks the positions held by the Nationalist Rebels in one color and the Republicans in another."

Even from where she sat, Sophie could tell the Rebels held far more territory. "What about the areas with no color?"

"Those are forest and mountains. They are held by no one." Emanuel spread an arm, as if motioning to the hills outside the cave. "Or so they think. They have no idea what these mountains hold."

Guilt seeped through Sophie's conscience as she thought about what else the mountains held. In the nearby cave was more gold than this part of the country had probably ever seen. She bit her lip and glanced around . . . knowing how much just one box could help fund these people's efforts. To buy them food. To give them enough supplies to make their work successful.

She glanced at Philip and noticed he was listening to their conversation. As if reading her thoughts, he ever so slightly shook his head.

She turned her attention back to Domingo and his maps. "So, if you know where the enemy is, why do you wait?"

Emanuel glanced up at her with a look of pity on his face.

"Señorita, knowing the right timing is just as important as the act itself. We must use our supplies well, which means timing them to achieve the greatest damage."

Sophie wondered if he meant damage to machines or men. She had a feeling it was both. "I see."

"I see, too," Emanuel said, studying her face.

"I mean, I understand."

"Sí, that is what I mean. I see anxiety on your face, and I understand you have many worries. Perhaps you cannot be of help as we first thought."

"You doubt I can help your cause?" She brushed her hair back from her face and sat straighter, trying not to be offended by his tone.

"No, it is simply that you worry about much. And if you are to be effective behind the lines, there is only one thing to worry about. Do you know what that is?"

"My task. Whatever that is."

"Sí, that is correct."

"I think I can do that."

"Can you? We will see. Because from what I hear you will be with us for at least a few weeks." He swept his arm around the cave. "So I have a task for you. I discussed it with Walt this evening."

"If Walt is in agreement, as you say he is, I will do what you ask." She held his gaze until she was sure he believed her words. "Although, if I tried to put together a detonator, that would be the end of me."

The man laughed. It was a loud, boisterous laugh that she hadn't expected.

"No, do not worry. Our plans are far different than that."

Emanuel glanced at Philip, who nodded and smiled. Sophie realized he was in on this, too. No wonder he hadn't said anything.

"Señorita," Emanuel said with a sigh. "The next part of the lesson is timing. As I have said, it is just as important as the act itself. But even more important is having the right man for the right job. Or in this case, the right woman."

"So, you have a job specifically designed for me?"

"Sí, that I do. It is an inside job, and one that is very dangerous.

But do not worry. We will have someone watching over you."

A chill settled over Sophie as she remembered Bilbao. The scenario sounded familiar. A man had watched over her then, and she didn't realize until later that it had been her dear friend Luis. Not only had he watched for her, he had died protecting her.

She also knew having a guardian meant she needed one. Sophie crossed her arms over her chest, hoping to hide their trembling. She offered a weak smile. "I know what this means. I've been asked to do such a thing before. And I have a feeling I should have volunteered to set bombs. I have a strange notion it's safer."

"Sí, I suppose so, but do you see those maps? The problem with them is that the information is old. We wait to act until we get a confirmation. But by the time our data is confirmed, the situation has changed. We need you to go on the inside . . . someplace to watch and report."

Sophie noticed he didn't use the word *spy*. She pressed her hand to her forehead. It made no sense. She thought their plans were to get the gold out of the country. Why had things changed?

"We have someone on the inside . . . although he appears to be a Fascist supporter, he works for us. His position is too critical. We need someone to smuggle out information for us to look at and then smuggle it back in again the next morning before it is missed. Our friend cannot make the deliveries himself, but he will help you. We already have a story for your presence."

"Walt agrees?" she asked.

"Walt agrees as long as we promise to take care of you . . . and only if your help is vital to our cause. I assured him of both."

"Where is he now?"

"He is outside, talking with some of the others. We have a man who is familiar with the castle at Granada—Alhambra."

"Just as long as you don't ask me to be anyone's girlfriend. I . . . I'm tired of having to spread out my affections—be it real or pretend."

"Do not worry, señorita. We will not ask anything of your heart—just your mind . . . and your acting abilities."

"Let me guess. Should I get used to being called Eleanor?"

For the next hour Emanuel told Sophie and Philip about the

rugged hill on which the Alhambra was built, especially about the subterranean passages leading from the fortress to various parts of the city.

Walt joined them, yawning widely but eager to join their talk. "More than once the tunnels carried royal damsels beyond the walls of Granada, where the cavaliers waited to bear the whole party over the borders," he said.

"It sounds like something out of a storybook," Sophie commented. "Will I have to sneak in?"

"Nothing of the sort. You are arriving as the niece of one of the most honored men in the city. Tomas, or rather, *Uncle* Tomas, lives within the Alhambra on the top of the hill. He is one of us, but we set him up there from the beginning of the war. No one questions his loyalty to Franco, which is exactly how we want to keep it. Within these various tunnels and passages of the fortress, it should be easy for you to get information to us."

"If they know the tunnels are there, why don't they watch them more closely?"

Emanuel cocked one eyebrow. "Walt mentioned the . . . *damsels* who used the tunnels. . . . When first constructed, the tunnels were used as passageways for the rich men to keep their sins hidden. Today, the travel is not much different. No one wishes to stop it, because in doing so their own indulgences would be made known."

"Wonderful! You're going to place me in a palace and give me the reputation of a harlot?" She glanced at Philip, and for the first time he appeared ill at ease.

"You won't be asked to do anything I wouldn't have my own daughter do," Emanuel replied. "Besides, you will be safe, *and* you will provide us with the information we need."

"Walt? Do you think I'm doing the right thing?"

Walt's eyes darted to Emanuel. "Yes, Sophie. Actually, I think it will help us get information for our . . . shipment, too."

"Philip?" She turned to him.

"It will be safer than having you work with bombs and guns." Philip took her hand. "If anyone can pull this off, Sophie, it's you. And . . . well, you've helped the Republican causes in many different ways before. I have no doubt you'll succeed again. Besides, it's only for a week or two. Isn't that what you said?" He locked eyes on Emanuel.

"Sí, just enough time for us to update our information."

Sophie pulled her knees to her chest and rested her chin on them. Amazingly, the first thought that came to her was the woman in the cave apartment. *When the Republicans win, I will have a home,* she had said. That woman had hoped, even though she could do nothing for the cause. How could Sophie not act when given the chance?

"Okay. Count me in. When do I leave?"

Emanuel clicked his tongue. "Not too soon. The timing . . . it is not right. Not until we prepare. And not until you know your duty." He slid the gun from his shoulder holster. "First of which will be to protect yourself. And you need to know how to make it back to safety whenever it is necessary. This mission will not be done in haste. After all . . ." He smiled. "This right person is greatly valued in our eyes."

Chapter Twenty-Three

José looked around in disbelief. He hurried around the small farmhouse, frantic. His eyes searched up and down the road. The parade of slow-moving vehicles and even slower-moving men and women on foot stretched from one hill to the other. His horse was nowhere in sight.

He leaned over, hands on his knees, and told himself to think. Calisto would never wander off. If someone had been watching, waiting, they would have had time to mount him and ride him in any direction. Still, Calisto would only allow that with someone he trusted. José had witnessed more than once the stallion's determination not to be ridden by a stranger.

Petra.

José hoped more than anything that Petra had taken him. But why? Was she working with Michael? José quickly pushed that thought out of his head. Impossible.

He heard the sound of galloping, and his heart leapt. He turned to see Petra on Erro, riding toward him. Calisto was not with her. A worried cry escaped José's lips.

Erro stopped right before José. Petra's eyes were wild, her face frantic. "A man came in a truck. He got out and rode Calisto away."

Michael!

She brushed her long hair from her face. A strand still clung to her flushed cheek, and José wished he could brush it away. Wished he could take care of her and offer her a safe place. But he couldn't. He needed her.

"What direction?"

"Back that way." Petra pointed to the bombed-out village the people were retreating from. Her hand trembled.

He knew he should thank her for coming—knew he'd be lost without her here. Instead he simply nodded.

"I think I know where they are going. There is a seaside cottage near here—in Santander." The memory of two childhood friends playing in the surf hit him, nearly taking his breath.

"But I don't understand. Calisto allowed him to ride away."

"That's because the horse belongs to him."

"You mean . . . Yes, it *was* the man we saw in Bilbao, when I got those photographs from the woman. He looked different—thinner. He walked with a limp."

José raked his fingers through his hair. "I need you to . . ." His mind raced. "I need Erro. Then go inside and let them know who you are. Tell the nurses I'm going to find Ramona. Stay with them, wherever they go. I will find you."

"And if you don't?" She climbed down off Erro and handed him the reins. Tears pooled in her lower eyelashes.

José thought about promising her that he would return, but the truth of the situation did not allow that.

"If I'm not back in two days, then you must find a way to travel into the mountains, back to the caves. Pepito and my father—I don't think they can survive alone. The horses either. Do you think you can find your way back?"

Even though she was a petite thing, she straightened, and José could tell she found a well of inner strength as she realized the responsibility he placed on her.

"Yes, I made a map." She pulled it from the pocket of her trousers.

Emotion overwhelmed him, and José hugged her. Petra clung to him, and José worried that her care for him was more than that of just a friend. Gently, he pushed her away.

"In two days. Be safe, José."

He mounted Erro and turned in the direction of Santander. José rode off, refusing to look back. He could only trust that Petra would be safe. And, if he didn't return, that she'd care for the two older men and the other horses. He'd never placed so much trust in another human being, and even now he couldn't believe he was forced to. After all, she was not much more than a girl.

Yet he couldn't think about that. He focused on the path ahead, on rescuing his wife. He didn't know why Michael had resorted to this, but things must be bad. In fact, the gold must be lost. He feared that Michael had returned to seek revenge. A friend turned enemy—that was the worst kind of opponent, because those who know you best also understand how to hurt you the most.

José urged Erro on faster.

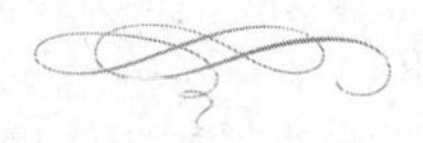

Ritter's eyes scanned the control panel. He leaned back in his seat slightly, finding a comfortable spot for the return flight to Berlin.

Monica sat in the copilot's seat, and a huge smile filled her face. Blonde curls peeked from under the leather flight helmet. "Amazing! I never get tired of flying. Isn't it wonderful? I remember going to school as a child on Long Island, memorizing all the European countries. I never imagined someday I'd fly from Germany to Spain and back again, just to ferry supplies. Can you imagine what the early explorers would have thought of this?"

Ritter laughed at her enthusiasm. "*Ja*, it is wonderful, isn't it? The thing I have trouble understanding is what is so important to your uncle Hermann for him to pay us so generously to make this long journey." He glanced at her again, appreciating her beauty that even the plain, drab flight suit could not hide.

At first when Monica had returned to Berlin, Ritter had

thought her a bother. She demanded his attention. Wanted to spend all their free time together. But the more time he spent with her, the more he enjoyed it. And while his heart still ached for Isanna, he was thankful that Monica had forced herself into his life—cracking open a part of his heart that had grown cold and dark.

She turned slightly in her seat, nearly shouting over the roaring of the engines. "You don't think it's those crates back there they care about, do you?"

"Why do you say that?"

"Because they tossed them inside with little concern. They didn't even tie them down well, even though they are marked *'Fragile.'* Personally, I think what they want is in that satchel you have tucked behind your seat."

"The satchel?"

"Oh, please, Ritter. You can't fool me. The only thing I wonder is if you've looked inside that bag? Perhaps you know more about this war than anyone." Her laughter filled the cockpit.

"Maybe I have. Are you challenging me?" Ritter glanced out the side window of the plane, peering over the top of the white peaks. Even after all the flights over the Pyrenees, he had a hard time believing that men—volunteers even—hiked across those mountains in order to volunteer for Spain. Giving their all. Facing extreme danger for a great leader was one thing . . . but their cause had no great leader. In fact, it wasn't even a great cause. He glanced over and noticed Monica's smirk.

"I'm not challenging you. I already know you've never looked. You're too honorable and noble for that. You respect Uncle Hermann and feel honored that he trusts you—you, of all people. Still, don't you wonder?"

Before he had time to respond, Monica leaned over and grabbed the satchel, placing it on her lap.

"What are you doing?" Ritter reached for it, but she sat just beyond his grasp. He tried to snatch the satchel again, but as he did the nose of the plane dipped, causing the whole plane to groan and shake. "Monica, you're going to get us killed!"

"What Uncle Hermann doesn't know won't hurt him. That's my motto."

Ritter grabbed his pistol from his shoulder holster. "Monica, I told you. Put it away." He waved it her direction.

Her eyes widened, and then laughter poured from her lips. "Ritter, you're no fun! You don't have to be so dramatic."

She opened the satchel and began flipping through the pages. She stopped, read some, and Ritter couldn't help wondering what had caught her interest.

After five minutes passed, Monica lifted her head and turned to him.

"Listen to this. It has nothing to do with the war in Spain—or at least what I can see." Her voice vibrated from the movement of the engines.

"I'm not listening."

Monica ignored him. "When do you have to turn this in? Right when we fly in? No, wait, you told me earlier. You have a meeting in the morning." She let out a dramatic sigh. "Well, I don't think we should rest tonight. We should read through it. It's about a guy's connection with Inca gold."

"I'm not going to read it." His curiosity was piqued—but there was the question of honor. He'd worked hard, had gone through a lot to earn Göring's respect. "I don't think we should."

"Why not? It's not as if we're going to go to South America on a treasure hunt. It's interesting, that's all."

"I'll think about it. But put it away for now. You're making me nervous."

Monica shrugged, and then put the papers back and closed the satchel. "You win. But promise me you'll at least glance at it."

Ritter nodded, even though he had no intention of doing so. Göring trusted him. He would not lose that trust.

But as the miles passed and the sunlight faded, Ritter had time to think. *Inca gold?* What could be so interesting about Inca gold? Why would Göring care about such a thing?

Before an hour passed Ritter had changed his mind. He would read it—skim it—just to ease his curiosity. As Monica said, it wasn't like he was going to head to South America in search of treasure.

❖ ❖ ❖

Ritter read the papers as if they contained an adventure novel. They told of a man named Barth Blake who found great treasure. He and a friend had followed something called Valverde's Guide and found the gold. Well, it was more than gold, really . . . silver handicraft, life-sized gold figures, emeralds. And much more.

Blake's partner, Chapman, died, supposedly by falling over a cliff. *Or perhaps killed by Blake,* Ritter thought as he read.

Blake made it out of the mountains without a partner, but with great evidence his story was true. His pockets were filled with Inca gold. After telling his story to a few, he headed back to England to raise money for an expedition. It was on the trip that someone pushed him overboard to steal his maps.

Monica yawned even though her eyes were bright. "I think I found something." She spoke no louder than a whisper, even though they were alone in her apartment. "This is supposedly a description from Blake."

Ritter took the paper from her and read it himself.

It is impossible for me to describe the wealth that now lies in that cave marked on my map, but I could not remove it alone, nor could a hundred men. . . . There are thousands of gold and silver pieces of Inca and pre-Inca handicraft, the most beautiful goldsmith works you can imagine, life-sized human figures made out of beaten gold and silver, birds, animals, cornstalks, gold, and silver flowers. Pots full of the most incredible jewelry. Golden vases full of emeralds.

"So how long would it take for us to fly to South America?" Monica laughed. She shuffled carefully through the rest of the papers, then sighed. "Too bad there's no treasure map here. But there is a translation of Valverde's Guide. Listen to how it begins."

She cleared her throat.

"Placed in the town of Pillaro, ask for the farm of Moya, and sleep (the first night) a good distance above it. And ask there for

the mountain of Guapa, from whose top, if the day be fine, look to the east, so that thy back be towards the town of Ambato, and from thence—"

"Enough. This is foolish. As long as there have been men, there have been rumors of hidden treasure. If there was such a thing, surely it would have been found by now." Ritter took the papers from her hand and returned them to the satchel in the order they had come.

Monica shrugged. "I'm sure to someone it's important, but you're right. It means nothing."

"It's time for bed, and I'm going to head home." Ritter rose, tucking the satchel under his arm.

"Why don't you stay? It's a pity for you to go all the way back to your place. I promise I won't look in the satchel again."

"Sorry. Not this time." Ritter walked to the door, placing his hand on the ornate handle. "But I'll stop by tomorrow to see you. Maybe we can have dinner?"

Monica rose and walked Ritter to the door, and though she tried to hide it, Ritter noticed anger in her eyes.

"I'm not sure. I might be busy." She placed her hand over his and opened the door without offering her usual embrace.

"Well, then maybe I'll dine with your uncle. He loves to tell stories. Perhaps he'll clue me in to what this is about." He stepped outside, feeling the cool night air hit his arms and face.

"Yes, perhaps. Good night." And with that Monica closed the door.

"Women," Ritter scoffed as he hurried to the side street where he'd parked. "You can never please them . . . never understand them either." He climbed into his automobile and placed the satchel on the seat. "Women are about as useless as fairy tales that speak about lost treasure. No, make that *more* useless. At least fairy tales sometimes have a happy ending."

Chapter Twenty-Four

José slowed his approach to the house when he noticed the lone figure sitting by an outcropping of rocks overlooking the ocean. Then he jogged forward, wondering why Michael left himself so unprotected. Surely, Michael must have guessed he would come.

He noticed Michael folding a letter, which he returned to its envelope and tucked into his pants pocket.

José rushed forward. "Where is she? Where is Ramona?"

Michael smiled. "I guessed right, on two counts. First, that you had left her alone. And second, that you would eventually come to find her. What I didn't count on was that a blown tire would keep us from getting too far down the road or that Cesar would spot Calisto as he'd finished changing the tire."

"I don't care about the horse. Where is my wife?"

Michael patted the rocks beside him. "She is safe. There is no need to worry. First, we need to talk." He moved his hand to his waistband, where José spotted a pistol.

"About what? I haven't been involved—" José remembered the photos and how he'd passed them on for Sophie. "At least it was never my intention—"

He refused to sit, but peered down at Michael and crossed his arms over his chest.

Michael pressed his lips together and placed a finger over his mouth, tapping it. Then he pointed to José. "Let me get this straight. I trusted you. I gave you a place to stay in Madrid. I asked you to *care* for Sophie, and then you got her involved"—Michael's voice rose in volume—"in *spying* on me? In turning on me?"

Michael jumped from the rock onto the ground. "I refused to listen to those who told me you couldn't be trusted. I listened to your advice and faked my own death." He spat the words out. "The one thing Sophie can't forgive me for." He poked his finger into José's chest. "And it was all your idea."

José took a step back. It was no use arguing whose idea it was or why he'd done it. There was only one thing that mattered now.

"I did what I thought was right. Protected what I believed was worth protecting." He touched the scar on his neck. "I nearly died protecting Sophie. But none of that matters now."

He reached forward and grasped Michael's shirt collar. "Where is my wife?"

The pressure of the metal of the gun barrel against José's stomach caused him to release his grasp.

Michael cocked one eyebrow, his penetrating gaze causing a weight to drop in José's stomach.

This man was not the friend he knew. Too much had changed—although José couldn't imagine why. How had things come to this? Facing the war was hard enough, but this . . .

"I am the one asking questions." Michael was seething with anger. "And only when I get the right answers will I speak to you of your wife." He nodded his chin toward the cottage. "Come, we'll talk like old *friends*. You remember this place, don't you, José? It was here that we met that first summer. Your father had come to care for the horses, and it was my first visit to Spain."

"Yes, I remember." José's steps moved him forward. "Although it seems like a different life. Two different people."

❖ ❖ ❖

José's stomach churned as Michael set a glass of cool water and a plate of fresh bread and cheese before him. Though anger coursed through him, his hunger won over. He guiltily ate and wondered how his father and Pepito fared with the little they had—not to mention his worry for Petra and Ramona.

"It was my parents who asked me to search for the gold when I returned to Boston. They had friends, fellow collectors, who knew its location and its worth. They were worried about the numerous conflicts in Spain. Months before the civil war erupted, I befriended those inside the bank. And although the war was not good for the country or the people, the decision to move the gold benefited me greatly. What I thought would be at least ten years of work narrowed to a few months when the government decided to move the gold. They hastily made a plan, afraid the Fascists would take the city before they could get it out. Stealing a portion of the shipment was almost too easy." Michael took a long drink of water. "But of course you know all this."

José acknowledged the statement with a nod. "I discovered it. Over time." He didn't mention that he'd also passed it on, much to Walt's appreciation. "So what do you want from me? We have the same information." He wiped his face with his napkin.

Michael rubbed his leg and frowned. José refused to ask him about the injury or the pain evident on Michael's face.

"I want to know where it is now." Michael pounded the table with his fist. "They tricked me. They stole the gold. I want to know where Sophie, Walt, and that . . . that volunteer . . . are hiding."

José leaned back in his chair. "I do not know. I have not heard from them since Bilbao."

"Maybe you haven't, but I am sure one of your contacts knows. Walt had a network of men and women throughout Spain. Walt was not a foolish man."

"Listen to me, Michael. I speak the truth. I have not heard from anyone in the network since the incident in Bilbao. The network—it no longer exists. The bombings . . . the war . . . those things have effectively broken it down." José pushed the plate back. "I am sorry. That's all I know."

Michael lowered his head as if defeated. Then with slow movements, he reached over and pulled on a bell rope.

The echo of shoes tapped on the marble. But it wasn't a cheery kitchen maid who approached; it was Cesar.

Michael lifted his gaze. "Kill the woman."

José jumped to his feet. "No, wait." He pressed his hands to his forehead. "There is one thing. Walt gave me an address—in Paris. He said that if I were ever in trouble or if I could not get information to him, to go there for help. It was a last resort."

Michael stood. "And you know this address?"

José nodded, hoping it was enough to save Ramona—save them both. He recited the address that had been given to him on a small piece of rice paper.

Michael repeated it, then approached the desk, taking up a piece of paper. He opened the desk drawer and pulled out an ink pen. Then suddenly he turned. "Wait. That cannot be correct."

"Yes, it is. I am certain. Please, do not hurt my wife."

The color drained from Michael's face, and José thought he would faint. Instead he reached for the closest chair and sat.

"That cannot be," Michael muttered. "It is my uncle's address. Uncle Adolfo . . ."

Cesar pulled on the rope that tied José's arms, cinching it tighter, and dragged José forward. The tall man moved with quickened steps, and José hurried to keep up. Cesar led him to the caretaker's cottage near the barn in the back. José let out a breath in disbelief. He would be killed in the very place he and Michael had played together as children. Since José was "the horse trainer's son," he hadn't been allowed into the main house, so Michael had come here, and they'd played in the meadows nearby. They'd climbed the trees at the edge of the property—played hide-and-seek in the small rooms of the cottage.

They stopped outside the door. Cesar pushed José to his knees and kicked his back, forcing him to the ground. José's cheek hit the rough wood of the weathered porch. The wind was knocked out of him by the force of Cesar's foot, and he fought the burning need to suck in a breath.

He heard the jingle of keys as Cesar worked with the outside lock. As he opened the door, Cesar pressed one boot into the small of José's back to hold him down, and José lay still, knowing it was useless to struggle. He stared at Cesar's dirt-caked boot. Beyond the boot, beyond the porch, José could see the large tree where he'd built a perch as a boy. It had given him a good view of the ships in the water. As a child, he'd spent days imagining he was a lighthouse owner whose lamps directed many to safety. José coughed again, trying to catch his breath. What foolish dreams. He hadn't protected anyone, not even himself.

The door creaked open, and he struggled to his feet, using his elbows and bound hands to push himself up.

A cry met his ears. "José!"

He lifted his head and saw Ramona sitting in the dark room. The windows had been boarded up, but for the most part it looked as if she were free to move around. He struggled to his feet, using his elbows and bound hands to push himself up.

A kick from Cesar to his backside pushed him into the room the rest of the way, and he sprawled on the floor.

"José!" Ramona scurried over to him, and he let out a low moan. He'd planned on coming to her as a hero, rescuing her. It was the second time he'd come to her broken and defeated; yet as he looked up and gazed into her eyes, he saw only love.

He struggled to sit.

"Let me help you." She eased him up, and he scooted to the wall, leaning against it for support.

She took his face in her hands and kissed him. Her lips were soft and moist, and he wondered, not for the first time, why he'd ever left her alone.

Then, without a word, she untied the ropes. Within a minute, he was free. He shook the rope from his wrist and embraced his wife.

José considered all the one-sided conversations he'd had over the previous months. In his mind, he had begged Ramona to come with him. In his thoughts, he'd also told her how angry he was that she hadn't. It had always been her fault. He was justified, of course. He had to check on his father. And the horses were worth saving. But never in the months that followed had he thought about how his wife felt. As she tenderly touched the sore areas on his wrists, he saw that she was made to care for others. She'd *needed* to help those injured soldiers. It was something she couldn't walk away from.

Their Creator had made her to care. God's nature, which reached out with love to the broken and the lost, had been implanted in her heart. By asking Ramona to leave, he'd asked her to cut off all her limbs in order to follow him. No, more than that, to dig her heart out of her chest and leave it behind.

"I have been a fool. I didn't understand you. I only saw what I wanted." The words spilled from José 's mouth as he embraced her. "I saw your love for me and didn't want to share it with the world."

"No, José, it was me. I should have explained. I feel so alive when I'm able to hold a hand or bandage a wound. But you thought only of my safety. I should have followed my husband. My grandmother would have scolded me for the way I treated you. I knew deep down that you loved me more than horses. It was just an excuse. I wanted to do what I wanted to do."

She curled her body next to him and tucked her head under his chin. "Will you forgive me?"

She didn't have to ask twice. José kissed the top of her head. Her hair smelled of the smoke and the ashes from the most recent bombing. He could have lost her. He paused.

He could lose her still.

"You are forgiven, but will you forgive me? There is so much I have done. I—"

"Shhhh . . ." Ramona stilled his confession with her whisper. "It is in the past. We are together now. We are two people at fault and two people forgiven."

José blew a slow breath out and felt the tension knotted in his shoulders release with her words.

"And the horses?" Ramona scooted back to look into José's face. "I saw Michael with Calisto."

"I don't know. I didn't see them." He took her hands in his and looked around. The room was familiar but different. Yet being there again, he could almost feel his mother's presence. He could picture her sitting by the sink where she used to peel potatoes and urge him to read his poems to her.

"José. Why did Michael do this? I don't understand. What does he want?"

"He wants his honor back. It's been stripped away by everyone in his life, including me."

"Do you think he'll hurt us? Will we have a chance to get out? The Fascists—"

José didn't need her to continue. Even if Michael didn't harm them, who knew what would happen when the enemy troops entered the area? They'd already sent their bombers to knock out those who dared to fight. It was only a matter of days—if that.

"Where there is life, there is hope." He swallowed down his emotion, then lifted his eyes to the ceiling, wishing a way of escape were written on the beams.

"Where there is life, there is hope," he said again, and kissed his wife's forehead, her cheeks, her lips.

Chapter Twenty-Five

Sophie sat next to Walt on the soft ground outside the cave. Across the open area, she noticed an armed man guarding the truck. Philip was on patrol with some of the others, getting a sense of the vastness of the mountains controlled by the guerilla fighters. The sun had set an hour ago, and the air had cooled drastically. She rubbed her hands on her arms to warm them.

"So what changed your mind—about my heading into the castle instead of our trying to make it to Barcelona?"

"It just seemed like the right thing to do. These men offered help and protection. Emanuel found us again when we needed his help. All the pieces seemed to just come together."

Sophie cocked her head and looked into Walt's face. Now that she knew he was Michael's brother, she wondered how she hadn't seen it before. The shape of their noses was the same. And their hands. Her stomach turned as she looked at his hands, remembering all the times she'd held Michael's.

Pushing those thoughts out of her mind, she bumped Walt's shoulder with hers. "So are you saying that maybe you could believe God had a hand in all this . . . and perhaps *He* sent Emanuel to us?"

Walt looked at her out of the corners of his eyes. "I didn't say that. But the more I thought about it, I also realized that you could help us get the information we need—about the right roads to take to Barcelona. And maybe send messages from there to my contacts." He shrugged. "I don't know. The benefits far outweigh the risks."

"I hope you're right. I feel totally unprepared."

"We're not sending you in yet. There are a few things you need to know."

"Such as?"

"Such as, some of the history of the area."

She leaned forward and rested her chin on her fist. "History—one of my favorite subjects as of late. Okay, since I am a visiting niece, what history would my uncle have told me?"

"He'd probably have told you this story to start." Walt lowered his voice to sound like an old, wizened storyteller. "In the hills there is an old Moorish castle. In the time of the Moors it was said this fortress could house forty thousand men."

Sophie swatted at his arm, laughing. "Oh, that will make the story so much more authentic."

Walt continued. "Rulers came and went, never staying for long. There was even a time when lawless invaders called this place home. This was their base for smuggling and thievery."

Not unlike today, Sophie thought.

"One great king lived there during the wars of Granada. It is said that the armies of Queen Isabella came to claim the land. The Moor king had no worries, for he knew he was safe from their reach. The path to the castle was unknown to outsiders."

As he spoke, Sophie thought of the outpost high in the hills near the cottage they'd recently left. And although she knew it wasn't the same one, she'd wondered more than once how the Moors had ever got up there—let alone built a large structure in the high peaks.

"The story goes that the Virgin Mary appeared to the queen and guided her and her army up a mysterious path in the mountains—a path that had never been discovered before this time. The Moors had no time to escape, and somewhere under that castle the Moorish king buried a great treasure. Until this day, it has never been discovered. Everyone believes it is there, and they think that when the Virgin comes again she will disclose the location."

Walt's voice trailed off, and he studied something over Sophie's shoulder. She turned to see Domingo exiting from the cave. He approached and sat by them. His gray hair had recently been trimmed, and when he sat he folded his legs as easily as a young man.

"Anything interesting in those maps?" Walt asked.

Domingo lowered his head. He picked up a round rock from the ground and moved it from hand to hand. "No. I am afraid not. The information was at least a few weeks old." He lifted his gaze, and his dark eyes met Sophie's.

She could read his question there—he wondered when she was heading into Granada.

"I was just telling Sophie of the Moorish treasure."

"Really?" Domingo's normally calm expression brightened. "Yes, it only makes sense that if you are familiar at all with this area you should know about it. I myself first heard the stories before I was able to walk. My father always dreamed of finding it."

Domingo spoke of various people who claimed they found the treasure. Every one of them, he insisted, had been killed in a tragic accident before they were able to disclose the location or retrieve any of the booty. What amazed Sophie is how similar the stories were. Whether in Spain or South America, they seemed to develop a life of their own.

Sophie yawned and glanced up at the moon high in the sky. "Yes, well, all this is interesting," she said. "But can you tell me about the castle itself?"

Walt nodded. "You, Sophie, have been given permission to occupy one of the vacant rooms in the Moorish palace. I am sure you won't be bewitched by the place, but I want to warn you all the same. The legendary halls almost seem to have a life of their own . . . as if a drama is being played out there."

Sophie nodded, noticing how Domingo's eyes widened with Walt's words, and she wondered if Walt spoke so flamboyantly because of their guest.

"The fortified wall is flanked by thirteen towers. The river Darro foams through a deep ravine in the north."

Sophie sighed. "It sounds beautiful."

"The name of the castle is Alhambra," Walt said. "It means *red* in Arabic—the color of the clay from which the bricks were made. Alhambra is now controlled by some of Franco's most faithful men. They have supported Franco for years, and are now rewarded."

Domingo's face returned to its bored state, and he rose and waved good night as he retreated inside the cave.

"Just like America," Sophie commented. "If you have trouble sleeping, just start discussing politics. It will either put you to sleep or fully wake you up—depending on whom you're debating with." Sophie laughed, but Walt's expression didn't change.

"Sophie, how much do you know about Franco?" he asked.

"Not much."

"Well, since you are a dedicated follower as of today, maybe you should know a little more."

She yawned and stretched again. "I'll give you five minutes."

Walt leaned his head back against the cave. "It will only take me two."

"Even better."

"In 1934, Franco took part in the massacre of Asturian miners. . . ."

"Miners?" Sophie's mind immediately went to Eleanor's journal. Mateo—Eleanor's husband—had been a miner, working for their very existence. A pain tugged at Sophie's heart, and her hatred of Franco grew even greater.

Walt cocked his head and studied her face by the light of the moon. "Señorita, you look as if you've lost your best friend. What are you thinking about?"

Sophie didn't know how to explain. "I . . . well . . . it's just that I've heard about the miners and the conditions they work in. It was—it is—a tough life."

"Yes, well . . . Franco, a general after the '33 elections, was put in charge of the insurgency by the miners' union. Over twelve hundred men lost their lives."

Walt didn't explain how, and for that Sophie was glad. She could imagine.

"So what happened after the massacre?"

"Less than two years later, after the elections, the Popular Front won control of the government. In spite of the demands of the Communists, they didn't put Franco in prison. Instead they sent him to be military governor of the Canary Islands."

"And that is where he was when this war broke out, right?"

"Yes, and he was called back to Spain right away. It was the Germans who ferried his troops from North Africa." Walt paused, and then smiled. "I dare to say that took *less* than two minutes."

"So that's it? That's all I need to know? That is surprising. You usually like to spend more time imparting your knowledge." She lowered her voice to a whisper. "But not as surprising as Domingo's reaction to the story of the Moorish treasure. I felt my skin burning. Did you see the way his eyes sparkled when he spoke of it?"

"Yes, he did transform into a different person before our eyes, didn't he?"

Sophie looked back into the sky just in time to see a shooting star. She made a quick wish that Philip would return safe from his guard duty, then turned her mind back to the conversation. "So many people talk about such riches. I never really thought about hidden treasure before. I feel bad that Domingo has no idea how close he really is to the sort of treasure he talks about. I almost wanted to get out one gold coin for him. Can you imagine how his eyes would have lit up then?"

"Yes, and if you had, the news of what our truck contained would fall to all the people in this area harder and faster than any rainfall. It is wise to watch yourself and your words carefully. These people lead simple lives, and anything out of the ordinary is great news. It's tricky enough seeking out help and food. If word got out to the wrong person about strangers—Americans —up in these hills, Michael and his friends would find us before the sun crested over the peaks."

He rose and offered her a hand. "Speaking of which, the day will be upon us before we know it. Your uncle Tomas is already making arrangements for your arrival. It will be a big day for you . . . Eleanor."

❖ ❖ ❖

Pain, which he had spent a year ignoring, rose in Philip's chest. He leaned against the cave wall breathing hard as if he'd just finished a race. In truth, he attempted to hold his thoughts at bay, attempted to dam up the tears that threatened to flow. Sophie would be leaving again—out of his sight. Out of his grasp. And there was nothing he could do about it.

He glanced over his shoulder and knew that she watched him. He had returned from the patrol and noticed her laying out her blankets to sleep. Her worried eyes studied him, but he didn't care. He had stayed in Spain for Attis. He had stayed in Spain because the Americans needed volunteers. He had stayed by Sophie's side even when he really wanted to be on the front lines. Then he had been taken from his duties because of her. His heart had broken a hundred times because of her too.

He took another drink from the wineskin. His new friend, Salvador, had given it to him as they'd walked up the road, back to the cave.

Sophie lay down on her blanket, but still she watched him. After a moment, she rose, drew near, and sat by his side. Philip ran a hand down his face, knowing he looked awful—smelled awful too—but he didn't care.

"Is something wrong?" she asked.

"Something wrong? Sophie, I was bound and taken to the south of Spain. Nobody asked if I wanted to go," he mumbled, as if trying to make a joke out of it. "Then I got roped into helping Walt. Nobody asked, 'Philip, what do you think? Where should we go?' Now I'm patrolling mountain trails around who knows where—and you're leaving."

"Walt thinks it's best. He thinks the information . . ." She glanced around, and her voice trailed off.

Yes, and I thought it was a good idea too, he wanted to tell her. Until he really started thinking about it. The men had talked excitedly through the day about how wonderful it would be to have her on the inside. They talked about her as if she were another weapon to help their cause. But to Philip she was much more than that.

He looked at her again. Her face was so beautiful; Philip didn't think he could bear to lose her. His chest throbbed as he imagined her going into the castle alone. Surrounded by the enemy. *Don't do it. I can't lose you.* He reached over and took her hand.

She leaned close and whispered. "Walt thinks it is best. . . . I can help us get the information we need for the rest of our journey. Each step now will take us closer to home, to America. Where we can be safe . . . together."

He brought her hand to his lips and kissed it. Then he released it abruptly. He was tired of hurting. Tired of worrying.

"Well, right now, Sophie, I honestly don't care what anyone else thinks we should do. What I should do. What *you* should do. I'm going to drink a little more wine, and then I'm going to get a good night's sleep. I'm going to dream. Maybe I'll dream about running that doesn't involve people chasing me. Or maybe I'll dream about actually having a fighting chance to win this war."

She didn't move. Didn't try to talk some sense into him. "Okay, Philip. If that's what you think best. I suppose a good night's sleep is a good idea." She went back to the blanket laid out by the crackling fire, turning her back to him.

Philip took another long drink from the wineskin. Then another for the mere fact that he *did* have a voice, and had all along. And if there was anyone to blame for what had happened in Spain, it was himself. He didn't like that fact. It was easier to blame others than to realize the truth.

And, when it came down to it, he would have chosen to follow Sophie, gold or no gold. He'd been tied up and taken down to the south of Spain; that was for sure. But in the long run it had made it easier for him. He hadn't needed to find his own ride.

He set the wineskin to the side and pressed his face into his hands, trying to hold back the emotion.

She'll be okay, he told himself. *She'll be okay.*

Dear God, please let Sophie be okay.

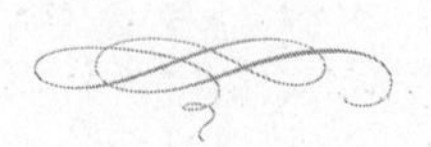

Each day Deion's small group moved. Some days it was forward. Some days it was back. Sometimes the only movement was lateral as they traveled down the dry riverbed to check on the others and see how everyone else was holding up.

His throat ached. He could never find enough to drink, and the continual thirst bothered him more than the sound of explosions in the distance.

In the rainy season there were rivers all around this area, but in July the riverbeds were dry. Bone dry.

Overhead, bombers flew. The same type that had bombed Guernica, he knew. Of course here there were no buildings to aim for, just lines of men in hastily dug foxholes.

Deion heard a plunk, and the man standing next to him fell dead. It was a surprise, but in a strange way not unexpected. He didn't ask why it wasn't him; he was just thankful that it wasn't.

In the light of the moon, Deion watched his feet move forward as if they belonged to another. He felt numb all over. He'd seen too much to try to feel any longer. Somewhere he had a memory of what life was before Spain, but it was too hard to draw out. Too hard to remember.

A friend called his name, and he turned. At least he remembered his name.

Chapter Twenty-Six

Ritter couldn't sleep, and he cursed Monica for ever opening that satchel. After tossing and turning for two hours, he decided to walk.

No matter how hard he tried, his mind wouldn't release its grasp on the gold. Obviously, if Göring was interested in it there had to be some truth to the matter. And the more he thought about it, the idea of traveling to South America didn't seem so crazy.

The night air around the city smelled of history. Of all things old. Things that struggled not to be forgotten. He thought about golden treasure and imagined leaving Berlin for good.

Before his parents' death they had told him he was someone special—that he'd do great things in his life. They told him that Germany would not always live in defeat, that great victories would come. And more than that . . . that he would also be great.

At the time it didn't sink in. Didn't all parents tell their children such things? But now . . . what they had prophesied was beginning to come true. And he had been a part. First in Spain, and now with this.

"Any coins to spare?" The voice rose to Ritter out of the darkness, interrupting his thoughts.

Ritter ignored the beggar in the shadows and continued on through the streets. He purposefully walked the opposite direction from where Monica lived. And it wasn't until the first rays of sunlight brought the city to life that Ritter realized he was near the home of Isanna's parents.

At first his stomach knotted; then he dug his fists deeper into his pockets, realizing it didn't matter. She wouldn't be there anyway. She was a married woman now, living with her pilot-hero.

But perhaps things had worked out that way for a purpose. After all, if he were a married man, the thought of traveling to South America would be out of the question.

Ritter thought about the look on her face when he'd last seen her. He'd been angry; that was certain. Looking back, he liked to believe he'd seen sadness in her eyes. And he realized that perhaps he wasn't the only one who'd lost out.

He raked his fingers through his hair, and then rounded the corner, deciding to find someplace to stop for breakfast. His footsteps stopped short when he noticed a man and woman approaching with a carriage.

"Isanna." The name escaped before he had a chance to stop it.

"Ritter." A smile filled her face, and then disappeared as she looked first to Xavier, and then the child in the carriage. "You're back from Spain."

Ritter quickly ran a hand across his wrinkled shirt. "I . . . I was just out for a walk. I didn't expect to see you."

Xavier narrowed his gaze and placed his hands on the handle of the carriage. "Yes, well, it was good seeing you. Welcome back to Berlin." The tone in his voice was anything but welcoming.

The baby from inside the carriage started to fuss. "Xavier, wait. Perhaps Ritter would like to meet Sebastian." Without waiting for an answer, Isanna lifted the child from the carriage. He noted her arms trembled as she pulled the baby to her chest and kissed his forehead.

In his mother's arms the baby hushed. He had light blond hair and round, blue eyes. His chin had a small cleft. He wore a light blue sailor suit and small black shoes. The baby cooed and reached a hand to Xavier. Xavier kissed it, then turned his gaze to Ritter. "This is Sebastian."

Isanna stepped forward. "Here, why don't you hold him? Don't be shy. He's six months old and very strong." Her voice quivered.

Ritter took the child in his arms. The baby was lighter than he expected. And his face so similar to his mother's.

"You say the child is six months old?" He quickly did the math.

"Yes." Isanna didn't offer more of an explanation.

This child could be his, of course. But . . .

Ritter scowled, remembering those times Isanna also spent with Xavier. Who could know for sure?

His mind returned to the day he saw her in the café. Her pregnancy had been evident. Yet perhaps this was simply another trick to play the two men against each other as she'd done in the past.

Ritter glanced at Xavier and saw fear in the man's eyes. Fear that he'd lose what he loved.

Ritter lifted the baby into the air, noting his eyes were the same color as the sky above. The baby, Sebastian, smiled and kicked his feet.

This could be my son.

He glanced to Xavier again. *But another is his father.*

A lump grew in Ritter's throat. Then he thought of the gold, and he knew what he had to do.

"He is a beautiful boy. His father must be proud to have such a son." With his words he saw Xavier's face soften. Ritter pressed the baby to his chest and kissed the top of the soft blond head.

He handed the baby back to his mother. "A beautiful child. Congratulations. I wish the best for . . . for your family."

Isanna offered a smile as she took the baby from his arms. "Thank you." The words held deep meaning. "And someday, when he is older, I will tell him of Spain."

Ritter nodded, and he watched as she placed the baby back in his carriage. Then with a lighter step she pushed the carriage down the street. Xavier walked by her side with a protective hand on the small of her back. Inside Ritter ached, but another emotion rose within him. It was a sense of pride. For once he'd thought of others more than himself. Strangely, it was a good feeling.

He walked back to his apartment with slow steps. When he entered his apartment building, he tried to clear his throat, but the emotion refused to budge. He approached his door and noticed a figure leaning against the wall. Waiting for him outside his door was Monica. He tried to speak but failed.

As she approached, he took her in his arms and wondered if it was so bad that he imagined he held another.

José waited until late in the night to whisper his plan to Ramona. Though he couldn't see her, just the touch of her—mixed with the fear they'd be caught—caused his heart to pound faster.

"I used to play hide-and-seek here as a boy. Underneath the house is a cellar with a door to the outside. If we can get down there, maybe we can escape."

"Just tell me what to do." The touch of her fingertips caressing his cheeks caused him to smile. Or perhaps it was her words.

"I'm going to see if I can find a soft spot in the wood." He crawled on his hands and knees toward the kitchen. Ramona touched his ankle to keep track of him and followed.

In his mind's eye, he tried to remember where the table had sat all those years ago. He pictured the pantry. The sink. The stove. He thought about the leak in the roof that his mother had asked his father to patch numerous times. Of course his father had given the same answer every time. "*Mañana*. I'll take care of it *mañana*."

José neared the spot, and it was as he hoped. The wooden boards were soft, rotting. He ran his finger against the seam, but they were too thick to pry inside.

"Ramona, I need you," he whispered. "Try to reach between

these boards and pry one up—even a little bit, so I can grasp it."

She did, and within a few minutes, they'd lifted one small piece of wood.

He removed his shoe and slid his hand inside. Then he used it as a lever to fix underneath. With all his strength, he pushed upward. The board broke with a loud snap. He reached his hand into the hole. It was cool and . . . his fingers entwined on a cobweb, causing a shudder to travel down his spine.

"I hope spiders are our biggest worries," he whispered to his wife. "I don't want to think what else could be living down there."

He pried away a few more boards. A whiff of dirt mixed with rotting . . . something . . . rose to great them. Ramona reached her hand down just as he'd done.

"Maybe we should wait until morning, when we'll have more light to see what's down there."

"We can't. It will be too late. I don't hear anything outside, which means Cesar must be sleeping in the main house. Either way, now is our perfect chance."

When he'd created an opening large enough to slide through, José poked his head down through the hole, hoping for a look. Amazingly, it was brighter there than inside the boarded-up house. He turned his head and saw why. The door to the cellar had either been taken off or had broken on its own. Moonlight filtered in from outside, and his heart leapt as he realized his plan would work.

"Let me go first." José lowered himself to the cellar, but he couldn't stand upright. His head poked through the opening.

"Come. I'll help you." He reached his hands to his wife and helped her down. With his hands before him, he cleared their path—sticky webs clinging to his hands and shirt. When he made it to the opening, he paused. "Wait here."

"No, I'm coming with you. It doesn't matter what is out there," she whispered. "Let's run for it."

José didn't hesitate. He took her hand and together they exited. He glanced around, didn't see anyone, and they began to run.

❖ ❖ ❖

Ramona squeezed her hand tighter around José's as he pulled her forward. She moved her legs as fast as she could to keep up. In the moonlight it was hard to see the ground, and she stumbled more than once. A gunshot sounded from somewhere behind them, and then nothing. José paused slightly, then tilted his head. The sound of a horse's whinny could be heard somewhere in the distance, and he wondered if it was Calisto.

José continued on. He led Ramona toward the hillside and behind a stand of bushes. To her surprise there was a *chamizo*—a very narrow gallery that farmers often dug to extract their own coal. Dried grass had been laid out on the floor of the gallery; others, no doubt, had used this very spot to hide.

José's voice was low. "Stay here. I'll be back. I think someone was trying to take the horses."

"Who? Like the Fascists? Or maybe the Moors?"

She couldn't see José's face, but she could read his pause.

"I'd guess Petra. A young woman who's helped me."

Ramona felt heat course through her. "A woman? Who is she?"

He patted her hand. "Not now. I'll explain. I'll be back."

"José, no!" Her frantic cry was no more than a whisper. He didn't pause, but rushed ahead, leaving her. He was gone, disappearing into the night.

Why hadn't he told her about this sooner? *Unless he has something to hide.*

She clenched her hands to her chest. "He came for me. He loves me," she whispered into the night. "He loves *me*."

❖ ❖ ❖

José darted from the gallery, ran twenty feet, and paused. He thought about returning to the barn, but then he heard the sound of a horse galloping and turned. There, in the light of the moon, he spotted two horses nearing. A small figure rode bareback on Erro. He waved his arms.

Petra stopped beside him. "I saw your escape. I knew it was

time to get the horses." He didn't ask why she had again disobeyed his request for her to stay with the nurses. He was just glad she had.

"I didn't have time to saddle them. And Calisto . . . Michael fired a shot. I'm not sure if it hit him or not. He stumbled."

José did a quick scan over Calisto's back and chest. "He seems fine. Wait here." José went back for Ramona.

"Petra is here; she has the horses." He motioned to Erro. "You must ride with her. The two of you will weigh less."

Calisto whined and pawed the ground, but José ignored it.

"Here." He cupped his hands for Ramona to use for a step, and she climbed on the back of the horse. He looked to Petra. "Follow me. We'll stay off the roads."

She nodded and pulled Ramona's arms tighter around her waist. "Hold on," she urged.

José grabbed Calisto's mane and vaulted onto his back. He looked around briefly to gain his bearings, then headed toward the hills in the distance.

The sound of a vehicle starting broke the still night air. He whispered a silent prayer that they'd make it into the trees before the truck caught up.

The scent of smoke that still hung in the air also reminded him of the approaching Fascist troops. He hoped they hadn't already descended on the town.

"Follow me," he called again, signaling to Calisto with the slightest nudge of his heels to carry him into the night.

Chapter Twenty-Seven

The towers of the Alhambra gleamed like silver in the sky. Sophie didn't know if it was the cool breeze from the mountains or the sight of the structure that caused goose bumps to rise on her arms.

Dozens of eyes were on her as she walked toward the market from the train station where Walt had dropped her off, to give the appearance that she'd just arrived in town. She carried a floral satchel—an upgrade from the battered one that had journeyed with her all over Spain. And she wore a crisp white blouse, a simple skirt that swished as she walked, and a red scarf tied around her head in Spanish style. She smiled slightly as she remembered the look of appreciation in Philip's gaze as he saw her all dressed up. But she'd noted something else, too. Fear, concern. His fingers had clung to her as she held his hand as they said good-bye.

It seemed everywhere she looked it was business as usual. Bread, potatoes, and hotel rooms seemed plentiful. And everyone she met praised General Franco. From the conversations she picked up on, Franco was a military genius and universally beloved.

She walked along a cobbled street. It was her first time in Granada, but the surroundings were so similar to other parts of Spain that it seemed she'd been there a hundred times.

Sophie adjusted her flannel skirt—too thin, too long, too big for her waist, but it looked similar to those of the other women who strolled along the street.

The small café had few visitors, mainly because it was still early morning, and most people didn't rise before ten o'clock. A cat walked toward her, twisting its thin form around the legs of the iron chairs. It met Sophie's legs and did the same. She didn't slow her pace and gently pushed the cat to the side with her new shoe–clad foot. She thought of Badger and hoped he was all right.

Her skirt swished, and Sophie added an extra sway to her hips. She had a part to play, after all.

"Eleanor," a voice called out, and she paused. She turned and saw a tall man who looked strikingly similar to Salvador.

"Uncle Tomas!" She opened her arms to him, noticing the gazes of the few sellers in the market.

He embraced her and quickly kissed her cheeks. "Sorry I missed your arrival. I unfortunately slept in."

She took a step back and forced a smile on her face. "It is fine. I am well. Thank you for inviting me. I'm eager to see Alhambra."

Sophie relaxed, realizing how easy it was to play this part.

"*Qui potest capere capiat*. He who is able to receive it, let him receive it." He waved a hand toward a waiting car. "I am glad you accepted my invitation."

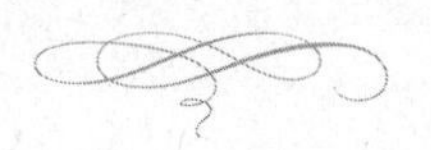

Ritter searched through five bookshops until he found what he sought. He bought the aged volume and hurried back to his apartment. After getting comfortable in his favorite chair, he brushed off the dusty book and read the title again. *Inca Gold*.

He told himself he needed something to keep his mind occupied. He didn't want to think about Isanna or Sebastian. He didn't want to face Monica, embarrassed by the way he'd wept in her arms. And so his thoughts turned to the treasure. It didn't even matter that it was only a story. It was an interesting story and something he could pour himself into.

He flipped through the pages, reading the personal accounts of men who'd traveled to South America. Some claimed they'd journeyed there to search for the remnants of primitive civilizations and native Indian tribes. Others longed to carry the grace of Christianity to heathen souls, ministering among the tribes. And all returned with stories of treasure.

As Ritter read, he was transported to the land of vivid sunlight, warm adobe houses, and stories from old women who seemed as ancient as the hills themselves. So many of the descriptions reminded him of sunny Spain, and a strange beckoning to return stirred within him.

He read, occasionally glancing at his pocket watch. Ritter was eager for his meeting with Göring. Göring had been thrilled when he'd delivered the satchel days ago, but Ritter hadn't heard anything since.

At first he wondered if the general had somehow found out he'd read the documents in the satchel, but when he'd spotted him at a social event and Göring offered a friendly wave, Ritter knew that wasn't the case.

Ritter hoped Göring would propose another visit to Spain. Ritter was eager to see what else the general was up to. And he hoped additional information needed to pass hands.

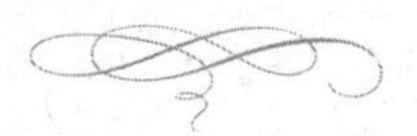

The shiny automobile carried Sophie up the road to what Tomas called the southern entrance. Lofty elms and chestnut trees lined the roadway, leading them to the horseshoe-shaped arch through which they entered. The automobile continued on, and she peered over cisterns cut into the rock.

"This is called the Place of Cisterns. Although the plateau has its own aqueduct, there was always a danger in times past of enemy troops cutting off the water," Tomas explained. The cadence of his speech also reminded her of Salvador; she was certain they were brothers, maybe twins. Of course, she wasn't given that information. The guerilla fighters had told her the less she knew, the better.

Because if I'm found out and tortured, I'll have nothing to disclose.

As the vehicle continued on, Sophie felt as if she was not only being transported someplace magical, but through a portal of time as well.

After they parked, the driver opened the door for her. She stepped from the car and took in a breath at the kaleidoscope of shimmering beauty surrounding her.

"This, my dear, is the last bastion of the Islamic presence in what used to be known as Iberia. Depending on the angle of the sun's rays, you will notice the walls of the Alhambra will change shades of red. The red is due to the bricks made from the richly colored mud."

"It's lovely," Sophie whispered. "And larger than I imagined. Larger than it looks from below."

Tomas took the satchel from her and offered his arm. Sophie gladly slid her hand into the crook of his elbow.

"The Alhambra itself is divided into three sections, although they appear as one," he continued. "The public esplanade is the first. The sultan's official residence is the second. The courtyard is part of this, and it leads to the loftiest tower—the Comares Tower, which rises 150 feet into the air."

Tomas pointed to the tower, which cast a shadow upon them. "There are only two windows in the tower, and they light the Hall of the Ambassadors, where—when seated on his throne—the sultan would receive his envoys."

"And the third part?"

"The housing for the harem. While the prophet Muhammad restricted each follower to only four wives, two loopholes made it possible for the wealthy or powerful to enjoy the favors of regiments of women."

Her surprise must have shown on Sophie's face.

Tomas chuckled. "Do not worry. This place has become Christianized since then. And Franco himself is an ambassador for Christ, remember? You will be staying in the Renaissance

Palace—added by Charles V, the Holy Roman Emperor."

From her place upon the high hill, she looked upon Granada below. The white houses and buildings with red-tiled roofs sparkled in contrast to the green of the hillsides around it.

"This view. It is like—"

"An oriental pearl in an emerald setting?"

She quickly glanced up at him, sucking in a breath. "Exactly."

Tomas laughed. "Don't credit me. I'm simply quoting an Arab poet from long ago."

He walked her to the northern side where a large gorge opened to a river below. "The Darro River. An impregnable defense. Come. We will enter through the Gate of Justice."

A shiver traveled up Sophie's arms at the name. *Maybe I will find justice within these walls.* At least it was her hope.

Tomas led her to a large door. "The Alhambra from the outside is impressive but not unique. Just as Muslim women hide their beauty beneath shapeless cloth, so the Eastern homes and palaces hide beauty within. Outside, there is nothing to envy—no treasures to be stolen or defaced. But inside . . ." Tomas opened the door and led her in. "Inside is a different story."

They walked through long halls, and Sophie almost forgot to breathe as she took in the intricate design and architecture. She paused before an archway that had to be the most beautiful masterpiece she'd ever seen. It was something she imagined from the story *Arabian Nights* that she'd read as a child. She wanted to run her fingers along the floral motifs and geometric designs, but she held back, reminding herself she was supposed to be a woman of culture who was used to fine things.

They continued on, and her eyes widened at the countless ornamental reliefs and mosaics. Each room seemed to top the last in beauty and intricacy of design.

"You will note some parts of the castle are still in disrepair. For many years this place was abandoned and used as the hideout of bandits and thieves." Tomas's eyes sparkled. "But there is more than enough repaired to enjoy . . . to paint."

Men and women moved about—mainly servants working at various tasks. None of them offered Sophie more than a glance, and she prided herself on the fact that she fit in well.

"Feel free to wander as you like," Tomas said. "I know as an artist there is much that will interest you." They walked to what she assumed was the palace, and he led her to a door on the first floor. He opened the door with a grin, and she entered the large suite and stopped short in delight and surprise. The windows of the room overlooked the town of Granada. An easel had been set up before it. A side table was filled with various painting supplies.

"You've come to paint, have you not, Eleanor?" Tomas asked with a twinkle in his eyes. "You can be assured my friends will ask for regular updates. You better not disappoint."

Sophie rushed forward and picked up a paintbrush, marveling at the feel of it in her hand. She turned and then offered Tomas a quick hug. "Thank you. I will begin today."

An hour into her first canvas, Sophie adjusted her weight from side to side as she studied it. Considering she hadn't painted in months and months, she did a fine job of painting the view from the window. But something didn't seem right. Though her specialty used to be landscapes, they now seemed boring and . . . uninteresting.

She considered taking her easel to the courtyard. Out there, she would no doubt have chances to meet many of the castle's visitors—which was one of her objectives. Instead, a strange burden weighed on her shoulders, and she had an image of the one painting she most desired to capture.

Sophie rearranged her supplies and set up a new canvas. She began with the face of the woman in the cave apartment. Then she painted Deion, disguising him as a Moor. His mouth was open as she remembered the memory of him singing gospel songs while lying in a hospital bed at the first-aid station where she'd helped.

She smiled to herself as she painted the uniform, realizing he'd be horrified to see himself as such . . . but it warmed her heart to shape his face upon the canvas. Sophie painted José next. And then Benita and Father Manuel. She disguised each one so she alone knew their true identity.

With each brushstroke she realized how these people—once strangers—had affected her. At the beginning of the war, it had been easier for her to think of the "big picture"—she had focused on the victory of a nation. But the more she experienced the war, the more she realized its unique effect on individual people. It wasn't a nation that hurt—it was the hearts of millions, one by one.

Painting the hands, the feet—each unique—Sophie also realized God hadn't given her a way of escape from Spain. He'd instead planned for her to be where she was—serving and being served.

"To live or die, it's not up to me, but to serve God. To do my best to help the one He brings before me. That is enough," she prayed as she painted.

The light outside the window faded, and Sophie realized that dinner had passed, and she had missed it. Her stomach rumbled, but her heart felt full.

And by the time she heard footsteps approaching from outside her door, Sophie realized one thing. In the long run it didn't matter much if the gold made it out or not. It didn't even matter if she made it out. If, in the end, when she approached the throne of Christ, He said, "Well done, good and faithful servant . . . for each small act of obedience and way of tenderness," then that would be enough. It would be her true reward.

With a sigh, she finished and laid down her paintbrush, gazing at the faces of her friends. Even in heartache, there were those who had hope and faith. And even if the victories on this earth could not be achieved by those who she thought deserved it, God could still be victorious in hearts and souls.

"God can win here, in the center of our hearts. We may die, yet we will live," she whispered. "We can lose, yet no one can take away what we carry in our hearts. And that is where true victory lies—in the whispers of deep recesses. Whispers that no one else can hear. A place where we and our Savior meet alone."

A knocked sounded at the door, and she turned and smiled as she strode to the door. Tomas was waiting. With him were two men with a large trunk.

"It is a sad thing, Eleanor, that you lost your luggage during your travels. What a dreadful thing to try to cross a country in the midst of war. A friend of mine heard of your plight and offered you a few things. There is a formal dinner tomorrow night, and I hope you can find something to wear."

He motioned to the men, and they placed the trunk in the room. The two servants left, but Tomas stayed, eyes eager to see her response. Sophie opened the trunk and saw everyday dresses on top. She lifted them out; beneath lay two Spanish-style gowns.

Sophie sucked in her breath and lifted a light blue one. She pressed it to her chest and did a slow twirl. Then her painting caught her attention, and she remembered why she was here. She remembered her prayer from only a moment before . . . amazed that in the midst of all that had happened and all that might happen, God had given her this unexpected gift, even if only momentarily—the freedom to paint gorgeous, lush surroundings and ancient craftsmanship. He'd even given her beautiful gowns. She smiled as once again she came face-to-face with the providence of God.

Tomas followed her gaze to the painting. "Amazing. I never knew my niece was so talented." He walked toward the painting. "I cannot believe you have created a masterpiece in such a short amount of time. Do you know these people?"

Sophie laid the dress upon her bed, amazed how Tomas always stayed in character. He never dropped his guard, never wavered. "Just faces I've seen on my travels, Uncle—composites of those who fight so hard for Generalissimo Franco."

Tomas nodded his approval; then he offered her another hug before leaving. "Good night, Eleanor. I'll have a tray of food sent up for you. And sweet dreams. I look forward to hearing about the great things you'll discover around these grounds *mañana*."

Chapter Twenty-Eight

José only considered stopping when he was certain they were far enough in the hills that Michael could not reach them by vehicle or foot. The sun now crested over the horizon, and it was strange to see Petra and Ramona riding together—two parts of his life intersecting. He hoped that the two women he cared for would become friends.

The sound of a creek met his ears, and he remembered this place from his journey down the mountain—a small place of refuge among the hills.

"Petra, stop in that clearing ahead," he called to her. "We will rest the horses . . . and ourselves."

"Yes, José," Petra called over her shoulder. She turned and looked back, and it was from the wild look in her eyes that he knew something was desperately wrong.

"What is it, Petra?"

"José! Calisto is bleeding!" The color drained from her face.

José quickly dismounted and saw the bright red stream of blood on Calisto's shoulder. Yet the horse had carried him to safety, and his steps hadn't wavered. Guilt washed over him for not stopping sooner to check the horse.

Petra helped Ramona dismount, and a few seconds later both women were at his side.

"Will he be okay?" Petra stroked his mane.

"Is it a gunshot wound?" Ramona took a closer look at the bullet wound in his shoulder.

"Michael . . ." Petra said. "He saw me leaving with the horses, and he ran out. He aimed the gun at me, but Calisto lifted his front legs and leapt—just as you'd trained him for show. I heard the gunshot, but I didn't know he was hit. I am so sorry, José." She fell to the ground, and silent sobs shook her shoulders.

José reached for her, patting her hair, and from the corner of his eye he noticed Ramona stiffen beside him.

He moved back to Calisto. "If there was any spot where he was hit, this would be the best place. It didn't hit any major arteries or enter his chest cavity." José turned and took his wife's hand. "And do not worry, Petra. My wife is a wonderful nurse."

Ramona's eyes widened. "I work on men, not animals." But her gaze softened as she turned to the horse. "Of course, the wound doesn't appear too deep. I only wish I had some supplies."

Petra lifted her head. "At the caves . . . your father packed bandages, needles. He had a very fine first-aid kit."

"Do you think Calisto can make it that far?" Ramona asked.

"It will take us longer, but I think he can make it if I don't ride him," José said. "You two can ride Erro, and I'll follow, leading the horse."

"Are you sure?" Petra straightened her shoulders. "I could go ahead and get the first-aid kit." She pulled the map out of her pocket. "I have this, remember?"

"Sí, good idea. We'll give Erro a chance to rest and graze before you head out. And then we will find a place nearby to wait. I'd like to stay with Calisto just in case."

Ramona took Petra's face in her hands. "José, why did you not tell me sooner God had provided you with a guardian angel?" She brushed the hair back from Petra's face.

A smile spread over Petra's lips, and she offered Ramona a quick hug. José smiled too.

After twenty-one days of living in dry riverbeds, their orders were to fall out. The action was over. This surprised Deion. During the days that were extremely hot, and the nights that were cold and caused him to wish again for the heat, he didn't expect that they'd ever be called back. This was their big offensive. He supposed they'd press on until they reached the end—wherever that was. Or until he met his end, whichever came first.

With slow steps, the troops marched to their reprieve. The men around Deion collapsed, and he had never ached with so much weariness in all his life. After withdrawing from the heat of the Guadarrama Valley, the Lincoln Bridgade moved to a rest camp at Albares, near enough to Madrid to permit the men to explore the capital.

"I don't think I could walk one more mile, even if they paid me in solid gold," Deion muttered to the man beside him. His back ached. His mind even more.

He had just drifted off to sleep when he awakened to see their commander, Steve Nelson, climbing onto a large rock before them.

A man shouted from somewhere in the crowd, "For Pete's sake, Steve, you're not going to tell us to go back, are you?"

"You know I would not do this if there were any other choice. The Spanish marines are surrounded. You, men, are their only hope. And even if we rest, it won't be for long. Word has it that we are threatened from the rear."

A low murmur moved through the crowd. And then silence, as if each man was weighing his options.

They'd do it fer us, Deion thought. *How can we not try to save them?*

"You're right!" someone called out.

"It's our duty. This is why we have come," another added.

Deion, with strength he didn't know he possessed, pulled himself from the ground and repacked his supplies—or what remained of them. They lined up for the trip back, but not five hundred yards out, another messenger arrived.

"Men, wait!" Nelson called. "The order has been reversed. Relax. Rest."

And with this announcement they somehow were more strengthened than they had been. Deion looked around at their faces and noticed their pride.

They'd been willing to give everything, to push past their pain. It was a good feeling—one that couldn't be explained.

Deion drifted off to sleep again that night with a feeling of hope.

The next morning came, and with it word that they'd been given ten days' leave in Madrid. Now what was he supposed to do with that? The six months he'd been part of the brigade ran together. He was either fighting, driving, or wounded in the hospital. Deion wondered if he even knew what to do with time to himself. Back pay also caught up with him from the International Brigade offices. He'd forgotten all about the *pestas*—which totaled a month's wages back home—promised him during training.

The drive toward Madrid was like a drive from death to life. From the barren land the road wound into green fields, and Deion even noted a river full of water. If he could have, he would have jumped into it and washed away the filth of the fight. Washed away the memories, too.

Instead of finding peace on the road, he had a strange feeling as others on the road turned and watched the truck pass. He noticed pointing and wide-eyed gazes, and he realized that perhaps it was the first time many of them had seen a black man.

When he entered Madrid, the first thing Deion thought of was Sophie's paintings of the city. There had been paintings of bombings overhead and people with terrified looks on their faces. It sort of surprised him that today the sky was clear and people walked around. Many buildings were pockmarked by bullet holes and some buildings had been reduced to rubble, but it appeared as if the city had done its best to clean up the mess.

If only it were as easy to clean up one's thoughts—pushing away the rubble. And one's heart, for that matter.

Chapter Twenty-Nine

Ramona checked Calisto one more time. He seemed to be faring well, considering his injury. She approached José, noticing that his gaze still followed the trail Petra had taken thirty minutes prior.

"They'll be okay," she whispered, slipping up to him and feeling his arm wrap around her. "All of them. You'll see."

They loitered along the creek, and Ramona found a small stick she used to hit the reeds along the shore. A fish floated by, dead and limp. The current carried it away. Ramona empathized with the limp creature. She too was being swept away, not only by her circumstances but by her emotions.

She gazed up at José, knowing she'd do everything within her power to make sure they didn't part again. "I've worked around hospitals long enough to know one thing. Brave men can be reduced to tears. The dark hours are far more frightening than the grave," she whispered. "They cry over nothing and everything. They are alone. Their thoughts strike blows at will. I have come to believe that hope is the greatest treasure on earth. Hope centered on the knowledge that with Christ you are never alone. You are never powerless." She dropped the stick and settled on the grass. "Petra. Your father. Pepito. They are not alone either."

José didn't respond, but he sat by her side, entwining her hand in his.

"As a child I used to visit the nuns," she continued. "They always welcomed me and appreciated my company. They cared for each other with such devotion, and I believe it was from them I learned why Jesus urges us to love each other as we love ourselves. Our joy increases with service. Yet their hope meant little to me when I didn't need it. Just as a banquet means nothing to a person who is not hungry."

A bird sang overhead, and in the distance she heard the rumble of a large gun.

"But when your stomach is empty, even one slice of bread brings a smile. And when I've witnessed so much hopelessness, I realize I wouldn't trade the hope I have in Jesus for anything in the world."

"Not even a greater treasure than you could imagine?" José asked. His gaze held a far-off look.

"Not even that." She opened her arms and wrapped them around her husband's neck, bringing him close.

"Neither would I," he whispered in her ear.

"But I have to admit, being here with you feels strange. Half of this day has passed, and no one has asked anything from me. I wasn't sought out to bandage or to clean a wound. No one died in my arms or asked for a drink of water."

José took her chin with a soft touch and turned her face toward him. "Oh, dear wife, I am asking everything of you. To love me as a forgiving wife. To come with me into the wilds. In my opinion that is much harder than offering a hundred cups of water, especially for a husband as foolish as I."

She nodded slightly. "Sí, but I never expected you to be perfect. When we married, I knew that there would be things that would force us apart. But we can remember this day . . . mostly by the fact that sweeter is a reunion after a long parting." She leaned up and offered her lips.

José kissed her deeply. "My dear," he whispered, pulling away. "I think you are the poet. The greater thinker."

"And you . . . even when you didn't realize it, were the caregiver

—to the old men, the horses, the girl. She is a sweet thing, isn't she? As we rode she told me of your journey into the mountains. She adores Pepito and your father. Maybe someday we will have a daughter like that." Ramona took José's face and turned it toward her. "I understand why you love her. But I know, as much as I know the curve of your lips, that your caring love for her never threatened your love for me, your wife. I loved some of the men I cared for, also. It's hard to keep compassion from turning into intense care. I think our Maker placed that in us. It's good if we both recognize this love for what it is. We offer our care out of God's love, and then . . . we offer our complete selves to each other. That is how we are designed."

As she studied her husband's face, Ramona saw peace settle over his features. They were together, and they understood each other. It was the reunion she'd worried would never happen—but one that turned out to be a perfect gift.

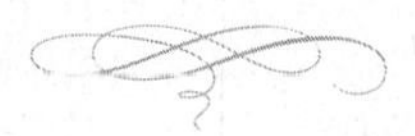

Philip waited in the shadows of the forest. He told the others he wouldn't bother them. He said he'd allow Sophie to pass off the maps and whatever else she found, without interrupting. He'd told himself it would be enough to see her from a distance. That he could watch her without asking anything in return. Yet even as he stood, partly hidden behind a tree, he fought a losing cause. It wasn't enough. Knowing she was there and not being able to be with her would never be enough.

If he would have remained on the front line, he had no doubt he would have run into battle, even a hopeless one, with thoughts of victory and duty. Even now, though his mind didn't understand it, his heart marched on to die. He'd given it to Sophie, even if he could never have her in return.

But his battle wasn't on the front lines. It was a solo fight. The weapon wasn't in his hands, but he knew if he lost it would lead to his destruction. He'd made a fool of himself in his last moments with Sophie, and now he'd do anything to take them back.

"Civilian-fighter," he whispered to himself. "Spanish volunteer. Loser in love." Even now those words defined him.

He waited for Sophie's return, but his waiting was not idle. He'd discovered that his speed was valued among the guerilla fighters. And now it was his job to place the explosives, light the detonators, and run.

How many lives were helped by his acts of destruction? Farmers and weavers. Bricklayers and potters. Still, he doubted it was enough. Though the war raged on, he saw little chance of their victory, and his mind turned to what would happen next.

How would the lives of these people change in the new Spain—the one they had fought off for so long? He thought of some of the Spanish soldiers he'd fought beside, including the friend who'd held Attis's head as he died. The Spaniard had carried a sharpened knife next to his heart, ready to fight to the death for a cause he believed in. Such a man would be hunted and killed in the new Spain. He wouldn't live in submission—just as the mountain fighters did not. Philip knew, Franco knew; it would only be a matter of time before the battles waged once more.

The more Philip thought about this, the more he realized that maybe he wasn't there to fight with them, but instead to urge the men to escape while they could.

He heard footsteps, and he sank deeper into the shadows.

"I have found these—maps and documents. I've discovered that Tomas is very forgetful—just as we planned. He usually leaves doors unlocked . . . and now I know to follow him. Look them over tonight and bring them back in the morning—I need to return them before they are discovered missing. I'll meet you here." Her voice sounded weary. "I hope they are of some use."

Sophie wore a cape. A hood covered most of her face, but in the moonlight Philip noticed the curve of her mouth as she spoke. She looked around, and he wondered if she searched for him. Her shoulders slumped slightly, and then without another word she returned inside the tunnel, no doubt hurrying to the safety of her room.

Philip let out a low sigh. Though he'd at first agreed with Walt, he agreed no longer.

Even though leaving the country without the gold didn't

make sense, Philip knew it would be their only chance for survival. He knew that even if Spain fell to Franco there would be hope . . . as long as they lived.

To live in a free country, such as France, would not mean freedom as they saw it. To leave the riches would not bring honor. But it would mean life. And right now that was enough.

Petra had returned as quickly as she could with the two older men, but by the time two more days passed, Calisto was failing. Petra watched as José held the horse's large head in his lap, speaking to him in a low, even tone.

The horse's gaze was wide, fearful. Petra could see the whites of his eyes. Pepito and Juan held the horse's legs steady as Ramona's gentle fingers dug into the incision, searching for the bullet.

Calisto groaned deeply. By tremendous effort he lifted his head. He met Petra's gaze, and she swore she could see compassion there. Forgiveness. She knew he did not blame her for the injury, though she blamed herself. A shudder passed over his bulky frame, and he sank back onto the straw.

A smile filled Ramona's face, and she pulled something from the wound. "I have it. I got the bullet!" For the next fifteen minutes she cleaned the wound as best she could; then she carefully stitched it up. By the time she finished, her hands and arms were covered with blood. There was even a spot on her cheek that José tried to wipe away with his fingers.

"What do you think?" José leaned down and touched the bandage.

"The wound isn't bad, but it's the infection I'm worried about. He should not be moved. I know it's not the safest place, but I think we need to stay here."

José nodded as he looked down into the valley. "It will be fine."

Petra could tell from his tone he was trying to convince himself as well as them.

He stared out at the sea, deep in thought. "Maybe it is better this way. We could not have stayed in the mountains through the fall and winter, anyway. Maybe this will force us to think of another way."

As he glanced over his shoulder, first looking to the older men and then stopping his gaze on Petra, she had a feeling what that meant. They would not return to the mountains. In fact, she had a feeling they would not remain in Spain if José could help it.

Chapter Thirty

José glanced at each face as he looked around the fire pit. He had left them for half a day—journeying down to the docks. Though Ramona had begged him not to go, he knew it was the only way. He must send the others away now, before it was too late.

He motioned Petra off to the side. She followed, eyes wide.

"There is a ship leaving soon, from the village of El Musel. Petra, you need to be on it. I will hear no objection. You must go with Pepito and Father. I need you all to take care of each other. I found passage for the horses as well."

"Yes, I understand." Petra squared her shoulders.

"There is more." He paused, noting how thin she'd become. She'd given so much to help them . . . and now he had a gift for her.

"José, what is it?"

"You came to us looking for Edelberto, remember? Well, that is where I am sending you . . . to his home. Or more accurately, to that of his father. You will be cared for."

Petra touched her hair, her face. Then she looked down at her clothes. "I am not sure. . . . Things have changed."

"Listen to me." José cupped her face in his hands. "You are beautiful. You are worthy. Any young man would be honored to have you as a friend."

Petra nodded but said nothing. When they returned to the campfire, José explained the plan to the others.

⁂ ⁂ ⁂

Pepito and Juan nodded, as if accepting their fate.

Ramona took José's hand. "Parting will be hard, but it will be even harder if we spend the night worrying and fretting. Let's think about other things." She turned to Juan and looked deeply into the older man's eyes. "You are amazing, you know. It was the poultice you made for Calisto that sucked the infection out. *You* saved him . . . not me."

José turned away, trying to hide his emotion.

"Perhaps I was born to work with God's creatures."

José could hear his father's smile in his words. He closed his eyes and memorized the sound of his father's voice.

When he had first come up with the plan for sending the old men and Petra away, Ramona had told him not to worry—they'd see him again. But José knew differently. His father was old, and José had no plans to leave Spain until they won the war. Until Franco lost.

"I grew up in the hills in which roads did not exist," Juan continued, weaving a story for Ramona with his words. "As a child one of my clearest memories was of the Spanish muleteers who chanted songs and ballads as if they owned the hills. They traveled alone, or in trains. Sometimes I awoke to the bells of the lead mules. Soon it would be joined by the voice of the muleteer, singing or cursing his animal—both with the same wild enthusiasm."

Ramona laughed, and the sound of it filled José's soul.

"It was the animals that impressed me most. The way they descended the precipitous cliffs. They were simple animals, yet they amazed me. And more than anything I wanted to spend my time with them."

The stories continued long into the night, and in the morning they rose and traveled to El Musel. José kept a lookout for

Michael, but thankfully there was no sight of him.

"José," Ramona whispered as they approached the docks. "Are you sure we shouldn't try to go too?"

"This is my country. I cannot abandon her. . . . I will fight for her honor until no hope remains." José squeezed Ramona's hand tighter. "But if you would like—"

"No. I'm staying with you."

José nodded, then led the horses onto the large fishing boat. He wondered, too, if it would be the last time he'd see the beautiful creatures.

Calisto's white and gray tail swung lightly as he boarded. Erro followed, as did the four mares.

After obtaining paper and a pen from the captain, José hastily jotted down a note, and then handed it to Petra for safekeeping.

> *Señor Adolfo, These three souls have served you well. They have worked to rescue what belongs to you. Any harm caused to your family rests on my shoulders alone. Care for them as I would. Gratefully yours, José*

Though tears filled his eyes at their departure, a joy filled José knowing he had succeeded. The horses would be safe. He had protected them. And he'd now sent them to their proper owner. Though Michael had failed him, José had no reason to distrust Adolfo. Michael's uncle had always been a fair man. A good man.

When they were boarded and secure, José and Ramona exited, and then they stood on the dock and waved good-bye.

Walt had paid José generously for his work watching Michael, and he'd always felt like too much of a traitor to spend it. Until now. The money would be used well, paying for their passage to France. He let out a soft breath knowing those most precious to him—those he'd protected—would be safe.

Petra curled herself as close to Juan as possible. Others pressed around her. Those with faces she could not see in the darkness of the hold. It felt strange being huddled so close to strangers. Every once in a while she'd feel breath on her cheek or the brush of a hand or foot as the person next to her adjusted himself. She could tell that the person was young. His breathing had a different tone to it than the nasally sound of Juan's breathing. He also had a smell about him like pine and soil. She wondered if she did too. She considered asking—speaking into the darkness, but knew she wasn't allowed. There was always the chance that passengers above would hear them. There was always the chance of passengers who would point them out to save themselves. She shuddered at the thought of the Nationalist boats that patrolled these waters, and she hoped that they would be some of the lucky ones to slip through.

As much as she could, Petra slept. It helped the time go faster. Then, when she awoke, she listened closely to make sure she could hear the breathing of the old men. Tomorrow she would be in France. And a few days later in Paris. She had first traveled from Guernica to Bilbao in search of Edelberto . . . and before the week was out she would see him. Her stomach trembled at the thought of it.

Ritter considered his new assignment—to ferry a war-weary Junkers Ju.52/3, with its cargo, to Granada the following day at dawn. These trimotor transports usually had a two-pilot crew to manage the complex fuel transfers and monitor the propeller rpm of the three 750 horsepower, nine-cylinder BMW radial engines.

Still, Ritter wondered if it were better that he went alone. It played into his plan nicely. The only trouble he had was the last time he'd seen Monica. She exited Göring's office the same time he entered. Monica hadn't said a word. Instead, she avoided looking at him and veered off the path to walk around him.

But even more than her silence was the look in her eyes. It was as if she was bidding him a silent good-bye with her gaze.

Ritter knew something was wrong, so he decided to carefully

check the Junkers before the morning flight.

When "lights out" finally darkened the airfield, Ritter—armed with a flashlight—started his preflight with the propeller on the front of the fuselage. He worked his way around the entire aircraft, checking each nut, bolt, clevis, and control cable.

He walked out onto the wing and checked the complex flaps and the ailerons to make sure no worn parts existed that could fail at the wrong time. The big, all-metal transport appeared to be well used but airworthy. Still, the feeling that something was wrong would not leave him.

Glancing around, he found a heavy-duty broom leaning against a hangar wall and swept the oil-spotted ground all around the aircraft to cover his tracks. Once finished, he hurried to the barracks where he'd stay the night. Then he tried his best to get some sleep before the flight.

The watch commander woke him an hour before dawn. Ritter showered, ate a quick breakfast, and headed out to his aircraft. He walked the perimeter, and something looked different. The broom marks appeared to be going in the opposite direction of those Ritter made last night. Or perhaps it was just his imagination.

In the cockpit, the crew chief ran up the engines. Behind him, the fuel truck pulled away. It was time to go. Göring had one plan, but Ritter had another.

He pushed his worried thoughts from his mind. *Nothing is wrong. I'm just mistaken about the strokes of the broom,* he assured himself, knowing he had time to recheck the aircraft while taxiing to the takeoff position.

As the aircraft taxied, he repeatedly moved all the controls from stop to stop, looked out the window, and checked for oil or gas pouring over the wing. Nothing. He applied the brakes. They worked fine. He slammed the rudder from left to right. The huge vertical surface followed every move of the control cables.

Just before he taxied into the takeoff position, he ran up each engine, checked the dual ignition for drop off, and found that all six magnetos were working within limits. He cycled the three props; all responded perfectly from maximum fine pitch to full pitch. Ritter knew that dozens of eyes—of the other pilots, those in the tower, and the ground crew—were watching him, and the precautions he had taken were all normal for any pilot to perform before takeoff. He scanned the office, almost expecting to see Monica there, but there was no sight of her. He blew out a low breath and told himself just as an adulterer often accused his spouse of cheating, so a thief and deceiver worried about being deceived.

Out of habit, Ritter rotated the plane 360 degrees, checking for other aircraft in the pattern before takeoff. The lightening skies were clear of approaching aircraft. It was time to go.

Ritter advanced the three throttles slowly, allowing the big radials to respond without loading up. The low-wing trimotor started on its takeoff roll. It sounded more like a moving sheet-metal barn full of running tractors than a modern warbird. He kept the plane headed straight with application of rudder input and a slight tap on the brakes.

As the plane gained speed, Ritter moved the control wheel forward a bit to get the tail off the ground for less drag and better visibility. The plane was easier to hold straight now due to the added air flowing over the rudder. With one eye on the airspeed indicator in kilometers per hour, and the other on his takeoff path, he waited until the airspeed needle bounced on 125 kph—the magic number for a lightly loaded takeoff. The rumbling noise stopped, and soon the only distraction was the shaking of the airplane as the unbalanced wheels started to vibrate.

A tap on the brakes, on top of the rudder pedals, stopped the wheel shake immediately. The big old tin bird was in the air and climbing out just the way her designers had planned.

Ritter scanned the engine instruments, his tense body looking for any movement through the air that didn't seem normal. Nothing appeared wrong. As if welcoming him to the sky, the sun's rays crept over the mountains, indicating clear blue skies for his trip to Granada.

All was well.

Chapter Thirty-One

Thirty minutes after takeoff, the Junkers reached its cruising altitude for the remainder of the short flight. Ritter trimmed the plane for level flight by reducing the manifold pressure of each engine and applying more pitch to the propellers for a faster cruise under lowered rpms. He leaned the mixture on each engine, checking the fuel flowmeters, looking for reduced flow without reduced rpms.

After setting the elevator, aileron, and rudder trim for level flight, Ritter settled back into the pilot's seat, opened his thermos of coffee, and prepared for a boring flight.

He'd just crossed over into Spain when a rattling noise woke him from his daydream. There it was again. He grabbed the control wheel and rotated it. A loud snapping noise caused fear to pound in his heart, and the control wheel went limp in his hand. Someone had cut the cables to elevator and ailerons—they'd most likely seared them enough to allow for takeoff before they failed.

He immediately thought of Monica. Had she told Göring of his knowledge of the satchel's contents? If so, why? She was the one who had urged him to look.

Or perhaps Göring still didn't know. It had never made sense why the American had pushed herself into Göring's inner circle. Perhaps she was using Göring as well.

She had got the information she needed . . . and to her Ritter was just extra baggage.

Does she think she can get rid of me this easily?

Ritter knew the rules of flight—fly high enough to pick out a good landing area if necessary, know where you are at all times, and know his airplane and how to cope with in-flight problems. Loosing the elevator and ailerons was a rather high-priority problem, but nothing he couldn't handle.

He tightened the straps on his seat chute, checked all the buckles and straps, and made sure the rip-cord handle would release from its pocket.

The plane had been trimmed for level flight before the emergency. He had plenty of altitude, and if the plane continued on for just a few more minutes he would be out of the mountains and over the Spanish fields of grain, which would certainly be a better landing strip than rocks, hills, and the huge trees he was leaving behind.

As the Junker lumbered away from the hills, Ritter knew his first priority was to make a thirty- to forty-degree course correction to starboard, thus avoiding the rising hills in his current direction. The fields of golden grain were just a bit off his current path.

Good old *Junta Ju* had engines on both wings and one in the nose, making the turn possible—even with the damage. This type of plane climbed and descended not by the elevator, but by engine power or lack of engine power. It was possible to get *Junta Ju* back on the ground in one piece in a rather hard, but survivable, landing.

About five miles in the distance, right off the nose, he spotted a wide farm road intersecting two wheat fields. The road was about five to seven meters wide.

Ritter prepared the plane for an attitude landing—nose high—controlled with the right amount of flap, engine power, and trim settings of the elevator. With gentle nudging of the two wing-mounted engine throttles, he lined up the plane with the road. He slowly reduced the power of the main fuselage engine and started rolling in an elevator-up trim.

Mother Nature was on Ritter's side for once, supplying a steady ten-knot wind right onto the nose, thus slowing the landing speed by ten knots. Ritter scanned the area again, hoping the farmer owning the field had slept in this morning. The last thing he wanted was to tangle with a huge wheat reaper being towed down the road by a team of oxen. Even *Junta Ju* was no match for a multiton oxen team.

Ritter prepared for the final approach. He held the big plane just above the road and slowly reduced the power. The plane settled and bounced once. With no elevator to hold the nose up, it bounced again and settled into a jittery roll down the dirt farm road.

Ritter kept the plane on the road by using his still-working rudder and brake controls. A minute later, the Junker came to a halt, right on the road. The road was slightly uphill. Just on the other side of the road was a wide, dry creek filled with rocks that Ritter had seen as he was setting up the approach.

Only when Ritter had landed, and his stomach had settled, did he consider what to do next. It took less then thirty seconds for him to decide the plan of action.

If she wants me dead, let her think she has won.

He threw his traveling bag with clean uniforms and other necessities out the window. He made sure the address Göring had first given him was in his pocket. If word got back that he was dead, then Göring—or Monica—would never expect Ritter to arrive, which Ritter was glad about. Now he answered only to himself.

He left his parachute on the seat and opened the pilot's exit door. He then reached over, pushed all three throttles to the wall, and dove out the open door. *Juanta Ju* came to life, climbing the mild hill faster and faster. When it reached the top of the hill, the plane had nearly reached flying speed. With full throttle and full-up elevator trim, it staggered into the air as the hill fell away from beneath it.

Ritter knew it was going to be a very short last flight, but the more horrific the crash, the longer the investigators would take to realize she was a ghost ship bound for no place, with no one on board except the devil. If they even investigated. With all that happened in Spain, he questioned if they even would.

The plane gained fifty meters when one of the wings started to dip. With no pilot aboard to correct it, the bank became almost vertical. As if doing a dying dance, the plane pivoted and then plummeted nose first into the rocky creek bed. It hit with an agonizing death yell, and then the almost-full fuel tanks of high-octane aviation fuel blew, causing an explosion and fireball that rose into the sky like a beacon. Those in the Spanish countryside would assume another enemy plane had been shot down.

Ritter bent down, threw open his bag, removed his uniform, and changed into civilian clothes. He'd survived on the ground in Spain before—he'd do it again.

Ritter was dead. Ritter was alive. It was time to bail out of his life in the Luftwaffe and head for more friendly skies. But first, he had to find a way to beg, borrow, or steal a lot of money to start his new life.

He tossed his bag over his shoulder, stuck a sweet wheat straw in his mouth, and headed south.

Even though the ground was hard, and a rock or stick poked at her side through the blanket, Ramona relished being in her husband's arms. José's arm was under her, and she snuggled with her cheek to his chest. She could tell by his breathing that he was still awake. Could tell by the softness of his breaths that he, too, lay there thinking.

"Are you worried about them? Wondering if they'll make it all the way?"

"Sí," José whispered. "And what kind of reception they'll receive in Paris. Adolfo abandoned the horses and their caregivers. How will he feel to have them show up on his doorstep?"

"Not to mention the girl."

"Petra, yes." José hesitated as he said the name.

"So . . . how did she come to be with you?"

"She arrived on the front steps looking for Edelberto. She had met him in Madrid two years before. She survived the bombing in Guernica. All her family was lost. After that she didn't have anywhere to go."

"She wasn't from Guernica. I've lived there my whole life and worked in every school and hospital. I never saw her. In fact, I don't think she was a poor girl, as she tried to make us believe."

"I know. If she knew Edelberto, it makes sense she wouldn't be."

"Perhaps her parents were Fascists."

"Perhaps. Or maybe some of the wealthy from farther south. Many were rounded up and killed."

"She lied to you."

"She was lost and scared," José shot back.

"You cared for her greatly." Ramona bit her lip, surprising herself. She thought she was over that—thought she'd dealt with it. Obviously not.

"I loved her like a sister, or a daughter."

"Nothing more?"

"I have to admit. There was a special feeling there. She followed without question. She looked up to me. She trusted me."

Ramona felt the pain in her chest. The younger woman had behaved more like a wife than she had. Why had she been so foolish? Ramona felt tears coming to her eyes, and her throat constricted.

"Ramona?"

"Mmm-hm." She dared not speak for fear a sob would escape with her words.

"It is you, only you, I wish to hold in my arms. Tonight. Tomorrow. Forever."

She nodded her head, but still the accusations would not leave her mind. *Why didn't you believe him? Trust him? You better than anyone should know his heart.*

"Darling. The time we were apart was hard on me. But everything turned out. God worked it for our good." José's breathing slowed, and she knew he was drifting toward sleep.

A peace settled over her.

"There is a reason we are still here," José mumbled. "I trust if we are meant to leave, we will. Until then, there is a war to fight."

She sighed. "I'm not very good at fighting."

"No, but you are good at mending. And that's what they will need." José's voice grew softer as sleep threatened to overtake him.

Ramona didn't ask who "they" were. She knew many in Spain needed her help. Yet even if she had the knowledge, what good would she be with no facilities or supplies?

"Lord, I commit myself and my husband into Your hands," she whispered as she drifted off. "May we be used as vessels . . . of Your peace. To bring hope to the hopeless and healing for the injured."

Chapter Thirty-Two

Sophie yawned. The long days and sleepless nights were catching up with her. She'd made many friends, if that's what one would call them, who were more than interested in her art. When the men and women took their daily siesta, she found it was the perfect time to wander through the castle "reclaiming" maps and bits of information for the cause.

Since she was American, no one wondered why she didn't rest. And as an artist, no one thought it peculiar to find her in remote rooms, copying the mosaics or reliefs onto her canvas.

Then, during the nights, she moved through tunnels to the place she met with the guerilla fighters. Tomas had shown her the path, and she'd become an expert at knowing which turns to take. She traveled alone, with a single candle as her light.

Today she'd joined her "uncle" on his weekly trip to town. He'd planned another elegant dinner party for that evening and invited Sophie to help choose fresh flowers for the event. She made an excuse to wander around the town, with hopes of seeing someone from the mountains. The men often came down to spy within the crowds. Something within her longed for a friendly face. She felt so very alone and playing the part of a self-involved artist was harder than she'd expected.

But there had been no one familiar, and she spotted the flower store ahead. Tomas saw her and waved.

"Eleanor!" he called.

Sophie waved back, recognizing one of the town's high officials standing beside Tomas.

She quickened her steps, and as she was about to pass a small crowd on the sidewalk, an older woman stumbled in front of her, falling hard to the ground. Sophie gasped and looked to Tomas. His gaze widened as if wondering how Sophie would respond. She didn't slow, but instead tilted her chin and continued on.

She knew Eleanor—the selfish person she'd created—would never stop. But as she continued on, Sophie wondered if she would stop even if she had the chance.

It's just one woman. Helping her won't make any difference. I could bend over and pick her up, but then what? I'd become involved in her life. I'd feed her and listen to her. And I'm tired.

Her shoulders sank in weariness. *I'm tired of giving and getting nothing in return. Where has reaching out gotten me? I'm alone. I don't know whom to trust. I'm living a lie. I don't even have my own name.*

The woman's hand reached out as Sophie passed, and Sophie scooted over so not even the woman's fingertips would touch her skirt. She kept walking.

"Please," the woman called behind her. "Please help me."

Sophie continued on with quickened steps.

She met Tomas, and they walked back to the automobile in silence. Shadows lengthened through the streets, and Sophie's eyes darted to others who mulled around in the crowd. Two children, dressed in rags, begged for *pesetas* with a tin cup. A man with a curved back and slow limp hobbled by. A young woman carried a crying baby, the infant clutched to her chest.

Among them strolled soldiers in uniform, priests, finely dressed women, men in business suits. It was the weak and feeble who drew her attention.

But with each one she passed, a cool indifference settled in her chest. And after she'd walked halfway to the parking area, she didn't notice them anymore.

They arrived back at the castle as people headed to the dining room for lunch. A net of safety settled over her as she laughed with the wealthy of Granada, and they talked about nothing of importance. Tonight she'd allow herself to be twirled around the dance floor. And she'd enjoy herself as if she lived only for this moment with no cares for tomorrow.

Or so she'd like to think.

⁂ ⁂ ⁂

The food, the music, the beautiful people—with so much to enjoy, Sophie dismissed the fact that she hadn't sent word that she wouldn't deliver any information tonight.

A guitar player sat in the corner, strumming lively Spanish music. She swayed from side to side, enjoying the silky feeling of the light blue dress swishing across her legs.

Her eyes moved around the room, and she had a strange feeling that someone was watching her. Sophie turned and paused. Then everything in her told her to run. Her charade was up. Across the room she stared into the eyes of Maria Donita. The woman who had carried, and apparently borne, Michael's child.

An older Spanish man approached and struck up a conversation. Sophie did her best to focus on his words and laugh at the right times. After thirty minutes ticked by, she could wait no longer. She saw Maria Donita head to the balcony, and she followed.

The night air was warm. Maria Donita stood by a balcony overlooking the lion fountain, with the city of Granada beyond that. She turned slightly when Sophie came out.

Sophie shut the glass door behind her. She breathed in deeply as she strolled onto the patio, smelling approaching rain.

"I was wondering if you saw me come out here. I hoped so. I want to talk to you . . . Eleanor. Isn't that what they call you?" Maria's tone was cautious.

Sophie stopped. "I don't understand. If you recognized me, why didn't you turn me in—or point me out?" Sophie cleared her throat.

"I can't do that. You are working for someone. And I need your help. I need you to help me get out."

Maria stepped closer, and desperation marred her face. "I have a son. He is all I live for now. My husband is dead. Killed, most likely, by someone who was angry at him for leaking information to the wrong people. We traveled south with a promise to leave the country; and now I am stuck here, living amongst people whose beliefs I can't adopt. They will win. And I can't . . . imagine what it would be like to live my whole life like this."

"Your son. Tell me about him." More than anything Sophie wanted to ask if the child was Michael's, but as she looked at Maria's face pity washed over Sophie. The pain was clear in Maria's gaze.

"We both fell in love with the same man. I will not deny the fact that I wanted Michael to be mine. And perhaps that could have happened, with more time. If you hadn't arrived."

"Your son . . . is it Michael's child?"

Maria shook her head. "No." She dropped her gaze. "No matter how I wish it was so." She turned again to the view of the moon and the sparkling lights of the city. "I gave everything for love. I would have given my body, too. But he didn't ask that of me. Michael wanted information. He wanted me to get close to a banker. I did what I had to. I did it to gain Michael's approval. In the end, I bore the child of a man I don't love. Michael had the information he needed, and then he was dead. I had no choice but to marry Emilio. I had no one to care for me. To be a single woman in that condition—it just isn't done."

"But I heard your sister at the funeral. She said the child belonged to Michael."

"I told her that because I was ashamed that I gave myself to Emilio. I wished it had been Michael's. I wanted it to be. For a time I thought he shared my affection, but now I know it was only part of his game. And in the end he was faithful to you. It was you he loved."

"I don't know about that. He lied to me, and then left me in the hands of soldiers with full expectations I would be imprisoned and killed. Then he flew off. . . . If a man loves you he doesn't leave you for dead."

"What are you talking about? He had no choice. He was shot."

"You don't know, do you?" Sophie rubbed her forehead. "Of course, you would have no reason to know. You were at the funeral. . . ."

Sophie looked at Maria Donita with a new perspective. Not as someone who had betrayed her, but someone who had also been betrayed.

"What are you saying?" Maria moved to a long stone bench and sat as if she knew the words to come would deeply affect her.

"Michael didn't die that day on the streets of Madrid. It was a setup—to make us believe he had. In order to follow . . ." Sophie paused, deciding to save Maria the burden of the whole story. "In order for him to follow another path."

"The gold . . . that's it. He succeeded. He got what he was after! And I helped him. He lives . . ." Maria broke down and began to cry.

Sophie understood too well the pain the young girl experienced. She approached and placed a hand on Maria's shoulder. "He lives, and he no doubt seeks me. I'm not sure if you want any connection with me—it could bring you even more trouble than you are in now. But I promise you this—when I do find a way out of this country, I'll make sure that you come along. I promise I'll help you and your son find a way to safety. You are as much a victim in this . . . this hunt for treasure as anyone."

The door opened, and a man walked out on the patio with a woman on his arm. Maria Donita quickly wiped her face. "It was so nice to meet you, Señorita Eleanor. I hope we meet again." She spoke loudly for the benefit of the couple. Then she reached down to give Sophie an embrace.

"Meet me tomorrow, at the lion fountain," Maria whispered in Sophie's ear. "We can talk more then." With that, she hurried away.

Sophie sat there a few minutes longer gazing over the mountains and the beautiful shimmer of moonlight upon tree limbs that danced in the breeze.

It was hard to believe that an unseen force could cause so much movement. What from a distance looked like ripples were actually gusts that could push a person any direction the wind desired.

She continued to ponder this as she returned to the fine party, attended by key people who hoped to someday conquer Spain. Though they were beautiful to gaze upon, an invisible death stirred within their souls. She prayed she and Maria could get out before they became the next victims.

Chapter Thirty-Three

They had ridden an entire day on the train from the coast of France. Now Petra stood in the stable on the outskirts of Paris brushing down Erro's side with long strokes. She noted the two marks on his shoulders—his brands that proved his bloodline, and to whom he belonged. The question was, what about her? To whom did she belong?

She had thought about this while they sailed. Many had asked Juan if she was his granddaughter. While he always answered yes, she knew it wasn't the truth.

Fear clung to her as she worried about Edelberto's cousin Michael—the one who'd kidnapped José. The one she'd stolen the horses from. José had insisted that Michael had nothing against her and would do her no harm, but she wasn't sure if she believed it. He'd shot at her, after all. If it hadn't been for Calisto, she'd be dead. What if Michael figured out who she was? Who would protect her?

Edelberto's father was out of town, but when he returned he'd likely welcome his two dedicated stable hands. He would rejoice that his horses were safe and sound—far away from the threats of Spain. But why should he care about her? Especially when she had nothing to offer.

It seemed foolish now that she'd tried to find Edelberto with the hopes of rekindling a friendship they started one afternoon in Madrid. They had only talked face-to-face for a few hours, years ago. So much—everything—had changed since then.

"I'm sorry, Erro, but this must be good-bye. I will never forget you."

The horse's ears flickered as if listening to her words.

"It is not fair to them. . . ."

From behind her, Petra heard someone clear his throat. She turned and noticed Edelberto standing there. Taller than she remembered, and so much more handsome.

"I see the old men taught you well. I remember even as a child going to the stalls and hearing them talk to their horses. Sometimes they talked about nothing of importance, but other times they poured out their hearts to the creatures. It was good for them. It's good for all of us to have someone to talk to."

"Edelberto . . . I didn't expect you here." She ran her fingers through her hair, wishing she'd taken time to look presentable.

"As soon as I heard, I came. Why didn't you come to my home?" He came a few steps closer. "Are you well?"

"Sí, as well as to be expected, I suppose."

"And your family?"

Petra lowered her eyes. She shook her head.

"I am so sorry to hear that. Some have endured so much heartache in Spain. Hopefully, things will be better now that you are in France."

He approached Erro and gave him a firm pat on the neck. "I remember when he was born. It was the first birth I witnessed. He's always been my favorite."

Petra smiled, daring to meet his gaze again. "Yes, mine too."

"So tell me, Petra. The things you spoke to the horse—was it just chitchat or something more?"

She tightened her lips and continued brushing.

"I don't think you have to tell Erro good-bye. You are welcome in my home for a time. But if that is not appropriate, I have many friends in the city. I have talked to a few families, and more than one offered you a place to stay."

"I could not impose on another's graciousness."

"But you wouldn't be imposing," he hurriedly continued. "One friend is a novelist, and she is eager to hear about your adventures in Spain. The other has horses in the country, and she is looking for someone to help care for them."

"Really?"

"Sí, and it will be not far from where Erro, Calisto, and the mares will be, which means I can visit often."

"You would do that? Visit me?"

"Of course. And during our days apart we can write letters. You are a fine letter writer."

Petra blushed. "I don't know about that. I agree to stay on one condition—"

"And what is that?" He came closer, and her heartbeat quickened.

"Promise you won't pity me. I have faced a lot, but if we renew our . . . friendship, I want you to care for me because of who I am, not what I've lived through."

Edelberto smiled. "That sounds wonderful to me. Of course, you have to promise to do the same."

"The same? What could you possibly have faced—safe and protected in France."

Laughter spilled from Edelberto's mouth. "You will see. It just might surprise you, señorita." He reached out for her hand. "Come now. I have someone eager to meet you—a family member who's invited us to lunch. We must not be late."

Michael reread the piece of paper before him. He'd gone through the stack of letters Philip's father had written him. He'd read the first one weeks ago, and he told himself he shouldn't read more. Yet he couldn't stop. The father's love for his son drew him. He read and reread the words, and as he did, Michael imagined *his* father had written the letters . . . to him.

The doorknob turned, and Michael quickly tucked the letter

back in his pocket, then retrieved the pistol from the desk and stood.

His uncle Adolfo entered and set a briefcase on the floor. He removed his hat and loosened his tie, then he turned—pausing as he noticed Michael and the gun.

"Did I surprise you, uncle?" Michael took a step forward. "Tell me, what surprised you more? Seeing me here . . . or seeing this gun in my hand? It tells you something, doesn't it? Your ruse is up."

Adolfo closed the door behind him. "Put that away. You'll frighten the help." He slowly walked to his desk and sat. Michael followed him with the gun. Adolfo sat with a long sigh. "So . . . tell me, what brings you to this?" He nodded at the gun.

Michael rubbed his chin. "Maybe that I talked to José. He told me who Walt was working for—told me your plan had been to steal the gold from me all along."

Adolfo shrugged. "Yes, well, what else could I do? What type of uncle would I be if I turned you against your own parents? Besides, Walt had a second mission while he was following you . . . and that was to make sure you were safe."

Laughter burst from Michael's lips. "How kind of you! Steal from my nephew, Walt, but don't kill him! Oh, yes, and make sure no one else kills him."

Adolfo leaned back in his chair. "Michael, there is something you should know. Something that might make sense of this—then maybe you will understand my heart. I not only did this for you and for Walt. I did this for our family."

"Really? I love a good story—go ahead." He pulled a chair across from his uncle and sat.

"Michael . . . Walt is your brother. Your father's child, conceived before he met your mother."

Michael would have laughed if it were not for the serious expression on his uncle's face. His mind flashed back to a time in Boston when he was still a teenager. Heaviness settled in his chest as he remembered his mother weeping. When he'd questioned her, she told him to ask his father about it.

Michael's knees trembled. He'd never asked. But now he knew.

"All Walt wanted was a relationship with his family, but he was never given the chance. He was bright and observant, yet lonely. We were a perfect match. We built a friendship and later sought a treasure together. Your mother is a wise woman, but she doesn't have the insight I have. She doesn't have the heart for adventure. My goal was never to steal all the gold—simply seven coins. Would you like to hear the story?"

Michael nodded, and the tale turned into something from a dime novel. When Adolfo finished, Michael lowered his gun. Then he stood. "I'm not sure I believe you."

"Ask your mother. She can confirm that Walt is your brother . . . and the rest, I suppose, you'll just have to trust me about."

Laughter from outside met his ears, and Michael looked out the window. It was Edelberto and a young woman, exiting the front doors. They talked and laughed as they walked through the courtyard toward the street. Her laughter reminded Michael of another.

"What do you know about Sophie?" Michael looked to his uncle just in time to see his eyes dart to his briefcase.

His uncle rose. "I know she is well."

Michael lifted the gun again; then he hurried to the briefcase. "Wonderful. I'll take this, thank you."

"Michael, no!"

Michael pointed the gun at his uncle's chest.

Adolfo backed away and then collapsed into the chair. "Please, whatever you do, do not hurt your brother. He . . . Walt did nothing to deserve the heartache your father has given him."

Adolfo took a step forward, and Michael cocked the trigger.

"You wouldn't shoot your uncle, would you?"

"Why not? There is a priest downstairs to give you your last rites . . . and absolve your sins before you pass away." Michael's hands shook, and then he lowered the pistol. "But I will not. I will spare you. But I do recommend you ask the priest if he will take your confession. With that story you've just told, and the mission you've orchestrated, I believe you've broken nearly every one of the commandments." And with the briefcase in his hand, Michael hurried away.

❖ ❖ ❖

Michael looked across the room to where his mother sat. She'd come to France for the gold he promised, and remained . . . waiting for him to come through. Michael had come to talk to her, but instead he'd discovered she already had company.

Edelberto was there with the young woman. She was too thin, too young, and trembled like a leaf every time someone looked at her. What did Edelberto see in her?

His mother cast him a simple glance. "Michael, we just finished lunch, but there is more in the kitchen—just ask the help." She offered him a quick hug.

"I'm fine. I just want to talk when you're through."

He could tell from her face his mother was in one of her good moods. Those who knew her saw her this way most of the time. Those who knew her *well* realized another lurked behind her smile.

"You poor thing. You're all alone in this world?" His mother moved to the sofa and put her arm around the girl's shoulders. "Your name is Petra, right?"

Petra nodded. She glanced at Michael from the corner of her eyes, but didn't say a word. She looked familiar, and Michael wondered if he'd seen her with Edelberto before.

"I remember what it was like to lose my mother," his mother continued. "My father did the best he could, but it was my brother, Adolfo, who understood me the best. Since I was a child he encouraged me. He told me I was beautiful and wonderful. Everyone should have that voice in their head."

His mother turned and looked out the window. Michael followed her gaze. As far as he could see, beautiful estates stretched in every direction.

His mother sighed. "Of course, one always tries to prove herself. And yet, when one looks in the mirror it's easier to spot faults rather than strengths—at least in my case."

Michael lifted one eyebrow and glanced at his mother. She played many games, did many things to win the approval of others, and he waited. Waited for the charade to end. Waited for her true motivation to come out.

"Come, Petra. Follow me. I have so many clothes." His mother rose. "Too many to wear. I think I can have some tailored to fit you. You are a beautiful girl. So beautiful. And you've seen too many hard things. . . ."

Michael was sure now that his mother had forgotten he was in the room, for she drew the girl to her and placed her arms around her. With a quiet sob, Petra placed her head on his mother's shoulders. And then, for the first time in his life, Michael noticed tears in his mother's eyes, too.

"Shhh, I have searched the world. I have obtained all I thought I desired, but I never found anything to replace my mother. To you . . . I will . . . well, I would like to be here for you," his mother said.

Michael rose in disgust. He stalked from the room, trying to ignore the feeling of rejection. He returned to his automobile, glancing at the briefcase he'd placed on the seat . . . and suddenly he knew what he had to do.

Chapter Thirty-Four

Ramona noticed how José's eyes scanned the hills as they hiked the mountain, heading for the caves he knew well. She didn't care about the hot sun or steep climb. She remained thankful they were together. But at the sound of a branch breaking in the small forest of trees, José paused, lifting his hand to quiet her. After a minute he continued on, holding his rifle erect and pointing it ahead of them.

"José, are you looking for someone? Michael? Or do you think the Fascists have come into the mountains?"

"No, that is not what I'm worried about. People have lived in these hills for years. There are small mining camps all over—some with women and children. But also within these hills are the remnants of a defeated army. Many of the men were not political to start with, but since they fought to protect their land, they can't return. They fight simply because they have no place to go. They have no training, no supplies, no arms caches, no radios. They form small guerilla troops, independent of the other. I've heard the same has happened in the south of Spain, around Granada, just as it has here in the Basque region."

"Why don't we join them? We can offer our help and receive theirs?"

"No, that isn't a good idea. You never know who is a true friend and who is not. I must remain on constant guard, and as hard as it is, I think we're better off on our own."

"But it seems if we work together, we could take turns on guard duty or finding food."

"The problem is knowing whom to trust. If someone happens to leave for the day, we'd have no idea if he was visiting his girlfriend or chatting with the *guardia civil.*" He shook his head. "I've heard of horrible things. Men murdered by those they believed were friends. No, our only hope is the sierra."

Hours later, as Ramona looked at the chunk of meat cooking over the open flame, she thought she would be ill. José didn't seem to mind eating meat night after night—the bounty of his hunting skills—but Ramona would give anything for fresh-baked churros, an artichoke, maybe even a fresh orange for dessert.

She noted José's gaze on her as she picked at her portion.

"You okay?" he asked.

"Sí, I am fine."

"You look a little thin. I notice you cut another notch in your belt."

"Well, it's all this hiking. It's good for me. I'm in the best shape of my life."

"A husband is supposed to care for his wife. I have failed much in that department."

Ramona scooted closer, balanced the tin plate on her knees, and reached for José's hand. "I am thankful God brought you back from the dead. You care for me well. Where would I be if you hadn't found me? I might still be running from the Fascists, or locked up in one of those concentration camps I've heard Franco has set up for those who've been brave enough to oppose him."

"Yes, well, providing you shelter and a fine meal is the least I can do." José chuckled.

Ramona took a large bite of her meat. "At least I have food. There are many others who do not."

Suddenly a noise came from the woods—the sound of someone running through the undergrowth. José grabbed his rifle and stood.

A gray-haired man darted into their campsite, and José took aim. "Who are you? What do you want?"

Instead of answering, the man turned to Ramona. "I hear you are a nurse. My son is injured. Please, can you tend him?"

José took a step forward. "How do you know this?"

"How could we not? I myself have lived in these mountains since I was a boy. Of course, with the battles below, many more have sought safety here. Everyone who enters these mountains is watched. I myself saw the way the señora tended the horses."

Ramona turned to José. "It is an answer to prayer. I prayed I could help."

The old man approached, smiling. "Señora, you are like an angel. A gift to us. Come with me if you will. I am afraid my son will die without care."

He took them a few miles away to some type of mining camp in the mountains. Ramona looked around and tried to imagine how someone could live in such a place his whole life. She also wondered what they thought of their hills filling with guerilla soldiers and others attempting to hide from the Fascists.

José waited outside the cabin, watching and guarding, while the man led her up the steps to the porch. She followed him inside. A woman greeted her and made the sign of a cross, muttering a prayer of thanksgiving under her breath.

The floor was tiled, even the closet. The man got on his knees and lifted what looked like a trapdoor.

"We dug a tunnel between our home and the barn. Three men sleep here at night. The other two are gone for the day, scouting the hills and watching out for us."

It took a moment for Ramona's eyes to adjust to the dim light cast by a lone lantern. She climbed into the hole. It was no bigger than the interior of an automobile. The young man lay next to a radio with towels wrapped around it to muffle the sound. A small stack of books sat next to the radio.

From the odor of the space she knew the infection was worse than he'd explained to her. She lifted the man's hand and set it on her lap so she could get a better look at his arm. The man moaned with the slightest movement.

"Shh." She hushed him. "It will be fine. I simply need a look."

He gritted his teeth and nodded. Sweat covered his forehead.

Slowly, gingerly, Ramona unwrapped the bandages. "So, how long have you been staying down here?" she asked, more to get his attention away from the pain than anything.

"Since the fall of Bilbao. We sta–started with a hole under the . . . the haystack. But then we h–heard they burned barns. We . . . I've been digging this out and living down here . . . since then."

The closer she got to the wound, the more dried blood she found, and under that, pus. The odor grew stronger, and she didn't need to finish unwrapping to know what she needed to do.

"Well, now that I've had a look . . . I just need to get some things ready before I can take care of you."

She climbed out of the hole and wiped her dirty hands on her equally dirty coveralls. Her eyes darted to the young man's parents and then to José, who had come inside. "I'm going to need your help. His arm . . . it needs to come off at the elbow."

The mother lifted her arms to the air and let out a wail.

"Are you sure? Isn't there anything else you can do?" the father pleaded with his hands folded, as if in prayer.

"I'm afraid not. The infection has set in too deep. If we don't take care of it right away, your son will be dead within a couple of days. Even now it's difficult to know how much infection has already gone into his system."

"Have you done such a thing before?" The woman's eyes were filled with fear.

"Unfortunately, more times than I'd like to remember. At first I assisted the doctors, but after awhile . . ." Ramona shook her head as if ridding herself of a memory. "Well, we nurses had to do more than we were ever trained for. We had no choice. There were so many. . . . And the more the war progressed, the fewer supplies we had. Soon any clean room with minimal instruments would do."

"What do you need?" the father asked.

"I can make you a list . . . but where in the world will you find these items? It's not as simple as finding a few herbs from the woods. I—"

"I'll do it." José's voice interrupted.

She turned to him and saw the compassion in his gaze. "Are you sure? Where will you look?"

"That is for me to worry about. I only want you to think about caring for him."

"Fine." Ramona ripped a page from one of the books and used a pen and ink to write down the items she needed.

She handed the list to José with a kiss. She didn't need to hear the details to know finding the items would be dangerous.

"I'm proud of you," she said.

"All I can do is try. Pray, my dear wife, that I succeed." And with that José hurried from the room.

He returned the next morning with everything on the list. "The nearest miner's first-aid station—it is not too far. I found friends there. And . . . your supplies."

Ramona thanked him and set to work. José stayed by her side through the whole procedure. He helped to comfort the young man's parents, and he assured them they would be back to check on him—to make sure he was still well in a couple of days.

When she walked from the cottage later in the afternoon, José turned to her with a smile. "While I was out, I discovered something else. Come . . . it is a surprise."

José took her hand and led her through the woods. It didn't matter that she was tired and dirty. It didn't matter that she was covered with blood. Her husband led her as if she were a princess, and he was a king, and they were about to find a castle on the edge of the forest where they would live happily ever after.

Ramona sighed. If only it could be so.

Chapter Thirty-Five

José led Ramona inside a windowless room—a small cave apartment—and spread his arms, as if it were the bridal suite at a fine hotel. There was only one piece of furniture—a large iron bed smothered with goatskins. She smiled, thinking it was the most beautiful bed she'd ever seen.

The next day they were met by a young boy who wore a poncho of rabbit skins. He gingerly led them toward a creek were a small band of men waited. As the minutes ticked by, another man joined, then another. Then three men were followed by five more, coming out of the hills. Ramona couldn't believe the sight. Just days ago, when they'd walked through the forests, she'd felt so alone. Now, she wondered how many eyes had watched their trek.

On either side of the group men perched on their legs, with straight backs and guns ready like sentries. Ramona drew up her knees to her chest and blew into her cupped hands, hoping to warm them.

"Señora," a man said, and offered her a chunk of dark bread.

Though she knew it was provided for the man by a wife or a sister back in the valley, or perhaps in one of the mining camps, she could not resist. She liked to think she was protecting his pride, but it was truly her hunger that forced her to accept the gift.

"Thank you."

She took a bite and then broke off a chunk for José. She offered it to him, but he shook his head. She knew he was hungry; she could see the familiar look in his eyes. But he cared more for her than his own stomach.

"God has sent us a gift." One man's voice rose among the rest. "For so long we have fought, and we've seen many die. But today we have an angel of mercy who will heal our wounds." He pointed to Ramona. "So fight hard, men, fight brave. For we now have hope on our side!"

"Don't you think I should actually offer some help before they call me an 'angel of mercy'?" Ramona murmured to José.

He took her hand and squeezed; then he lifted her fingers to his lips and kissed them. "They know. To meet you is to know. . . ."

Ramona felt joy settle over her. One that surpassed any since this war had begun. They were together . . . not just the two of them, but many. This was *their* fight. And she knew *this* was exactly where God wanted her, trusting in Him no matter the forces that waged around her.

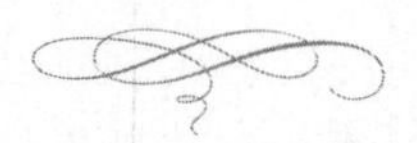

Deion met a new group of Spanish men the first night he returned to the trenches. The battalion returned to the front lines in the middle of August, taking positions outside Azaila. They planned to begin a new offensive in Aragon, which would take pressure off the Euzkadi and Asturian fronts—two areas under siege by Franco's legions.

But before the first shot was fired, Deion was called back to the command center.

His commander approached him with quickened steps. "We need you to drive a doctor and a nurse to Barcelona. They seek medical supplies for the hospital."

Deion heard footsteps behind him and turned to see Gwen smiling at him. He almost thought he was dreaming.

"And after you drive them there," the commander continued, "you will return home."

"Home?" Deion scratched his forehead—the word seemed unfamiliar.

Gwen touched his arms, and he could read an apology in her gaze. "They've asked me to go back—after I find supplies. They're looking for someone to go back and tell the news of Spain. Someone who has been here, to share what they've seen. I told them I'd go if I found you. And you could go with me. We can travel together—raise money and help the cause."

Deion straightened his shoulders. "But what if I told 'em the war isn't over yet—and I want to stay?"

Her smile fell.

"The truth is, we could you use more at home," Steve Nelson interrupted. "To tell others of your fight. To get them to send more help to Spain. Few have witnessed as many battles as you and made it through. You will be leaving tonight for Barcelona, and taking a ship from there."

Deion nodded his answer, and Gwen took his hand. He was going home. Going to urge others to help their fight. Somehow it seemed good. It seemed right. He squeezed Gwen's hand.

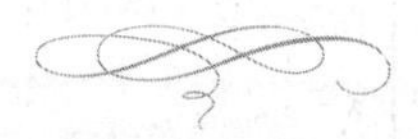

Sophie chatted with Maria as they walked. They laughed as baby Carlito clapped his hands at the sight of the water.

"I think he wants to jump in," Maria commented, offering her son a kiss on his cheek. He had curly black hair and large, dark eyes. Sophie thought he was the sweetest baby she'd ever seen.

Sophie had sent word to Walt that there would be two more passengers when they left. Walt had sent a message back for her to meet him in the tunnel this evening. Sophie only hoped he didn't argue. She couldn't bear the thought of telling Maria they couldn't help her.

They strolled in front of the Hall of the Ambassadors. A long pool of water stretched half the length of a football field. On either side of the pool, myrtle trees stood. And at the end of the Hall of Ambassadors a statue sat cross-legged. It was said he could dispense favors or dispense death to those who asked it of him. Sophie knew no idol held such power, but she whispered a prayer that God would hear her plea for this mother and child.

In the distance, a man entered the courtyard. He was too far away for her to recognize his face—but his walk, his body structure, even his slight limp caused Sophie to pause in her tracks. "Ritter," she whispered.

"I'm sorry; what did you say?" Maria asked.

"That man." Sophie turned her back to him before he could see her. "I know him."

"The German? That's Hermann von Bachman—he's a German advisor. I heard some friends talking last night, and it seems he's here for a short stay before heading to South America. When did you meet him?"

"South America? Hermann? No, never mind. I'm mistaken. I thought he was someone else."

Sophie turned and noticed Ritter approaching. She knew better than to run, for others mingled in the garden. Instead she placed a hand on her stomach and took a deep breath. *Don't panic,* she told herself. Apparently Ritter was in hiding once again. He had as much to fear from her as she did from him.

Maria reached out her hand. In her arms Carlito cooed. "Hermann, I'd like you to meet Eleanor."

Ritter stretched out his hand. "Eleanor?"

She took his hand and bobbed a curtsey. "Hermann . . . so nice to meet you."

Sophie's heartbeat quickened. Perhaps their way of escape was going to come from a very unlikely source.

"Hermann, would you like to walk with us?"

"Thank you for the offer, but I won't be here long. Perhaps we can talk another time? To share how we both ended up here. Talk about what we seek in Spain?" His gaze fixed on Sophie.

"Yes, I would like that very much." She touched his arm with her hand. "Let's make sure that happens, shall we?"

❖ ❖ ❖

Sophie waited impatiently at the opening of the tunnel. She paced back and forth, eager to tell Walt her news. Finally she heard footsteps, and she nearly threw herself into Walt's arms. "I've found it! I know how we can get out."

She spent the next ten minutes explaining how she knew Ritter, and her plan for their escape.

"Are you telling me I should approach a German pilot, who once deceived you, and ask him to help ferry priceless gold out of the country?"

"Anyone can be bought," Sophie insisted. "And he's hiding too. He used a different name, Hermann von Bachman. . . . I think he might be searching for the gold, too. I heard he plans to travel to South America. And while I don't completely trust him, I know there is a softer side to Ritter. I saw in his eyes he still considers me a friend."

"Hmm." Walt scratched his head.

"Of course, if you have a better idea, let me know," she added. "For now it's something to consider."

Walt sighed. "Well, I suppose it wouldn't hurt. I have no other answer." He placed a hand on her arm. "I'll be in touch. You better hurry back now."

"Thank you, Walt." She reached to give him a hug, nearly knocking off his hat. "I'll meet you here tomorrow. Maybe we'll know something then."

"Let's hope so. It seems the stakes are rising with each day that passes." He sighed. "And just think—for so long I was only concerned about a few coins."

Chapter Thirty-Six

Walt ascended two flights of cement stairs, then used his key on the door of the studio apartment rented by James Kimmel. He knew there could be people still watching this apartment. James Kimmel had many enemies, but also many friends. Maybe in Granada the latter still outweighed the former.

The room was nothing much to look at. Dark, dusty, dank smelling. Yet Walt tossed his suitcase on the sagging bed, hardly noticing the dimness as he strode to the small window and opened it, not appreciating the view outside.

He moved to the mirror, almost not recognizing himself. He looked old and ragged. The gray that had appeared at his temples gave him pause. His eyes reflected his weariness. Had he come this far only to fail?

He'd created a spider's web of people and layers of stories. For a time he'd kept each straight. He'd known who worked for whom and what they offered to him, and to Adolfo. Now Walt's mind was tired. He couldn't explain it other than that. He even questioned whether the treasure would be worth the cost. Maybe it too was as fictional as the personalities he'd created for his cover. Was it no more than a dream, an illusion he'd formed in hopes of gaining the approval of his family? In hopes there was something worth living for?

He thought about Sophie and her trust that God protected them . . . protected him. The change in her hadn't happened overnight, but she had a deep inner peace he envied. And at this point in his journey, it almost seemed what Sophie possessed was greater than any treasure cast by man or forged by human hands.

"I don't even know where to begin," Walt muttered to the reflection in the mirror.

Just accept and believe.

It was Sophie's voice that filled his thoughts. *Surrender . . . trust.*

He laughed at the words she offered. To others that may seem easy, but for someone who'd spent the last three years controlling not only each move he made but those of the pawns he'd set in place, it seemed beyond his ability. He had created a life of second-guessing everyone, running from one end of Spain to the other to stay ahead.

For years he'd campaigned to find the treasure that would cause this world—and his father—to take notice. When it was clear the Spanish conflict would erupt, he'd justified his work by arranging with Adolfo to make sure that the people of Spain would receive the majority of the stolen wealth. He hoped the funds the treasure promised could help the poorest among them.

But maybe that was simply an excuse too. Because deep down Walt somehow felt he was on the wrong side—not in the fight of the Nationalists against the Republicans, but in the fight between light and darkness.

He ignored his troubled gaze in the mirror and raked his fingers through his hair. Then he sat upon the bed, and his eyes focused on the few rays of light filtering into the room.

Walt had sent a message to the name Sophie had given him, and he was pleased to see the tall, blond German striding into the quaint café. The German's physical appearance could not be denied. Many women turned his direction when he entered, including a beautiful blonde at the bar. She quickly looked away when she noted Walt's gaze, blushing over the fact she'd been caught with a gaping mouth.

Ritter nodded to Walt, then approached.

"Herr von Bachman." Walt rose and shook his hand.

A twinkle lit Ritter's blue eyes. "Sophie referred to you as James Kimmel, the Fascist reporter." He nodded. "I've been a fan of yours since you wrote that piece about the Reds burning Guernica from the ground. Of course, we both know that is only one of your covers."

Walt shrugged. "What can I say? The truth always comes out."

Ritter sat and ordered a drink, then turned his attention back to Walt. "So, your note said you had a proposal for me?"

"First, I want to know how much you know about Spanish gold."

Ritter pursed his lips. "I know there is word of a hidden treasure in South America . . . or maybe that is just a fairy tale. I have come here to discover more about that very thing."

Walt felt the weight of the five coins in his pocket. "Yes, I've heard that too. But as I've checked into it . . . well, I personally believe it is legend. Nothing more." He leaned forward, steepling his fingers on the table in front of him. "But there is another treasure—closer and more precious. One already discovered. The problem is, I need a way to get it out of the country. I'm looking for someone to help me. How hard would it be for you to secure a transport plane?"

"And what would I receive for my efforts?"

"More wealth than you could imagine."

Ritter cleared his throat. "And you think I can be trusted? How do you know that I wouldn't take it all for myself?"

"I don't. But I do know you're hiding something. You've already turned over your key to the room at Alhambra. It would only take one phone call from me to let Göring's office know you aren't dead, as they assume."

Ritter chuckled. "You've done your homework. I'm impressed!"

"I wouldn't have made it this far without my research skills.

Besides, for some reason Sophie believes there is a good soul beneath that tough exterior."

Ritter ran a hand down his face. "She said that?"

"Yes, she did."

"Sophie is a dear girl, but as we all know, friendships change with the tide of war and the needs of the players."

"Sí, you are right. So how much will it take for you to consider rekindling those embers of friendship?"

"Enough that I will no longer be at the bidding of others. Enough to be in control of my own destiny and support a future wife and children." He lowered his gaze. "And enough to walk away. To start over."

"Fine. That can be arranged." Walt leaned close. "Now . . . here is what I need from you."

Sophie hurried down the tunnel with eager steps, hoping that Walt waited at the end with good news.

When she rounded the last corner, she saw him standing in the tunnel opening. He held a rifle in his hands as he scoured the area with his eyes.

"Did you talk to Ritter? I didn't see him today around the castle grounds. I was hoping—"

"He's considering it," Walt interrupted. "Actually, more than considering it. He likes the idea. He's going to check out a few of the airfields in the area to see what he can find. It's a heavy load—one larger than most transport planes can handle. But he's hopeful."

She studied Walt closer and noticed dark circles under his eyes. She patted his hand. "Are you okay? You don't look so well."

"Tired, that's all. Ready for this thing to be over."

"Me too. I miss . . . well, that's not important now." She thought of Philip and considered asking about him, but changed her mind. "Get some sleep. We'll have plenty of time to catch up on the latest news in a few days."

"I hope so." Walt offered a tired smile. "You can't imagine how much I hope so."

Sophie watched him walk away; then she turned to head back up the tunnel. She'd only gone a few steps when she heard footsteps behind her. Someone touched her arm.

Sophie sucked in a breath and turned, then relaxed when she saw who it was. "Philip!" She smiled as he swept her into his arms.

"I'm sorry, Sophie. I know you have work to do. But I had to come. I miss you." He placed a kiss upon her head.

"I miss you, too. I just talked to Walt. . . . I think I've found a way for us to escape—"

The sound of a rifle being cocked interrupted her words. She turned to see a soldier with a rifle pointed at them. Philip released her and reached for his gun.

The soldier lifted his weapon. "I wouldn't do that if I were you, señor!"

Three more men, all wearing Nationalist uniforms, emerged from deeper in the tunnel.

One man looked familiar; in fact, Sophie was sure she'd danced with him on one occasion.

"We have watched you, señorita. When our papers and maps started disappearing, we knew we had a traitor in our midst." He motioned for the men, and they grabbed her arms, pulling them behind her back and snapping handcuffs in place. They did the same with Philip.

"But look here," the soldier exclaimed. "Today is our lucky day! For it seems we caught not one, but two foxes in our trap."

Chapter Thirty-Seven

Walt approached the waiting truck, but his steps slowed when he noticed an automobile parked to the side. Two men stood beside it under the light of a street lantern. It was obvious they wanted to be seen.

Walt's heart pounded, and he stopped in his tracks. *Michael.* He pulled his rifle closer to his chest, tightening his grip.

Michael approached Walt. He narrowed his gaze and studied Walt's features. Then he nodded, as if in recognition. "I hear you've been following me."

"I was."

"But not now?"

"I have no need."

"I know. Maybe that's because you have what you were after." Michael looked at his own hands, then Walt's. "I always wondered how you kept up with me. I never understood it. It was as if you could read my thoughts."

"Maybe I could. Or . . . rather, maybe I just pondered what I would do if I were in your shoes."

"Really?"

"Yes, I imagined how I would steal the gold. Where I would go. Who I would seek help from."

"And it worked?"

"I think the results prove so."

"Until the end. You surprise me, Walt . . . Walter. I thought you'd be long gone by now. I read about the seven coins. Five of which you have. My uncle kept detailed notes. You could have left long ago. You have what you wanted."

"My focus changed."

"Because of Sophie. And Philip." He spat their names. "I would have left—"

The sound of a man's hurried footsteps interrupted Michael's words.

Salvador approached. "Walt, come quick! They've been captured!"

"Who?"

Cesar lifted a pistol and pointed it at Salvador's chest.

"Sophie and Philip," Salvador continued.

Walt cursed. "Philip? What was he doing? I thought he had a mission tonight."

"He canceled. He said he had to talk to Sophie—convinced me to bring him."

Fury flashed in Michael's gaze, and he turned to Cesar. "Let's go."

"Where to?" Walt asked.

"To save Sophie, that's where."

"It's not going to happen."

Michael and Cesar climbed into their car, and Michael started the engine.

"Wait! We need to talk!" Walt called. "To figure out a plan."

"Talk? We don't have time to talk," Michael shouted through the open window. "Do you know how these soldiers operate? They worked hard to take control of this part of Spain. And even harder to keep it."

"Yes, but—" Walt took a step back. "I know what to do. Leave Sophie to me. It's the only way!"

Walt watched as Michael sped away. He lowered his head in defeat.

⁂ ⁂ ⁂

Instead of heading to town, the truck wound up a steep mountain hill through the dark night. Clouds covered the moonlight, and Sophie strained to see Philip's face.

"Where are we going?" she asked. Her body tossed from side to side on the wooden bench in the back of the canvas-covered truck bed.

"Silence!" The young soldier pointed the gun her direction. He looked like dozens of other soldiers she'd seen, helped, painted. Only the uniform was different—and his allegiance.

She bit her lip, and her eyes met Philip's. She could see the apology in his gaze.

The truck pulled over, and Sophie stood.

"Not you." The soldier pushed her to the floor of the truck.

Two others yanked Philip to his feet and pulled him out of the truck.

"Sophie, I love you. No matter what happens . . . remember that!"

"Quiet!" One of the soldiers slammed the butt of the rifle into Philip's face. It gave a horrific *crack*, and blood spurted from his mouth.

She yanked on the handcuffs in front of her, but it did no good. They were locked securely and held together by a thick, heavy chain. She rose again and tried to push past the soldier in the back of the truck. "Where are you taking him? What are you doing?"

"I said *quiet*!" The soldier pushed her back. Her head cracked against the bench as she fell, and Sophie fought to keep consciousness. The light faded even more, and then the soldier neared. His angry face distorted her view. He gave her a quick kick in the ribs.

Sophie gasped as pain shot up her side. A moan escaped her lips. Through her blurry vision, she watched in disbelief as another automobile sped up the winding road and stopped. The guards looked at each other. Surprise registered on their faces.

Two men jumped from the car. She recognized both of them.

"Michael?" Sophie spoke his name. She could see Philip looking at her, pain in his expression.

"Silence!" The same soldier covered Sophie's mouth with his hand.

One of the soldiers holding Philip's arm seemed to recognize Michael.

"Señor Michael. I haven't seen you—"

"In months, I know, but I need a favor. I want the woman." Michael's voice was firm.

"Sorry. I have a direct order. I will lose my own head if I do not bring her in. She made a fool of all of us—passed on vital information."

Michael refused to meet Sophie's gaze. "If you can't grant that request, I ask another."

"Sí, señor." The soldier's head bobbed, hoping to please.

Michael pointed to Philip. "This man has harmed me. He's taken what was most precious to me. I want revenge." Michael opened his hand to Cesar, and Cesar passed him the pistol with a smile.

Sophie shook her head, trying to free the man's hand from over her mouth. His grip was too strong. She struggled harder and felt tears springing to her eyes.

Michael, no!

Michael motioned to the shovel in one of the soldier's hands. "Cesar, grab it. I've learned never to leave my dirty work unfinished."

Cesar approached, lifted the shovel, and forced the handle into Philip's back.

Philip cried out, then crumbled to the ground. Sophie looked away. She couldn't watch—couldn't believe what was happening. It was all her fault.

Hatred coursed through her like she'd never felt. Hatred greater than any love she'd ever felt for Michael.

Michael grabbed one of Philip's arms, Cesar the other.

She closed her eyes but could still hear the sound of Philip's feet being dragged into the forested area beside the road.

A minute later, the sound of three gunshots split the air.

"Sophie!" Philip screamed once. And then silence.

Sophie's whole body trembled. She fell to the bed of the truck and curled up in a little ball. More than anything she wished her hands were free so she could cover her ears. Worse than the gunshots were the sounds of the shovel's head penetrating the ground.

❖ ❖ ❖

The guard pushed her into the tiny, dark cell, and Sophie collapsed to the ground. Sobs shook her body.

Philip.

The tears came, and she couldn't stop them. The sound of those three gunshots rang in her head. Over and over.

"Why, God? Why did You bring me here?" She curled up in a ball and tried to block out the world. "I never wanted this. I never asked for this."

She thought about Michael and swore to herself she'd hate him until the day she died, which she knew might be this very day. She worried about Walt and wondered what part he'd played in all this. She wondered if he too had been captured. If he too had died like Philip. Or if he would.

Nothing mattered anymore. Not the gold. Not Spain. Not her life. She glanced around at the small cell and considered her fate. She'd come for Michael . . . she'd tried to give all she could to help. And now . . .

Sobs shook her body. "Why, God, why?"

The answer that came to her soul wasn't what she expected.

Why not?

Why not her? Many had lost so much. Who was she to think she deserved anything different? Jesus had offered her salvation, but He never promised an easy life.

Sobs shook her shoulders again. She held her ribs, sure they were broken. She gasped for a breath of the filthy air.

Images filled her mind. Of Philip when she first saw him in the foxhole, and the surprised look on his face when he noticed a woman on the battlefield. The tenderness as he'd carried injured José. Their talks. Their laughter and the way he had watched her as she painted the soldiers at the field hospital, months ago.

And finally she thought of the last kiss he'd placed upon her head only hours ago.

The cell had no bed, so she curled in a ball on the filthy floor that smelled of urine. The shouts of guards carried down the halls. From somewhere a man's pained screams split the air. It was the most horrific cry she'd ever heard.

Sophie drifted off in a fitful sleep, not caring if she ever awoke. Not caring about anything. Knowing all was lost.

Chapter Thirty-Eight

The sound of the solid metal door opening pulled Sophie from her fitful sleep. She'd woken throughout the night to the sound of the tortured man's screams, but they were no worse than the demons that danced in her nightmares. No worse than the memory of Philip's last cries.

"Señorita." It was the guard's voice.

She lifted her head and pushed her hair back from her face, wincing at the pain that shot through her side. It was a different guard from the one last night. And if she weren't mistaken, his eyes hinted of compassion.

He opened the door wider. "I have come to tell you that you are free to go."

"What do you mean?"

"We thought we had captured a key spy when we got you, but we were mistaken. There will be a truck to drive you out of town today. The ship will be waiting on the coast. It will take you to France. You will not be stopped."

"I don't understand."

"The man we've sought the whole time . . . he has made a trade."

"A trade? Are you talking about—?" She sealed her lips, not wanting to incriminate herself. Or her friend. Maybe this was their plan all along.

He smiled. "You are learning. The trade was one spy for another. A small pawn for, well, one greater."

She stood, brushing the filth from her clothes. "I still don't understand."

"I believe you know him as Walt Block. But to us he has many names."

Sophie eyed the open door, yet heaviness settled on her heart.

"You have Walt?"

"Did you not hear the screams of pain from the dungeon?" The guard chuckled, and his gaze hardened. "I thought you would recognize your *friend*."

He stepped forward and took Sophie's face in his hands, leaning close. His breath smelled of liquor. She tried to turn her head, but his grip was strong.

"If I had a choice, I would keep you both. But it was not my decision to make. You are free to go. I will give you a ride myself."

"Can I see him before I leave? Can I see Walt?"

"No. I would let you. But he doesn't want you to see him . . . in such a state."

Sophie swallowed hard. It pained her even more to realize the cries had been those of her friend, her rescuer. A sob escaped her lips, and she clung to the wall and then slid to the floor, wishing she could die where she lay.

Sophie found herself in the same truck as last night; only this time she sat in the passenger's seat. She had refused to leave—after all, where could she go? What did she have without those two men? The guard didn't listen to her pleas.

"Walk away or die. It is your choice," he stated firmly.

The truck drove through town, and in the bright morning sunlight she saw men and women walking to the market as if it were any other day. One woman laughed at her child as she hoisted him onto her hip. The sound of the child's laughter joining his mother's caused Sophie's stomach to turn as the truck rumbled past.

Sophie thought of Maria Donita—yet another person she'd failed. As if Walt and Philip were not enough.

I can't go on anymore. I don't want to live with this pain.

The truck exited town. She refused to turn and glance at the gleaming castle on the hill. Not only was she leaving Granada behind; she was leaving all hope. Sophie slumped lower in her seat, when suddenly gunfire sounded. Bullets hit the cab, and the sound of breaking glass filled her ears.

She screamed and tossed her aching body onto the floor of the cab.

Isn't it enough that You let me be defeated? Must You kill me, too!

The driver shouted in surprise and then in pain. She looked over and saw a bright red spot on his shoulder. In agony, he released the steering wheel just as the truck sped around a curve.

"Dear God!" Sophie cried, reaching for the steering wheel. She was too slow. The truck missed the curve and plowed into a field of thick brush. Her body slammed forward, and she hit the dashboard of the truck. Then only blackness.

Sophie awoke to find herself hanging halfway out the passenger door. Her gaze darted to the driver, and she noticed a large gash on his forehead. His eyes were wide—staring into the broken windshield, and she knew he was dead.

A moan escaped her lips, and the driver's face blurred. Everything around her faded to gray, then black.

Something stirred outside the truck. She heard the sound of the passenger door opening, and then a voice. "Here, let me help you."

She felt her body being dragged, then lifted.

If Sophie hadn't known Michael's voice so well, she would have thought she had died. She would have imagined it was an angel who carried her to her Maker.

She tried to focus her mind. "Are you here . . . to kill me?"

"No, Sophie." Another voice broke through. One she also knew well. "He's here to help."

Sophie opened her eyes. "Philip." She gasped for breath and then coughed.

"I'm here. And you . . . you'll be okay."

"But . . . but . . ." She looked at Michael. "You took him away. You killed Philip. I heard the gunshots. The sounds of the shovel."

Michael smiled. "Do you think I do not know how to fake a death? To make it believable?"

"He told me to play along," Philip explained. "Michael saved me, because he needed my help to save *you*."

Instead of meeting her gaze, Michael turned his look to Philip. "Philip will never abandon you," he said, emotion choking his voice. "Even until the last moment—when he was sure he was about to die—he pleaded for *your* life. Not his own."

Her eyelids felt as if they weighed a hundred pounds each, and she let them flutter closed. "Walt," she whispered.

"We know." Philip's voice was compassionate. "By the time we returned to the camp, he'd already turned himself in."

"He traded himself . . . for me." She felt a tear escape and journey down her cheek.

"I know, but we'll see what we can do."

"Dear Walt," she muttered again. Sophie felt her body being lifted. She didn't know if it was Philip or Michael who carried her. But she focused on the beating of his heart, and allowed the weariness to pull her into its grasp once more.

Chapter Thirty-Nine

Sophie awoke in the cave. She opened her eyes and noticed Michael and Philip talking, looking at her with concern. It was strange to see them together. Others she recognized—Salvador, Emanuel, Diego—sat with them.

Philip pulled away from Michael and walked toward her. "How do you feel, Sophie?"

She tried to lift her hand to her face but winced at the pain in her shoulder. "Like I've been hit by a truck."

He smiled. "Close enough." He glanced over his shoulder to Michael. "We're trying to figure out a plan . . . to save Walt."

She nodded.

"He left you something." Philip pulled a small brown pouch from his pocket. A piece of paper with her name on it had been pinned to it.

Philip helped her sit, and she opened the top of the pouch with shaky fingers. She turned it upside down, and five coins fell into her palm.

"He thinks he's not coming back."

"I know."

"And the rest of the gold?"

"We're sticking to the plan. Michael will be meeting with Ritter."

"And you?" She looked into Philip's light blue gaze.

"I stay with you."

She held up a coin to the light. "Do you think if I give this away, I'll regret it?"

"Yes, I do," Philip answered. "They cost him a lot. You could give it away. But if you did, I think for the rest of your life you'd wonder if you took the easy road out. And you'll wonder if you would have made a difference had you followed through."

"I don't want to think about this anymore."

"You don't have to right now." He placed the softest kiss on the tip of her nose. "Rest. We have a lot to talk about."

"But Walt . . . he may not have time."

"Don't worry, Sophie. We'll talk fast."

Walt felt his body thrown into the cell. Even if his legs would have held him, he could have not stood in the small space.

The cell was long and narrow. *Like a coffin,* he thought to himself. Iron rings hung from the walls, like the handles of a coffin turned inward.

He crumpled to the ground and tried to ignore the pain. He refused to look at his hands, to see the damage, and instead pulled them tight to his side—as if that would somehow ease the throbbing.

"Are you rested?" a voice asked.

Walt forced his eyes open and realized he must have fallen asleep. For how long he did not know. All he knew was that the faintest beam of sunlight slanted in a tall window, one he had not realized was there.

A man stood in the doorway holding out a cup of coffee. From the scent wafting up from the tin cup, Walt knew it was real coffee, not the chicory most of the country drank as a poor substitute. Walt shook his head, refusing, mostly due to the fact he knew his hands could not grip the cup. He also considered it might be drugged—yet another way for them to try to pull information from him.

"Not thirsty?" the man asked. Then he drank from the cup himself.

Outside, from somewhere in the courtyard, Walt heard the sounds of marching feet. The clump of boots against the stone pavement wearied him. Keeping his eyes open and gazing into the man's smiling face tired him even more.

"It is sad that someone such as you, who has commanded so much, should end up like this. There are generals who have commanded the troops, but you have controlled so much more—the coming and going of men and women. The shipment of treasure."

Walt refused to reply, or even to look at the man.

"You carried more in your mind than others in books of troop placements and battle plans. It's a shame you could not turn off your sympathies. You could have left this country a wealthy man if not for your tender heart." The man spat the last two words as if they created a foul taste in his mouth.

"You're in pain. I can see that." The man's voice held no sympathy. "But do not worry; it will not last long. I am not cruel. In two nights it will be over. The plans. The schemes. Your life."

And with that the man turned and strode from the doorway.

A sob caught in Walt's throat. It wasn't something he expected. Then again, he hadn't expected to be here either.

The man was right, though; he'd become soft. If he'd stuck by his original plan none of this would have happened.

Yet even now Walt didn't regret the changes. He'd thought of everything. Well, almost everything. One thing he hadn't considered was the people. He didn't realize how they'd change not the plan, but his heart.

He sighed, then eased his head back against the damp, moldy straw. He would be dead in two days and wished it were sooner. He had no doubt that, if his friends were still alive, they'd try to rescue him. It was the last thing he wanted.

"Señor, can you hear me?" A voice spoke through the walls.

"Yes." Walt turned. "I can. Who are you?"

"I am a prisoner, too."

Walt considered telling the man not to speak for worry of the guard's wrath, but changed his mind. He needed a friend. And for a strange reason he immediately considered this man a friend.

"What are you here for?" Walt asked.

"I tried to help . . . those who didn't want it. Then I was wrongly accused. A friend turned me in. Or at least, someone I thought was a friend. And you?"

"I had something they wanted. But I didn't tell them where it was. I'm not sure why, because even when I found it . . . it wasn't what I thought." Walt adjusted himself against the wall, the pain of his body nearly causing him to black out. "I did it for myself. Then for others. But it made no difference. My soul was still empty. I wanted my family's approval, but I failed at that, too."

"And your friends?" the man asked.

"I put them in danger, and I'm afraid they still are. I either need to escape or to die. I worry for them if I don't."

"Maybe you should wait and trust instead." The man's voice was gentle. "Maybe they have a plan."

"That's what I fear."

The door opened, and a guard shoved another man into the cell. A man as broken and bruised as Walt.

"Thank you for listening," Walt said after the guard had stalked away.

"Are you talking to me?" his cell mate growled.

"No. To the prisoner on the other side of the wall."

The eyes of the man widened. "Are you mad? There is no one over there. It's an outside wall. We are three stories high."

Walt glanced up. Sure enough, he leaned against the wall with the window. A chill moved up his arms. "I was mistaken," he said hastily, remembering the words spoken to him. "I am mistaken."

Sophie stared into the fire. "I think we should do this alone." She looked at Philip. "We can't bring any more danger to these men. If anything, perhaps they could help by finding Maria and the baby—but as for the rescue . . . they shouldn't risk their lives."

Emanuel crouched before her. He gently touched her hand. "Señorita. You are an American. You were born in a country filled with freedom of choice. Yet you come here—into a country that is not yours, and you believe you know better than we do? My family has known no other country." His voice was firm. "This is our land. Our home. We have fought the Moors. We have fought ourselves. You cannot grasp all our fight involves."

She glanced away, ashamed. Then she looked at Michael. "You are right. I've been a fool. Michael—he has told me this from the beginning. I don't understand. I wasn't raised here." She folded her hands on her lap. "But I do know this—suffering happens. Countries are forged out of hardship. I grew up in Boston. The very ground cries with the blood of martyrs."

"Then let us go with you. Let us try. Some for the woman and child. Some for Walt. We know what it means to die for a cause—many of our friends have done that very thing."

"Are you sure?"

"Señorita, you do not understand," Salvador echoed. "In our country we are raised with the knowledge there are important people, and then there are the rest of us. For a few months we had hopes that the people's voice could win. That what we cared for, as a group, could stand up to powerful men."

"But don't you understand? That is the truth. Every person is special in God's eyes. Your voice *does* matter."

"And that is why I am doing this. You are important—a gifted painter and one whose work has touched hearts for our cause. But more than that, your heart is tender for the people—the lowliest among us. Your voice with your heart will make all the difference. I am one man, and the people I influence are few. You have a fighting spirit that you barely see for yourself. It is the same with your friends. I believe in them because you believe in them. I will help them with hopes they will continue the fight."

Sophie nodded and lowered her head. "Yes, I can't stop you. In fact . . . I appreciate your help."

"Good." Emanuel patted her hand. "But now we must sleep. Tomorrow is a big day, and we must all be rested."

He rose and looked at her with a twinkle in his gaze. "And maybe the next time you fall asleep, you will do it as a free woman, in a land of freedom."

Chapter Forty

Sophie tossed and turned throughout the night, to the point that looking back it was hard to know which thoughts were hers and which belonged to dreams. How could they get Walt out of that prison?

She met Philip's gaze across the campfire the next morning and was surprised to discover he looked rested and had an excited look in his eyes. The words spilled from his mouth before she even had a chance to ask.

"Sophie, remember how we were saved at the airport when we first stole the gold? Walt didn't try to overpower Cesar or Michael. Instead, he made them believe everything was as planned." He took her hands. "I spoke to our friends about the executions. They told me the guards usually take the prisoners outside the gates somewhere, shoot them, and bury them in shallow graves.

"First, I thought we should ambush the vehicle. Or try to overpower them when they stop. But what if we simply have a different truck pick him up? You told me yourself they have so many soldiers coming and going that they don't know who is who."

"You mean drive to the prison, pick Walt up, and drive away?"

From somewhere the smell of frying bacon wafted to her. Her stomach growled, reminding her it had been too long since she'd eaten . . . but she couldn't eat if she tried.

"Yes. We have two days to watch first. See just what takes place. Tomas said he could get the keys for us for one of their trucks. He can even find someone to pose as a driver."

"I don't know. It sounds too simple."

"That's the beauty of it. Men know how to react when they are confronted with conflict, but when everything seems as it should be, there's no need to even question. It comes down to having faith—faith that Tomas knows the right people. And that the guards won't see anything unusual."

"Then what happens after we get Walt?"

"Michael went to get Maria and the baby. He's then going to travel with Ritter while we journey to the coast, find a ship, and sail away."

"You make it sound so easy."

"Let's hope it is." Philip reached over and stroked her cheek.

A man entered the cave, and Sophie turned. She recognized him from somewhere and knew he was one of the guerilla fighters. As he neared, Sophie saw he was bloody and beaten. He walked with a limp, and a great sadness filled his gaze.

"Are you the ones trying to find a way to rescue Walt? Are you Sophie?"

"Yes." Sophie rose. "Do you have information about him?" She looked behind the man. "Is he here?" For the briefest moment Sophie dared to hope Walt was free.

The man lowered his gaze. "He is not here, but I have information. A message for you, actually. I was released from prison this morning. Walt and I shared a cell. Come, señorita; sit so we can talk."

Sophie did as she was told—her knees already growing weak. She eyed the man with suspicion. "How do I know Walt sent you? Why should I trust you?"

"Walt said you'd believe me. He said your heart was tender, and you would trust me. Out of all people, he said you wouldn't let the war turn you into someone distrusting."

"Maybe I'm learning to see the world as it really is," she interjected. She felt Philip's hand on her back.

"If that is the case, that would be a sad thing. Spain is full of people without hope."

"What did Walt tell you?"

"He said to tell you that you won. The treasure you spoke about was true . . . and you have done more for him than he managed to do for you." The man cleared his throat. "He said that when he saw you on that train heading to the Spanish border he thought he had helped you cross over to the other side . . . but in truth you helped him to do just that."

Sophie let out a little cry. Her chin dropped to her chest. "The other side?" She didn't know whether to smile or cry. She did both.

From the corner of her eye she saw Michael enter the cave. He stepped to her side as if understanding something terrible had happened.

"Walt's dead," the man said solemnly. "They took him again, for interrogation. He never came back. But he asked me to give you a message. He told me that if something happened, I was to find you. He said he learned to believe what he could not see." Tears filled the stranger's gaze.

"But that makes no sense. He told me that in order to continue seeking the treasure, he learned to have faith in the great treasure house." The words caught in Sophie's throat.

"Yes, but this is a different treasure he speaks about." The man slipped a small piece of paper into her hand. She unfolded it and read Walt's handwriting. *Streets of gold. A bridge to the other side. Jesus.*

Sophie knew that for the rest of her life she'd never forget Walt. And she'd never forget how in the end he'd found what he'd always sought—truth, treasure, acceptance.

She'd have time to mourn Walt later. More than anything, she knew, he would want her to complete what he had started.

All the other men left, to give them space, leaving only

Michael and Philip to comfort her. Sophie wiped away her tears. "Well, our job isn't done. We still have to find Maria."

Michael looked at Sophie, and she knew something was wrong. "She is gone. I went for her this morning, and one of the maids said Maria had already left for the coast."

Sophie's head pounded, unable to absorb the mounting news. "We have to go. We have to find her! I promised Maria . . . she needs a way of escape. I'm afraid she thinks I am not coming back. She's desperate. She thinks it's all up to her now."

"Sophie." Philip took her hands. "Either that or she's decided to stay."

Sophie jerked her hands away. "Maria married Emilio for Michael. She carried a child because of *this* man." Sophie pointed to Michael's chest. "*He* asked her to do whatever it took to make sure they were able to get into the bank. She trusted me. I gave her my word. More than that . . . I promised to help her."

Philip placed a hand on her shoulder. "We can't risk any more. We have the gold. We have plans for escape."

Sophie shook her head. "I've made my choice. I'm not going without her. Gold or no gold."

"Sophie, please." Michael added his plea to Philip's.

She turned to him. "Go ahead. Ritter is waiting."

"Why are you doing this?" Michael asked.

"You may not understand this, but I'm saving the one thing worth saving. And that's not the gold."

Michael's gaze narrowed. "Sophie, you can't be serious."

"The gold belongs to Spain. It does not belong to me. Or either of you." She glanced at both men. "Just promise me you'll sell it and use the money for the good of the people."

"You are confused." Philip's voice was gentle.

"Am I? From the moment the gold was taken hundreds of years ago, people have chased it. Greed kills and destroys. People will continue to die for this treasure—"

"That's why we must get it out," Michael interrupted. "Before more people die hunting it. Before more people are lulled into its trap. What has been sacrificed: life, families, truth, souls?"

Philip reached for her hand, but Sophie pulled away.

"This gold has trapped me since the moment I entered this

country." Sophie distanced herself from the men. "It will not hold me anymore. I am leaving. I'm going to find Maria, and we'll figure out on our own how to get out of this country."

Chapter Forty-One

Ritter's disguise had been simple. A pair of handmade crutches, tattered clothes, and a full facial beard hid his true identity. His downcast eyes kept everyone away. The fact that he smelled bad helped, too.

Through the afternoon and evening, Ritter had shuffled through the streets near the air base where he'd previously been stationed, hoping to locate one of his former friends. He needed the help of someone still assigned to the local squadron. It was the only way.

He'd asked Philip and Michael to make sure the gold was transferred to canvas moneybags. From there they were to be secured in the bomb bay of a Dornier Do.17—called the Flying Pencil. The Dornier was capable of carrying fifteen hundred pounds of bombs. He hoped the gold didn't weigh much more.

Night had nearly descended, and Ritter was about to give up hope when his shuffle took him past a park where a small gathering of pilots and mechanics played cards. It was then he spotted his former wingman, Erik Schomburg.

Ritter shuffled by and caught Schomburg's eye. With his right hand, Ritter flashed Erik the sign they'd used when flying formation to determine who would break away first when an encounter was eminent. Schomburg's eyes lit with recognition, and Ritter could almost see the blood drain from his friend's face. Ritter kept on moving toward another bench a good distance away. He eased down, got comfortable, and waited.

In a few minutes the card game broke up, and the men headed off in different directions. Ritter turned and watched Schomburg come toward him at a natural pace to avoid the attention of his departing squadron mates.

Schomburg looked around, then grasped Ritter's hand with both of his. "Friend, it is great to see you alive."

It took Ritter nearly an hour to tell his friend how he happened to "go missing," and why he needed help now.

Schomburg's eyes sparkled at the promise of gold for his help.

"Send the truck with the gold tonight," Schomburg said. "Meet me there. We can work together to load the gold, and in the morning I'll convince the base mechanics to allow me to preflight the large twin-engine bomber."

"Perfect. I knew I could count on you," Ritter said with a smile.

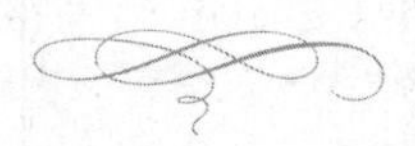

Philip drove Michael to the airfield. In the distance he saw the transport plane. Parked beside it was the truck that had carried the gold for so long, now empty. The cargo was loaded, and he could see Ritter and another man doing a final check of the plane.

Michael opened the door and turned to climb out.

Philip stopped Michael with his words. "It seems we both ended up here because we love the same woman. And that is no fault of ours. The problem is, you hurt her . . . and I have hurt her less. Still, I *trust you.*" He emphasized the last two words.

"Yes, well, I'll be waiting in Paris. Let me know when you arrive . . . and together we can work to get the money from the sale into the right hands."

"I'll be sure to do that."

Philip noticed Michael's gaze soften.

"There is one more thing I have to tell you." Michael cleared his throat, then glanced away. "I read your father's letters. First with amusement. What foolishness. Then with curiosity. Why did his words stick with me? I asked myself. I wondered why I could not shake them. Then . . ." Michael sighed. "I read the letters with hunger. I wanted to know more. I wanted to know how someone with so little could have such hope."

"When I get there, we can talk about this more. And maybe someday you can meet my father. I think you'd like him."

"Yes, I would like that." Michael shook Philip's hand. "In the meantime take care of Sophie. She's a stubborn woman."

Philip nodded. "Yes, I know that well."

"Take care of Maria and the baby, too."

"And you take care of the gold . . . for the gold will take care of many."

Sophie's heart was heavy every time she thought of Walt, but she urged herself to continue what he had started. She even imagined him looking upon her with a smile as she kept her promise to her friend.

It had been easy to find Maria. At the train station, she and Philip had simply asked the man at the ticket counter to tell them which direction the beautiful woman with the small child had traveled. Then together, Eleanor Howard and Phil Attis bought tickets for Gibraltar. Sophie would return there, but this time for a different treasure.

Eleanor and Phil booked a room at the finest hotel they could find, and then Sophie waited in the lobby. Sure enough, a few hours later Maria exited with the baby in a carriage. Her face filled with joy, and she embraced Sophie.

"Come with me," Sophie said, taking her arm. "Philip should be ready."

Philip patted the paperwork in his pocket, adjusted his cap, and drew in a breath to make himself seem taller. A voice met his ears as he entered the doorway to the command post of the volunteers. The polite and proper intonation told Philip the man was British.

"Bugger this rain," the burly soldier guarding the door complained to no one in particular.

Philip approached them. "Excuse me. I'm looking for the doctor. I hear he's looking for volunteers to transport wounded men?"

The Englishman scoffed. "Don't be daft. He's looking for men stupid enough to drive unreliable vehicles to the front lines and most likely wind up in the middle of enemy fire. Dang the Reds." The man crossed his arms over his chest and studied Philip from the top of his head to the toe of his shoes. "Still interested?"

Then he lifted his eyes and met Philip's gaze.

"Yes, I suppose I am. Didn't come to volunteer for Franco because I expected rest, relaxation, and roses."

Deep laughter burst from the man's lips, and he nodded his head and patted Philip's shoulder.

"Hey, I like you. Usually the volunteers come shaking in their boots. You seem more like a veteran of this war than someone just arriving."

Philip stomped one foot. "No shakes—at least showing on the outside, anyway. I wish I were a veteran," he quickly added. "Then at least I'd know it's possible to survive this thing."

"Sure, you'll survive. I can tell those who will—call it my sixth sense." The man paused as if a parade of faces of all those who didn't make it filled his mind. "I'll walk you to the docks. Put in a good word, even. They're transporting troops north by way of ship, you know."

"Yes, I know."

The man reached his hand to Philip. "I'm Gregory, by the way."

"Phil. Phil Attis."

"Gregory Wiersbe, at your service." He didn't take time to introduce Philip to the others, and Philip was grateful. His mind was already full of the duties he had to complete by the time darkness fell.

Philip strolled with a relaxed posture as he followed the man through the halls leading past offices. The command post overflowed with people moving with purpose in their step. He wondered if there was ever a time when quiet filled these halls. His guess was that even late at night the office was staffed with people waiting to get news of the latest events—good or bad, but always colored so Franco looked liked the victor.

Philip didn't need to think about that now, or how he'd find the right ship so that they could steal away unnoticed. Instead he focused on walking along and answering the man's questions as convincingly as he could.

"So, Phil, what do you think of Spain so far?"

"Spain is beautiful, and so are its women. But I've heard that as someone new I shouldn't try to get to know the others by joining card games—if I want to keep my wallet, that is."

The man laughed again. "In that case, can I talk you into some flamenco dancing? Pretty women, *and* you get to keep your wallet. Well, unless you fall in love, that is. I know one volunteer who took a wife only to discover that she expected him to support her family, too."

"And maybe her friends as well?" Philip laughed; then he scanned the docks. "I think I can take it from here. Thank you. This is just what I needed."

Sophie hurried down the dock, head down. Rain softly fell. She saw the small boat, just as she'd expected. She saw Philip, in his disguise, sitting on the bow. He rose when he saw her.

"Do you have Maria and the baby?"

"Yes, they are below," he said. "What took you so long?"

She climbed onto the boat. "I sent a telegram ahead. I told Michael where to meet us—on the coast."

"Do you think he will?"

Sophie shrugged. "I'm not sure. For all we know he could have taken the gold and run." A baby's cry rose from down below. “Even if he does, we have the most important part.”

“Maria and the child.”

Sophie nodded, and then drew a small pouch out of her pocket with five coins. “Yes, that too.” She placed a quick kiss on Philip’s lips. “It’s time to go now.”

With a smile, Philip used his foot and pushed away from the dock.

Sophie watched the coast of Spain grow dim. Tears filled her eyes.

“I know it’s hard. With Walt—” Philip placed an arm around her shoulders.

“Shhh, you don’t need to say anything. Just hold me.” The tears refused to stop. “Just hold me and let me know that I am worth it.”

“Worth what?”

“His sacrifice.”

“In his eyes you are.”

“Yes.” Sophie sighed. “You are right. In his eyes I am . . . and that’s hard to accept.”

The boat continued onward until Spain disappeared in the distance. She had entered with Walt’s help; now she exited the same way. And yet in between she had become a patriot of Spain and a saint. An unusual mix, but both due to Walt’s sacrifice.

“He knew what he was doing, Sophie—trading his life for yours.”

Sophie sighed deeply. “I know. And I pray that the rest of my life will show my gratitude.”

Epilogue

EIGHTEEN MONTHS LATER

Ramona held the blanket tight to her shoulders, and she focused on the coastline ahead of her. *France.* It seemed a dream. It also seemed strange that Spain was behind them. They had fought for their country, but she died before their eyes. The International volunteers had been sent home months ago, and it was only a matter of time before the government agreed to declare Franco the victor.

José wrapped his arm around her. "I sent word ahead. I believe there will be friends waiting."

"Really, who?"

"A priest named Father Manuel. Do you remember him, from Guernica? I hear he has opened a home in Paris for stragglers like us. I'm not sure where he received the funds to do so, but many have benefited from his care."

Ramona closed her eyes and nodded, then pressed her cheek against his chest. "Yes, I remember him. But that seems a lifetime ago. It will be strange to live in a real home—to sleep on a bed." She chuckled. "In a strange way, I'll miss our cave . . . it's where we truly had a chance to love each other." She opened her eyes and peered into her husband's face. "Do you think we will ever come back home?"

José set his chin. "It's my hope. Maybe we can unite with others and return someday to reclaim what we have lost."

Ramona nodded. It seemed hard to imagine such a thing coming true, especially with Hitler's war machine bent on controlling Europe.

"At least we have each other." She placed a kiss on his lips. "And at least we know our Lord is with us . . . wherever we are."

"It is enough," José agreed. "It is enough."

Acknowledgments

John, thank you for sharing me with Spain for three years. I hope you liked how the story ended! Your love for me is more overwhelming than I can put into words.

Cory, Leslie, and Nathan. Thanks for being great kids!

My loving family . . . grandma, dad, mom, Ronnie—who always rejoice with me.

Stacey, Kimberley, Lesley, Melissa, Bruce, and Susan—unexpected and special gifts.

Robbie, my brother-in-law. No, I wouldn't tell you how the book ended, but now you can find out for yourself!

Amy Lathrop, my right-hand-gal. You are the best!

My small group, Job and Marie, Casey and Allyson, Tara and Skyler, Kenny and Twyla. Dearest friends and fellow God-seekers. Thanks for your encouragement and prayers!

My agent, Janet Kobobel Grant. I'm thankful for your wisdom and dedication.

My editor, Andy McGuire. This book is here because of your enthusiasm over my spark of an idea! Thank you for believing in me.

The whole Moody team whose partnership was a true gift from God.

LB Norton. You make me look good. I consider you a friend.

My "unofficial" editors, Cara Putman, Ocieanna Fleiss, Amy Lathrop, and Jim Thompson. Thanks!

Finally, this book wouldn't be written if not for the wonder ful men and women who help with my research:

Alun Menai Williams. February 20, 1913 – July 2, 2006. Veteran of the Spanish Civil War.

Karen Lynn Ginter. Thank you for making Spain real to me!

Norman Goyer. Though we may not be related, I'm thankful for all your expert aviation advice! I have no doubt God sent you to me.

And others from the Abraham Lincoln Brigade Associated who answered my questions and provided insight. Thank you!

World War II stories of Honor and Promise

ISBN-13: 978-0-8024-0855-6

ISBN-13: 978-0-8024-1556-1

Dan is shot down and captured by the Japanese while Libby is called into the service as one of the first female fighter pilots in a time of war. Their love is tested across an ocean.

At the New York Tribune, Mary and Lee are competitors as war breaks out. But then Mary's coverage of a bombing in Germany leads to new adventure and a narrow escape.

by Tricia Goyer

Find it now at your favorite local or online bookstore.

www.MoodyPublishers.com